AFTER DARK

Short Stories by:
Brigid Barry
Chris Campeau
C.W. Stevenson
Gayle Siebert
Glenn Dungan
Jessica Clem
Jonathon Palmer
Justin Alcala
Kaye George
Ken Foxe
Kent Priore
Ken Teutsch
Mister Bad (Kyle Owens)
Mark K. McClain
Mike Sherer
Natasha Grodzinski
Pamela Kenney
Rik Hoskin
Terry Campbell
Tracy Falenwolfe

Cover Art Design by: Kelly Moran/Rowan Prose Publishing
Photo Credit: Adobe Images/Deposit Photos
First Edition
ISBN: 978-1-961967-71-7
Rowan Prose Publishing, LLC
www.RowanProsePublishing.com
Published in the United States of America

The Widow's Hand

BRIGID BARRY

Even on high, Miah's wipers couldn't keep up with the deluge pounding the windshield. Pulling over to wait for visibility to improve was an option, but she was only a few minutes away. She just had to hope the downpour hadn't washed the road out.

The rain let up to a fine mist as she reached the cabin. Miah released her white-knuckled grip on the steering wheel. Cutting the engine, she frowned at the squat building. Nothing moved, and despite the dimness of the day, no lights were on. The overhanging pine branches shuddered in a gust of wind. Heavy drops of water hit the car like stones. A shiver ran up her spine, and the delicate hairs on the back of her neck rose.

"Don't be stupid. Jack is probably still sick in bed, right where I left him." She shook her head. "Maybe next time he'll listen when I tell him to not drink out of streams in the woods."

Her voice didn't dislodge the dread in the pit of her stomach. Searching for any sign of life in the squat building, she grabbed her grocery bags off the passenger seat and stepped out of the car. Five steps later, she pushed the unlocked front door open and froze.

Silence roared in her ears.

"Jack?" A high-pitched noise repeated. The refrigerator? Shivering, Miah entered and kicked the door closed.

The back of the cabin beckoned. The fridge's white light spilled over wide pine floorboards, worn and scarred with years of use. Her body tensed, but she forced herself forward. She flipped the light switch. Her heart jumped into her throat, and the grocery bags fell from her hands.

The contents of the fridge had been ripped out and scattered throughout the tiny kitchen. Cabinet doors dangled from bent or broken hinges. Her heart pounded like a wild thing trying to escape. Something crunched under her foot, and she sprang back. Cereal, strewn across the floor. She couldn't breathe. Was whoever—or whatever—had done this still here?

Miah had to clear her throat twice before she could speak. "Jack?"

She took a step, and slipped. Miah landed on her hands and knees in a puddle of viscous liquid. Holding her breath, she brought one of her trembling hands to her face. Red fluid glistened in the overhead light as it ran down her palms and wrists to drip onto the floor with wet plops. She released her pent-up breath as she rubbed her fingers together. A mix of maple syrup and ketchup. Not blood.

Her jeans soaked from the knees down, she stood and wiped the sticky mess onto her thighs. Two more steps. The steel entry door stood wide open, the knob embedded into the plaster behind it. The flimsy screen door lay broken and twisted in the mud fifty feet away as if it had exploded from the house. A mashed trail in the high grass headed straight into the trees.

Miah darted back into the cabin and slid across the floor. With a curse, she pulled her wet sneakers off and ran down the short hallway in her socks. She skidded into the bedroom door, shoving it open. The empty bed was neatly made. Colorful pillows leaned against the oak headboard. There was nowhere else to hide in this tiny room, not even a closet or space under the bed.

She opened the narrow bathroom door next to her. "Jack?"

Empty. Jack's cell phone sat face down in the sink. Miah swiped the screen. He'd taken a photo of them yesterday, smiling at the end of their hike, and set it as his background screen. She tucked it into her back pocket. He wouldn't have gone far without it. Voluntarily.

The only other place to look was the loft. She scrambled up the narrow ladder and peered into the dim space. Nothing but two rusty footlockers and a pile of dusty blankets. She pushed away from the ladder and dropped into the living room. Jack was gone. If he'd gone into the woods, he could be hopelessly lost.

A photo of her father stared at her from the wall. *Whatcha gonna do about it?* his eyes asked.

She stared back. What choices did she have? There was no cell reception, and no landline to use within an hour's drive. Even if she could call the authorities, it would take the Staties five hours to respond from Houlton. Longer if they were tied up with something else. The temperature was dropping as night approached. No, she couldn't wait for someone else to ride to her rescue.

Her father had given her all the tools she needed to go find Jack herself, so that's what she'd do. At the very least, she needed to canvass the area. And they'd have a good laugh when she found him lost in the woods nearby. Or so she hoped.

She unlocked the gun cabinet and pulled out her thirty-aught-six. She leaned the weapon against the ladder and scrambled up to the loft. The hinges of the steel footlocker squealed as she thrust up the lid, and then emptied her pack onto the floor. The gear she'd needed for a day hike with her husband was not the same stuff that she'd need to camp in the woods in November. She layered every MRE bag from the locker into the backpack. Not knowing how long she'd be gone, she shoved several pairs of cushioned socks and clean undershirts into her bag.

She sat back on her heels. What if Jack had just gone off for a walk?

The sweet scent of maple syrup and the faint sting of vinegar wafted up from her hands.

She stuffed a set of her old woodland camo Army BDUs into her pack.

The two cold weather sleeping bags were tossed to the floor below. Along with her Cabela's survival kit, she packed a waterproof first aid kit and fleece gear into her bag. She yanked the straps viciously to secure it before kicking it over the side of the loft. Miah stripped down to her underwear and pulled on a fresh shirt and another set of BDUs, tucking her pants into new Gore-Tex boots. Her thick, dark hair hidden under a flat cap, Miah heaved the full pack over the ladder to the floor below and jumped down after it.

Signs of Jack's passing would have been obvious even to a complete novice, but after three days tracking him through the woods, Miah still hadn't caught up. How much of a head start could he have gotten?

The fourth night she pulled out her flashlight and kept going, convinced she would catch up with him. She struggled to remember what he had been wearing when she left to go get supplies. Cut-off sweatpants and a t-shirt. As far as Miah could tell, Jack hadn't taken anything with him. But he was alive—and she was getting closer. Despite her best efforts to rest, her racing mind and a sense of urgency spurred her on until she couldn't go anymore. She dozed fitfully and was up before daybreak.

Frost covered leaves crunched under her boots and her breath hung in the air as the new sun crept over the horizon. The air vibrated before the rumbling of an engine reached her. Miah held her weapon half up, her finger hovering over the safety as an ATV approached. She tensed as the vehicle came into view driven by a familiar green uniform.

The forest ranger smiled and waved, pulling up close. His friendly smile didn't reach his narrowed eyes, hidden in the shadow of his flat-brimmed hat. They raked over Miah, lingering on her rifle. His bulbous nose and thick brows overpowered an otherwise average face.

"You're out awfully far, aren't you?"

"Not terribly."

He dropped the smile. "You shouldn't be out wandering alone, Miss."

Miah tipped her chin up. "It's Missus, actually."

His shoulders tightened, and he thrust his jaw out. "You're Billy Michaud's girl, aren't you?"

Miah nodded. Death hadn't diminished the weight her father's name still carried in these parts.

The ranger looked pointedly at her weapon. "You plannin' on shooting something with that?"

She gave him a smile as brittle and cold as ice. "I'm wandering out here all alone. I wouldn't want some mean old bear to come get me."

He snorted. "If you have half the balls your father did, every bear, coyote, and bull moose in a ten-mile radius already headed for the hills."

Miah's fingers tightened on the cold weapon in her hand. "Funny how you people never appreciated him when he was around to hear it."

His brows came up, and his hands dropped to his thighs. He rubbed them on his pants and cleared his throat. "You seen anyone while you been out here?"

"Not a soul before you." Miah relaxed her grip, and the muscles in her shoulder ached with relief.

"There are a few people missing from the camps by the highway. Keep an eye out."

Miah winced at the word *missing*.

The ranger rubbed his thumb along his jaw. "You said you're married now, right? Where's the mister?"

"He stayed home this time."

The ranger's brown eyes hardened to flint. "You got something to tell me?"

Miah pursed her lips and shook her head. "Nope."

He tugged on the brim of his hat and grabbed the handlebars. "Watch yourself out here. I know your daddy taught you better than coming out into the woods on your own." He waved a beefy hand in the direction he'd been heading. "That storm the other day has the stream up ahead over the banking so take care."

He took off, dirt spraying from his tires.

Once the sound of the engine faded, Miah dropped to her knees and pulled out her father's map. A few quick calculations in her head verified her suspicions. Intent on tracking Jack, she'd completely missed the obvious. She traced the undulating line carefully drawn in blue ink. The stream they'd hiked through the day before he'd disappeared. Jack had taken a drink from it just before they'd returned to the cabin, after she'd told him not to. He'd been following it. A chill crawled up her spine. Coincidence?

She folded the page carefully and tucked it back into her pocket. Her father's voice rang in her head. *There are no coincidences.*

The bright sunlight filtered through the canopy to dapple the forest floor when Miah finally spotted Jack ahead of her. Only the elastic waist of his sweats was still intact. The rest of the garment hung in tatters on his thighs. His bare torso glistened with sweat as he staggered far ahead of her, barely visible through the trees.

Her heart leaped. "Jack!" She dropped her heavy pack, and keeping hold of her weapon, ran to him. "Jack!"

He looked over his shoulder. His blue eyes widened, and he stumbled into a shuffling jog. Away from her.

"What the hell?" Miah broke into a sprint. Her tactical boots sprang up from the spongy earth.

Jack ran faster, bouncing off trees in his haste to get away. He tripped and Miah sped up even more. With a final push, Miah collided with him, knocking him to the ground. She fell on him and straddled his hips, pinning him to the ground.

"What is wrong with you?" She double-checked her safety and set the weapon aside.

He rolled onto his back without dislodging her. "Miah—"

Her hands fluttered over his face, their deep tan a sharp contrast to his pale skin. "You scared me to death, baby." She pressed her palms against his cheeks as her mouth caressed his eyes and forehead. "You're burning up. What are you doing out here? Why did you run away from me?"

"I didn't know what else to do," he moaned and grimaced. He caressed her back, then gripped her upper arms and threw her off of him. "You have to get away from me."

Miah jumped upright and brushed her palms on her pants. "Have you lost your mind?"

"Just go away!" Jack staggered to his feet and lurched into a tree.

"You have lost your mind." Miah trotted the few steps and put a hand on his shoulder.

Jack's arm came up, but this time, instead of pushing her away, he clung to her. "I didn't know—" a groan started deep in his belly, "—what else to do."

He didn't make sense. She stroked his forehead again and glanced at his eyes. Instead of the normal blue, the irises and sclera had turned black as onyx. The grip on her elbow tightened, and she struggled against it. The fingers of Jack's other hand dug into the bark of the tree, then deeper into the wood. The muscles beneath his skin rippled as he straightened. Miah yanked herself out of his grip with such force that she fell to the ground. Scrambling backwards on her hands and feet, she couldn't tear her eyes away from him.

Normally around six feet tall, Jack now towered at least eight feet high. The center of his face bulged forward, and his cheekbones and jaw widened.

Jack hid behind his hands. They had long, thick fingers now, all sprouting hair. The elastic band of his tattered sweats dug into the flesh at his waist. He turned away, hunching over.

Miah lay stunned, staring up at Jack's trembling back. His muscles spasmed and ebony hair burst from his skin as his shoulders broadened still further.

"Jack, what's happening?" Her voice was calm, detached.

"I don't know!" He looked at her over his shoulder, pleading with his strange black eyes. He swung around, his head and shoulders swaying to a rhythm only Jack could feel. His fingers shaped into wicked claws as his pale skin filled in with more coarse, dark hair and his nose lengthened, darkened.

He sank to all fours, heaving and panting. When the changes finally stopped, Jack growled, swinging his massive, blocky head.

"You turned into a bear?!" Miah pushed herself to her feet, shaking her head, unable to believe her eyes. "This isn't real. This isn't happening."

Jack stared at her with black eyes. Miah shook her head again. Stories her father had told her as a child ringing in her head. The world stopped as her thoughts fell into place. "You drank from the stream."

He regarded her sadly.

Miah covered her face and inhaled against her hands. She took another deep breath before she could look at him again. "Will you change back?"

He sat and nodded, his rubbery lips bouncing.

"Do you know when?"

The bear—Jack—shook his head.

"Let's get to the cabin, and we'll figure this out."

He shook his head again and ambled farther into the woods, then paused to look over his shoulder at her.

"You want me to come with you?"

He nodded.

"Let me get my pack." As swift as a rabbit, Miah snatched her rifle off the ground and sprinted back to her bag. She shouldered it with a grunt and trotted back to him as she buckled the strap around her waist. He waited patiently until she was a few yards away, then ambled into the trees.

Miah followed.

By sunset, Jack had changed back into himself, albeit larger and hairier than usual. They sat together over an MRE. He picked at the rehydrated chicken as she popped Skittles into her mouth.

"It's been cold at night, Jack. Are you okay?"

Jack glared at her. "I turned into a bear and you're worried that I've been cold?" His voice had deepened.

Miah stopped chewing. "Tangible problems are easier. I know what to do if you're hypothermic. Not so much if you're turning into an animal." She crumpled the candy wrapper and stuffed it into the empty MRE bag. She placed her hand on his forearm, stroking the silky hair with her thumb. "What happened at the cabin while I was gone?"

His hand clenched, and the muscles jumped beneath her fingertips. "You know I was sick because of drinking from that stupid stream. Pretty much as soon as you left for the store, I got hot. I chugged both gallon jugs in the fridge. Then I felt...I don't know what I felt. It was unreal. I looked down and saw my shirt shredding and the hair...I freaked out. I trashed the place pretty bad." He looked at Miah, his glassy blue eyes earnest. "The worst part was just this intense feeling that I had to *go*, but not why. I needed to leave the cabin. I just kept heading along that stupid stream. I couldn't stop. When I needed to rest it was like a bell was clanging in my head. I couldn't even think, it was so loud. As long as I followed the stream, everything was fine. I tried to go back once, and it was like I was being electrocuted." He kicked his bare foot at a clump of grass and wrapped his arms around his knees.

Miah stared at him, wanting to comfort him, but not knowing how. "Where do you think you're heading?"

Jack shook his head. "I don't know, but I think I'm close."

"Why?"

"The noise is really bad right now. I can see your lips moving but I can't hear you very well."

Miah collected the remaining wrappers and stuffed the garbage into her pack. "Then let's go."

His bushy brows drew together. "What do you mean?"

"I mean, let's go. Let's figure out where you're headed. Maybe we'll get some answers." She stood and swung the heavy pack onto her back. "Well?"

One of Jack's eyebrows rose. "See if there's a solution to me turning into a bear?"

Miah grabbed her rifle and cradled it in the crook of her arm. "Yes. My dad always said there is a solution to every problem." She held her hand out and helped Jack stand. He tried to pull his hand away, but she brought it to her mouth to kiss his palm. "We'll figure this out."

Jack searched her eyes from his new height and stroked her cheek. He leaned down and brushed his lips against hers. "I wish I had known your dad. You're one hell of a woman, you know that?"

Hand in hand, they walked deeper into the woods.

As the sun peeked over the horizon, Jack and Miah came to a small, white-washed cabin. The red light of dawn filtered through the clearing, giving the building an ethereal and ominous fairy-tale quality. The immaculate yard didn't have a single leaf or pine needle to obscure the grass dying in the autumn cold.

Crouching behind a tree, Miah tightened her grip on the weapon. The cold metal in her palms reassured her. "Is this the place?"

Jack frowned and shook his head. "I think so. The ringing isn't as bad."

Miah looked over the pale skin of Jack's furry chest and back to his face. "You aren't very stealthy. You do know that, right?"

Jack tweaked the bill of her cap. "You'll have to be stealthy for both of us."

The blue front door opened, and a petite woman stepped out, wiping her hands on a dishrag. A long, heavy skirt swung to a stop at her ankles, and she pushed up the long sleeves of her shirt. "Hello?"

Jack looked at Miah, panic on his face. She shrugged.

"I know you're out there," the woman called. "I've been waiting for you."

Miah tipped her head in the direction of the cabin and nodded. She peered around the trunk of the tree as Jack entered the clearing.

"My, my, my," the woman said, shaking her head. "Aren't you just fine?"

Jack cleared his throat. "Ma'am, can you please tell me what's going on? And why I'm here?"

"Why don't you come in and have some lunch. You must be hungry." She smiled, and dimples appeared on her cheeks. She reached for Jack.

He stumbled toward the cabin, the tension in his muscles screaming his reluctance.

"Come on, now." She waved impatiently.

Jack tripped forward as if she had tugged on an invisible leash.

The muscles in his neck tensed and Miah held her breath. *Don't look back*, she willed him. *Don't look back.*

Jack disappeared into the house and the door closed with a soft click. Miah crept silently around the back of the small cabin, keeping to the shadows at the edge of the clearing. Voices drifted out an open window as the woman yammered on about nothing in particular. Jack responded quietly and without interest.

With her eyes glued to the house, Miah settled behind a wide oak only a few yards away from the window. A sudden silence sent chills down her spine, and the hairs on the back of her neck rose.

"I suppose you want to know why you're here," the woman said.

"That would be nice."

On silent feet, Miah crept across the narrow strip of lawn and crouched on the ground, her back against the rough wall. She inched up until she could peer around the edge of the window. Jack sat at a round table, hands in his lap and head down. A bowl of something hot steamed in front of him, untouched. Miah couldn't see the woman except for one slender hand resting on the dark wood of the table.

"What's your name?" the woman asked.

"Jack. Yours?"

Miah heard the smile in the woman's voice. "Ada Chamberlain. You aren't from around here, are you?"

Jack shook his head. "No, ma'am."

Ada laughed, an earthy sound that stirred something primal and angry in Miah. "I swear I haven't been called 'ma'am' in decades. You are so polite." She sighed, and a chair creaked. "So many of my guests have such deplorable manners." Ada drummed her fingers on the table. "I don't suppose you would be interested in staying here with me, Jack?"

Jack shook his head. "I'm married."

"Oh, that doesn't matter to me." The slender hand moved to his knee and slid up his thigh. Her thumb disappeared under the edge of his tattered shorts.

"You aren't leaving here, regardless. You'll be just another hiker lost in the Maine woods, vanished without a trace. Why not be here with me?"

He pushed Ada away. "I said, I'm married."

Her hand slid over his shoulder and Miah had a view of Ada's narrow back and a long, dark braid as she slithered into Jack's bare lap. Miah gritted her teeth as Ada caressed his cheek.

"I've been here a mighty long time and it's getting lonely. It would be nice to have someone here with me." She caressed Jack's chest and toyed with the worn elastic band at his waist. His jaw tensed, but he did not move.

She pushed away, her cheeks scarlet. "Well, fine." She disappeared from view and Miah ducked down before Jack spotted her. She flicked off the safety with her thumb.

Dishes clattered together and Ada reappeared. After swiping the steaming food to the other side of the table, she set a bowl of salt, a lit black candle, and a vial of cloudy liquid in its place. She murmured under her breath words that Miah could barely hear. They didn't resemble any language she knew. Light flared and Miah bit her lip to keep from crying out in surprise. When she peered through the window, a halo of green radiance surrounded Jack, ebbing and flowing.

Ada held the vial to Jack's lips. "Drink this."

He pinched his lips shut and turned his head.

She slapped his cheek, leaving an angry red handprint. "You *will* drink this."

She spat out some more of the strange words. He sat upright and froze, staring straight ahead. When She poured the vial into his mouth, he didn't resist. She ordered him to swallow, and his throat worked.

"We could have done this the nice way, but you've forced my hand."

Ada backed up and stretched her arms over her head. More weird words. Jack shuddered, a low moan escaping his lips. His body spasmed, and he hit the floor hard. Within moments, the black bear lay prostrate on the floor, partially under the table. His unfocused onyx eyes found Miah and the rubbery lips pursed. As the chanting continued, the flowing green light drifted close to Ada's boots, and swirled around her like a fog. Writhing, the bear's breathing became labored, and his eyes closed.

Crap. The glow was Jack's aura. The bitch was sucking it like a drink, taking his life away from him. The massive rib cage heaved upward and fell down like bellows. The light flared.

Jack was going to die.

Miah stepped backward and brought the butt of her weapon to her shoulder. "Hey, Ada."

Ada turned wide brown eyes to Miah. The rifle exploded and recoiled in the same moment a quarter sized hole appeared in the center of Ada's forehead. Her mouth dropped in a surprised "oh" as blood and brain matter dripped down the wall behind her. Ada stood for half a heartbeat before she crumpled to the floor.

Miah shoved the muzzle of the rifle through the bullet hole in the screen and popped it out of the frame with a quick twist. She pulled herself up and through the window to land on her feet in the tidy kitchen.

The ebony hair on Jack's body melted away, and he shrank back to normal proportions. Miah gripped his clammy hand, feeling for a pulse. His eyes opened, and he sucked in a deep breath. She smiled at him, her eyes tearing up as she stroked his blond hair away from his face.

"What happened?" Jack asked.

"You don't remember?" Bending, she pressed her lips to his forehead and breathed in his scent. His fever had gone.

Jack shook his head and sat up, the shredded remains of his shorts barely covering him. "I've been sick all day. I think you were right about the water."

Miah's brows drew together, and her fingers touched his face. His eyes had lost their glassy look. She helped him into the chair he had so recently vacated. "I want you to wait here."

Miah tip-toed around the table, not ready to see the corpse but needing to. She expected lifeless eyes to stare up at her. Instead, a thick layer of dust coated the floor. A silver belt buckle winked in the flickering light of the candle. Miah touched the clean white plaster. Her index finger traced the hole where the spent round was embedded in the wall.

With Jack safely at the table, Miah crept down the hall and, standing against the wall, she pushed the first door open. Her stomach rolled as the thick scent of game hit her nostrils. Piles of pelts filled the tiny room. She entered, her hand reaching for the fur of its own accord. Her fingers sank into thick black and brown bear pelts. Were there ever grizzlies in Maine? Nothing smaller than a coyote was represented in the piles. The hides had been home tanned. She paused at a neat stack of what she knew were wolf pelts. The species had been gone from the state since the late nineteenth century. Where had Ada gotten these?

Miah turned to the single sepia photo on the wall. A man in a Union uniform sat in a high-backed chair, staring somberly into the camera. Behind the chair with one hand on the man's shoulder and holding a bible in the other was Ada, wearing a long dress cinched at the waist with a wide belt before it flared over wide hoops.

"A lost Maine hiker." Miah's fingers clenched in the fur. What better way to hide a human body than make sure it wasn't human at all?

After removing the photo from the wall, it took a few seconds to free it from the wooden frame. Fortunately, it was a print and not a tintype. Carefully, she tore Ada away with only a twinge of guilt for destroying such a beautiful artifact.

The Union soldier went into her cargo pocket, but Miah crumpled Ada's image in her fist. The black candle wouldn't go to waste today.

Back in their cabin, with Jack fast asleep in the bedroom, Miah took a worn book off the shelf and pulled a piece of paper from between the dog-eared pages. Her eyes skimmed the legend he'd scrawled there. A widow, distraught at the death of her beloved husband, hid herself deep in the woods and cursed the running water of the land. If any man drank from it, he would be called to her like a siren to meet his doom.

She slipped the torn photo and note between the pages, and then replaced the book. Her fingers stroked the broken binding. Her father had been right. Nothing in life was coincidence, not even the stories he'd told her as a child to teach her how to be safe in the woods.

Anchor Tenant

CHRIS CAMPEAU

Jody remembers when the Wasteland was a Nordstrom.

She remembers when she'd coined it the Wasteland, too. Back in 2026, three years after the last seasonal rolled in to get swallowed up, shuttering the unit's maw-like entrance at the east end of Paradise for good.

She tries to remember what that last business was, but after Nordstrom pulled out, so many others moved in, then followed suit, gone with the mall's dwindling daily head count. At a certain point she'd stopped caring. And then they'd stopped renting it.

She also remembers when it was a Sears, the original anchor tenant. It closed, too, of course, but she wasn't working at Paradise then. She'd been a tween at the time, too young to work, but young enough to still like the mall, back when boys still liked her.

Now, approaching Tagz like she might give a shit about luggage, Jody almost laughs at the prospect of associating any sort of positive emotion with the Paradise Shopping Centre. She *almost* laughs, but a noise behind her chokes the humor.

Jody holds her key in the lock. It's too early for customers—the mall's not open yet—and besides, Tagz is the last store along the east wing before the aisle meets the Wasteland. It's the end of the line.

She looks over her shoulder, toward the vacant department store. The black kraft paper veiling its shutters gives it the illusion of a gaping mouth. She shivers and tunes her ears.

Was it one of the maintenance guys? Slipping into a staff corridor? It couldn't have been. The janitors make their rounds well before the retail staff lug themselves in. Jody knows this. She's been working at Paradise for sixteen years. An assistant manager at Tagz for five. Doing this *very same thing*.

She hears it again, a sort of dampened commotion. No mistake this time, it's coming from the Wasteland. She checks her phone, 8:22 a.m. She's late but can spare a minute. Angie doesn't check the timesheets anymore. Manager or not, she's over *her* job, too.

Jody leaves her keys in the lock. Approaching the Wasteland, she eyes the ghost of the old Sears sign above her head. *Ironic*, she thinks, as the phantom letters sear another hole into her spirits.

It's better than the food court, she reminds herself, remembering her first job at Paradise, on the other side of the mall, and the acne that'd colonized her cheeks. *At least you're not hooked on fucking Cinnabon anymore.* She fingers the scars on her face, still visible beneath a sheet of foundation.

She takes the mini flight of steps toward the Wasteland's entrance but doesn't race down the accessibility ramp like she used to as a girl. Nor does she sit on the steps like she did with Linda and Margot the summer before junior high, their chokers flexing against their necks as they'd powered back their Big Gulps.

In the morning-dark of the mall, Jody can't help but wonder what her old BFFs are doing these days, but she also wonders what good it'll do her to wonder. Last she heard, Margot was running a charity (a fucking charity!), and Linda was getting her PhD. She considers looking them up on social, the self-sabotage cruelly addictive, but knows they've probably got new last names.

Thruuunk!

The sound brings her out of her head. This close, Jody places the noise instantly. Someone's dragging a piece of furniture.

Are they setting something up in there?

She brings her ear closer to the vacant store, suddenly aware of her heavy breathing, but an unwavering certainty pins her in place. It's like a flame catching in her core, flooding her limbs with a soothing surge of blood.

Today's the day I quit.

She can't explain it, but she *feels* it, knows it, like she knows the first four digits of every backordered SKU in her store. Then, as if she's lost control of them, her fingers tear a hole in the craft paper. She brings her eye in, breath lodged in her throat.

The shutters are gone.

The lights are...*on?*

There's a table in the center aisle.

Jody squints at the brightness of it all—the walls and pillars, white and gleaming—as if the building manager primed the space for a new tenant. Everything is clean, not streaked with dust and cobwebs like she'd imagined.

Jody rips the paper enough to step through. Inside, the scent of fresh paint hangs tangy in the air. Beneath it, another smell fights to dominate, like someone lit a match in a bathroom. Jody can't name it, but it clings to her skin like dirt.

"Hello."

Jody yelps as a woman steps out from behind a pillar down the center aisle. Her hair is sun-kissed caramel, teasing her shoulders like it was tousled by God herself. In her tan blazer and black skinny jeans, she's everything Jody wishes she was, the Pinterest epitome of a professional millennial.

"Shit, you scared me." Jody hunts for words, not sure which ones will justify her being here. "I just...I heard a noise."

The woman stares like she's waiting for more. She's so put together, Jody feels the blood flush her cheeks as she considers her own attire, her Lululemons pilling where her thighs meet.

"Sorry," Jody continues, already turning to leave. "I'm not sure where I was going with that. I don't know what I'm doing here."

"Where?"

Jody stops. "I'm sorry?"

"You said you don't know what you're doing here. Where's here...this room or this mall?"

She chews it over. "Good question." They laugh together, so in synch it sends another flash-freeze through Jody's nerves.

"Hang on." The woman disappears behind a pillar then immediately returns. Jody can't be sure she moved at all. She places a tent card on the table then scrawls something on it in thick black Sharpie. She unfolds two chairs and motions for Jody to come over.

"Ta-da!" she says as Jody inches close enough to read the words inked on the makeshift sign. "You're a day early, but I never turn away an applicant."

"I don't understand."

"What's not to understand? It's a job fair. Says right here."

Jody scans the empty department store. "Yeah, but no one's here. No one *comes* here." She wants to say more but catches herself, wishes for the three-thousandth time that Paradise hadn't made her such a monster.

The woman doesn't reply, and Jody feels a hook catch in her stomach. She hopes she hasn't offended her, though the thought doesn't stick around for long. Up close, Jody notices the woman's hands on the table. Each is impossibly long, with what looks like an extra knuckle studding each finger. The skin around her cuticles looks mottled. Aged.

Maybe she chews them, she tells herself, *like a nervous habit*. But she's not convinced. The hook pulls in her stomach as she looks back up.

The woman watches her with a gritty gaze, like she's sizing her up. She leans forward and clasps her hands over the table. It takes everything Jody's got not to look at her fingers, so instead, she opens her mouth without knowing what to say.

"Okay," she starts, "what kind of job fair?" The words just tumble out. She forces a smile, still not sure what she's doing here but unable to walk away.

"Thought you'd never ask," the woman says. "I'm from a staffing agency. We represent a lot of businesses. Marketing, the energy sector, tourism. Like I said, you're a day early. I don't have my—" she pauses and looks to the ceiling, as if she's searching for a word. For a second Jody swears she sees the woman's left iris slip, like she's wearing an unruly contact lens.

But her eyes look so…believable.

"Pamphlets," she continues. "I don't have my pamphlets. But it doesn't matter. The point is, this is a job fair. A *career* fair. A shot at a fresh start!"

"But why here?"

Her lips form a knowing smile. "My experience? You find the most fruitful talent in improbable places."

"Talent," Jody mumbles, testing the word. She tries to think up a talent of her own but comes up empty handed.

"Listen, you must have a lot of questions," the woman says. Her voice is over-enthused but scripted, almost sedative, like the white noise of a late-night infomercial. "But let's not forget that answers come at a price."

Jody can't help it. She laughs, *squeals*, unsure if she's amused or nervous. But then she looks around. The eighty-five-thousand-square-foot space feels new, pristine, in total contrast to the rest of the mall. It's a blank canvas, like her life could be.

This could be real, she thinks, recalling the feeling that swarmed her minutes ago. *This could be my ticket out of here.*

"What kind of price?"

The woman stands up, and it's only now that Jody sees how tall she is, surpassing her own five-and-a-half feet by at least a foot.

"A leap of faith," she says, eyes hinting at hidden knowledge. "A commitment to change. To *embrace* it. The whole process. You have to step into the unknown with the belief that you deserve more than what you're doing today. You deserve more than nine hours of senseless commercialism daily, children wreaking havoc on your displays, their parents overdemanding, syphoning the color from your soul every time a product goes out of stock, as if it's *your* fault, as if you're hiding it in the stockroom in a little neat corner, like you don't know how to do your job.

"You have to *believe*," she continues, "that it's not too late to make something of yourself. You can have something better."

Jody can't tell if she's excited or insulted. Every word from the woman's lips feels invasively tailored, but also like syrup on a toddler's tongue.

"Oh, and your email address." She smiles. "For new job listings."

Jody's heart pumps double-time. She looks at her hand. It's holding a pen that she doesn't remember picking up. The woman pulls a notebook from her back pocket, lays it on the table.

"Jot it down here," the woman says. "I promise I'll follow up."

Promise, Jody thinks, and the word debases her until she's seventeen again, promising herself it's just a part-time job to save for a used car, then to mitigate her mounting debt during college, then a full-time job to keep her apartment when her internship doesn't amount to an offer, just a few more months at Paradise while she hunts for a real job, then a few more when no one calls, then the months become years, more jobs at Paradise, then an assistant management position opens that sounds like it *could* be something, even though it's still retail, but it turns out it's just a set of keys, more work, and an eighty-four-cent raise.

"Promise?" Jody says.

The woman nods.

Jody jots her email down. The elusive smell from earlier surfaces again, only this time it's potent. Unmistakable. Jody would know. She's cleaned the fridge in the lunchroom too many times to count.

Rotting meat.

She hears it before she looks up, the laugh bubbling up the woman's throat. Her voice is deeper now, a devilish drawl. She sets the laugh free, sputtering a mouthful of dirt across the table and into Jody's eyes. Jody screams and brushes it away to find the woman tight-lipped now, both irises running down her eyes like yolk, vanishing behind her bottom eyelids. A chunk of her scalp slips off with a wet sucking sound. It lands at Jody's feet with a hideous slap.

Jody doesn't have time to run. The woman's hands find her wrists and pin them in place. Her skin feels like wet pulp—irregular, breaking apart.

"Just as gullible as the last," the woman says, before a mix of teeth and gum matter spills from her mouth onto Jody's hands. Her breath is like steamed sewage. Jody gags through a face full of tears.

As the overhead light fixtures click off one by one, ushering them into darkness from opposite ends of the store, Jody doesn't bother screaming. Even as the decaying woman sneers and tightens her grip on her wrists, her sodden flesh giving way to bone, Jody doesn't put up a fight. She closes her eyes and accepts it.

It's always been easier that way.

It's been a while since Angela's had to fire someone.

Not because her current staff are a bunch of rock stars (wouldn't that be nice?), but because it's too much effort to onboard someone new, and the resume stack is thinning.

Today, though, Angela knows she needs to put her business hat on. She's been lax for too long with Jody, and on too many things: her clothes and punctuality, her attitude toward customers. But not opening the store? Without even calling? And leaving the keys in the door? Thank god the mall administration notified her. It's not just irresponsible. It's a security issue. There's only so far she can bend.

Angela takes a breath, fiddles with Jody's keychain in the back office. With the day behind her now she tries to piece it together again. There has to be an explanation. *Has* to be. She sighs, already dreading the conversation.

She considers trying Jody's cell again, for the eighth time, but after covering for her all day, she puts the landline back on its receiver. Her feet feel like bludgeoned meat, and she's already left three voicemails.

As she sets the alarm and locks the door, she steals a glance down the hall.

A missed opportunity, she thinks, eyes trained on the forgotten department store. *Maybe if they'd put something good in there we'd get more traffic down here. Hit our numbers for once. Hire some decent staff.*

It's the only thought she gives it, though. She's not in the mood to daydream. It's days like today that she wishes she had other options.

LORCÁN

C. W. STEVENSON

He'd bought the castle for its history, to help preserve and restore what was left, aware of what long, brutal, and bloody past Lorcán Castle possessed... as well as its hauntings.

From Vancouver originally, Julian had finally given in to his desires, making the Green Isle his permanent home after a few trips.

Standing guard over large tracts of pasture near the foot of the Slieve Bloom Mountains, Lorcán stood erect in a near ruinous state. Enveloped by trees of Alder, Ash, and Birch, Lorcán towered above their canopies, its upper floors and battlements visible to the several surrounding farms.

Julian slept on a cot in the great hall the first night, keeping the looming fireplace constantly burning. The walls were furnished with antlers and shoulder mounts. Even a fox head poked out above the main double doors.

Old books, covered in cobwebs and dust littered the chipped, built-in shelves along one wall. The back wall had a small opening, leading to a make-shift conservatory where dozens of plants had thrived without proper care for years. Feeling drowsy, Julian made a mental note to trim back the horde of vines.

Then, there were footsteps.

Because of the clutter, he'd placed his cot next to the winding, stone staircase that led to the lord's chambers, ending with the upper floor—the chapel. Hearing what he swore were small feet climbing up the stairwell, he immediately regretted this decision.

"Hello?" he called out to the darkness.

Cats, maybe?

He'd seen a couple when he'd walked the grounds that evening.

No. He couldn't explain it, but this presence was something benevolent, something he could not explain. All he knew was, besides a few spiders, he was the only *living* thing here this night.

He rubbed his eyes at the mist, almost sparkling in place at the top of the stairs. Then, to his horror, it formed into woman.

Julian stayed still, but he knew that *it* knew exactly where he was. It was staring right at him.

His eyes matched her widening smile as it curved upon her lips.

Her hands reached out toward him, as if beckoning for him to join her on the stairs. Julian saw there was no color to her skin. Even her long, flowing dress was a translucent white mist, hovering there, as if a soft breeze was moving the fabric. But Julian felt nothing.

He stayed motionless as she began withering silently into the blackness of the hall behind her, retreating back into solitude. Floating backwards, dead eyes gazed into Julian's, her hands still gesturing he follow, and her smile...never ceasing.

Once she'd gone, Julian all but ran to his car. Then, driving nearly half a kilometer down the road, he parked to the side and slept.

Julian woke to the sound of something clinking on glass. He expected the garda to be looking back at him, but instead, a man sporting a large, drooping mustache was standing next to the driver's side window.

His neighbor, John Kelly, tapped the window once more, the metal of his wedding ring hitting the glass.

Julian rolled the window down.

"John," he said. "How are ya?"

"I was inclined to be less worried about m'self, seeing the state you're in. I was strollin' to the other side of me pasture when I saw *you* here shiverin'. The spirits kick you out then?"

Julian wasn't sure if the old man was joking.

"Just about," he said. "I saw a woman on the stairs."

John nodded. "I've seen her m'self as a lad, the *White Lady*... in one of them stained glass windows, that is. Figured you'd see them soon, just not *this* soon."

"Them?" Julian asked.

"Mmm," John said. "*Them*. Not sure how many. I overheard Lorcán's previous owners, the O'Bannons, claim there were five. But the woman... they never mentioned."

"Who is she then?"

"Best to stay clear of that one, ya hear? Nothin' good can come meddlin' with the spirits. Best to ignore them all, lad."

Julian smiled. "Better said than done, eh? But why didn't anyone tell me?"

"Well," John began. "You didn't ask. And *you* try tellin' a person such a thing who don't believe in the such or haven't experienced it, and you might as well try convincing'm you're the second comin' of Christ."

With that, John made the sign of the cross.

For the next week, there was no sign of the spirits.

Julian spent this time hard at work, replacing old stones with the new. He repaired the stairwell, adding rails to one side for the tourists he hoped to one day lure in for a few euros apiece. It winded to the second floor, leading to the lord's chambers and ending with the third floor, Julian's least favorite area. The room chilled his very bones each time he emerged onto the open floor. *The Black Chapel*, it was called.

John helped with some of the more laborious tasks, hauling stones or tools to Julian while atop a ladder. On the battlements, early in the morning, just as the sun began to rise over the southern moors, the *boy* made his presence known.

John noticed him first. Passing up fresh plaster, John saw the child standing in an opening on the battlements, as if he were preparing to jump.

"Lad," John urged. "Don't do it."

"What?" Julian chuckled, but when he looked past John, he almost screamed.

Like the White Lady, the *boy* smiled, looking straight at Julian and ignoring John's plea entirely.

For a moment, he tried to convince himself the boy was a local, and that he'd come at the behest of his peers to play the role of a lost spirit to mess with the foreigner.

But when the boy looked to the ground and jumped, Julian's worst fears came alive.

He hadn't imagined the White Lady.

He hadn't imagined the boy.

The tormented souls were here, bound to these old ruins he now called home. Like the unexplained sense of the White Lady's presence on his first night in Lorcán, he *knew* the boy was no living thing.

Startled, Julian fell backwards from the ladder, as both John and what he guessed were his own screams, pierced the morning air.

The world dimmed, and he felt John by his side.

Then, a boy's voice whispered in his ear before all became black.

"Mother...will be looking for me."

A broken leg and a broken collar bone were the cost of his fall.

For the next few months John, and his wife, Marie, helped care for Julian during his recovery. When they'd insisted Julian come stay with them, he politely refused, citing, "The spirits would miss my company."

For the months that followed, Julian studied the castle's history, calling professors at several universities across Ireland and beyond, questioning the men considered the top of their field when it came to Irish castles.

They faxed him records and many other documents containing histories with clues as to who the restless spirits may be.

The White Lady, Lady Clodagh O'Brien, and her youngest son, Tomas, were both victims of suicide amidst the Irish Revolution in April of 1916. A domino effect, Tomas's elder brother had fallen ill, passing swiftly within the course of a few days. A fever took him in the night. The next morning, Tomas took to the battlements in his grief and threw himself from the ledge. His mother followed.

But the most disturbing account had come from John.

Sharing the burden of pouring through the piles of historical text, John uncovered the darkest of atrocities committed in *The Black Chapel*.

As bloodthirsty chieftains of the land, the O'Calloghans had hired Norman mercenaries to help drive off nearby rival clans. Once victorious, the two factions celebrated with a feast. Cut short, the O'Calloghans poisoned the mercenaries before hacking them to death. Those unfortunate enough to live were tossed down a bottleneck dungeon adorned with spikes. The dead were thrown down on top of them. It was said those who survived the fall screamed for days in constant agony before succumbing to their wounds.

"Trapped," John said. "For *days*...amidst the darkness and rats. From the other side of the pasture," he pointed, "I've seen faint light coming through that upper window...when there should be none. My entire life, I've seen those lights from time to time. I thought by helpin' you I might quelch my fears of the dead. Not after this," and he put a finger on the passage depicting the gruesome murders.

For a time, only Julian toiled away on Lorcán. John still came by to chat about this or that, but he never stepped inside, even when Julian hinted at the need for company. Mostly, they conjugated with the other townsfolk at the local pub.

One day, while attending business in Cork, Julian met an Irish lass who caught his eye called Cara. Within the year, they were wed, making the haunted halls of Lorcán their home. For a while, the spirits were silent. A few books scattered, some footsteps unaccounted for, but no apparitions appearing before them. Soon, they had a little girl they named Ciera.

A week after her birth, Julian found the bottleneck dungeon.

He'd been removing the crumbling wall away, replacing it with recycled stone from an old barn on his property when he found a walled-off opening. Looking down, the drop must've been nearly twenty feet. Rubble mostly, piled atop two centuries worth of loose earth, web, and *bones*.

After the excavators wheeled the remains away, they'd claimed to have recovered more than three cartloads of human bones, considerably *more* than the single massacre John had read of. It was apparent that the descendants, future lords, and owners of Lorcán had continued using the dungeon, or, an *oubliette*, according to the excavators. For another two centuries it'd been in use, proven by a watch manufactured in the 19th century, still wrapped around the wrist bone of its master.

Cara had been furious at him for keeping the severity of Lorcán's bloody past relatively secret.

"You would've never accepted it as your home," he'd told her. "Forgive me. Please. What spirits there were have found peace. We can as well, finally."

"Then you believe in the stories?" she asked.

"No," he replied. "I believe in the history and for what I've seen for myself."

Deep in the night, Ciera would scream until Cara or Julian came to calm her. The family doctor's diagnosis was colic, but Julian knew better, and in time, Cara did as well.

The door to Ciera's room would be left open, but only slightly. Upon entering, they would find it colder than the rest of the castle, regardless of it being the nearest chamber to the fireplace.

Then, footsteps began to be heard regularly around the castle again. Come dawn, Julian would find books and objects strewn about on the floor, or their possessions placed in strange places. What'd sent Cara over the edge was finding Ciera's stuffed rabbit on the edge of the oubliette—the henge Julian had fitted to cover its opening undone, its door swung open wide.

"They were waiting for her to get near the edge!" Cara screamed.

Julian countered, "They don't touch like that, they've *never* touched us."

"A *hand* grazed me on the stairwell," she tried to reason. "You've felt it too! How many times? I know I've lost count. It's *her*, Julian."

The White Lady had made herself known more and more since Ciera was born. Many nights, he'd spy her leaving he and Cara's chambers, heading back to the lonely dark of the stairwell. Julian couldn't understand her fascination with him and his family. Perhaps she was jealous his own child lived while hers did not... there was no way of telling, and from what Julian had studied, communicating with her and the *others* within Lorcán would only be seen as an invitation.

When they'd found Ciera at the other end of the crib Cara had *sworn*, she'd placed her in, Cara packed her and Ciera's things and left. Julian refused to leave, proclaiming Lorcán as his home and theirs. A week later, there were divorce papers weighed down by a rock on Lorcán's doorstep.

Julian lost himself in his work. There was an actual toilet now, where for years he'd been using an outhouse. For the tourist's sake, Julian did not add electrical wiring to the stairs or that of the upper floor. He *wanted* their sense of fear to come from the darkness. Afterall, he couldn't rely on the White Lady grazing past *every* tourist on the stairwell.

Soon enough, he began to let folks from all around go on self-guided tours throughout his home. Being that Ciera still came to visit, he kept his working hours strictly to during the week. She was enthusiastic about his venture until one day, he'd found her sobbing near the county road, sitting her back against the gate.

Calmy, he sat beside her.

"Who did you see?" he asked.

When she could speak, she looked at her father and told him, "There were lots, I think..." she stifled, then continued, almost haphazardly, "I think it was the soldiers who were murdered. They had axes, Da. They were lookin' at me. The oubliette is open again."

Julian tried to reason with her, "They're little more than memories, Cee. The paper their lives are written on is more real than they are. Do you understand?"

She shook her head. "I *understand* you've given your life to this place, and it's left you half a cripple. You sit there, next to the fire with your books and your ghosts, and you act as if it's perfectly normal when it is anything but."

It was the last time Ciera would come to visit he realized, but in truth, there was a weight lifted from his shoulders. Julian could finally open up more to those who cared about his little piece of the past, without judgement. Soon, he was opening Lorcán's doors on the weekends as well.

Julian began receiving calls from film production companies and media outlets, wanting to schedule interviews, or make documentaries. Largely, it was the ghost hunters and paranormal experts bringing him in the *real* cash, their main goal being to capture an otherworldly occurrence, negative in nature. But Julian didn't mind, his capitalization of Lorcán and her dark histories had provided the castle with the renovation it needed to last. Lorcán had been standing for six-hundred years, and now, it'd be standing another six-hundred, or beyond.

An old man now, John Kelly used his cane to assist his old legs to the great, double doors of Lorcán Castle. After a long walk, he was looking forward to sitting beside the hearth of Lorcán once again. He needed the rest, and besides, he promised he'd be there for the concert Julian would be hosting in the great hall next week, so, getting over his fear within those old stones would need some mending.

Julian opened the door and light poured into the gloomy hall.

"John," he smiled. "Come on in."

"I don't see ya down at the pub much these days," John inquired.

"No, no, she's got me pretty busy."

John wasn't sure if he meant *her* as in the castle itself or... *her*. For the moment, John didn't question it.

"Wasn't sure I'd be able to make it inside. But now that I'm here, I must say lad, you've done fine work. I do believe the O'Calloghans would be proud."

"Well, I thank you for the kind words, John."

"All these years," John said, gazing around the great hall as he spoke, "Restoring the damnedest stones in all the county, maybe the Éire... I never asked you *why* you did it."

"Well, I can tell you it wasn't for the money," they both laughed knowingly. The trust had dried up long before he'd made Lorcán a roadside attraction.

"Not doing too bad for yourself now though."

"No," Julian admitted. "In fact, I've got a couple staying in the chapel tonight. *Thrill seekers*, Cara calls them."

"No disrespect, but would you not put your own self in that category?"

Julian grinned at that and said, "I'm just a man who fell in love with a country other than the one he was born in, and I love her history most of all."

Shaking his finger at Julian, John told him, "I'd say you got more than you bargained for when you bought this accursed pile of rubble. But you changed it, made it your own. I never told you, but I was glad you stuck with it all these years. Would've been a wee bit lonelier without you around."

"Thanks John," and he meant it. Then, leaning back in his chair next to the crackling flames, he took a sip of his beer, staring into the same flames many of the dead walking his halls had done centuries before. He wondered then, if after his death, he'd be walking these very halls, confined within the walls of Lorcán forever. Further, he wondered if the White Lady would beckon him to the battlements, to follow her Tomas, as she had.

Then, John brought him back to the present.

"So then why?" John asked. "Why go through it all? I know plenty of folk who love the histories, I'm one of'm, you know it's true. But your fascination goes beyond your love for history, I suspect. Livin' with the spirits..." and he shook his shoulders, "That's more than a love for history."

"You're wrong," Julian said. Then, he raised his glass, and John tapped Julian's glass with his own. They drank before Julian continued, "The spirits... the White Lady, the men trapped in the dungeon, the boy, all of'm... they're the biggest part of history in this place. I used to think it was these stones and the—"

Just then, they heard footsteps.

John stopped searching for the source when he found Julian gazing at the top of the stairs. He turned his head then, dreading what he knew he was about to see, and *who*.

The White Lady peered down on them, her dead eyes unblinking, her smile, the very same Julian had detailed to John so many times before, and the same he'd seen as a child, so long ago.

Drifting back toward the stairwell, her hands gently floated outward, beckoning they follow.

Standing up from his chair, Julian stared at the spirit, their eyes linked as she settled further back into the shadows.

Stopping at the foot of the stairs, Julian looked back at John.

"Don't be afraid," he said quietly.

Unable to speak, yet unable to look away, John watched in paralyzed fear as the lord of the castle went after his lady.

Jackson

GAYLE SIEBERT

It's a lovely evening for a stroll, but Nikki isn't enjoying it. She spent most of the day at the beach. She's covered in sunblock and sand. Her feet already hurt, and she still has about an hour's walk. To top it all off, now that the sun is setting the mosquitoes are coming out. It was a crappy thing to do, and she still can't believe they did it to her.

She's not used to walking or doing anything physical so she's tiring. It's almost more than she can manage to keep putting one foot in front of the other. She begins counting, "One, two, three, four," and so on. When she gets to a hundred, she begins at one again. When she gets to a hundred for the second time, she says, "Two hundred," and begins at one again.

An unpleasant, pungent smell assaults her. There seems to be something rustling around in the underbrush next to the path just behind her. She stops and turns around to see what it is. The branches on the low shrubbery move a little as if stirred by the breeze, then are still, and the bad smell fades.

"What was that?" she asks of no one. There's no breeze so why did the branches rustle? She stands statue still and quiet, watching that spot in the bushes to see if one of the feral rabbits that live everywhere around here might come out. Or maybe it was birds.

But all is quiet except for the steady hum of the traffic on the nearby freeway, and the bushes remain still. She thinks she must have been imagining things or whatever was in the bush is long gone. She continues on her way. But she's lost count of her steps, so she gives up counting, turns on her iPhone playlist, and puts her earbuds on.

It's getting late, and she feels an uneasy twinge of nerves when she realizes if she doesn't speed it up, she won't get through the part of the path that goes through the forest before it's dark.

The bushes next to the path just a few meters ahead move. Again, she stops and watches. It's something bigger than a rabbit. There have been bear and cougar sightings here, but more likely, it's a deer. She draws a deep breath. That smell again! The branches are still. All is quiet. But she is filled with the feeling of being watched, and the hairs on the back of her neck prickle. She begins singing along with Taylor Swift, loudly but tunelessly, and walks faster.

As she comes to the beginning of the forest she starts jogging. This isn't easy in flip flops. She mutters, "God damn you all to hell, Lily Mae!"

Tears sting her eyes when she thinks about the other girls leaving the beach while she was in the washroom. They had done the same thing to others before, but Nikki never thought Lily Mae would do it to her! But now she had.

The first time they took off on someone was last fall. They were watching the boys show off at the skate bowl. Lauren was on the other side fooling around with Jackson, and when the two of them went down the path that leads behind the skate bowl and out of sight, Lily Mae said, "Let's take off on her!" They bolted for the car, jumped in, and went racing out of the parking lot, spewing gravel. It was thrilling! They laughed so hard they cried, thinking how shocked Lauren would be when she finally took her eyes off Jackson and realized they had left. Payback for her coming on to Jackson. Everyone knows he's Lily Mae's boyfriend! But at least Lauren had a chance to get a ride home because Jackson and some other guys were still skating.

But she never got home. Jackson said she didn't want to wait until he was ready to go, so she started off hitching, and hasn't been seen since. Foolish girl! Everyone knows hitching is dangerous.

A couple of other girls have gone missing since Lauren disappeared. The city is beginning to get national media attention for the number of missing girls. The RCMP have set up a special task force. A bunch of people at school have been interviewed. The last time it was on the news, the RCMP spokesperson said there were no leads and called for the public to come forward if they have any information, no matter how unimportant it might seem.

Today, Lily Mae and the new girl left when they were the last people at the beach, and the sun was low in the sky. Lily Mae knew it would mean she had no way to get home other than to walk and it would likely be in the dark. She not only didn't care, but planned it. It would be a nasty thing to do any time, but especially with all the missing girls!

Now she's breathing too hard to sing and can't run anymore. As she approaches the part of the trail nearest the swamp, clouds of mosquitoes attack. The smell is stronger here. She identifies it as sewage. Kind of smoky sewage. She wishes she could hold her breath. *There must be a sewer pipe running through here, and it's broken,* she thinks. Or maybe it's just that the level of water in the swamp is higher than usual because of the rainy summer.

The forest is not only dark, but feels ten degrees colder. An intense chill knifes through her, and she wishes she had more than the flimsy cover-up over her bikini. A big sweatshirt like those worn by girls who have no boobs to show off would be welcome now.

To top it off, the feeling of being watched has intensified, and several times, she's so sure she's being followed that she looks over her shoulder. She stops and turns on the flashlight on her iPhone. The low battery warning flashes on the screen. She has to get through the forest before it goes out. Her guts clench.

"It's not much further," she tells herself. "You're halfway there!" Once out into the open stretch, she'll be safe.

Something catches her toe, and she sprawls forward, landing painfully on hands and knees. She jumps to her feet. The heels of her hands and both knees are scraped. Burning. Stinging. She picks up her phone, but just as she does, the battery dies. No more flashlight! It's enough to make her cry, but she tells herself, *nothing's broken, get moving before it's completely dark.* She gives an anguished sob and walks on, more slowly now, desperate to stay on the path. Branches seem to be reaching out to grab her, and something, likely a blackberry vine, nearly wraps around her ankle.

"It's just branches, just branches," she mutters.

Suddenly, a dark figure steps out of the gloom right in front of her. He is dressed all in black, and his face is so deep inside the hood he appears faceless. She screams.

"Nikki," the figure says, "it's just me! Did I scare you? I'm sorry." He pushes his hood back and Nikki recognizes him.

"Jackson! Yeah, you scared me! Scared the shit outta me, actually!" Nikki takes a few deep breaths to calm herself, then walks up to him. "What are you doing here?"

"Lily Mae told me what, er, happened at the lake. It was a joke, she said. She has a rotten sense of humor sometimes."

"Ya think? So ... You came to find me?"

"Yeah."

"My hero!"

"That's me! My car's parked up at the storage lot. I thought I could intercept you here and give you a ride the rest of the way."

"Oh, that's great. But the storage lot? It's quite a walk still."

"I know a shortcut through the bush. The trail starts here." He turns and indicates a break in the underbrush.

"Oh! Okay," Nikki says. It's not much of a trail, but it does explain how Jackson was able to materialize on the path right in front of her, seemingly out of thin air. She takes a deep breath and falls in behind him as he leads her into the deeper gloom.

"I can't see a thing! Don't you have a flashlight? At least your phone?"

He turns again and says, "It's okay, I have really good night vision. Like a cat! Just stay with me. Here, take my hand."

Did his eyes suddenly flash? Nikki is reminded of her cat's eyes, golden, and with the pupil a vertical slit. But she must have been imagining things. He did say cat, after all. That must have tricked her brain. His eyes are perfectly normal, and he's smiling as he offers his hand. She clasps it and feels a vast sense of relief as she allows him to tow her along.

It's so dark she can't see much of anything, least wise where she's going, but Jackson goes on without hesitation. She thinks, *he really does have cat-like vision*, and stays close behind him. So close, she can smell him. It's a scent of smoke and sweat, masculine, but rather unpleasant. She'll have to ask him what cologne he's wearing and suggest he get something else.

Just as Nikki has that thought, Jackson stops so abruptly that she bumps into him and steps right out of her flip flop.

"Aggghh! A little warning would be nice! I've lost my flip flop. Find it for me, would you? I can't see where it is. What did you stop for?"

There's movement in the underbrush several meters off the narrow path, much more powerful than the rustling noises Nikki noticed earlier. She screams.

"It's okay," Jackson tells her, and pulls her roughly into his arms. "It's my, er, cousin."

"Cousin?" When she fantasized being in his arms, she thought it would be nice, but he's holding her as if to stop her from getting away. "Jeez, Jackson, not so tight. You're hurting me!"

The underbrush rustles as though a powerful whirlwind is passing through, and a funnel cloud of tiny swirling stars forms. As it comes closer, the stars coalesce in the center, becoming more and more solid until they form a creature. It looms up over them, staring with the lidless eyes of a snake. It is covered in glistening scales. There are two holes that must be nostrils and the drooling, red-rimmed mouth has double rows of long teeth. Flaps like small, jagged elephant ears run up the sides of its head, joined together on its crown by a glowing green ridge, illuminating a sphere around them. Its forelegs are thin and undulate as the creature's body sways like a snake charmer's cobra. There are long, saber-like claws on its hands? Paws? But the appendages appear useless, like vestigial legs, left-overs of evolution.

This is Jackson's cousin? Nikki can't suppress a sobbing squeak. She shrinks back and tries to hide behind Jackson, but he turns her to face the creature, his hands like vice grips on her arms.

"Thissss issss a nissssss one," the creature hisses. Plumes of smoke come from its nostrils.

"This is the last one I'm going to bring you," Jackson says.

"Thissss issss not your choissss."

"The cops are starting to get suspicious. You've seen them going all through here with their dogs, right? They're hunting ussss!"

"You hafff to be more careffffulll."

"No! I'm done! I've changed my mind. I don't want immortality, or magic, and I don't want to live in the marssshhhh with you."

"You don't hafff a choisss."

"No! I'm not gonna do it! I won't be a ffffreak like you! I…"

With astonishing speed, one of the creature's little arms slices the air. A saber-like claw slashes Jackson's neck. His head falls and rolls across Nikki's feet as she's covered in hot arterial blood spray.

She has time to think, *oh, those arms aren't useless after all.*

It's strange how the mind works.

Then the creature enfolds her, and her nostrils fill with the choking, nauseating stench of smoke and sewage as she's pulled against him. She isn't able to utter more than a squawk before it bites through her neck.

The creature picks up Jackson's body, and everything disintegrates into a swirling mist of tiny stars and disappears.

In the morning, all that is found is a torn, discarded flip flop, and of course, Jackson's head. Instead of skin on the back of his neck, there are shiny, iridescent scales. His grieving parents explain that the family is cursed with a rare, severe form of psoriasis that affects a few unfortunate individuals every generation. To respect the family's privacy, this detail is never disclosed to the media.

The Bark

GLENN DUNGAN

You do not recognize the bodies in the forest.

I implore you to listen to me, just listen.

No one knows when the bodies started appearing, hanging from the gnarled branches of Cog Hollow. Little Janine says she sees the body of her grandmother hanging like a broken chicken wing at the edge of the school. Postman Milton swears he sees the checkered house dress of his sister flapping in the wind like laundry out to dry. They say there is a rule of threes for examples, but I think you get it.

You do not recognize the bodies in the forest.

Sometimes they appear out of the corner of your eye, like a little light flash. Other times they appear in the middle of errands, or trips around town, staring directly at you with vacant, lifeless eyes. The time does not matter. People have seen them over their morning eggs and coffee, outside of the window of Pat's Diner. Dusk makes only the ones wearing darker clothing more difficult to see, but no one usually dies wearing flashy clothing. Most of the bodies wearing lighter clothing are children or little siblings. I've always seen them, too, without pattern or prompt.

You do not recognize the bodies in the forest.

The bodies always hang, always sway. No one knows why the bodies appear. No one knows why two people can see the same body. Or why Robert from the corner of Bleeker and Rye sees his estranged sister while Hannah, the bartender at Jacob's Tavern, sees her father who died of cancer ten years ago. Even more, the bodies will be of loved ones strangled by a rope and hanging like a limp scarecrow, always, regardless how they died. And you will want to save them.

The bodies only sway in the branches, latticed by gnarled, dying leaves. They do not come into town, and everyone from Adam knows not to go into the forest. They won't hurt you, we tell the children, and they don't. Until they do.

Last autumn, same time around now actually, Paul McCoy was taking a walk down the fields, keeping very clear of the forest. Paul has seen the bodies. He has gotten used to seeing Mama McCoy dangling from the rafters, a coarse rope cinching her liver spotted neck. He is used to seeing his brothers and sisters bent at odd geometries, sunspots of blood splattered on the clothes they died in, not the ones they were buried in. Paul understands this of the forest, knows this is just a trick, knows its ruses. His constitution is strong, as is everyone's in Cog Hollow, but once he hears the voice of his estranged son who ran away from home at sixteen and missed every Christmas since, Paul came a-runnin into that dark forest, past the dangling bodies, past the tattered remains of those he recognizes but knows isn't real. Can you imagine that? Ducking underneath the boots of your brother, scuffed with grime and fish flecks from the docs. Running in between the heels of the semolina dusted shoes of his cake loving mother, fat but weightless, held up by a thin reed of a branch. Paul goes into the forest, into its stomach, finds his boy stuck in time, still at sixteen. The next morning, we all see Paul in the middle of Main Street, his body snapped at all joints, spleen ballooned out of him, entrails coagulating underneath the crisp air. No teeth. No tongue. It is little Janine and her school friends who find him on their way to morning classes. This is not a coincidence. I'm trying to help this make sense for you.

You do not recognize the bodies in the forest.

The FBI came and visited our little town for Mr. McCoy's murder, because even our local law enforcement could not lie about the bodies in the forest. The first wave was simple protocol, invasive because they existed. Black vans parked along the side of the main road, suits and sunglasses taking residences in the Clarence's Inn right on McGowen. They interviewed everyone, myself included. It was the forest, we said, the forest took Paul McCoy.

"The forest?" they said, as if we were crazy.

"The forest, not the bodies."

The FBI directed their attention to the forest, their backs turned to us. We watched them from our windows, watched the sun set as they waded through the long, browning grass, stepping over the plants getting ready for the great resurrection of next year. We saw them nudge one another, point at bodies that we all recognized. I saw an agent point a shaking finger to my grandfather who died in '82 and claim that she was his little sister, Samantha. We saw minds begin to break, and it was both fascinating, yet sad. Pistols drawn as if this could dispel the illusion. Into the brush they went, pulled by the need to save their siblings, their parents, their lovers. Those that remained were shattered afterwards, and yes, it was heartbreaking.

The second wave consisted of chemists, botanists, all the eggheads. They shut down poor Rosie's Pub and Pat's Diner, for a place to hold their beakers and test tubes. They set up a perimeter around town, long barriers with twenty-four-hour surveillance. Riflemen posted at the corners of all junctions, aimed at the forest. They worked in shifts of two hours, consistently moving up and down the rickety ladders. I get it. Enough exposure to seeing your mama, or little sister all twisted and hanging limp is enough to break you emotionally, even though you know it's fake. When they went into the forest, they wore quarantine outfits. I saw some of the agents returning to town with tears in their eyes, some with splotches of blood from suicides of their colleagues.

Occasionally, one of the hazmatted FBI agents will appear like a crumpled candy wrapper in the middle of Main Street. Tossed aside like trash. No teeth. No tongue.

The third wave overlapped with the second. They brought psychologists to talk to us before they pricked at us with needles and little rods. They thought we were causing the bodies in the forest, that we were playing a giant trick on the FBI. Why? We are plagued with it as much as they, we've just learned to live with it. Me, Bill Montgomery, and Anna Beth, all think this is what makes them so suspicious of our little town, that we have just learned to live with it. We have no other choice.

You do not recognize the bodies in the forest.

The fourth wave was seances, shamans, people with Ouija Boards and funny incense. Made our little town look like a gypsy carnival. Who knew the FBI had this division, this paranormal sector? It was all so silly. Here is a list of theories that the FBI revealed to us during one of the mandatory town hall meetings where they locked the doors from the outside:

1) Spores in the forest inhibit a neurochemical response that evokes the emotional effect of seeing a loved one hanging from the trees.

2) The townsfolk have all been infected with some invasive bacteria in the water or crops which makes us perceptive to illusions.

3) Communism. Just that. Communism.

It goes without saying that after all these months the FBI has determined nothing. Perhaps it is the separation of church and state. They did not bring in any priests, any holy men of any kind. In all their knowledge, no one noticed that our little town of Cog Hollow has no church, no pews of worship, no sacred spaces. We have our little diners, our watering holes, our corner stores. But no church. We've had churches but they've all caught flame, and you do not recognize the bodies in the forest and not once did they ask us if we are religious. We are. We believe in The Bark because we must. We believe in The Bark because we have no option not to. We do not know where The Bark comes from, or how long it has resided in the forest. All we know is that The Bark needs to feed.

I've seen The Bark, once. I was at the edge of the forest on a crisp autumn morning much like this one, much like the one which took Paul McCoy, much like today. I was a boy then, fascinated with the impending doom that I could allow myself if I just stepped forward. A child's game. My neck hurt from staring at the dangling legs of my grandfather. Behind him was my aunt who was taken by cancer last year, and next to her, dangling from an adjacent tree, was a brother who died in a car accident. I have not seen him in years, but I could tell he died by the bludgeon to the head, the busted cervix. I stood at the edge of the forest, the toes of my sneakers pressing upon the cold and shadowed Earth, the leaves moving like little tendrils. Wind whistled through the trees, moving in the empty spaces of the darkness. The lifeless eyes of my loved ones looked down at me from their bondages, their faces blistered and purple from asphyxiation, eyes bulged. I wanted to save them, I did. It is human nature and The Bark preys on this.

I told myself that I did not recognize the bodies in the forest. I just wanted to stare at the abyss, like a sort of game, a controlled dance with death. A tug of war of wills.

The Bark appeared in the thresh of the woodland, a figure looming behind the trees. A juggernaut of cosmic insult. I swear the trees parted like curtains for it, or else reality warped, twisted, and broke as I gazed upon it, waiting, salivating to mangle my body, take my teeth and tongue. Smells of rotted vegetables and moss bombarded the forest and I swear all the trees were in on it.

The Bark is tall, looming, and bends at odd angles. A dry and dusty cloak, like a moth's wing, wraps around a hollowed, skeletal torso. Gnarled fingers look like roots. It wears a crown that has sprouted naturally from its head, and its skin is a white bark, both petrified and flaky. No eyes. It stands with its arms folded behind its back, guarded by the bodies it wants you to see, the bodies *you* want to see. And it waits. The Bark waits, clicking, and clacking, the distant sound of twigs breaking, the knotty creaking of wood bending.

Without moving, I could tell it was beckoning me into the forest, a gravitational pull that blackened out my peripheries. I ran faster than I could that day, and still I woke up with splinters.

I've seen The Bark, yes, and I hope I never see it again. Now all I see are the bodies, some new, some old.

Lately...well, lately they look a little bit like you.

The Return

Jessica Clem

Alexa eyes the stranger in her living room with cool, calm composure. The man, dressed in black from head to toe, watches her with wide, bloodshot eyes, while an empty syringe trembles in his hand. "What the hell took you so long, Neko?" he asks as he shakes his head patronizingly. "This could have gone wrong. Really wrong. Like, 'sorry, the cancer's spread to the fuckin' liver,' wrong."

Somewhere in her atavistic brain, Alexa knows her survival depends on playing along. However, due to the crumpled body of her husband lying between her and the stranger, this proves challenging.

Her eyes flick down to the bloodied carpet and into Brian's wide, dead eyes. His swollen tongue protrudes rudely at her from his open mouth, still coated with foamy spit. The needle in his chest casts a slight shadow on his gray t-shirt.

Her mind whirls.

It's a hit. Who would put a hit on Brian?

"I got held up," she said, sliding a hand through her short, blonde hair to hide her trembling fingers. She reaches behind her and locks the door. The stranger lets out a loud exhale.

"Goddamnit," he mutters as he lowers the syringe. "Chase has got to do better with coordination. What if you had been a neighbor? Or this idiot's wife?" The stranger gestures to the dead man at their feet—the man who is, in fact, Alexa's husband.

"Don't blame me. Blame Chase," she snaps.

The stranger's brow furrows. Alexa was sure she'd been caught and was almost ready to fall to her knees and beg for mercy. But he laughs. Alexa's skin crawls at the cruel and lighthearted sound.

"I'm Chris," the stranger said. "And holy shit, am I glad you showed up when you did."

She smiles thinly and almost reaches for the closet door but stops before her arm twitches in that direction. A hit woman wouldn't hang up her jacket. Instead, she tosses it on her beloved ivory couch with the light pink pillows.

"Neko. But you already know that."

Alexa shakes out her newly cut and dyed hair, marveling at how a meaningless yet dramatic change has saved her life. Just an hour ago, she'd exchanged her waist-length brown hair with a pink pixie cut. She'd come home and knocked coyly on the door, excited to surprise Brian with her new look.

The stranger caps the syringe, drops it in the open briefcase on the end table, and scratches his bald head. "I gotta admit, I don't understand why pink hair is back," he said. Alexa doesn't respond. Instead, she focuses on his gloved hands–hands that had taken her husband's life.

"Chase said you liked to make an entrance. Hey, I'm not one to judge."

Alexa looks past him and to the pink couch pillows. Brian had resisted the pillows at first. She had defended her choice in Target like a child bargaining for a puppy. "You have to think about the whole color scheme," she had said, her hands splayed and raised like she was explaining the symbolism in a piece of art. "It won't be the focal point. It will be an accent. You won't even know it's there." He had laughed and planted a kiss on her forehead.

"Whatever you want, Ms. Ridgemont," he said. "You know best."

Flickers of rage and grief dance inside her guts. She recognizes this feeling and wants to stoke and baby the urge for as long as possible.

Yet she knows focus is the key to the return.

"This line of work is tough," she said. "I have to keep it interesting."

Twenty years ago: The crash

Alexa's father sputtered and wheezed behind the truck's steering wheel. His eyes bulged out of his head as he groped at his chest. "Hurts," he wheezed. Eight-year-old Alexa, barely old enough to see over the dash, grabbed the wheel from the passenger seat and yanked it to the right. The truck swerved sharply out of the opposite lane.

"Good girl," her father gasped. Tears shone on his twisted, leaden face. He let out a high groan. "Okay, grab the pills, honey."

With one hand still on the wheel, Alexa fished in her father's shirt pocket for the nitroglycerin bottle—the gift of time for good men with bad hearts.

Her hands shook as she fished out the bottle. The truck swung back and forth like a fishing boat on a violent sea. "I have to let go of the wheel, Daddy," she said, her voice an octave higher than usual. "I can't open the bottle with one hand."

Her father nodded and grimaced as he returned one hand to the wheel. The realization that her father's funeral was just a pill away turned her fingers into feathers. She struggled with the cap as sweat stung her eyes.

Suddenly, her father's mouth slackened, and his hand slid off the wheel. His foot dropped heavily on the pedal. Alexa's eyes widened.

"Daddy, that's not the brake," she panted. Anxiety bound her fingers together. She struggled with the cap, her heart pounding so hard she could barely hear her father's agonized moans. His knee bounced. But his foot stayed heavy on the gas.

"*Fuck*!" Alexa shouted, knowing her daddy wouldn't care that she swore. She had to act fast. Death was just a tire scream away for both of them. She fumbled open the bottle. Pills exploded onto the console like confetti from a cannon. The engine roared.

Alexa leaned forward and scooped two pills up from the floor mat. She brought them to her father's gaping mouth, but both tablets slipped through her fingers and tumbled down his sweat-soaked shirt.

"*Fuck*," she shouted again as she reached for the spilled pills. She didn't see the telephone pole rushing toward the windshield.

The truck spun hard to the right and roared through a ditch. Alexa flew up from her seat and hit the headliner with a sick thud.

The truck slammed into the pole.

Alexa hit the dashboard.

Darkness pulled her down its throat.

Now: The apartment

The hitman steps over Brian's prone body and pulls a new pair of surgical gloves from the briefcase. "Don't touch anything," he says. "You got gloves on you?"

She keeps her voice as steady as possible. "Of course. You think it's my first job?"

Her heart thuds loudly in her ears. She has no gloves on her, but there are some in the cabinet under the sink. She just has to distract Chris for a few minutes.

"Just take these," he says, handing her a pair of black gloves from the briefcase.

She peeks inside the briefcase as she slips on the gloves. Inside are two more syringes, each filled with a murky liquid. "Morphine and epinephrine," Chris says. "It puts on quite a show—you see their hearts explode." He laughs again, and Alexa forces a grin.

"Well, isn't that lucky for us," she says.

He nods and turns back to the kitchen. Alexa scans his broad shoulders and his squat, fat neck. The zipped leather jacket would render the syringe useless unless she could get it into his neck. Unfortunately, he has a bulldog's head, and the thick leather hides most of his neck.

Her eyes travel to the knife block in the kitchen.

Chris caught her eye.

"We cleared the kitchen beforehand," he says. "The knives have been swept."

He kicks Brian's limp foot.

"This guy didn't have a chance."

Twenty years ago: The crash

Alexa woke to a pain-filled world.

White smoke slithered through the cab. Pain commanded her body like a demon hellbent on possession. Her daddy was silent. She moaned and tried turning her head away from the passenger window so she could look at him, but the bent headliner trapped her in place. As she did, shattered glass sank into her cheek like millions of tiny teeth.

Her scream ricocheted in the dilapidated, steaming truck cabin. She closed her eyes again and counted her breaths. When she was calm enough, she lifted her left arm. It was bloodied and stiff, but the arm still rose on command. Breathing steadily, she forced her arm outward to the driver's seat. Her hand landed on her daddy's leg.

"Daddy?" she croaked.

No answer.

She made a fist and shoved it into his thigh. Nothing.

She inhaled sharply and pushed her head into the headrest. It gave her just enough room to turn her head to the left. Glass sank into her face and drew more blood, but she didn't care.

She looked at him. She wanted to scream again, but her throat wouldn't allow it.

Her daddy lay on top of the steering wheel with his eyes closed. His head was at an odd angle, and his spine rose from his broken neck like a lighthouse in a bloody sea.

"Dadddyyy," she moaned. Tears stung the bloodied rivers on her face. "D-Daddy, no."

The grief and horror slid out of her like a child taking off a costume. It stood behind her daddy and leered at her cruelly. "I want my daddy back," she bawled to it.

The thing inside the darkness grinned.

Then bring him back.

Something shifted inside her head. It crepitated through her skull with searching, probing fingers. Thick blackness blinded her and cut off her tears. Another world opened up inside her head.

Alexa inhaled and stepped into it.

She was no longer in the truck. She wasn't anywhere. She stood alone in complete darkness. An alarm rang through her. Yet, the darkness was comforting. It was like going home. She raised a hand and hit a rough, stone ceiling.

It was a tunnel.

She walked down it with her hands outstretched.

Inside the truck cabin, her eyes rolled back, and she lost consciousness once again.

Now: The apartment

"I suppose we should get this cleaned up," Chris says, gesturing at Brian's body like roadkill. "But first, I gotta take a leak. You don't mind being left alone with him?"

Alexa wrinkles her nose from the couch.

"Do what you have to do. Next time, spare me the details."

He smiles. "Back in a flush."

He walks down the short hallway toward her and Brian's bedroom. Alexa hears the bathroom door click shut, and her calm expression disappears. She leaps from the couch, tears stinging her eyes–all composure gone instantly. She falls to the ground and cradles Brian's head in her lap. "Oh, my sweetheart," she moans, carefully keeping her keening to a low roar. She nuzzles his cold face, as enraptured with him as a Labrador.

A soft knock at the door snaps her out of her hysteria.

"Chris?"

Alexa gently lowers Brian's head back to the floor and stands slowly.

"Chris," the voice repeats. "It's Neko. Let me in."

The blood drains out of Alexa's face. Without breaking her gaze on the door, Alexa walks to the briefcase on the coffee table and pulls out another syringe. With the needle in her hand, she rushes to the door and swipes her keys from her fallen jacket. She tucks them into her jeans pocket and looks through the peephole.

A young woman stands on the other side. She wears a black beanie and an unbuttoned dark peacoat. The girl's hat reveals a streak of pink hair that is more neon than Alexa's.

The girl knocks again, louder this time.

"Chris," she says. "What the fuck is happening in there?"

Alexa's hand slides down to the lock. She has to move fast, or she will lose her cool.

She unlocks the deadbolt.

Neko sighs. "Thank God," she says. "Hurry up."

Alexa grips the doorknob. Her gloved hand slides across the smooth metal, and an odd, coppery taste fills her dry mouth.

Now.

She opens the door.

Neko has enough time to furrow her brow before Alexa buries the needle into the side of her neck. The girl sputters beneath her like a cold engine. Alexa turns the flailing girl down the hallway as Neko's arms beat against Alexa's sweating back. Empowered by her dominance, Alexa shoves the girl faster down the hallway. Alexa's storage unit is just down the hall from her apartment. She needs to get the girl there quickly before any inquisitive neighbors stick their heads into the hallway.

"Chris," the girl calls weakly. Her light green eyes fixate on Alexa's face.

"Who are you?" she whispers.

The girl's voice crawls up Alexa's shoulder and tickles her ear. It slips inside her head and wiggles its legs inside her brain. Alexa hisses, unlocks the storage room door, and drops the girl on the floor. It's almost fully dark inside the unit. Only a single, tiny window lets in a hint of hallway light.

Fury boils inside Alexa.

"Why did you do it?" Alexa demands. "Why Brian?"

Neko's eyes shine madly in the dark room. "It was just a job," she pants. "I don't ask for details." Before Alexa can ask any other questions, her head drops against the wall, and her eyes glaze over, frozen forever in horror and surprise.

Twenty years ago: The crash

The tunnel seemed to go on forever. Alexa walked tentatively, her footsteps echoing in the thick darkness. Occasionally, her fingertips slid over the tunnel's rough walls. Silence yawned around her. Then, a few minutes later, a low hum filled her head.

She stopped and dropped her hands. "Hello?" She spun in a circle, her eyes straining to see the source of the noise. The humming intensified. Goosebumps flared across her skin. The sound was coming from the end of the tunnel. A strange desire flooded her body, and her fingers twitched longingly toward the sound. She ran down the tunnel with her mouth open and her hands balled into fists. It was so close. The hair on the back of her neck stood at attention. Her mouth watered.

The darkness thinned. She was almost there. Alexa closed her eyes and ran faster.

Then, the darkness was gone.

She opened her eyes in the passenger seat.

Her father's eyes were open, too.

Now: The apartment

"Yo," Chris says when Alexa walks back into the apartment. "Where did you go?"

"I thought I heard something, so I went to check it out."

Neko's foaming mouth pops back into her head. She clears her throat and shakes her head. "But it was nothing." She shuts the door and locks it.

Chris's eyes narrow. "You look rattled," he says.

"Nope," she says evenly. "Just have to pee. Are you done in there?"

He steps aside and gestures toward the bathroom. "Go ahead."

Keeping her head high, she walks confidently past him and into the hallway.

When the bathroom door shuts, Chris raises the briefcase lid and looks inside. The used, capped syringe is there, and another unused syringe lies beside it.

One is missing.

He lowers the lid slowly, his eyes trained on the bathroom door. An odd, clammy feeling scampers through his guts. He smells more than a mildewy bathroom.

He smells a fuck up.

He picks Neko's jacket up off the couch. He quickly rifles through the pockets, his fingers buzzing with nervous energy. Finally, he finds a small wallet in the front pocket. Dropping the coat on the floor, he flips it open and looks at the woman in the ID photo. She has long brown hair and dark eyebrows, but he recognizes her face.

Alexa Ridgemont.

The address is this apartment.

Shock squirms in Chris's gut like a bloated tapeworm. He squeezes the wallet until it crumples like paper in his hand. *That fucking bitch.*

The bathroom door opens. He returns the wallet to the coat and drops it on the couch. He could have ended it right then, but now, he is too curious.

Why would she play along with the hit?

Alexa walks around the corner, still wringing her hands. Chris narrows his eyes at her, furious at her composure.

"What's your problem?" she asks flatly.

"I got a funny feeling, Alexa," he says.

Alexa maintains eye contact even though her knees want to buckle.

"Why are you calling me that?"

Chris ambles around the couch and touches the closed briefcase. His boots thump on the hardwood, the sound a reminder of how heavy he is compared to her. Alexa's heart rate skyrockets. The tension is so thick she could bite through it.

"Where did you say you was from again?" he asks as he opens the briefcase.

She feigns irritation. "I told you already," she says. "Chase sent me."

Chris rifles through the briefcase without looking at her.

"From where?"

Alexa knows the game is rapidly ending. It rushes in front of her like water flooding from a dam, but she couldn't give up—not with Brian's body before her.

The return is all that can save her now.

"Why the fuck do you need to know?"

Chris smiles. It has all the kindness of a lion baring its teeth. He looks at her and raises the final syringe from the case. "Cut the shit," he says. "I know you ain't Neko."

The silence yawns between them. "I don't know what you're talking about."

Chris sighs and lowers the syringe. It rests on the open briefcase like a gun protruding from a trench. "I saw your ID," he says softly. Black dots swim in Alexa's vision. She takes a heart-steading breath. "You went through my stuff?"

His calm, dark eyes watch her like a crocodile stalking prey.

"Alexa Ridgemont," he says. The needle gleams in the overhead light. "Five foot four, one hundred thirty-eight pounds. An organ donor. Very nice."

Alexa takes a few slow steps toward the door.

Chris's lips pull back in a sneer, exposing his red, inflamed gums.

"Oh, no, not yet," he says, raising the needle. "We ain't done talking."

Alexa looks down at Brian's body, and her eyes go wide. "He's moving," she whispers.

Chris's eyes stray from her to Brian's prone body.

She grabs the oversized vase on the end table near her and swings it at him like Babe Ruth at the top of the ninth. It connects with his head in a sick crunch and splinters. Large ceramic shards rain down on her feet. Chris lets out a grunting sigh and crumples to the floor like a sack of flour.

A humming sound fills her head, and dark spots elongate in her vision. She lets out a bellow as her eyes roll back. The room disappears, and the tunnel opens.

The return is here.

She drops to her knees, arms dangling and shoulders slouched. Her hands slap to the floor as she crawls blindly to Brian. Chris fights the intense pain in his head and forces himself to his side. Dizziness throttles him. He needs to orient himself before she attacks him again, but she isn't in front of him.

She is beside the man's corpse.

"What the fuck are you doing?" Chris croaks.

She doesn't respond. Chris grits his teeth as he sits up and reaches for a large ceramic shard near his feet. *I'm gonna cut her fucking head off.* But before he can move, the corpse rears up from the hardwood. Its limp hands flop onto the tops of its thighs. The head cocks toward Chris.

Chris freezes, his eyes bugging from his head, the shard dropping to the floor.

Alexa grins and stands up. She backs away a few feet and opens her arms. Her eyes are two silver bullets in her skull.

"You're a witch," Chris sputters, scooting clumsily away from the grinning corpse.

Alexa's fingers curl into claws as the return surges through her. Twenty years ago, she'd laid her bloodied hands on her daddy's chest and made him return. He'd blinked at her, surprised as she was at his second chance. It hadn't lasted long–he was dead again before the ambulance arrived, but Alexa had honed it over the years. She'd practiced on dead squirrels, cats, and even a cow. The reanimation, and her time in the tunnel were always brief. But this time, she would keep going.

She would finally see what waited for her at the end.

Brian stands up. Chris tries to scream, but he can only moan helplessly.

An ecstatic thrill hums through her like a current. She is running down the tunnel. Hell, she is *flying* down it. The corpse lunges for Chris, and Alexa keeps running. She bursts through the tunnel's end—further than she'd ever been able to go. She hears squealing truck tires.

Then, the darkness swallows her whole.

Moonstruck

Jonathon Palmer

Sunlight melted over the horizon, washing away two weeks of perpetual night. To the day, it marked another year on that lonely rock. It wasn't something to celebrate, although I admit, there were times I couldn't help thinking that it was.

I performed my daily rounds of the charred and melted station, sweeping aside any new debris and making the usual checks. The air pumps were still working, barely. The food storage was still airtight. The lunar surface was as barren as ever. In the first few months it had seemed unchanging, a still photo pasted onto the windows of moon station Aldrin to relieve claustrophobia. Gradually, though, I had noticed the shifts. Patterns in the rock that would disappear and re-emerge. A new crater here and there, where something had ploughed into the tundra with no atmosphere to slow it down. The fact that I never had anyone with whom I could share these observations made them that much more surreal.

I spent the rest of that anniversary tinkering with the corpse of the radio. I'd managed to get a makeshift solder going and thought that by rewiring the thing from scratch, I might coax it into picking up a signal. I'd done my best to keep my hopes low—to temper them with a healthy dose of cynicism—but was still bitterly disappointed when I twisted the tuning dial and got nothing in return. No voice, no coded beep, not even static. Just the same, everlasting silence I'd heard since the crash.

I was conscious enough of my frustration to remove myself from the radio before I smashed it to bits. Instead, I went back to the window with my fists clenched, the tremor I'd earned from the landing still a regular occurrence. The empty plain was beautiful in its blue grey light, and after a deep breath I at last admitted the truth to myself. Even if I had gotten the radio working, the antennas outside were no doubt in as bad a condition as the rest of the station. Any heartfelt call for help I yelled into the mic would have gotten no further than my rarely used voice could carry. I was never getting off the moon, and I'd known it all along.

I took my rehydrated lunch in what had once been the rec room, but that I now think of as the mausoleum. A thin layer of grime—a combination of charcoal and melted fiberglass—had settled on the rest of the crew, or what remained of them. I blew it away as reverentially as I could. Captain Martisano's skull had rolled askew, and I straightened it to what I hoped was a hallowed arrangement with the rest. I counted the others, as was my habit by then. The captain, Hassan, Levick, and Takahashi I remembered by rote. The other two I could not reliably place a name on. The rest of the team—there were eleven of us in total—were unaccounted for, their bones melted, or lost, or simply too jumbled with the rest to make an accurate account.

Back in one of the tethered hammocks, I sipped at my canteen of coffee—the seventh brew on the same grinds. By that stage, it was hard not to imagine the crew speaking, and I'd long since given up resisting it. Martisano narrowed her burned and hollowed eyes. "What the fuck do you want, Tom?"

"Happy landing day, boys and girls," I returned, raising the canteen. "As ever, I'm sorry for all of it."

The next day, perhaps fueled by nostalgia of what should have been a treasured memory, I found myself in what had once been the landing dock but was now a tangled mess of solar foil, astral ceramics and, of course, the remains of the shuttle. The entire trip has been a shitshow from the start, and I'd been the only one unlucky enough to survive. It had also been my fault.

Slung off course by my substandard flying, the paperwork for which I'd forged at no small expense (an investment, I'd told myself), Martisano and I had spent the first two days punching numbers into calculators and fiddling with the fuel gauges, while the rest of the crew watched in ashen silence. As captain, it was Martisano's job to get us to Station Aldrin and the skeleton team who ran it, but as pilot, it came down to me to actually make it happen, and that made my lies and their consequences all the worse.

I later figured I'd missed by about two degrees. A laughably small angle, but enough for the shuttle to slice right through the Kevlar-bound landing dock, through the western end of the station, and into the oxygen tanks. By the time the fire had sputtered out, everyone else was dead.

I'd only doctored my references. I knew how to fly the shuttle, had practiced a million times on the simulator. But I wasn't going to let politics and nepotism shunt me to the back of the queue, was I? I'd worked too hard and for too long to be denied my dream of space, although it turned into a nightmare quicker than it had taken to rework the document. A lifetime of training, two Goddamn (mostly legitimate) degrees, and all I ended up getting was three years alone in a cosmic graveyard that I had created. Why had I even been bothering to get the radio working? What had I been expecting back on Earth? A hero's welcome parade? As far as they knew, the shuttle had simply missed its angle and hurtled off into space. So sad, what a shame, them's the breaks of space exploration. Blah, blah, blah. They were better off not knowing what had happened. *I* was better off holding that secret alone.

Such was my mood in those final days—the culmination of thirty—six months living amongst the carnage, talking to the skeletal remnants of my teammates, slowly running out of tanked oxygen and drowning bit by bit in guilt—that it was perhaps no surprise that in the middle of that night, when a burst of scratching static filled the station, I did not immediately run to the radio, as I'd always imagined I would.

The sound, though, insisted I attend to it, and I was eventually coaxed into bouncing slow motion down the ring-corridor, clambering over parts of the inner wall that had collapsed. By the time I got to it, there was, buried in the hiss, an unmistakable voice.

"Come in." Crackle, fizz. "Station Aldrin, do you read? Come in, station Aldrin."

I sat next to the thing and listened for several minutes, still half asleep and half not believing that my DIY soldering job had worked—that after all the complex tuning and recalibrating I'd done, simply gluing the stupid thing back together was what had fixed it.

"Station Aldrin... does anyone read?"

"I'm here," I muttered without pressing the transmission button. My voice was colder and harder than I remembered, and I realized that much of my conversations with Martisano's skull had probably taken place in my head. "Jesus fucking Christ, I'm still here..."

My chest was pulling in on itself and I could feel tears on my cheeks. This impersonal military *schlub* was the first human voice—the first real voice—I'd heard in three years. Even from before that, I remembered only screams. And they were clearly still looking for us, trying to ascertain why such an important mission had disappeared so suddenly and quietly. They were trying to bring us home.

But what would I tell them? That I screwed up my one job and incinerated not only the crew, but their trillion-dollar research station as well? They wouldn't give me a welcome parade. Falsifying my credentials was an imprisonable offense even if nothing had gone wrong. The punishment for what *did* happen...

"Station Aldrin, please... if anyone is there, please, come in."

I fingered the transmission button, listened to the expectant static, felt the bated breath of all those listening back on Earth hoping, praying, for Martisano's voice or a loud cheer from Hassan and Levick and all the others. Voices that would never be heard again.

The static died, its well of patience dry, and I slunk back to the dorms without answering.

They tried making contact every day for the next week. The voices changed and spoke with a variety of registers—some military, some academic, some personal and pleading—as though they were trying to bring a shy dog out from under a car. I found them easier to ignore with each passing day. Where at first, I'd sit by my little Frankenstein radio, rocking back and forth between homesickness, guilt, fear, and self-loathing, by the sixth day I was regarding the crackling messages as little more than background music. I worked to it, splicing the feeder pipes into the last oxygen silo and re-rationing the dwindling food stores, the way my dad used to weed the garden with classic FM emanating through the open windows. I'd just about made my peace with the decision not to respond when I heard her.

"Tom? Are you there? It's Amina..."

I dropped the wrench I'd been using—it floated away rather than clanging to the floor—and hauled myself down the outer ring corridor as fast as I could. Her voice had turned the whole situation like a switch. My heart felt as though it was beating for the first time in years, as I clambered over wreckage and propelled myself down the passages that were still clear. The lack of gravity kept me to an agonizingly slow pace, like that classic nightmare of trying to run with your legs glued down by some unseen solvent, only instead of a monster or bad man behind me, I had sweet, beautiful Amina up ahead, ready to give up at a moment's notice.

Finally, I glided into the comms room, leaving clouds of ash and particles of smashed equipment in my wake, and thumped into the bulkhead housing the radio.

"Tom? Anyone? Please, if you can hear me..."

I jammed my hand on the transmission button.

"Amina, it's me. It's Tom." She didn't reply at first, and for an utterly gutting second, I thought perhaps I'd only fixed the thing so that it could receive, but not send. Then I heard a sob, followed by a wordless, broken voice. "I'm here, Amina. I'm okay. God, I missed you. I missed you so much..."

And then I was sobbing, too, and no doubt for the listening pleasure of a crammed control room, my fiancé and I cried, laughed, and told each other over and over how much we'd yearned for and still loved the other.

When we could no longer talk—squeezed dry of bottled emotions—Amina told me that a Commander Osborne needed to speak with me. I nodded with no one there to see the gesture, then swiped my eyes and told her "Of course," promising to say goodbye before the transmission was terminated. I then summoned every ounce of cunning I had, to deal with what was about to transpire.

Osborne's voice was deep set and confident. Despite her words, she seemed all business. "Bana, we can't tell you how pleased we are to be hearing your voice down here. Big smiles all-round the room." As if to punctuate this, a chorus of cheers distorted the mic.

"Thank you."

"Now, listen. Straight to it. What the hell happened up there?"

I lied only once. That was something, at least. A shred of decency that reduced perhaps a little of what I owed. "An oxygen tank blew when a solar panel overheated. Ripped apart the hangar, the shuttle, and sent flames through every vent. We were asleep when it happened. It was chaos from the get-go, commander. We never stood a chance."

"Jesus... Listen, Bana, there's no easy way to ask this. How many of you survived?"

"It's just me. It's been just me for three years."

Murmurs and chatter drowned the first part of Osborne's reply. "... your situation. But you'll be relieved to know that a rescue shuttle is already on its way. As you probably know, securing the funds for this was the biggest delay, what with the loss from last time and those bastards in...well, it doesn't matter now. We were hoping to bring back more of you, but...one life saved is enough for us."

"When will..."

I couldn't even finish the sentence. Already, I was looking toward the hangar, where the ruined ship sat as it had done since the day of the landing. It would take all of two seconds for the rescue crew to realize it'd crashed, and that pilot error was the only logical explanation. Then would come the investigation, and the discovery that I was culpable in a legal sense, as well as a moral one.

"Bana?"

I jumped. "Yes, sorry. When will the shuttle get here?"

You could tell she was smiling, just by her tone. I was glad she couldn't see the look on my own face. "If all goes to plan, you'll be shaking hands by this time tomorrow."

They let me say goodbye to Amina—more tears—and then I was on my own again. Less than a rotation of the earth until I got a miraculous trip off my self-made prison. Less than a day to make it look like I hadn't killed every single other person up there. Amina had waited this long in hopes of seeing me again, but she wouldn't, I'd decided, share her life with a man who'd single handedly destroyed the international lunar base and gotten his crewmates, some of them long family friends, roasted alive or crushed in a mangled ship.

God, the ship. After several hours of just staring at the ghastly wreckage, wondering what the hell I was going to do, I decided the only reasonable thing would be to take it apart piece by burned piece, and tell the rescue crew I'd stripped it for repairs around the complex. All eight struts of the spiky design had snapped off, and half the cabin had been crushed where we'd slammed into the outer wall of the station. There was simply no reconfiguration that would make it look like it'd been fire alone that had destroyed it.

The shuttle was only small—more of a skiff or barge than an actual ship—and most of it had been melted anyway when our second rocket, fully fueled for the trip home, had exploded. Still, it was some seven hours later by the time I'd wrenched all the pieces loose, pulling apart the screws and rivets of some and carving up the rest with the station's one surviving plasma cutter. I placed some of them around the more damaged parts of Aldrin, riveting them onto shredded paneling and splicing wires into equipment that would never work again, to make it look as though I'd tried and then given up.

Satisfied that the place did in fact look as though an oxygen silo had exploded, and not had an out-of-control shuttle tear it apart, I spent several hours tinkering with the aesthetic before finally, I was ready to confront the one job I'd been putting off.

The bones.

Martisano's skull was as disapproving as ever, and whilst I tried to offer her and the others a last, groveling explanation for everything I'd done, I felt she could sense what I had planned. "Don't you dare, you lying sack of shit."

"I'm sorry, cap, but I'm no doctor, and even I could tell that half of you were dead before the fire even started. Hassan's got a crack in his skull three inches wide, for Christ's sake. And since the rescue team will be here tomorrow, I don't have time to dress you all up."

"You need to tell them the truth."

"If it weren't for Amina, I would. I'd tell ground control that I lied about the recommendations...and yes, okay, embellished my simulator record a little, and that it was a massive mistake. That I got you all killed, fair and square. Then I'd pay whatever dues are owed. But I need my fiancé. I need to go home, and I'm not going all the way back there just to sit in a military prison."

"Fuck you, Tom."

"No hard feelings."

I placed Martisano, Levick, and Hassan (and whoever else was sitting in the pile) into an empty rations sack, tying it off quickly so I'd no longer need to look at them. I slung it over my shoulder and hopped my way to the airlock.

"Don't do it!"

"I'm sorry," I told her. "This is the only way."

There was a hiss as the artificial air was sucked out and a hush fell over the soundscape, the vacuum of the moon open before me. Martisano, though, would not be silenced.

"Bana! There's no coming back from this!"

"There's no coming back from anything, cap. What's past is past."

I bounced across the plain, over the moon's undulating face, until I reached the lip of crater Zappa, the deepest such thing within the perimeter of the station.

I scraped the hole first, following the contours of hard rock and pliable soil, until I thought I had something deep enough. Then I laid the sack of bones over a flat piece of ground and picked up the largest boulder I could find.

Levick and the others joined the protest this time.

"Bana! No!"

I raised the stone above my head. "As ever, boys and girls..."

"*Bana!*"

"I'm sorry for all of it."

The first blow crushed the majority of the bones in the bag. Another five, tugging the rock gently through the soupy gravity before pushing hard back down, reduced the crew to powder.

A minute or two later, they were buried at the bottom of the crater.

The rescue shuttle arrived early.

I woke from a nightmare-filled sleep to find a new star in the sky, glinting against the sun and growing larger by the minute. After a final tour of the empty station, imagining myself as a standard issue inspection crew and satisfied that the look of the place matched the story I'd given them, I sat down to watch the shuttle land. Even as it made its final approach, all sound of it was vacuumed off into space. Station Aldrin mirrored the silence.

In mockery of my own landing three years earlier, the pilot brought the shuttle in at a gentle glide, reverse thrusters firing in coordinated bursts from the struts until, when it was propped safely on three of its eight legs, the crew tip-toed it into position. God, what they must have thought of the ruined hangar.

I met them at the airlock, face burning as they greeted me with a reverent round of applause. There were only three of them. Perhaps control did not want to risk losing anymore personnel. The captain introduced himself as Akhtar and after shaking my hand, wrapped me in a hug.

"Am I glad to see you," I said to all of them at once.

"Likewise, lad, likewise. We're all just so amazed at the human spirit you've demonstrated up here."

"Please. All I did was survive."

"For three years in a ruined moon station!" chimed one of the others.

"This is McLeod and Poku," Akhtar told me. "They're structural analysts and electricians."

"Here to fix the place up?" I joked with my stomach in a knot.

Poku shook her head. "Just here to figure out why the place burned up so quickly. Control is obviously not too keen on letting it happen again."

"Big job for just the two of you."

Akhtar put a hand on my shoulder and led me toward the central mess hall, which was now, ironically, an actual mess. "They're only doing a cursory check. The priority of this mission is to get you home safe and sound. We figured you'd spent enough time here."

"You can say that again..."

"I take it you're all packed?"

"Almost."

"Go get yourself sorted. We're going to make this a quick turnaround." Then he stopped and smiled. "In three days' time, you'll be having dinner with your fiancé."

I'd been so busy dressing the station, I hadn't packed at all. Not that I had a great deal of things. Most of my essential belongings had perished in the crash, and I'd made do in the succeeding years by pilfering whatever had survived of the other crew members' possessions. In divine irony, it was personal items that had fared the best. A photo of Amina and I kept safe in my pocket for good luck during the flight and a plush toy alien she'd bought me as a joke.

Packed and ready as ever to leave, I allowed myself a moment or two on my bunk, and it wasn't long before I was caressing the photo with my throat constricting. We'd taken it the day before launch, on the balcony of the restaurant in which I'd proposed to her. It was a promise, I'd told her, that I was coming back, and that despite the adventure I was about to embark on, we still had our entire lives together ahead of us. I remembered my hand shaking as I offered her the ring, as though to forewarn that my 'adventure' would eventuate as a karmic odyssey with no end in sight. She'd been too excited to ask about the 'issues' the institute had had in finalizing my qualifications, the complications I'd told her had gone away, but had gone anywhere but away. I'd been too happy to remind her.

I slipped the photo into a zip pocket on my jumpsuit, the same pocket it had travelled here in. Then I gave the alien a squeeze (it was nicknamed Martisano, another joke that didn't age well) and shoved it into the transport container. Amina would be proud to have me back. And despite everything, perhaps Martisano would, having had three years to forgive my deceit, also be glad that at least one of us had made it home—even if it was me. Maybe Akhtar was right, and I had inspired some kind of hope or amazement down there on Mother Earth.

Maybe I'd paid my dues, after all.

I was carrying the transport box out to the hangar when I heard a clang from the far end of the corridor. I stopped and waited for the sound to reappear. There was nothing down there, just a dead end that had once been a passage to the laboratories, and which was now an ungainly blockage of ruined structures. Another sound rattled through the station—the crinkling of solar foil. I followed the echoes with my stomach knotting.

McLeod was on his hands and knees, busily digging around the bottom of a collapsed bulkhead. Small piles of random debris sat either side of him. He turned when he heard me approach, but otherwise did not change his position.

"I was trying to get through to the labs, see if there's anything there to salvage."

"Believe me, I've tried. All the hydroponics stuff is down there." I stopped when I was right behind him, the box still in my hands. "But there's no way through."

McLeod hunched over even further, extending his arms around the base of the mangled steel wedge. "I think if I just give it a…"

He heaved back with all his might, and the ruined bulkhead slid out from the wreckage. A small avalanche of material came with it, rolling or tumbling off to either side, and when the detritus had settled, the only thing left was the body.

My heart seized in my chest while McLeod sat in shocked silence. I recognized who it was straight away. It was Levick, whose skull I thought I'd been apologizing to every night for three years. She'd barely even decomposed. Her hair was spread beneath her, and her skin was waxy, like old leather. She lay in a pool of congealed blood, and whilst I was thankful that she had turned in such a way that we couldn't see her eyes, which were undoubtedly jelly by now, they were not what horrified me.

Her legs were buckled out of all natural shape, zig zagging up to her spine like an accordion. Her arms and one side of her face were desiccated—ripped to shreds in what could only have been a window shattering in an out-of-control shuttle.

"Jesus Christ," McLeod managed at last. He inched toward her, still on his knees, and poked her gently with his fingers. I was still frozen, a thousand impossible options screaming through my head. "Jesus, look at her. This doesn't make any sense." He waved a vague hand at the bulkhead he'd dragged aside. It had blocked the corridor, but had not been overly heavy, and it had not been sitting on her, only masking her from view. I knew it. He knew it. She must have survived the initial impact—just—and dragged herself here to escape the fire. "What the hell happened to her legs? To her *face*? Fuck me, she looks like she was in a car crash…"

He got no further. I brought the transport box down on the back of his head as hard as I could, and he dropped straight to the floor and didn't move. My mouth had turned dry, and I could feel the blood in my ears. I didn't move him or try to cover him. I wheeled away down the corridor, calculating the fastest possible route to the shuttle, praying Akhtar hadn't put any kind of lock on it, or that the piloting systems had not changed dramatically during my sabbatical.

I'd come this far. I was going home. I was marrying Amina. I was not going to prison.

Poku and Akhtar were both by the surveillance console in the comms room, the station's black box that I'd failed to repair. Poku looked up and spoke before I could say or do anything. The solder—my improvised stupid fucking solder—was in her hand. "Hey, Tom, did you make this? Clever boy. I think

I've almost got the hard drive back online. We can watch how the fire spread so quickly. Shouldn't take too long, don't worry."

I was no longer listening. I was already at the radio, so lovingly and delicately put back together. Only Akhtar noticed what I was up to, and even then, it was only when he heard me tear away the covering. "Tom, what the hell *are you doing?*"

I wrapped my fingers around as much wiring as I could and ripped the guts straight out of it.

"Jesus, Tom, no!"

"Hey, I've got it! Videos all backed up to... oh, my God..."

I didn't look at the screen. I only glanced back long enough to determine that Akhtar and Poku were too occupied by what they were watching to notice that I was headed for the hangar. I'd seen the footage already, replayed a thousand times in my sleep.

The shuttle screaming in, thrusters all firing in wrong directions. The catastrophic impact that tore the station apart and killed half the crew in one go (but not Levick). The exploding oxygen silo, the mangled survivors stumbling from the wreckage, choking as they hammered on the airlock door.

The lying, trembling pilot, miraculously unscathed, too paralyzed by shock and guilt to help anyone.

That same airlock door slid shut right as Akhtar and Poku appeared around the corner, careening awkwardly into the walls and each other. Akhtar got there first and hammered on the thick glass. He'd recognized what was about to happen.

"Tom! Tom wait, it was a mistake, okay?" His voice went muffled as I fastened my helmet, all but disappeared as the air was sucked away. "It was human error, that's what we do *Jesus Christ, Tom, stop!*"

I put my hand on the glass and because I knew he couldn't hear me, I mouthed every word in over-acted pantomime. "I'm sorry! Both of you! But I'm going home to Amina."

I ducked out of the second door before it had fully opened, and I was soon inside the shuttle. The controls were familiar. Only small aesthetic changes seemed to have been made, and I had the thing fired up in no time. My hands were calm and fluid as water. Below the edge of the cockpit, I could just make out Akhtar and Poku in the airlock, yelling at the dawdling mechanism.

With nothing left to lose and no way to turn back, I banked the shuttle around step by step, struts extending and middle body rotating like the sea-urchins they'd been designed after, until I was staring across the stars at beautiful Mother Earth. Akhtar and Poku, I knew, would be directly behind and underneath the shuttle, where the airlock opened.

I did not look back.

"I'm coming, Amina."

The shuttle lurched as I hit the ignition, and a few seconds later, I was on my return journey.

It was the smoothest takeoff I'd ever performed.

I do not know if Akhtar and Poku are still alive up there—whether they made it back inside, or if they copped the launch blast full in the face. To be honest, I don't know which would be worse.

Either way, I'll give them a hero's death. McLeod, too. It wasn't their fault, after all. Maybe a story of impossibly strong solar winds, or malfunctioning oxygen tanks, or sudden medical complications known to happen during space travel. I don't know. I'll practice them aloud, see whichever has the ring of truth to it. It'll still be a couple of days before I hit Earth's atmosphere. A further twenty-four hours by the time I've parachuted into the Pacific and the retrieval crew have arrived. I have time to decide.

And in twenty years' time, when I'm wrapped up in bed with Amina, perhaps with a kid or two down the hall, I'll know that none of this was in vain. That Martisano, and Levick, and Akhtar, and Poku, and Mcleod—all of them—did not die for nothing.

My dues will have been paid, my lies accounted for, my promises made good.

At least, for now.

Friends in High Places

JUSTIN ALCALA

Dad went to jail, and we went to Wrigleyville. It felt like our ninety-sixth move in three years and the latest apartment was the worst. A grubby, stone, three-flat with cracked bay windows strangled in pest-filled ivy. Atop the roof's east corner, the ugliest gargoyle ever sculpted glared down in resentment. On the west bend, a pillar of stone where it's partner once mounted—taken, just like Dad.

It was Halloween week, and our Chicago neighborhood of Wrigleyville hadn't seen a blue sky in days. I hiked the mile from middle school to my reprehensible apartment, petrified I'd run into Hector Montanez. The should-be-sophomore who went to some alternative school for bad teens, but frequently skipped to smoke pot with his friends under the Red Line. He welcomed me to the area by force-feeding me dumpster leftovers, then left my cheek purple for good measure. I outran his latest effort to embarrass me and was due for the beating of my life should we cross paths.

"Danny," yelled Pat at the first block of my route. "Why are you always running?"

"Survival," I said.

"Hector?"

"Nothing gets past you."

Pat was the only person who ventured to be my friend, a fellow outcast for timeless reasons—wits, uniqueness, and honesty.

"Why don't you call the cops?" Pat asked, ginger pigtails over an anime shirt and plaid skirt.

"Mom drove me to the station. Cops stopped by his house, but couldn't find him."

"Early intervention prevents the onset of adult criminal behavior."

"Thank you."

"So, listen, you want to go trick-or-treating Friday?"

"Pat, we're twelve."

"And?"

"Eh, guess if I mask up, Hector won't recognize me."

"Brilliant. We can go after school."

"Alright, now can we like...run-walk home?"

"It's called Jeffing."

"Sure. Let's Jeff."

We sped to my apartment, greeted by the gargoyle's unapproving leer. Pat walked me to the glass framed door, staring skyward as I fidgeted with the lock. The bolt released and we shuffled in. The porch smelled like cat piss from our landlord's pride of felines.

"Dude," said Pat, "that statue is bizarre."

"The gargoyle?" I asked, collecting mail from our postal wall-coffin. "I know."

"What's with the red teeth?"

"It's just weathered. Acid rain and stuff."

"Or its last victim."

"Hey, not that I don't love your unique perspective, but don't you need to get home?"

"Yeah, I guess. It's family therapy night."

"Must be nice."

"What therapy?"

"No family."

Pat placed their hand on my shoulder. "Hang in there, bud."

Pat exited into the October cold, but not before getting another eyeful of gargoyle. I didn't watch Pat go down the block. I knew they were okay. People like Pat didn't let the world maltreat them. Not like me with Hector.

I squeaked up the creakiest stairs in Wrigleyville where our neighboring landlord, Ms. Schneider, donned in her pumpkin-patterned Snuggy-swept cat hair.

"Danny," she said, a shedding calico curling at her slippers. "Your friend came by."

"Friend?"

"Big guy. Hanson."

"Hector?"

"Yes, Hector."

"He's not my friend."

"I truly don't care. Tell your mom rent is overdue."

"Sure." I jingled the keys in my door. "Good to see you, too."

Our apartment never left the 80's—wood panel and orange ceilings accented by leftover furniture from the house we sold to get by. I went to my room, flipped on some music, and stared at my self-sculpture. My art final bore the makings of a real person—arms, legs, and a head, but none of the details to feel real. Still, even though it wasn't due for months, sculpting a half-sized Danny kept me distracted. After toothbrushing textured hair, I shaped an aluminum foil hand, but stopped midway as a mystery along my bedroom window caught my eye.

Four claw like scratches drew along the glass. Too big to be a bird's work, too congruent to be coincidental, the marks left me dumbfounded. I took a closer look before examining what lay below. Bushes and stone steps only added to the mystery. Maybe spooky season, an unrelenting bully, and my solitude were getting to me. I quit molding and spent the rest of the night watching public access horror in the front room until Mom came home. She lived in a state of exhaustion since Dad's embezzlement charges, so I kept it brief. *School is great, trick-or-treating with Pat on Friday, and rent is overdue.*

Zombie Mom thanked me for my report.

School came and went. Pat left early for the orthodontist, so I trekked home alone in an autumn shower, changing my path like prey evading predators. Unfortunately, a Wrigley Field *Hell-aween Eve* event blocked my path, so I rerouted through an alley umbrellaed by the Red Line. I was a half block from home when a blow like a mule's kick bucked me in the back. I fell face first, smashing my nose on gravel, blood spluttering from my nostrils.

"Look, it's Dandy boy," said Hector as hands lifted me by my shoulders. A skinny kid with a stringy mustache and a round guy who looked like a grown man held me while Hector flicked my nose. Electric shot up my sinuses.

"Oh, hey, Hector." I winced. "Good to see you."

"You met my bros?" asked Hector, looking at Thin and Stout.

"Yeah, I think so," I said. "The number ten, right?"

Hector's fist thrust into my stomach, stealing my breath.

"I visited your shit apartment like you made the cops do to mine," said Hector. "You're going to pay me as an apology."

"Sure," I said, "you want it in singles or a whole Lincoln?"

"Fifty bucks a week," said Hector. "We'll start today."

"Jeez, Hector," I said. "I'm kind of short at the moment."

"Then you get another." Hector pounded me in my guts again. This one was nastier, projecting cafeteria pizza out of me.

"Gross," said Thin as they tossed me down.

"Tomorrow is Halloween," said Hector. "I'll be looking for my money. Get anyone involved and it'll be fatal."

Rain swelled as I curled in blood and vomit. It took ten minutes to get up and limp home. I reached the three-flat drenched, fighting oppressive belly pains as I dug for keys. By accident alone, I looked up, noticing the chimpanzee-sized gargoyle. The winged devil's horned head didn't stare back as usual. Instead, it tilted ever so slightly over its shoulder at the empty pillar where granite feet without a body mounted. The gargoyle's four-clawed hand pointed in its absent partner, and its shark-toothed jaws glowered.

"No way," I groaned. "It's the beating I took."

I hobbled up the stairs, where Ms. Schneider taped a witchy kitten cling to her door.

"Danny, you better be close and lock that entrance," Ms. Schneider hissed. "Tobias is missing."

"I promise, Ms. Schneider," I said, gripping my stomach.

"What happened?"

"Hanson."

"You're weak, boy."

I didn't respond, instead shuffling to my door and pushing inside. Lightning flashed through the empty unit. I didn't flip on any lamp. I just flopped into bed, the tapping rain my only comfort. Sleep gave respite to my agony. I don't know how long I lay damp in my bed until a scraping, like a fork on a bottle, intruded my slumber. My room was pitch black. I thrashed through floored clothes and dodged an errant swivel chair which thirsted for shins, leaning over my desk to tilt my face on the glass. Another flash of electric and a crack of thunder revealed a grotesque face staring back, nails scratching at the panel.

"Holy..." I leapt backwards.

I couldn't tell if the monster lingered through the obscurity and I second-guessed flicking on my nightstand lamp. In an act of stupidity, I did, and the repugnant gargoyle face persisted. I don't know how long I stared, but it must've been significant because the grisly statue took initiative, directing its talon at my self-sculpture.

"Fan of art?" I blurted.

The creature snarled.

"Dumb question," I said. "Not sure what you want, but I'm totally scared right now."

The creature focused its gaze upwards to the west corner of the building, the same spot where its missing partner once resided.

"Oh, um, okay. You want a replacement?"

The creature beamed like the devil at crossroads.

"Sure, I could do that. Just need time."

The gargoyle nodded, then instead of absconding in flight, clawed back up from which it came. Dumbfounded was the understatement of the year. I locked in place, no idea what to do. So, with my stomach throbbing, I followed my instincts and began altering clay Danny.

Morning came with hurried indecency. It was Halloween. I checked out my room. Scars remained on the window and my sculpture bore a new pair of bat wings. I grabbed my clown mask from under the bed and hurried to eat breakfast. Mom left another *working late* note topped with a poorly drawn pumpkin. *I missed her.*

Halloween made the school day tolerable. We read Poe, studied Samhain, and worked on pumpkin geometry. By final bell, it didn't hurt to breathe and the prospect of trick-or-treating delayed the aftershock of battery victimization and demon appeasement. Pat and I met up in front of school and hit the ground running, storming every house with an open door or decorations. After an hour, our bags were filled, but our ambition still yearned.

"Man, people are generous this year." Pat the green-haired Oompa Loompa ogled their bloated pillowcase. "Your house is close. Let's dump this candy."

"Uh." I recalled last night. "Maybe we could stash it in bushes?"

"Yeah, right," said Pat. "Come on, we'll give that gargoyle our Butterfingers."

"Eh, okay. Let's hurry. Looks like rain."

We tried our luck at North Halsted, a street crammed with parents escorting costumed toddlers and employees returning home. To my chagrin, we nearly ran directly into Hector and his goons at our intersection sharing a beer. It was too late to turn around without raising suspicion, so I pulled my mask down and tried to act natural. Clueless Pat bobbed along humming *Thriller*. Hector's glazed eyes followed me, but as we passed, he just kept drinking his Heineken.

"Holy crap," I said after a few feet. "That was Hector."

"Hector?" Pat shouted. "Where?"

"Please, shut up."

"Well, we know where he is. Let's just go the opposite way once we drop our candy off."

We turned the seven-minute walk into four and soon were in front of my three-flat. Mrs. Schneider stood on the porch stairs, grasping a can of tuna.

"My Church is missing?" she sobbed.

"Well, what's your denomination?" asked Pat.

"It's a cat," I said, lifting my mask.

"Have you seen him, Danny?" Mrs. Schneider grabbed my jacket.

"Sorry, Mrs. Schneider," I said.

"I'm afraid something terrible happened to him." She looked down at the steps, defiled with what looked like bits of sausage and cherry pie.

"I'll keep an eye out," I said.

"Useless boy," she said as distant thunder rumbled. "You better lock that damn door."

I hurried inside while Mrs. Schneider made the *pspsps* sound, but I knew it was for naught. Pat and I hurried to my unit and emptied our bags inside my kitchen.

"Okay, I need to tell you something," I said.

"You don't need to apologize for her."

"No, not that. It's about the gargoyle."

"Atop your roof?"

"Pat, I swear what I'm about to tell you is true. Yesterday when you went to the dentist, I got my ass kicked by Hector again. I hid in my room that night until something came scratching at my window. It was that gargoyle. It wants me to sculpt it a partner."

"Well, let's cancel Halloween and make us a sexy monster statue."

"Come on, I'm serious. I think it's killing the cats."

"Did Hector give you a concussion because you're talking *loco*?"

"Okay, this was a bad idea. Never mind."

Pat chewed their lip. "I'll tell you what. If we go out there and the gargoyle is scarfing kitty, I'll believe you. But if it's still there, promise you'll go to Mr. Gildiner?"

"The school counselor? Fine. Now, come on."

We left the three-flat into the beginning of a brisk thunderstorm. Mrs. Schneider must've gone back in because all that was left was the can of tuna.

"Well, at least your crazy landlord is gone," Pat said.

"Dang, I'd better close the door before—" Something pressed the back of my neck like a vise, sending pain through me.

"Think I didn't see you, Little Dandy?" said Hector as he squeezed my collar. Thin blocked the sidewalk from onlookers while Round moved and pressed against Pat.

"Hey, let him go," said Pat.

"Look, Danny's dating the Joker," said Hector.

"I'm an Oompa..." Pat stopped themselves. "You know what, I don't have enough crayons."

Round shoved Pat to the ground.

"You got my money?" asked Hector, peeling off my mask.

"Listen, I know you think you're a contemporary gangster—" I said.

"Contemporary?" asked Hector. "Speak English, Dandy."

"Eh, it doesn't matter," I sighed. "I'm not paying you."

"*Oh*, but you are." Hector balled his fist. "Or I'll beat you and Joker's faces in."

"Please leave Pat out of this," I said.

"Eat shit, dude," said Pat before Round kicked them.

"Alright," I said as an odd *thwap* echoed in the downpour. "We have two bags of candy upstairs and one of my mom's beers. Will that buy us another day?"

"Holy shit," Hector snorted. "You hear that, Dave? Candy?"

But Dave didn't answer. Collectively, friends and foes alike looked to Thin-Dave blocking the sidewalk. He was still obstructing the pavement, but more in the traditional sense. His body lay on the pathway, pooling in blood. Round hurried to his side as a blaze of lightning blinded us. When our sight returned, Round's body drunkenly danced about, a clean red stump where his head should be. The body fell atop Thin-Dave's as thunder rolled.

"Yo, what the hell," said Hector.

"The gargoyle," I shouted. "Everyone inside."

I helped Pat to his feet, then we hurried up the stairs. Hector forgot how to think, eyes locked on his dead friends. We shut the glass framed door just as a graphite-colored shadow of the horror descended along the miniature front yard. Hector awoke from his trance, hurrying to the door. But as he pounded on the pane of glass, I looked to Pat, who nodded. My fingers went to the deadbolt and secured it. Hector frowned before his face smashed into the glass. A streak of red burbled from his lips before his body whiplashed upward towards the roof.

On the wet rooftop where it lived, bones of three boys lay. Days piled into weeks, but no one mentioned Hector or his friends. Pat and I lived a blithe life, free to walk through Wrigleyville wherever we wanted. As for my sculpture, it finally had all the details to feel real, and will look great on the three-flat's roof.

Meanwhile, Mom said she missed me, too, and stopped working overtime. And even though she worries about rent, I tell her not to. The world might not be fair and it might not be right, but sometimes, problems like rude landlords take care of themselves. You just need a good friend to get by.

The Bathroom

Kaye George

I t had taken months to convince Leonard to move into the building my family
owned. He kept saying it would make him feel too much like a "kept" man to
live in a building my family owned, one that my grandparents had bought twenty
years ago. But, from the time I was very young, I had looked forward to living in it.
Everyone in the family stayed in one of the apartments or another for a short time
when they were young, before they settled down and bought a house. Sometimes
they stayed a long time.

My harping on the subject didn't work, but when the apartment stove started
leaking gas and wasn't fixed after three days of calling the landlord, over and over,
he finally agreed to move.

We moved on a mild, sunny spring day. As soon as we were settled in, Leonard
threw all the windows open, and the curtains floated with the gentle breeze. The
traffic noises came in from below, too. I was afraid that would bother him, but
we were both too happy to let that happen.

I was delighted with the master bathroom. The apartment had both a master
bath and a powder room. This would be a luxury for us. We'd spent two years in
that cramped little two-room walkup on the third floor. Here, even though we
were on the fifth floor, there was an elevator that worked and a superintendent
who had the appearance of being able to fix broken things. My father had always
spoken highly of him, so I looked forward to getting quick response when the
dishwasher or disposal acted up. Unlike the pokey little place we'd just left.

I found the box with my bath salts—I loved soaking in bath salts—and hefted
it onto the generous counter space next to the sink. The air coming into the small
window felt chilly, so I pulled the sash down. It still felt cooler in the bathroom

than the rest of the apartment, but I knew a steaming bath would warm the room up. Our last apartment had only had a shower. I was in heaven!

That first night, I told Leonard not to wait up for me. Sweaty and tired from unpacking all day, I headed for the bathtub, looking forward to soaking all my aches away. I had a new package of lavender salts, so I shook some crystals into the stream of hot water. The package jumped from my hand, and all the salts went into the water. It probably wouldn't hurt anything, but it was a waste! The box had held enough for at least six tubs full. Oh, well. It smelled wonderful.

My soak was relaxing and I fell asleep, waking only after the water had turned cold. I glanced at the clock on the counter and was surprised that I'd only dozed for ten minutes. Rather than run more hot water, I dried off, joined Leonard, who wasn't quite asleep yet, and we celebrated our move in our own special way.

None of my baths were ever as nice as I had envisioned they'd be. The porcelain tub seemed to cool the water quickly, almost as soon as I ran it. I kept a grip on my bath salts, though, and didn't lose any more whole packages.

Our second week in the apartment, a sudden thunderstorm sprang up in the afternoon. Leonard and I both returned from work bedraggled and dripping. I stepped into the bathroom to get a towel for my hair. After I dried off, I reached for the faucet to pour some water for a drink in the plastic cup I had put in that bathroom. All the rain had made me thirsty.

I woke up, slumped against the opposite wall, tingling all over. I heard Leonard calling my name, but I couldn't speak above a croak. He found me, and I told him I was numb. He rubbed my hands and feet until I could feel again.

"I reached for the faucet," I said. "That's all I remember." Except for a faint cackling sound, but I may have imagined that.

A nearby clap of thunder rattled the glass in the window.

"Must have been a lightning strike," he said, gazing at the raging storm outside.

He tried to talk me into going to the emergency room, but I felt better as soon as I got to the couch. I took it easy and watched TV the rest of the evening. Leonard brought me a sandwich and a bowl of soup on a tray so I could eat on the couch. My heart swelled with love for him.

We'd been together for a little over three years now, and I was waiting for the first crack in our relationship. I had had two of them fall apart in the two years before I met him. Maybe, soon, I could stop holding my breath and realize that we were together for good.

I washed up in the powder room before bed and took a sink shower in the same room the next morning before work. I'm not sure why, but I avoided the big bathroom.

That night I tried a bath again. No storms, no lightning, just a nice long dip in the lovely wide tub. The back sloped just right, and I found myself drifting off, and the water even stayed warm that night. That was a nice change. As I got out, my skin nicely pink, and reached for the towel, I lost my balance for a split second.

"Be careful," sounded a faint whisper near my ear.

I recovered my balance in a split second and looked around for the source of the voice. I shivered, even though the room was steamy hot. The whisper had sounded like an old woman's voice. A vision of a hanging body flashed in front of me, then vanished.

As I snuggled with Leonard that night, I asked him if he'd ever heard voices in the apartment.

"No, the walls are pretty solid. I heard a TV one night, but we had the windows open."

"You haven't heard a whisper in the bathroom?"

Even in the dark, I could tell he was giving me a funny look. "Uh, no. No whispers."

I began to enjoy my baths. The water stayed warm, and I emerged, lulled and drowsy, ready to sleep soundly. I ignored the voice that came to me about once a week. I would start to lose my balance getting out of the tub, and a woman's voice would whisper. Once it told me to "Get out." Another time it said, "You don't know." And a few more times it told me to be careful. I got the faint feeling of something old and evil. But I'd be feeling so good from my long bath, I dismissed it. Only sometimes I imagined I was sensing the whiff of malevolence.

The whispers grew stronger, though, and I knew I had to admit I wasn't making them up. After another couple of months, I started bathing less often. At first it was every other day, then it went to once a week. Leonard commented a few times on my hygiene. Or lack of.

"I don't care if there's a ghost in the damn bathroom, you have to wash yourself. It's summer, it's hot, you're sweaty. God, you stink."

That stung.

In bed, he scooted away from me when I wanted to cuddle. Something had to be done.

I decided to conquer the damn bathroom. What could it do to me? I had gotten a bad shock, but that was the storm, not the evil spirit that lurked near the tub. The very next day, I returned from work ready to bathe in the tub I had abandoned, only to find water all over the floor. I called the super, who came to fix the leaky pipe.

"We've had so much trouble with the plumbing in here," he said.

"Why is that?" I asked.

"You got me. But ever since old lady Snell strung herself up on the shower rod, twenty years ago, funny things have happened here. The last tenant, healthy young man, fell and damaged his shoulder in the tub. Had to have surgery."

Twenty years ago? That's when Grandpa bought this building. Someone had once told me that my grandfather did something underhanded to acquire the place, but I hadn't listened to any of that talk. Lots of people seemed to have it in for him, since he was so successful in the real estate business. Had he somehow had a hand in old lady Snell's death? Was he not the person I always thought he was?

"Talk is that she might not have hung herself," the super said. "She might have been helped out of this world." More of the sour grapes gossip, I told myself. My grandpa was a nice man. He had bought me ice cream and read me stories.

With the leak repaired, I settled in for a lazy bath. I fell sound asleep, as usual, and awoke to see a shadow hanging above me. I blinked and it was gone. As I emerged, however, I slipped and banged my knee on the edge of the tub. The cackle I heard was louder than usual.

When Leonard got home—I could tell he'd stopped at the corner bar for a beer or two—I told him I wanted to move.

"We signed a lease for a year. No way can we move."

"That bathroom is out to get me."

"What? Can you hear what you're saying?" He plopped down on the couch and switched on the TV.

"Can you hear what I'm saying? That's really the question." He turned up the volume. "If we stay here, something bad is going to happen. Something bad."

I hounded him until one Saturday, he got up, and started packing his suitcase.

"Where are you going?" He was scaring me. Was this relationship cracking apart, too? He did take occasional business trips, but I always knew about them, and he hadn't told me of any recently. Not that we were talking all that much.

"I can't take it anymore," he said. "I'll keep paying my half of the rent."

"You're leaving me?" I couldn't quite take it in. Leonard, the light of my life, was dumping me? I fell onto the couch, stunned.

"I never realized before how crazy you are." He threw his clothes in without folding them. They'd be terribly wrinkled.

"It's just the bathroom," I said.

"See? That's crazy." He slammed his suitcase shut and stomped out the door.

He'd been in such a hurry to leave, he hadn't taken even half his clothes. I knew he'd be back. I hoped he'd be back.

"Come." I felt the voice in my head more than I heard it.

"Come, relax. You'll be okay."

The soothing voice drew me toward the bathroom. I fought back, gritted my teeth, and squeezed my eyes shut, resisting the silken invitation.

I thought I was winning, but when I opened my eyes, I was running water into the tub. I tried not to, but I peeled off my clothes and sank into the warmth. It felt benign, friendly. Every muscle in my body relaxed. The welcoming water felt so...right. The voice hissed, "Yes, you deserve this. Give in to me." I slipped deeper into the water. When my face went under, I came to. I pulled the plug and jumped up. I swayed.

I heard a harsh laugh.

My heels slipped on the bottom—I hadn't put the bathmat down—my body rose. I was airborne for a long, long second, then I crashed down. Headfirst. I heard my skull crack.

Paralyzed, I watched my blood swirl down the drain with the last of the bath water. Nothing hurt, but I couldn't move. I wondered if Leonard would find me in time.

The room grew cold.

Once Bitten

KEN FOXE

Mosquito bites are a peculiar reason to break up with your girlfriend of nine years. Your fiancée of eleven months. To have the diamond ring you bought on Vestingstraat in Antwerp pushed back through your door in a blank white envelope. Maybe it's wrong to say the bites were the reason, rather the last-most one. But for your life to end. To be bitten to death, that would surely be stranger still.

Cliona and I were in Venice, and I don't think either of us liked it, though we were too affected to admit it. It was teeming with tourists who we thought less cultured than us. Every restaurant we chose seemed to be the wrong one. Each night, as we made our way back to the apartment we rented off Via Giuseppe Garibaldi, we got lost so that our feet were aching and sweaty. It was hot by day, clammy by night. Worst of all, the air conditioning in the Airbnb wasn't working properly.

On our final night there, it was after 3:00 a.m. and I was still wide awake. I opened the window of the converted attic, hoping that it might bring a whisper of fresh air. Cliona was in a restless sleep, dreams vivid in the humidity. I began to feel the barest of breezes so that I slept for a few hours, but not well.

That Sunday morning, Cliona had been devoured, eight or nine different insect bites each of which were all red, angry, and itchy.

"I asked you not to open the window, Andrew," she said.

"What was I supposed to do? I couldn't sleep."

"How will I be able to sleep with these?" she asked, holding her arms out, one of the bites already turning yellowish.

"They'll have some cream in the pharmacy."

"And if I need an antibiotic, how will I get that?"

"Don't be so fucking dramatic, Cliona."

The water was choppy as the Vaporetto chugged by the island cemetery on the way to the airport that evening. The sinking city seemed just about the least romantic place on earth, as our Aer Lingus jet backed out from the bridge at the Marco Polo terminal to bring us home to Dublin.

There had been rows before, plenty of them. As Cliona sat beside me on the plane, scratching, then trying not to scratch, and scratching again, I sensed this was our last fight. When I got home from the advertising firm where I worked Monday evening, she had packed up her belongings from the Stoneybatter cottage we rented together. Her sister Carol came to collect one last bag, pushed the engagement ring back through the letterbox, no longer even trying to conceal her contempt for me. Carol and I got off on the wrong foot, and never did find the right one.

I submerged my sorrows with my pal Conor that night in a pub, then a late bar, and later a lap-dancing club. The last was his idea, and I sat morose in the corner drinking €10 bottles of Heineken, and mumbling to under-dressed women that I was only interested in beer. Just after 3:00 a.m. on Temple Bar lane, I vomited so that the bile ran gloopy in the gaps between the uneven cobbles. Conor's whereabouts were unknown and of no interest, as I hailed a taxi on Parliament Street in the Dublin piss drizzle.

It hardly needs saying that I was not fit for work that morning. A fortnight before my thirty-seventh birthday, the time when I could have endured a nine-to-five hangover at my desk was long past. I'd had the presence of mind at least to set an alarm on my phone for 9:00 a.m., so that through half-closed eyes I was able to send a short email to my boss Marcus saying I had come down with a stomach bug.

"Would it be at all possible for you to do some work from home?" Marcus wrote back immediately, and I could almost see him striking the keys of his personalised MacBook Pro.

"No," I replied. "I can barely leave the toilet."

A little after midday, I made it as far as the kitchen and let two aspirin tablets dissolve in a glass of water before crashing on the sofa. The bookshelves were now half empty and there was a brighter patch of paint on the wall where Cliona's favourite piece of art had hung. As I waited for the painkillers to take effect, I began scrolling on my phone. My once-fiancée had already unfriended me on Facebook, and set her Instagram to private.

I was one part terrified, the other excited. One moment I would be thinking of the never-to-be wedding. In another, the fifty-something divorcée in the office who sometimes flirted with me. A few times, I tapped out the beginning of a text message, asking Cliona if we could talk, but I never did press Send. Mostly, I felt sorry for myself. After all, how much could a few insect bites hurt?

Our trip to Venice was only a long weekend, and I never got around to unpacking my clothes. That Tuesday evening as the last grains of the hangover washed away, I tossed my red travel suitcase up on the bed. There was nothing I needed from it except to put the dirty socks, t-shirts, and underwear in the washing machine. As I began to open it however, I thought I could hear the faintest of hums.

As I undid the zipper, the sound began to intensify. I lifted over the top of the case, and a swarm of small insects flew out. The shrill sound they made was like two blocks of Styrofoam being ground together, only amplified through a dozen Blaupunkt speakers.

I quickly opened the bedroom window, hoping most of them would fly away. There was a copy of the New Yorker on the bedside locker, so I picked it up, and began to swat them wherever they landed. Little splatters of blood like microcosmic murder scenes appeared on the dull Farrow & Ball paint after each mosquito was crushed.

I spent at least fifteen minutes going between the four rooms of the cottage seeking them out. I opened every window, then the front and back doors, propping them open so they wouldn't slam. It was a warm evening, and I could feel the perspiration wet in the underarms of my shirt as I tried to track down each of the invaders.

Every time I sat down, though, I would see another fluttering around, or one would come screeching from behind and land upon my neck or forearms. I had always been lucky when travelling to places where mosquitoes were plentiful, they never seemed too interested in me. People always think they are choosy about who they bite. But that's not necessarily true. Some believe it's just how your skin and immune system react, not how 'attractive' the insect finds your scent.

I consoled myself with that fact that mosquitoes had never bothered me before. My New Yorker magazine was smeared with the thoraces and abdomens of a hundred of their kin. If a handful had survived the onslaught, they would do me little harm. Still, that night in bed, I did my best to wrap myself up tight in a light quilt to leave as little skin exposed as possible.

My sleep that night was untroubled, which in hindsight seemed odd. As usual, I had set two alarms, one for 8:50 a.m., so that I could hit the snooze button, and a second for 9:00 a.m., when I actually had to get up. As the first chimed on my iPhone however, I was immediately awake. I could say I itched all over but that would not quite be true. There were instead two dozen different places that stung so that it seemed my mind could not compute where first to scratch.

I sat on the edge of the bed. There were five bites on my left arm and seven on my right, three of them rainbow-like in the web between my thumb and index finger. There were six more on my left leg below my boxer shorts and seven on my right, the most painful and swollen in the pit of my knee.

In search of some cream or lotion in the medicine cabinet, I could see my face had not escaped either. There were three blotches on my left cheek and another two on my forehead, so close together that they blended into one. Cliona had left behind some Anthisan cream, though there was only a small bit left so that I had to squeeze it out like the last toothpaste from a tube. I dabbed it on sparingly, assessing the ones that pricked most.

Out in the kitchen, I made myself a pot of coffee and the bites stung so much that I was tempted to add a measure of whiskey. Going to work was the very last thing on my mind as I opened my email.

"Will we be seeing you today?" Marcus asked. His message was sent at 6:57 a.m., probably just before he went for his morning run. I fiddled around with a response, trying to answer his passive aggression with some of my own. When my future was filled with prospects of wedding banquets, mortgages, and perhaps a new family, I had clung to my job.

"Not today, but I'll keep you posted," I wrote, wondering if I annoyed him enough, if would he pay me off to leave? He had a nasty reputation around town, so it wouldn't matter what he said about me later.

There was a chemist just around the corner and as I checked my watch, it wasn't yet 9:30 a.m. Would they even be open? I walked around anyway, hoping but not hopeful. The pharmacist was pushing up the shutters. And as I approached him, it took every milligram of resolve not to start scratching like an ape in front of his shop.

"What can I do for you?" he said once we were inside.

"I'm after getting eaten by mosquitoes," I replied.

"Where were you travelling?"

"I was in the Veneto," I said, "but the bites, they happened here."

He looked at me, pulling at the lobe of his ear, trying to remember my name.

"Mr. Rogers?" he said

For the past two years, I had been visiting every month to collect my antidepressants after a flurry of crippling panic attacks. Mostly since resolved.

"We don't get many mosquitoes in Ireland," he said, "must have been a delayed reaction."

"I know, but ..."

I paused—for the first time thinking of the unlikelihood of a swarm of insects finding their way into my luggage and then surviving a three-hour trip in the hold of an aircraft.

"I've never really suffered any reaction before."

"How many bites do you think there are?" he asked.

"Two dozen, at least."

He turned around. He was tall but a little stooped as if he spent much of his time worried about banging his head. He took some cream from a shelf, the same type Cliona had left behind in our cabinet.

"This will help," he said, "but keep an eye out. If any of them get very sore or seem to be getting larger, you might need an antibiotic. If there are some that are really bothering you, you should mark their boundary with a pen, and if it overlaps, you might need to talk with your doctor."

On Thursday, all but the bite on the back of my knee were much improved. That morning, there were a few new spots where a proboscis had pierced my skin, but it seemed like my body was adapting to the insectile raids. As much as I tried, I could find no more trace of the mosquitoes in the cottage.

Late on Friday afternoon, it became apparent that the one on my leg was not going to mend itself. There was a red circle around it like the aura of a sun, raised flesh at the center, and a tender pinpoint from which a small amount of pus had oozed. It was hurting even when I walked, because with every extension of my leg, I could feel a synaptic dart in my body. I called an online GP service, which allowed for Zoom appointments.

The doctor rang me back about two hours later. He said he knew well the scourge of mosquitoes. He told me he was from Eritrea, even though he spoke perfect English with an accent like he had been schooled in the Home Counties. I explained to him how I had been travelling in Italy, but was already back home when the bitemarks appeared.

"Perhaps some kind of delayed allergic reaction," he suggested.

I was about to tell him how the mosquitoes had flown out from my suitcase, but even as the words formed on my tongue, it struck me again just how irrational this would sound.

"I can try to show you the one I think is infected," I said.

It was awkward trying to manoeuvre the camera of my phone so that it focused on the underside of my leg, but I managed it eventually.

"Yes," he said, "that looks quite inflamed, indeed."

"It's torture," I replied.

"I am going to prescribe you a short course of antibiotics and a topical antibiotic cream. Do you have any allergies I should know about?"

"I don't think so."

"Are there any other medications that you take?"

"Just something for anxiety attacks."

"Well, that should not be a problem. If you could just give me the name of your pharmacist, I will have the prescription sent over."

"How long do you think it'll take to heal?"

"It should not take very long at all."

I cycled down to the nearest late-opening chemist in Phibsboro. It was an unwise choice, as with each turn of the pedals, the skin behind my knee was stretched further. By the time I got there, it was agony to walk, and I was relieved to sit on a plastic seat for half an hour while they got my medicine ready. Back outside on the pavement, I tore open the packaging, dabbed on some of the cream, and dry-swallowed my first dose of flucloxacillin.

By the next morning, it had improved. The redness had shrunk so that the ink circle I'd drawn around it was now bigger than the rash. My boss Marcus had continued to email me with one final communication on Friday at 6:00 p.m. saying my so far 'uncertified illness' would now have to be handled by HR.

"Grand," I wrote back, hoping it would push him into writing, saying, or doing something foolish.

The weekend felt free without Cliona making plans for me to visit an art gallery or a flea market. I spent most of Saturday watching horse races, soccer, and rugby on TV. On Sunday, my leg was much better so that I was able to take a casual spin around the Phoenix Park on my bike. That evening, I met Conor in Mulligan's for food and beer, before one final sweet pint in Walshs. We got talking to two women, and for the first time in nearly a decade, I arranged a first date. As I walked up Oxmantown Road after midnight, I felt lighter, unencumbered. As if life was set to resume.

That feeling didn't last even six hours. Overnight, I came under attack again from my nocturnal enemy. It was as if the insects had taken a pause in battle, to renew, and rearm. This time, there were at least fifty fresh bites. It was difficult to count exactly, not least because there were several swellings on my eyelids, leaving my vision slightly blurred.

I used the topical ointment, but with so many different bites, I had to be conservative. It was Day Three of my course of antibiotics, but maybe I needed something stronger. I rang my doctor's office, was fortunate to get a 3:00 p.m. appointment. In the meantime, I looked up home remedies online: honey, oatmeal, baking soda, toothpaste, and ice. I tried the ones I had on hand, while I waited for the chemist to open so I could stockpile calamine lotion and aloe vera.

When I got home from the pharmacy, I began a hunt to see if I could trace the source of the insects. Cupboards, cabinets, drawers, presses, and wardrobes. Not a sign. The house had an old wooden floor, with sizable gaps between the planks. That seemed the next most obvious place to look. I used the torch on my iPhone to see if I could see what was below, or if I could roust the mosquitoes from their day slumber.

After half an hour, I gave up and sat down on the couch, so many individual pinpoints of pain that they coalesced and became indistinguishable. It was then that I saw a single insect, sitting right on the bright patch of wall where Cliona's favourite painting once hung. I rose from the sofa like a cat burglar, tiptoed across the room, and lashed out so hard with the battered New Yorker that I knocked a crystal candle holder from the mantelpiece. I saw my nemesis flutter away towards the kitchen. When I followed it there, it had disappeared.

Dr. McManigan was the family GP, still working, even though he was well past retirement age. He had been my parent's doctor before they retired and moved to Cantabria. Out of force of habit, I remained his patient, and because he had been seeing me since I was a child, he still spoke to me like one.

He had me strip down to my boxer shorts and lie up on an examination table.

"They certainly look like mosquito bites," he said, and with each fingered touch from his rubber gloves, there was a fresh dart of pain.

Yet again, I found myself weighing up whether to tell the truth or not.

"The mosquitoes were in my bag when I got back from Venice," I said. "A swarm of them flew out."

"Hmm," he said, kneading his fingers.

"I wouldn't have believed it myself," I said.

In his face, I could almost see the gears of his brain grinding as if in fifty years of general practice, this was finally something new.

"We don't really get many mosquitoes in Ireland," he said. "Perhaps it is a delayed allergic reaction. I think a stronger antibiotic and an antihistamine, and you keep in touch during the week and let me know how you are getting on."

"Have you anything for the pain?" I asked, as I scratched roughly at my left bicep.

"If it gets too much, you can use Solpadeine, but be very cautious about that as it can be habit-forming."

"I know that much."

He seemed on the verge of admonishing me.

"How has your anxiety been?" he asked.

"Good. Although this isn't helping," I said.

"And any big changes in your life? Personal? Professional?"

"I broke up with my girlfriend, but I don't see—"

He cut me off. "Maybe we could increase the dose of your antidepressant. Just a little. Nothing too significant, but to make sure we are out ahead of things."

I was tempted to ask what on earth that had to do with my beleaguered body, but I was so tired, sore, and itchy that all I wanted to do was go home. I filled my prescription first and asked for two packets of Solpadeine. The young assistant tut-tutted, and we argued over whether my pain was sufficient. Still unconvinced, she sold me only one.

Maybe she was right, because when I got home, I dropped two of the soluble tablets into a glass of strong Belgian beer and drank it all in one gulp. I quickly polished off another bottle, took a Xanax from my small 'emergency' supply of anxiolytics, and curled up in bed like a sick toddler. In my dreams, I was resting in a desert tent beneath a mosquito net, but then it was full instead, thousands of the insects, a cacophony of their ear-piercing screams.

I awoke for real then, and it was almost midnight. The pain had subsided, and the outer borders of the worst bites had contracted. The ones above my eyelid had shrunk so that I could see clearly again. There was already the foreshadowing of a hangover, so I took two more Solpadeine and sprawled on the couch, watching *North by Northwest* from beneath a soft Avoca blanket. By the time the film was over, I was drowsy again and went back to bed.

The next morning, there were no more bites, but I was terrified that the mosquitoes were just regrouping for the next offensive. I searched for pest control companies on Google and rang the first number I came across. It took until the ninth phone call before I found somebody who could come that day.

The exterminator arrived in a ramshackle HiAce van, already wearing a boiler suit and with a fumigation mask slung around his wrist.

"Mosquitoes you said?"

"Yes, definitely mosquitoes," I said, showing him arms that looked like I was afflicted with a pox.

"That's a new one on me," he replied. "But wherever the little bastards are, I'll snuff 'em out for you."

"And how long will I need to stay away from the house?"

"You could come back this time tomorrow. But two days might be a better bet."

I packed up my travel suitcase, first ensuring there were no insects—alive or dead—lurking inside. Maybe a little break was just what I needed. A couple of days away from the house, a nice four-star hotel, and a swim in the pool, if my bites had healed enough. Sitting in my car, I searched for last-minute deals and found a bed and breakfast offer at a country manor estate in County Clare.

Driving westwards from Dublin, leaving the city behind, I felt a little more at ease. I had the passenger window down, my Spotify playlist blaring, a skinny cappuccino in my cupholder, and a large bar of Cadbury Whole Nut on the seat beside me. My body still itched, but no longer so much that I could not resist the urge to scratch.

When I got to the hotel entrance, I drove up a long avenue lined with chestnut trees, while older men and women were out whacking balls with their woods and irons. I hadn't played golf since I was a teenager. Perhaps I could rent some clubs? A receptionist, so pretty it was hard for me to look at her, asked if I wanted to pay for an upgrade to a junior suite as they'd just had a late cancellation.

"Why not," I said.

It was one of the nicest rooms I'd ever stayed in, a king-sized four-poster bed with silk-soft duvets and pillows. There was a free-standing bath so, I added bubbles and chamomile lotion to the steaming water. As I dried myself after my long soak, I could already feel the improvement, the fluffy fresh towel no longer so harsh upon my skin. Dinner was exquisite. And afterwards in a quiet drawing room, I drank, ever so slowly, two Negronis.

Walking back up the grand staircase to my room, I decided I would contact Cliona the next day. Nine years was too much of my life to let slip without a fight. I knew I could be a better boyfriend, fiancé, husband. I could be more accommodating, less headstrong. That it was finally time to grow up. I sank into the mattress of the bed, let the duvet rest half across me, no longer fearful for my skin. It couldn't have been more than five minutes before I fell asleep.

When I awoke, I wasn't sure if I was just dreaming. My throat felt constricted as if there was a ligature around my neck. It felt like trying to breathe when a spoonful of water had gone down the wrong passageway. As I continued to gasp, I somehow managed to turn on the bedside lamp. I could see every surface of the room, the ceiling, the walls, the furniture, and the duvet crawling with mosquitoes.

I opened my mouth wide, desperately hoping to gather more air, when three insects flew directly out from my mouth. My entire body was raw and ravaged, more red than milky white. I reached for the telephone, pulled the receiver towards me. My head began to spin from lack of oxygen. I tried to remember which button to press to call reception. Was it nine or was it zero?

I pressed zero, and I could hear the calling tone. It rang and rang until, at last, it was answered.

"I can't breathe, I can't bree, I ca ..."

A State of Emergency

Kent Priore

I awake to find myself spread across a gurney, being rushed from the emergency room and into the hospital's hallway. At my side are two EMT workers pushing me along. I can't seem to move. My body feels heavy and drenched in some sort of fluid.

The two EMT workers carry me into a room and onto a bed. They leave in a hurry. Dazed, my eyes dart all around. *Why I am here? What earned my spot in this hospital bed? And, come to think of it, what is even my name?*

"Still with us, huh? Bummer," says a voice to my left, out of sight.

I turn to face it, and what I see is a man with pale, pasty skin, and black hair weaving around stubby horns that protrude from his forehead. He seems familiar, but I'm unsure why.

"Jesus, you sure did a number on your head, didn't you? You don't even remember your closest friend? It's me, Judas. I came to see how you were doing, buddy."

"W-what happened to me?" I ask.

His face freezes into a frown. He continues to think for a moment, as if he is trying to summon forth the best words to use. "Well, you see..."

Judas is cut short by a nurse's sudden appearance. She's short in stature and mildly obese, as well as the latter end of middle age.

"Hello there! I'm nurse Hopewell. First name's Joy. Call me whatever you'd like! Now, it seems like you've had an accident. But first things first, let's get you out of those cold wet clothes."

This woman is way too cheerful and upbeat. I don't like it, but I must suffer her for the time being as I am too weak to move. Nurse Joy Hopewell undresses and redresses me into a hospital gown. She digs her hands into the pocket of my black jeans and finds my wallet, from which she pulls my driver's license.

"Very sorry for the intrusion, but I heard from the EMTs that you can't remember much. So, let's see just who you are." She inspects my license. "Jesus Martinez." Out from my wallet, she unearths a small square piece of paper, written upon with jagged, indecipherable words.

"Seems like you may have been on your way to fill a prescription. For Seroquel? Well, that's not something you can go without. I'll have the doctor fill this and then I'll return shortly."

Forgetting for a moment about Judas, I am surprised to hear his voice once more after the nurse leaves.

"You're not actually going to take those, are ya? You know they're no good. All they do is dull your personality and make it that we can't talk anymore!" he says. "These people don't want what's best for you. I mean, take those EMTs and that insufferable nurse. In and out as if you're a checkbook, not a person. I mean really—"

My friend Judas here seems like quite the talker, and while I don't like Nurse Joy Hopewell much either, when she returns with a bottle full of pills, I will at least be saved from his ramblings.

"Hello there again! The doctor was going to come check in with you, but we decided it would be better to let you rest for the night without any more distractions. You've had an awful accident, after all. Though regardless, it's no good to have people go off their meds, so open up!"

She feeds me a tiny pill and serves me water to help it go down. She doesn't say another word and is promptly on her way out of the room. When she turns her back to me, I see long feathered wings rising high above her shoulders. They are as bright and white as fresh, untainted snow. A feature I didn't notice before.

Judas rolls his eyes in disappointment and leaves the room.

About twenty minutes have gone by, and I have still yet to see either Judas, the nurse, or any doctor enter the room. Truth be told, I'm enjoying the silence. For reasons I cannot explain, my heart feels as heavy as my body.

Nurse Joy Hopewell pushes a man past my room in a wheelchair. I catch a quick glimpse. The man is stout, blond, and has studded horns like Judas. A knife is lodged through his left eye, and blood drips from a wide horizontal slit across his throat.

"Oh, my goodness, just how did this happen?" asks Nurse Joy Hopewell.

The man replies, "Well, lesson learned! Never piss off the wife!"

I stare at the man in awe. Some people really can endure quite a bit of pain. I feel I was once that kind of strong person.

"Lesson learned, indeed, you silly man. A happy wife means a happy life, is what I always say!" says Nurse Joy Hopewell, whose voice should have been fading away by now as they proceed farther down the hall. Instead, I hear her clearly and at full volume, as if she is speaking inches away from my ear.

But then they are gone, and silence returns once more.

I hear a woman give off a violent screech.

Judas returns to my room and comes bearing gifts. Under his arms are two white feathered wings.

"Consider this a last meal before we both disappear for a bit. Angel wings are a delicacy where I'm from!" Judas says, taking a large bite out of a wing, feathers and all, baring his shark-like teeth as he chomps down. "Wanna bite?" he asks, wiping a bit of blood from his lips and plucking a feather that is stuck to his right cheek.

"I'm not too hungry," I reply. "To be honest I've felt off since I got here. How did I get here?"

"There was an accident," Judas replies coldly. "It's understandable though. It's been a foggy night, and I'm sure you just swerved off the road to avoid a deer or something. Anyways, you drove off a bridge, and your car landed in a lake. Thankfully they got to you before you drowned. The car is lost though. Either way, I rushed over as soon as I heard."

"Explains why my clothes were drenched."

"So, you really don't remember anything?" Judas asks.

"Not yet, but I feel like I have some thoughts lingering in my mind. Thoughts from before. Thoughts that give me a vague sense of who I am. They've been coming back slowly so hopefully my memories will return soon."

"Let's hope so. The sooner you're feeling better, the sooner we can get back to our home," Judas says.

"We live together?"

"Sure do, pal. We've been roommates for...the last decade or so? Well, long enough for me to forget."

I take in these bits of information about my life and who I am, hoping that it won't be long before I can remember everything on my own. I start to feel the effects of the pill Nurse Joy Hopewell gave me. In the hall, the man with the knife in his eye and the gash in his neck is speaking to a doctor.

"The nurse? Don't know, doc. She went off to grab something and never came back to me. Could you take me to my room? She never got me there."

I peer at him, but the view becomes hazy. His horns melt away, leaving his head with only his blond hair. The man himself blurs out of existence and—

Wait, what was I just thinking about?

I turn to Judas. The shape of his body becomes hazy and spills away into the void of the room.

"Well, glad I was able to eat before it was time to go," he says.

"Where are–"

I awake with my head feeling as if I had been hit by a freight train. Daylight is slipping through the curtains of the hospital room's windows. The room is empty. My mind feels heavy and blurry. Parts of myself have become lost in this thick, unabating haze.

Perhaps it's because Judas reminded me of the accident, or maybe it's the effect of a good night's sleep, but I feel my memories starting to slowly trickle back. The memory of icy cold water on my skin, the shattering of my car's windshield, the dirty lake water filling my lungs.

Noticing my waking, a doctor enters the room.

"Ah, good morning," he says plainly. "I meant to check in with you last night, but you were already asleep."

"Where's Nurse Joy Hopewell?" I ask, having expected to be woken up by her excessive enthusiasm rather than by a doctor.

"She's gone AWOL. Stole some pills and bolted. I always wondered how a person could be so cheerful in a dump like this."

"A dump? The hospital?" I ask.

"The hospital, the world. I guess the answer would be different depending on who you talk to." There is something strangely relatable in his words. "Anyways, you've had an accident."

"Yes, I've actually begun to remember some of it."

"Fantastic. Less work for me then. Well, miraculously you've sustained no vital injuries, and you're fine, really. We'll be releasing you later in the afternoon once you've gotten more rest." He pauses. "Oh, and here are the rest of the meds that were administered to you last night. That'll last you a month. Take them with you on your way out later."

He places the bottle of pills onto the nightstand to the right of me and leaves without another word. I shove the bottle deep into the pocket of my jacket that is laying across a chair, thankfully in arm's reach. My muscle function has begun to return.

I continue to rest, my head still in a blur, wondering what could possess Nurse Joy Hopewell to steal a bottle of pills. I guess the pressures of life would cause anyone to need some form of escape from time to time.

The sedative effects of the pill I took last night are lingering. I promptly drift back to sleep, wake up, and back to sleep again many times, until suddenly it is 1:58 p.m., and I'm being discharged from the hospital. On my way out, I take a couple dollars from my wallet and go over to a vending machine. I buy a bottle of water, as while my head *is* feeling a bit less heavy than before, Seroquel proves to be a potent drug, and I figure I can benefit from some water. I take a swig, dial the number for a taxi, then I make my way outside.

The taxi driver asks, "Where to?" But I have no idea *where to.*

"66 Maple Ave. Apartment 6," says a familiar voice to my left.

It's Judas, sitting at my side with a hazy smile.

"Ah. Yes. 66 Maple Ave. Apartment 6," I repeat with a dull voice, as the memory of our apartment complex returns to me. A few buildings, piss yellow in color and dilapidated. Not a place one would want to bring a date to for a nightcap. At least not without great embarrassment.

The cab driver nods and puts the address into the GPS on his phone.

"See, no one wants anything to do with ya. That doctor and nurse. This asshole here." Judas made a gesture with his hands toward the cab driver, who doesn't seem to care and refuses to react. "But don't ya worry yourself because you've got me. You've always got me."

"Where have you been?" I ask.

"Well, I had to go away since you didn't listen to me. But I'm here now and that's all that matters!"

The weather becomes glum. Dark gray clouds fill the sky above, and raindrops splatter hard upon the cab's windows.

"Whatcha thinkin?" Judas asks.

"About me. Memories are slowly returning, but I still don't know who I am. You do though. Could you tell me about myself?"

"Well of course, my friend," Judas responds.

"Do I have a family? Do we live with them? Am I religious? Do I believe in God?"

Judas pauses for a moment, his eyes scattering all about as if he is in a garden of words, trying to pick the very best flowers for the occasion.

"We don't speak about them, remember? And I wouldn't waste your time on religion. God has no saving grace left for the likes of you," Judas says.

Before I can respond, I notice the cab driver glaring strangely at me through his rear-view mirror. He pulls up to the piss-colored apartment buildings.

"Twenty-three fifty," says the cab driver.

I pay him and we get out of the cab.

I recognize the apartment as my own, as it's labeled Jesus Martinez across the door. Judas's name is nowhere to be found. I suppose it's my name on the lease, and he pays me rent. Living in a dump like this, I must not be that well off, so I'm sure the extra cash helps. "Home sweet home, eh pal?" Judas says. He kicks off his shoes with such vigor that they shoot off his feet and ram into the walls. He goes over to the fridge, takes out a beer, pops it open and sits down upon the ragged couch. Stuffing spews out from within the cushions as he lays his weight upon it.

I decide to look around. To the left of the living room is a door that leads to my bedroom. A single bed lays there at the far-right corner of the room. Its sheets are stained and strewn across the floor. Next to it stands a busted-up dresser with a couple of drawers hanging loose. Otherwise, the room feels empty. I return to the living room where Judas is peacefully enjoying his beer. I grow more uneasy by the second. I decide to pop open a beer myself.

"That's the spirit, mate! Take a load off. You've had a rough go of it these past couple days after all," Judas says.

Walking through the kitchen doesn't take long, as it's a measly four feet wide. But the sight of it makes me gulp down my Corona, then grab another. It's even more disgusting than the living room and bedroom, with oily grime thickly spread across the stove and countertops. There is a rusty frying pan resting upon one of the stove burners. I step on something sticky and wish I hadn't taken off my sneakers at the front door. I grab another beer.

Good Lord. Who would live here?

I reach for the paper towel roll which hangs underneath the cabinet closest to the sink. I run water to wet a piece, only to see brownish yellow liquid spewing from the faucet. I toss the paper towel aside and opt to wipe my foot with a dry piece instead. Making my exit from the kitchen, I notice a landline phone at the edge of the counter. I pick it up and press the call history button. Most recent on the call log is one I placed rather than received, and it was labeled "Martinez." *Family perhaps?* I redial the number.

Judas glares at me from the couch as the phone rings. I wait and wait, anticipating who might answer. The ringing stops, and I can hear a faint breathing sound from the other end.

"Hello?" I ask.

Silence.

"Anyone there?"

"I thought we told you never to contact us again," a woman's voice says.

"I'm sorry. I'm not sure what—"

"Yeah, that's just great!" she interrupts. "Acting all confused and oblivious. You're as delusional as ever! I still can't understand...how you could...the fire..." The woman's voice is cut short by loud weeping.

"I gave birth to a monster, you know that?" The woman continues in a rage. "Thinking God told you to set fire to the house, to slay monsters you claimed were following you around? You're sick in the head, Jesus! And because of you...my baby girl...your own flesh and blood!"

Stricken with panic, I'm without the words to respond.

"This is the last time I'll tell you. Don't you contact us again," she hangs up.

I can't breathe. My body slithers onto the floor. I crawl to the fridge and upon opening it, I realize there is no beer left. Glancing up at the counter, I see five empty bottles and a sixth one in my right hand. I now know why I'm living here and why I've been forced to rent out the living room to Judas to make ends meet.

"My sister," I mutter, as my eyes summon forth a flood. The panic ravishes my body, constricting my muscles, tightening my throat, *Ican'tbreathe.*

"Buddy? You alright in there?" Judas asks.

His footsteps approach me. I reach into my coat pocket and take out the bottle of pills. Pouring two tablets into the palm of my right hand, I lodge them into the small opening of my throat. I take a swig of my beer and swallow them down.

It occurs quicker this time, my body's motor functions cease. Tumbling over, I knock the top of my beer against the grimy floor. The bottle shatters in my hand. A tiny puddle of beer and blood blends together near my face. The last thing I see before the darkness takes me is Judas's dirty and jagged toenails, which also disappear as quickly as they came.

Flames overtake the building. They bellow and roar as they burn everything from the inside out. A woman, restrained in the arms of a man, tries and fails to run back into the building. She lets out blood curdling screams. "My baby girl! Please, you have to save my baby girl!" she shouts to the firemen who are now entering the building, and of whom reassures the woman that they will do everything they can to help.

I sit there upon the front lawn in awe of the scene I've put into motion during my divine quest. The holy flames devouring the evil spirits which haunt me every night. I gaze proudly into the flames, when the man holding the woman back shoots me a look of malice. The house crumbles in upon itself, and my mother's cries grow louder. The firemen emerge from the flames, giving up on saving the building and relinquishing it to its fate. One fireman is holding a small child. About three feet in height, but missing its hair. Its eyes and mouth are melted shut. The flames destroyed all identifiable traits. But my mother, father, and I know the child for who she was. My sister. As my eyes gaze upon her, the fabric of the world shakes around me. My sister's eyes and mouth are torn agape through the melted skin, blood and ash spilling out as they reopen. Her left arm raises and points toward me. Her mouth does not move, but I swear I can hear her mutter the word:

"Monster."

I awake to a hangover that could slay a walrus. My body feels three times its weight. And as life blurs slowly into focus, I can't move. My face lays across the floor. A small puddle of blood and beer smears across my right cheek. I try to push myself up, but the cut in my hand refuses to bear my weight. The arm gives out, my face slams against the floor. Using my other arm, I struggle onto my feet and stumble to the couch, the journey seeming far longer than it had been before. I sit, then remove the bottle of water from my coat and take a swig of it, hoping it will soothe my head. I drink about half the bottle, leaving the rest for later. Having seen the rust-colored water spew from the faucet before, I can't imagine it would ever be safe for drinking. I lay my head back, expecting a soft cushion. Into the backside of my head pricks a sharp spring that has pierced through.

"Fuck! God dammit!" I scream, clasping my head.

"Pal, you really need to stop doing that. What did I tell you about those pills?" Judas says, now standing before me with a scowl.

"I killed my sister," I say.

Judas glares at me.

"Didn't I tell you? We don't talk about your family! And that little bitch deserved it anyway," Judas says. "They were never there for you and when they weren't, who was? Me, that's who! I'm the only family you need now."

Fear overcoming me, I realize I need to leave. I rise to my feet, put on my coat, slip on my shoes, but I fall over as soon as I try to find my balance. Finishing the should-be-simple action on the floor, I somehow manage to get myself up and out the door.

I must have blacked out for a while because I now find myself down a quiet country road. I recognize it to be a few miles away from the apartment, even though it feels like I've only been walking for a couple minutes. I have no destination. All I know is that I can't be there. Perhaps I can't be anywhere. Who would have me? I turn and look over my shoulder. Judas is walking a few feet behind.

My mind is still brooding upon the return of that horrible memory when my foot is caught on a large tree branch. I trip and scrape my face on the road, tiny pebbles piercing into and becoming one with my skin. Blood trickles down between the pebbles, like water weaving through the rocky cliffside of a waterfall. I return to my feet and continue walking.

"So, where are we going?" Judas asks while stomping violently upon the branch that tripped me. He kicks the snapped pieces away from the road.

"I don't know," I say.

Judas doesn't answer. His attention is pulled elsewhere.

"Score! Look what I found, bud!" Judas says.

In his hands he holds a dead rabbit. It's quite plump, fatter than average. From a wound in its abdomen slides out a handful of slimy, unborn baby rabbits.

"What luck! I was thrilled enough to find the one rabbit to sink my teeth into, but it came with extra treats! Not as good as those angel wings, but it'll do!" Judas says, quite excited over his find.

Judas bites the head of the mother rabbit clean off. I notice his horns again. They aren't as small as before, but longer, sharper, no longer hiding beneath his hair. He slurps the unborn babies down, and I realize that I must be so far gone if I'm just now seeing that something isn't right.

I pull the bottle of pills out of my coat pocket. The doctor gave me a month's supply, about thirty tablets. Having already taken three, I unscrew the cap and empty the other twenty-seven pills into my mouth. Judas notices and rushes toward me.

"What the fuck did I tell you? Don't you dare take those pills!"

His hands make way for my neck, but not before I wash the pills down with what was left of my water bottle. His hands make contact, and he pins me to the ground. His dirty, sharp fingernails pierce the skin of my throat. All air leaves my lungs, and I feel my consciousness waning. He really seeks to kill me. *Yes, kill me. Let us both die.*

A blinding light emerges from the darkness of the night. A car pulls up beside us.

"Hey, you there! Are you alright?" says a young woman's voice. She only addresses me and pays no mind to Judas who is standing upon my chest, choking the life out of me. "Are you having trouble breathing? Are you hurt somewhere? Either way, you should let me take you to a hospital and in the meantime, it probably isn't helping too much that you're holding onto your throat so tightly."

Confused by her words, I glance downward toward Judas's pasty hands, which for a moment blur and morph into my hands, then back again to Judas's. The intervention of this kind stranger brings me back to reality. I'm sure of what Judas is now. In my lonesome, I made friends with my pain and even let him move in.

I break free from his clutches and push him back with all my strength, shouting "*You're not real!*" Suddenly, I look around, but Judas is nowhere to be seen. The kind stranger is now backing away from me. Her eyes appear to hold great fear, and I can't blame her as I feel that same fear. Panic surges beneath my skin, and I feel that there is no escape from it. I rise to my feet and start running.

I find myself on a bridge that crosses over a lake below. I don't know for sure just how long I've been running, but I see that the sun is beginning to rise, just enough for me to see what lies below the bridge. Alongside the edge of the lake is a small park with a few picnic benches, or rather, the crushed remains of picnic benches. There are also tire tracks creased into the grass that lead into the sandy shore of the lake. Back in the hospital I couldn't wait for my memories to return to me. Though now that they have, I wish they hadn't. While I thought that all my memories returned, I was wrong. As I look over the edge of the bridge, another comes back. This is the lake where my accident occurred and is the reason I was sent to the hospital. But the scene doesn't match up with what I was told.

Judas said that I swerved to avoid a deer and as a result, I went off a bridge and into a lake. But the bridge contains no damage. The guardrails are in pristine condition. I didn't drive off a bridge. I was down there at the park. There weren't any deer either. No—I drove into the lake, and I did it on purpose.

Sins were committed, and they needed to be paid for. I look around me and though the morning light begins to shine brighter, it is still early enough in the morning that the roads are silent and devoid of life. The effects of the medication are also hitting quite hard, so much so, that I feel that I could collapse at any moment. *Now or never.*

I glance down at the dark waters below. With both my arms I grab hold of the bridge's guardrails and lift myself up and over, beginning my descent. The water slaps hard across my back, but I am so sedated from the medication that I cannot display the pain. My body is stretched out like a cross upon the water's surface, before beginning its journey to the depths.

Water fills my lungs, its icy touch piercing my chest. *Yes, let us both die.* My body sinks deeper and deeper. As it does, up above the waters I see sparkles of ethereal light. They appear to me as angels. *Are they here to save me?* I sure hope not. *Sins were committed and they needed to be paid for.* I've done so much wrong, and I would like to finally do something right. *Please allow me to do something right.* As my descent to the cold, mossy lakebed coffin continues, I get my wish. The angels and their divine light retract one by one, dissipating into the void...and so do I.

Monster Size Monsters

Ken Teutsch

An enormous black bat, red-eyed, the size of a condor, swoops down onto the back of a fleeing figure. In the bat's inky shadow, only the top of the doomed man's head is visible above fleeing legs in white leggings and out-thrust arms, gnarled fingers grasping at nothing. Flashing fangs are poised above the shock of red hair, about to plunge into exposed flesh. Red letters are written in splashes of blood. *Bat Out of Hell!*

House of Mystery #195. Cover by Bernie Wrightson. Walt held it resting on his palms, his expression amazed and something akin to reverent.

"Well, I'll be damned," he said.

It had been a bad day, but what else was new? Walt decided to slip out a little early, but just as he crossed the showroom, Kevin, the sales manager, popped up in his path with a bunch of questions about the month's sales figures. Snot-nosed little creep. Jesus, hadn't he ever heard of a slump?

So, Walt had to yessir, yessir his way around that pissant (*Lecturing me? I was selling cars before you could drive...*) and then, before he could even get in his front door, there was Brenda, also popping up like something in a box on a spring, just suddenly *there* with that "now don't start" look on her face. Don't start what? What *now*, for God's sake?

"A package came," she said. "From Polly."

A month earlier Walt's mother had finally died. Fine. Whatever. His sister, Polly, had handled everything else, so why not this, too? But Brenda wouldn't let it go. Next thing you know, they're out twelve hundred bucks between them for airfare. *Twelve hundred!* Airlines don't do bereavement fares anymore, it turns out.

Bereavement? That's a laugh.

After the funeral, Polly wanted them to accompany her to the house. Some kind of stroll down memory lane or something. He might have forgiven Brenda for such a clueless suggestion, but Polly should have known better. He hadn't been back to that house, and he wasn't going back now. He was already worn out just from the effort of sitting through the funeral without screaming. Some droning Methodist rambling on about what a wonderful woman she was. Everybody all solemn. Having to pull a long face for all those people. Who were they, anyway? *Cousins,* for God's sake.

So anyway, forget it. The house? He told his sister to take it with his blessing. All of it. Sell what she could and trash the rest. Just leave him the hell out of it. Whatever was there, he wanted none of it. But now here was this box.

His sister's cramped handwriting on the note inside,

Walter,
These things were in the closet in your old room. I thought you might want them.
I know what you think, but she loved you.
-Polly

The woman was delusional. But okay, what did he have here?

Junk. Some notebooks from junior high and high school. Social Studies. English. Doodles in the margins. A little league trophy. Everybody on the team got one, he had spent the whole tournament in the dugout. A few battered LPs, some not even in the sleeves. A moment of hope at Led Zeppelin III, but it looked like somebody had been at it with steel wool. Paperback science fiction novels. A plastic harmonica. Detritus. Junk. And...

House of Mystery #195.

"Well, I'll be damned."

A little scuffed, a little creased, and tattered around the edges, but in pretty good shape, considering.

"Well, I'll be *damned*."

Walt sat at the table in the foyer where he had opened and unloaded the box, holding the comic book gingerly on his two hands like a curator in a museum. Brenda had scoped out the box's contents with great interest and now looked over his shoulder at the comic. "Ooh," she said, "Creepy!" He almost said, "No, not *Creepy. House of Mystery*!" But she wouldn't get it.

"Makes no sense," he said. "The old lady keeping this, I mean."

Brenda poked at a yellowed paperback on the table, something by Robert Heinlein. "She was your mother," she said. "A mother doesn't just throw out all that's left of a son." Walt guffawed, and Brenda looked offended. She seemed to look that way a lot nowadays.

"I'm talking about the comic book," he said, holding it up. "She hated my comics. She got rid of all of them, and I don't mean she just tossed them. She *burned* them. Right in front of me. Don't know how she missed this one." He had had a pretty fair collection, too, as he now recalled. He had always preferred the horror comics. He'd never had much use for superheroes. *House of Mystery, House of Secrets, Weird War, Creepy, Eerie*. All those comics. Today they'd probably be worth something. He wondered if this one was worth anything.

He opened it and carefully flipped the pages. "Ha!" he said. "Look at these ads!" The memories gave him a feeling of vertigo. "Man, I wanted all this stuff! But I could never get any of it, of course. Even when I had the money, she wouldn't let me."

"Just as well, don't you think?" Brenda leaned closer over his shoulder. She was chewing gum, and he winced as it popped near his ear. "I can't imagine a five dollar Polaris submarine would have been very seaworthy." She snorted.

Walt grunted and flipped to the next page, resisting the urge to turn away, hide the book. He didn't like people reading over his shoulder. And anyway, this was *his*. Then another ad caught his attention, and he smiled. "This one!" he said, tapping the page, "This is the one I wanted most of all."

"Monster size monsters!" Brenda read. "A seven-foot Frankenstein?"

"Glow in the dark, too. Yeah." Walt chuckled. "God, how I wanted that. Funny how kids can be. I was scared to death of Frankenstein. Nightmares and everything. But more than anything in the world I--"

"A seven-foot Frankenstein for a *dollar*?" Brenda barked. "Gives new meaning to 'let the buyer beware!'"

She thought that was a good one. She began that wheezy, clicking noise she made instead of normal human laughter. She poked a finger toward his comic book. "Real floating ghost!" she said around the nasal snickering, "X-ray glasses! Little boys must have been pretty stupid in those days!"

"Yeah, we were real morons," he said through clenched teeth and slapped the comic closed face down on the table.

"You're done?" Brenda asked, her laughter mercifully winding down. "You only looked at the ads. What's the story about?"

"As I recall," he said, "it's about a guy who kills his wife and seals her body up in a wall."

Brenda sniffed disapprovingly. "And they sold stuff like that to children? Violence against women, rip-offs to steal kids' money…" she reached over his shoulder. "Maybe your mother had a point!"

"Yeah," Walt said, snatching the comic up before she could touch it. "Maybe so." There followed a moment of cold silence after which Brenda finally vaguely realized that she had somehow annoyed him. She shrugged, said, "Well," and walked into the living room. When she was gone, Walt studied the comic again.

How did this one survive? He couldn't remember saving it. He had a non-stop, admittedly blurry, stream of shitty memories of his mother, but the comic book episode was one scene that stood out clear as a bell. The burn barrel in the back yard. Her in her blue waitress outfit with the stupid lacy apron like Hazel on the TV show. A stupid woman in a stupid dress for her stupid job, throwing *his* comic books into a trashcan and squirting lighter fluid. "This stuff will rot your brain!" Rot his brain. And what finally got her? Brain cancer.

He smiled. He liked irony. *Maybe that's why I liked the horror comics,* he thought. *Or did I get it from the horror comics?*

He carefully laid the book aside. He'd save it for later, in the Office. The rest of the stuff he carried to the garage and dumped unceremoniously into the garbage can.

The "Office" was a room over the garage that Walt had fitted out with a desk, a computer, a few envelopes, and some notepads. More importantly, if less relevant from an office work point of view, there was the mini refrigerator in the corner with its interesting cargo of ice, orange juice, and Smirnoff. Walt dropped the comic on the desk and with these and a plastic cup, made himself an extremely strong screwdriver.

The room wasn't much, but it had a couple of things going for it. The first was privacy, or something approaching privacy, there was a lock on the door, and anyone coming up the steps (as in who else?) could be heard several seconds before arrival. And then there was the small closet. Walt was no carpenter, but he had enough know-how to saw a hole in the back above the shelf and make a little hidden niche where he could keep a few private items.

Walt moved to the closet now, after locking the door. He moved a box aside, pulled out the ragged square of sheetrock, and took out a pair of binoculars. The binoculars were for the other thing that recommended the Office, which was the view.

He took a sip of the drink and plopped into the rolling chair, the momentum carrying it over to the window. It was getting late, but he still might luck out. He raised one slat of the blinds and peered out across the lawn, over his back fence, and into the neighbors' back yard.

Jackpot!

A few months back the Morrises, a drab pair of nobodies who had lived in the house behind theirs since before he and Brenda came to the neighborhood, sold out and moved to Arizona. A new couple soon moved in and the first time Walt glanced out the window and saw the wife, he drove immediately to Dick's Sporting Goods and asked for the best pair of binoculars they had. Since then, he had spent a lot more time in the Office.

Brenda had gone round to say hello and reported back. The husband was a firefighter. The girl worked part time doing something admirable with children. She told him their names, but to him the woman was just The Goddess. The husband was The Hulk. The Hulk worked long shifts at the firehouse and that suited Walt just fine. The lonely Goddess passed much of the time with exercise routines in front of the TV near the glass patio door, and that suited Walt even better.

The Goddess also liked flowers and spent long stretches in the back yard futzing around with them. She tended to do this in shorts, sometimes of the Daisy Duke variety, sometimes skimpy ones made of terrycloth. Along with the shorts she wore loose, low-cut muscle shirts or the occasional *(oh, glorious days)* halter top. She squatted, hunched, and hunkered over the flowerbeds, thrusting her little trowel repeatedly and rhythmically into the moist, dark earth, a fine sheen of sweat slowly spreading over her flawless, honey-colored skin. Her gold-and-amber hair, tied loosely atop her head, inevitably began eventually to come loose, and she periodically had to sit up and shake it all free before leaning languidly back to tie it up again. At these times, an attentive listener at the Office door might have heard moans of frustration or low, mumbled obscenities.

But eventually The Hulk always returned, and she disappeared inside. Walt imagined in great detail what they must be getting up to, but though he squinted until his head hurt at the shadows on the window shades, what went on inside the house was always closed to him.

Today The Goddess was watering the flower beds. Her clothing choices: ter‑rycloth and t‑shirt. The t‑shirt was voluminous, presumably one of The Hulk's. He focused the binoculars, and she seemed to leap within his reach.

"Hello, sweetheart," he said softly. "I missed you. Did you miss me?" Her expression was impassive. Her eyes were cobalt blue.

As his own eyes, with the help of the binoculars, wandered up and down her form, Walt's mind wandered, too. To Brenda. She wasn't holding up all that well. It was the simple truth. The years weren't being kind. He thought more and more nowadays about how he had been rushed into his marriage. *Let's face it. Call a spade a spade.* And (*simple truth, let's face it*) he could have done better. *That's not boasting, it's just fact.* She had been cute, sure. But almost right from the wedding reception she started to get frumpier. Now look at her. *Me, though. I'm not so bad. Maybe a little thicker around the middle than I once was. A bit thinner on top. But women still take a second look at me. Some do, anyway. A girl like this, now...*

At that thought he took another deep swallow from the plastic cup. Then another.

A girl like this, now...

He raised the binoculars once more to focus on her face. What was she? Twenty‑five? He frowned. Grim reality nagged at him. The depressing thought that he would never (*face facts, spade a spade*) get another shot at a girl like that. The vodka helped keep at bay the further (*spade a spade*) thought that he had never really had a shot at a girl like that in the first place. He thought now of the comic book on the desk, and of the boy who had owned it all those years ago.

If I had just played my cards right...not let women push me around... Like my dad...he didn't hang around to get his balls busted...he made the smart move and...

Suddenly a huge hand grabbed The Goddess, abruptly snatching her from his view. Walt cursed and jerked, sloshing vodka onto his sleeve. The binoculars caught in the blinds, and it took a moment to twist them free. He looked through the now bent slats.

It was The Hulk, damn him. Home unexpectedly. Dark, unlike his wife, and massive. Fireman mustache, fireman biceps. He had sneaked up on them. And now The Goddess was laughing and slapping at him, threatening him with the water hose. The big lummox was laughing, too. He grabbed the dainty hand with the hose and pulled her to him. She said something and laughed. He said something and pulled a mock diabolical face. He jerked her hand, and a jet of water arced over their heads, showering them with a brief mist.

Like two actors in a cheesy silent movie, he gave a wide‑mouthed, "Oh! How did that happen?" gawp, and she gave an "Oh no, you wouldn't dare!" simper. Then he twisted her hand around again, this time dousing them both. The

Goddess' shocked/delighted squeal was audible across the yard and through the window glass.

The water soaked her t-shirt. Walt raised the binoculars again. Now the hose fell to the ground, and The Hulk pulled her closer. They kissed, spun around. He lost them and lowered the binoculars. The Goddess now had her legs wrapped around The Hulk's waist. His large, hairy hands were under the t-shirt.

"You're kidding me," Walt said. He jerked the binoculars up again so abruptly that he whacked the bridge of his nose, and his eyes began to water. He couldn't keep things in focus. Where did they go? Dropping the binoculars once more, he watched The Hulk carry her toward the patio door. "Nooo," Walt said, "Stay out here!"

For a moment he thought they would. They paused, leaning on the wall by the sliding glass door. Walt frantically focused the binoculars. The big man's hands were all over her. Then he lifted her again, and carried her through the open sliding door. He set her down and turned to slide the door closed, and behind him The Goddess, with one smooth motion, whipped off the wet t-shirt and tossed it aside. There was just a split second—a nanosecond—before the big bastard jerked the curtain across the doorway, and she was gone.

With a whimper of frustration, Walt swept the binoculars from window to window, finally coming to rest on the one he knew belonged to their bedroom. All curtains drawn. He thumped the binoculars onto the windowsill and downed the rest of his drink. He took a deep breath and exhaled it in the form of a long string of obscenities. Then he mixed himself another drink. Stronger this time.

He woke up on the living room couch.

At first, he wasn't sure what had awakened him, then came a crash from the kitchen. Brenda was loudly and deliberately banging dishes. He slowly pulled himself upright. A wave of nausea passed over and around him, and his head began to throb. He took stock. His shoes were nowhere in sight, but he was otherwise dressed, except that his belt was unfastened, and his shirttail was out. He tried to think. He had been upstairs in the Office. There had been the thing with the neighbors. He had had a few drinks. He remembered reading his old comic book. When had he come back downstairs?

Brenda walked into the room, already dressed for work. Her mouth was tight, and her brow deeply furrowed.

"Big night?" she asked.

"Aw, leave me alone," he mumbled, lowering his head into his hands. He felt a jab in the back and reached around to find something rolled up and jammed into his hip pocket. The comic book. He dropped it on the coffee table.

"This is getting out of hand, Walt," Brenda said. He did not reply. She waited a moment and sighed. "If you want breakfast, there's oatmeal. I'm going to work."

"I'm going too," he protested weakly.

"Sure," she said. She turned to the table by the door and picked up a small, brown parcel. "This came," she said, holding the box out toward him.

He raised his head. "Huh? What is it?"

"How should I know? It's addressed to you." She looked at the label. "Actually, it's addressed to *Wally* Krulwich. Did you order something?"

He tried to think above the booming in his head. "Order?" Something vaguely flickered in the back of his mind. "I don't..."

"I heard the knock, but by the time I got there the van was pulling away. Who delivers packages this time of the morning?" she thrust the box at him again. He took it.

Wally Krulwich? Nobody had called him Wally since...

"Listen, Walt. Like I said, I have to go to work. But we need to have a talk. A serious talk. Do you hear me?"

Something was bumping up against his memory as he looked at the brown parcel with the printed label. No return address. He *had* ordered something, hadn't he? But this couldn't have anything to do with that... He tore the paper off the box. The lid was not sealed.

"I mean," Brenda went on, "this mid-life crisis thing, late life, whatever it is... I guess it happens. Okay. But there's a limit. You know?"

In the box, on a bed of deep red velvet, lay a pair of eyeglasses. Black, horn-rimmed eyeglasses. The lenses were strange, they weren't transparent. Walt lifted them out of the box. They were heavy.

"Walt, are you listening to me?"

The lenses were etched with a swirling pattern that curved around to meet at a pinhole in the center. They looked familiar somehow. They looked like...

X-Ray Specs?

"Walt?"

Not knowing exactly why he did it, he put the glasses on.

"*Walt!*"

Walt looked up at her and spasmed as though he had been tasered. With a choked yell he threw himself back across the couch. He pressed himself against the couch arm, gasping, frantically trying to move away, his kicking feet knocking the cushions onto the floor.

Brenda was stunned for a moment. "Very funny, Walt," she said bitterly. "Very funny." She turned away.

Walt lay there speechless as the living, speaking skeleton picked up Brenda's purse and walked out the door.

He vomited, and that helped a little.

Afterwards, he sat and looked at the glasses on the coffee table, trying to get things straight in his mind. *Last night.* He had gotten a little wound up...let the whole Goddess thing really get to him. Then he had way too much vodka. He had read his comic book...*Wait a minute...*

He picked up the crumpled comic and smoothed it out on the tabletop. He flipped it open. A page was torn. Torn...It finally began to come back to him.

He had stared at the neighbors' house until he had almost decided to go climb the fence and peek in a window. Then he had picked up the comic and seen the ad for x-ray specs. He had become furious at his mother. If she had only let him buy those...What? Something. This was quite a few screwdrivers into the evening. A lot of maudlin self-pity ensued. It was all very, very dim and distant. He closed his eyes and slowly rubbed his temples. It began to coalesce.

Sometime around midnight he had decided that he was a big boy now, and if he wanted x-ray specs, he would by-God *have* x-ray specs.

Walt opened his eyes and looked again at the torn page. Now it all came back. He had ripped out the order blank, scratched his name onto it, scrawled an envelope, and gotten loose change out of the desk drawer. He had staggered out to the street, put the envelope in the mailbox, and returned, a weepy, rubber-legged mess, to pass out on the couch.

And now, a few hours later, these glasses lay on the table before him.

What the hell was going on?

Carefully, gingerly, Walt picked them up. He held them up and turned them around. They were well made. Real glass, and the lenses were thick, frosted and etched, like in leaded windows or fancy desk ornaments. He held them up a foot in front of his eyes. They seemed opaque.

With great trepidation Walt slid the glasses onto his face again. The room became soft. Shapes oozed and swirled. Light flickered. He held up his hand and gasped.

Bones. His hand was just bones. He lifted the glasses. His hand was normal. He lowered them again. Bones. He swallowed and took a deep breath. He flexed his fingers, and the white joints bent and moved. He concentrated for a moment, and the hand turned red, blurred, and looked normal. When he relaxed, it flickered and turned back to bone.

Walt closed his eyes until his breathing returned to normal. When he opened them again, he turned his head to the right. The living room wall swirled and smeared like a watercolor painting, and suddenly he was looking at the front yard. He heard a motor outside, watched a car go down the street. He snatched the glasses off his face. "Son of a bitch!"

He set the glasses on the table. He leaned back on the couch, staring at them and the comic book lying next to them. "Son," he said again quietly, "of...a... *bitch!*" This wasn't possible. He leaned forward and picked up the glasses once more, holding them carefully with his fingertips. *Absolutely not possible. No way, no how.* Then another thought came into his mind.

I wonder if these things work with binoculars?

Walt sat in the Office and watched Brenda creep up the stairs and stand listening outside the door. As she raised her hand to knock, he called, "What is it?" That took her aback, and he chuckled.

"Have you been up here all day?" she asked. She rattled the doorknob.

"What if I have?" he said.

He hadn't. He had spent a lot of the day downstairs looking through the walls and attempting to peel the clothes off of passersby on the street, getting the hang of it, so to speak. Clothes were frustrating. Almost impossible to lose the cloth and leave the skin. Then he had come upstairs to look into the house next door, but to his dismay he found no one home. As some consolation however, he also found that the vodka bottle was not entirely empty.

"There are about six messages on the phone from your sales manager," Brenda called. "He sounds pissed. Are you going to open this door?"

"Oh," said Walt. "I don't think so." He slipped the glasses off his face and into his pocket, he didn't need x-ray vision to know the expression she wore. He'd seen it often enough. He reached over to the desk for his comic book.

Brenda's voice was cold. "Walt, we need to talk."

"No," he said, "*you* need to talk. Like a shark needs to swim." He flipped the pages.

"What is wrong with you?" She rattled the doorknob some more. "Let me in!" Walt did not answer. Brenda's voice became shrill. "You think I don't know what you do in there? Like some kid locked in the bathroom? It's disgusting!"

I know you are, Walt thought, *but what am I?* He giggled.

Brenda went silent, and Walt finally reached for the glasses to see what she was doing. Before he got them out of his pocket, he heard her clumping back down the stairs. Fine. He turned his attention back to his comic book.

Yes. After some consideration, he had decided. *This* would be his next purchase. It worked once. Maybe it would work again. He spun the chair and spread the book out on the desk. With great care he began to tear out the small, colored square.

The next morning found Walt once more on the couch, but more or less sober this time, and more or less awake. He had tried to do everything the same way. He'd waited until midnight to go to the mailbox. Now he sat on the couch. Would it work again? Had it really even worked the first time? Or was this just some weird dream?

The house was silent. The dull glow of dawn slowly grew stronger outside the windows. In spite of the anticipation, Walt began to nod. Then he really did begin to dream. In a honey-and-amber room a golden goddess surrounded by a golden glow reached toward him.

The knock snapped him back to wakefulness. He looked around, startled. Had he dreamed that, too? Then another knock, loud, reverberating. He scrambled to his feet, smacking his shin on the coffee table.

He snatched open the front door to find no one there. He heard the sputtering sound of an engine. He stepped out onto the porch in time to see a long, gray vehicle like an oversized station wagon disappearing around the corner. There was the briefest flash of lettering on the side: DELIVERY. The choking, growling sound of the motor quickly receded. He looked down at the doormat between his feet, and his heart jumped at the sight of a small, brown parcel. He picked it up with a trembling hand.

To: Wally Krulwich.

Brenda was standing in the foyer. She was even frumpier than usual in her purple bathrobe over blue flannel pajamas and her pink, fuzzy slippers. Her hair stuck out every which way. "What was that?" she said sleepily. "What's going on?"

Walt smiled, clutching the little parcel tightly. "You want to know what's going on?" he asked. "Sure. I'll tell you *exactly* what's going on."

Brenda pulled her bathrobe closed and cinched the belt. "What is it?" she asked said.

Walt held up the box. "You see this? I ordered it. Out of my comic book. With my own money!" He pulled the comic out of his hip pocket and held it up in his other hand. "See? That's where the glasses came from, too. The x-ray specs. I ordered them out of the comic book, too, and they came. They came, and they *work!* How do you like that? I can't explain it. I don't even *want* to explain it!" He began to laugh, first with simple glee, and then at the mixture of confusion and fear on her face.

"Walt," she said, "are you alright?"

He dropped the comic onto the foyer table and began tearing the paper off the package. "Sure, Brenda," he said cheerfully, "I'm alright! Don't you want to see what I ordered? It's super cool!" He slipped the lid off the box, pulled something out and took a step toward her. Brenda took a step back, bumping into the living room door jamb.

"Walt! Stop it!" she said, her voice shaking.

"Just look!" Walt said. "That's all! Just look!" he held up his hand. Brenda flinched, blinked, stared.

"The amazing Hypno-Coin," he intoned. "Look at it, Brenda! Waaatch the amazing Hypno-Coin!" The disk in his hand was surprisingly heavy for its size. It was a shiny, red, and gold. He turned it this way and that, moving it in small circles. The design on it seemed to swirl. "Hypnotize anyone in seconds! Amaaaaze your friends!"

"Walt!" Brenda barked, "Have you completely..." She paused, her voice trailing away. She slowly blinked again, looking at the disk. It glinted, even though the room was dim. "Are you..." she began again, but her words faded into a meaningless mumble. Her jaw went slack. Her hands, releasing the front of her bathrobe, fell limply at her sides.

Walt watched her in triumph. "*Yes!*" he said. He slowly lowered the disk, and Brenda continued to stare at the spot in space where it had been. "Brenda?" he said.

"Yes, Walt," she said placidly.

"Can you hear me?"

"Sure!"

Walt paced back and forth for a moment, considering. He stopped in front of her. "You know what?"

"What?" she said dreamily.

"You haven't been making me very happy lately."

She frowned. "No?" she said.

"No. From now on, I want you to make me happy. You got that? Make me happy!" He snapped his fingers. Brenda stood up straight and looked around, confused. Her eyes focused on Walt, and she smiled.

"Hi, hon!" she said. "Hey! You're up early. How'd you like a nice big plate of bacon and eggs?"

Well, this was a start. "That would be great," he said, "but we don't have any bacon." Bacon had been banished from the house long ago. Cholesterol.

Brenda looked alarmed. "No bacon? But you *love* bacon! Bacon makes you *happy*!" She shuffled past him to the table. "You lie back down and catch a few winks. I'll run to the store and be right back!" She snatched up her purse and grabbed the doorknob. "Hey! And how about a bloody mary? Or two? Would that make you happy?"

"Sure," Walt said.

Brenda beamed at him, blew him a kiss, jerked the door open, and ran down the front steps, purple bathrobe billowing. One fuzzy slipper popped into the air as she turned the corner at the sidewalk.

Walt looked at the disk lying heavy in his hand.

"Okay then," he said, and he sat down on the sofa to ponder the possibilities.

After a surprisingly short interval, Brenda burst back into the house and rushed into the kitchen, flinging grocery bags and pots and pans in all directions. It was the best breakfast Walt had had in years, and when Brenda brought him a bloody mary in the living room, plumped up all the pillows behind his back and started rubbing his neck, that improved his outlook even more. But after a few minutes, he had another thought. He would go in to work for a while.

Brenda was distraught. "But what will I do if you leave?" she asked, wringing her hands. "How will I make you happy?"

"You'll think of something," he said dismissively and walked out the door.

As Walt crossed the showroom toward the break area for some coffee, Kevin popped out of his office like a bird from a cuckoo clock. He looked Walt up and down with some disgust and said, "You look like crap. My office! Now!" Eyes all around the room pretended to look elsewhere. Walt smiled, slipped his hand into his pocket and followed the little shit into the office.

One minute and fifteen seconds later, Kevin left the office and walked up to the receptionist at the raised desk in the middle of the showroom.

"Donna," he said, "Get some boxes and have some guys move my crap out of Walt's office."

"What?"

"I mean my office." Kevin glanced over his shoulder. "It's Walt's office now."

The receptionist blinked in astonishment. "You're giving Walt your office?"

"Yeah," said the young man a little dreamily. "Hurry up and get all my crap out of there. And burn it. Yeah, burn it all. I gotta go." He looked troubled. "I gotta. I gotta go." He turned and stiffly walked away. The shocked young woman watched through the plate glass window as he got into his car and drove lurchingly out of the lot. She turned then to see Walt standing in the door of his new office, grinning. "Chop-chop, Donna!" he said.

By noon, Walt had sold five people eleven cars and decided to call it a day. He drove home without regard to speed limit or traffic signal. He just *wished* a cop would stop him.

He found himself driving through a new and different world. The colors were different. Brighter. The air was different. Sharper. Details he had never sensed leapt out at him, the color of leaves, the sound of birdsong. It was as though he had been dead, a zombie staggering across a gray and ghostly planet, and now he was resurrected into brightness and possibility. Oh yes, the possibilities! They were endless, but he knew exactly where he would start.

The Goddess.

His hands twisted the steering wheel as he ran the scenario in his head. *Hello! I'm your neighbor, Walt. Can I come in for just a moment? Only a moment! Now...take a look at* this. He gave a whoop of pure joy.

First home to take a shower and change. Had to look his best for her. The thought of home made him remember Brenda. Ah yes. Brenda. He would get rid of her of course, but not before he made her do a few more tricks. First, he would—

He turned onto his street and had to suddenly swerve almost onto the sidewalk to avoid a vehicle headed straight for him. He perceived a flash of gray, heard the gnashing of gears and the reptilian cough of an engine. He looked into the rear view mirror and saw a square shape disappear around the corner in a cloud of stinking blue smoke, a word across the side, mirror-reversed: YREVILED.

Did he imagine it, or had he caught a glimpse of the driver, a sallow face in a peaked cap, touching one finger to his cap brim in a passing salute?

He pulled up in front of his house. His front door stood open. He warily moved up the walk and onto the porch. He tried to peek into the foyer but couldn't see past the table by the door. Brenda's purse lay on it as usual. Next to the purse, he saw his crumpled *House of Mystery*.

Something wasn't right about this. He moved nearer the door.

"Walt!"

He gave a yelp as Brenda appeared, once again popping up like some damned spring-loaded toy. She laughed, hopped from one foot to the other, clapped her hands.

"Walt! I'm so glad you're home! You'll be so happy!"

"What?" he said. "Brenda, what's going—" she grabbed him by the arm. Her grip was startlingly strong. He was yanked through the doorway before he could resist.

"You said make you happy! You said think of something!" she cried. "And I remembered! I remembered what you said!" Walt managed to regain his balance, bracing himself against the foyer table. "I saw the funny book and I remembered what you said!" Brenda's face glowed with joy. "About the one thing you always wanted!"

What the hell...?

In the foyer next to the living room door stood a crate. A huge, wooden crate at least eight feet high and four feet on each side. As Walt stared, open-mouthed, there came a *thud*.

"Brenda?" Walt said weakly, "What did you do?"

Brenda hopped up and down. She clapped her hands some more. "I got it for you! To make you happy!"

There was a sharp *bang,* and the crate suddenly jumped and wobbled from side to side. One of the boards on the front cracked and splintered. Three or four nails fell pinging to the tile floor. Something snarled, something big and nearby.

Walt turned to run, but Brenda was in his way, her face ecstatic, her eyes filling with tears. She had the comic book in her hand and thrust it into his face. "What you always wanted!" she shouted, hugging him, knocking him back against the table, keeping him from getting out the door.

A board exploded from the front of the crate. A huge arm reached out of the hole. Walt glimpsed coarse, black broadcloth, pale skin, ragged black stitching at the wrist. An animal roar, and the whole front of the crate splintered and flew across the room. A piece of lumber bounced off Walt's forehead, but he didn't feel it. He watched the huge, hulking shadow come toward him.

"Monster size monsters!" Brenda shrieked happily. "Monster size monsters! Only a dollar! Only a dollar!"

Tell Me a Nightmare

MISTER BAD

Peter Scott stood at the window watching snow cover the ground like blood from a war scene as he began calculating all the losses in his head.

Behind him, a line of vacant chairs and tables were laid out along the edges of the gymnasium. Empty name tags laid piled inside a box, ready to have names written on them with black markers, while banners introducing everyone to the inaugural Halloween Horror Convention of Norton, Virginia hung from the ceiling rafters. Cardboard skeletons were hung from the basketball nets and held signs in their hands that indicated to register below.

Peter and his business partners, Frank "Cakes" Manford, whom looked like a cross between Bruce Lee and a 'Little Debbie' snack cake, Kathy Walsh, a blonde woman in her early thirties, whom was a horror movie poster dealer, and William Brody, a refined Black gentleman obsessed with pulp magazines and 1950s era crime comic books, sat at one of the tables staring off into space.

The quiet was interrupted by a discouraged voice. "Is it still snowing?" asked Cakes.

"It'll be snowing for the rest of my life," said Peter in a very depressed tone. "Who thought it would snow on Halloween? That's crazy talk. All I've been hearing about is global warming this and global warming that and here I stand looking out at almost a foot of snow! The weather forecast gave a chance of flurries, and we get this. You know, back in the old days when someone made a prediction, and they were wrong, they were killed by the townspeople."

Cakes, Kathy, and Brody ignored Peter's common comments of overreaction as they slowly began to realize all the work and money they put into the convention was for naught.

But Brody was trying to stay upbeat, a difficult task with Peter around, so he just blurted out to neither one in particular, "The last time you went trick-or-treating what did you go as?"

Everyone stared at Brody as if he just told them he could unscrew his head and bounce it like a basketball.

"What?" asked a confused Peter.

"The last time you went trick-or-treating, what did you go as? I was a corn-stalk."

This was not an answer Cakes, Peter, Kathy, or civilized man as a whole was expecting.

"A what?" asked Cakes.

"A cornstalk. My grandfather owned a small farm, and he thought it would be great advertising. So, every time I went to a house, I would give them my grandfather's business card for all the produce he sold. I have to admit, it was an odd costume, but thank God for my mom's creativity and the miracles of poster board. What did you go as Cakes?"

"Wonder Woman."

"Wonder Woman?" Brody asked Cakes for clarification, not fully sure if he was kidding or not, as Kathy tried to hide her laughter with her hands.

"I just wore the mask. I didn't wear the outfit. Mom thought it was a Spock costume. Her eyes never were any good. So, I just wore the mask. I didn't have the heart to tell her that she was an idiot."

"I went as a cornstalk and you went as Wonder Woman," thought Brody aloud.

"Technically, I was still Spock," interrupted Cakes.

Brody shook his head, "It's a wonder we didn't grow up to be serial killers or something."

Kathy said, "I went as Snow White searching for my Prince Charming, which in this case was candy."

"That sounds normal," said Cakes.

"Not really. I made the mask out of a paper bag. I looked more like a construction worker's lunch than Snow White."

"What about you Peter?" asked Cakes.

"Me, what?"

"The last time you went trick-or-treating, what did you go as?"

"I was a pirate, but my leg kept falling off."

Cakes, Kathy, and Brody laughed as they came to the understanding that the four of them had very misguided childhoods.

"I kept getting it caught in the car door. In my defense I had no depth perception because of that stupid eye patch. I eventually had to turn it around to the back of my head before I ended up killing myself by walking into another mailbox."

Cakes, Kathy, and Brody just kept laughing while Peter ignored them and stared out at the snowstorm that was becoming his new villain, which would rival any of Batman's, or perhaps this white beast that stacked the ground was evolving into his own Moby Dick.

A few minutes later as everything grew quiet, Brody asked, "What time is it?"

Cakes looked at his watch and reported, "Two o'clock."

The large vacant room took on the aura of a party that had ended hours earlier, and they were the last ones there waiting for their rides.

"Should we go on home?" asked Brody.

"How?" replied Peter, as he turned from the window to his friends. "No one can get out of town with all of this snow. Snow that is never going to stop by the way," he added with a frustrated emphasis.

"I called my wife," said Cakes. "I told her that I might be stranded here for a while. Didn't seem to bother her any. I think she's exhausted from the new puppy we got. She's trying to housetrain it, but it's not going too well. I have to be honest, I think the thing poops out both ends. Either that, or we're going to have to take him to the vet or buy some sort of poop stopper to insert into him or something."

"What kind of dog is it?" asked Brody.

"Just a mutt we got for free at the pound. I can see why too. We heard cheering when we left with him."

All four of them were quiet, seemingly trapped by their passion for horror and science fiction inside some diabolical plot of the Weather Channel.

"What do we do now?" asked Brody.

"Kill a meteorologist," quipped Peter.

"I'm in," said Kathy.

"It is getting dark up in here," replied Brody. "I hope I never get in a life and death scenario with you all."

"We're in a life and death scenario right now," exclaimed Peter as he threw his hands up in the air then pushed a folding chair with his foot, causing it to scoot across the floor until it suddenly fell forward with a loud bang that echoed throughout the gym.

Cakes responded, "It's not a life and death scenario right now. We have electricity. We have water and a bathroom. We've got a snack machine and pop machine that has twenty-four ounce 'Mountain Dews' just outside the door. So, we're far from a life and death scenario right now."

"The human bladder can't hold twenty-four ounces, can it?" thought Brody aloud. "Why would they make a drink that's twenty-four ounces for?"

"I'm sure it was invented by a man," said Kathy.

"What makes you think that?" asked Brody.

"Men always make things too big," responded Kathy. "The only surprise is that they didn't put boobs on the twenty-four-ounce Mountain Dew, too, and I agree that the human bladder can't hold twenty-four ounces of anything."

"Mine can't hold anything anymore," said Cakes. "I might as well eat supper in the bathroom now. Turning forty is like being pushed down the stairs or something."

"Oh, my God," exclaimed Peter, as he stared out the window, which brought concern to Brody, Kathy, and Cakes.

"What is it?" asked Cakes as he, Kathy, and Brody made their way over to the window.

"I see a Yeti," said Peter in the most manner of fact tone imaginable.

Brody, Kathy, and Cakes stared down the parking lot and through the blinding snow they saw, without any doubt, a dog running along the snowdrifts.

"That's a dog," said Cakes.

"You're letting all of this go to your head," mumbled Kathy.

They all stood staring out the window quietly watching the snow build up on the terrain as the day slowly droned on.

"It could have been a Yeti. It was white," said Peter in a defensive tone.

"Yetis aren't white," volunteered Brody.

Peter stared at Brody and said, "I guess you're going to tell me that they don't bounce either."

"You shouldn't get your scientific knowledge from a Christmas special," retorted Brody.

"I don't think that Rudolph the Red Nosed Reindeer would lie to me," said Peter. "He just doesn't seem like that kind of cartoon to me."

"Man, this day is turning into an episode of the 'Twilight Zone' which needs a serious rewrite," said Cakes.

The four of them then retreated back into their silence. Brody and Cakes walked back to different tables and sat down. Kathy walked over to the wall and sat down on the floor with her knees bent up where she rested her head on them. Peter continued to look out the window at the snow, which seemed to be eating the surrounding terrain like a 'Pac Man' game brought to life.

As time ticked on, and the sound of the wind and snow pelted up against the window glass, Cakes happened upon an idea.

"You know what we should do?"

"Draw straws to see who we eat first?" asked Peter.

"We don't need straws for that," said Kathy. "We'd eat you first because you're such a downer."

Cakes continued, "We should write a story. You know have a little horror story contest."

Brody smiled, "You mean like Byron's challenge inside the Villa Diodait in 1816?"

"Exactly," replied Cakes. "They had a thunderstorm, and we have a snowstorm. It inspired Mary Shelly to write 'Frankenstein' so maybe it could help us come up with something just as good. If nothing else, it would help us pass the time."

"Do you all think Mary Shelly was hot?" asked Brody.

Cakes, Kathy, and Peter stared at Brody, and then all looked at each other.

"What in the world would make you ask that?" asked Cakes.

"It just came to me is all. She seems a bit homely in the drawings of her."

Cakes twisted his mouth as if he was Samantha Stevens then asked, "So, are you interested in writing a story, or not?"

Brody smiled, "I kind of like the idea. Writing a horror story on Halloween is the perfect setting. I'm in, how about you, Peter?"

Peter humped his shoulders as he walked over to them and stood between their tables, "I don't know. I guess it could give us something to take our mind off of this lousy day. It also might help Brody to stop thinking about homely girls."

"Not going to work," said Brody.

"How about you Kathy?" asked Cakes.

"Sure. I like the idea."

"Should we have any rules?" asked Peter.

"Rules?" asked Brody. "What do you mean?"

"I don't know. Just should we have some sort of rules is all."

"Just make it scary," replied Cakes.

"How much time do we have?" inquired Peter.

"I don't know. When does it get dark? Around seven?" asked Cakes.

"Yeah, I'd say seven," said Kathy.

Cakes held out his hands to the side, as if he had just perfected a magic trick that stunned the audience. "Then seven o'clock will be our deadline. We'll have our stories done by seven, or when we're rescued by a Saint Bernard or something and then read them aloud and vote for the winner. But you can't vote for your own story," stated Cakes as he made the rules up on the fly.

They all scrambled to their laptops and began punching away at their keyboards until the seven o'clock deadline.

As the top of the deadline hour approached, a sudden burst of thunder echoed the room. They all looked up from their keyboards and an eerie feeling seemed to settle over them, as if Byron and his rebel writers from the original horror story contest had joined in.

Then, seven o'clock hit, and they all gathered around the center table with their laptops in hand.

"I have to admit that this was kind of fun," stated Peter.

"I liked it, too," replied Cakes. "Now who is going to go first?"

"I will," volunteered Brody.

"I'll turn the lights off for more atmosphere," said Cakes, as he hurried to the light switch and turned it off, then returned to his chair.

"Okay, tell me a nightmare, Brody," said Peter with a smile, to which Brody began his little tale of the macabre inside the reflection of the amber light of his computer screen.

"The Ghost House"

What becomes of a rational mind when it witnesses the darkness move?

This very scenario spilled into my world in October of 1976, and it would change the perspective that I had on everything that I hold dear.

Inside the coolness of an autumn morn, I arrived at my office at nine a.m. and awaited my first patient, Henry Gallatin (not his Christian name). He had given my secretary, Mrs. Dimple, no indication of what the appointment concerned, so I didn't really know what to expect.

At ten a.m. Mr. Gallatin entered my office, bathed in the broken sunlight that streamed through the window overlooking New York City. He appeared to be in his mid-forties, with gray swept hair along the sides of his temples and stood approximately six-foot two. He also appeared very fit, alert, and friendly.

"Please, have a seat," I said after I shook his hand, and he sat down in the chair across from my desk.

"Thank you for seeing me on such short notice," he said.

"That's no problem. I always try to adapt to a patient's schedule."

The room stood quiet as an uneasiness washed over his face. His eyes danced around the room, and his right leg began to bounce, which indicated a nervous tension had built inside him.

"How can I help you now?"

"I don't really know how to explain it."

"Don't feel apprehensive," I said, as I tried to reassure him. "Just explain your concerns in a way that is most comfortable for you. The more honest you are with me, the easier it will be for me to give you the help you are looking for."

"I understand. I just don't want you to think I'm crazy, I guess," he added with an embarrassed smile.

"Everyone feels this way at first when they see me, but you're not afraid of what I think. You're more afraid of what friends and family will think, aren't you?"

"I guess that's true. I never thought I'd see a psychiatrist. I even told my wife that I was just going to the dentist."

"I can't defend lying to your wife, but I do understand the perceptions that people have about my profession and how that impacts my patient's state of mind. But you came here because you felt you had no place else to turn. Now just tell me what brought you here today."

Mr. Gallatin stared down at his hands and a grave concern appeared across his face. He then took a deep breath and-

"I've been seeing things that aren't there."

He wouldn't look me in the eyes. He glanced about the office as if he was trying to find a way out of the room, almost as if he regretted coming in to see me today.

"How so?" I asked.

His mind searched for words, but only the quiet of the room filled the air. He became exasperated, leaned back in his chair, and breathed out heavily in a surrendered state.

"I don't know if I can go through with this."

I knew that I had to take control of the situation to help him feel more at ease.

"You are seeing things that aren't there you say?"

"Yes, sir. And hearing voices."

"That alone shouldn't worry you. It could simply be a misinterpretation of something common. It's happened to me before as I'm sure to many others as well. We all see and hear things occasionally that we can't understand, but when we take the time to tell another person, or to step back and reexamine it from a different angle, an answer comes. Now, please just look at this as a problem-solving exercise not an evaluation of your mental state. If you do that, I think you'll be more at ease."

"Yes, sir, you see me and my family moved into a new house in Hill Front. It's just outside of the city, but not far out enough that it's a long travel to it."

"How long have you been living there?"

"Three months exactly come Friday."

"Are you comfortable there?"

"My wife and daughters are."

"And you?"

With that question he appeared afraid that his shared, true thoughts would cast him in a low persona in my eyes.

"It's okay to tell me what you're thinking," I stated, as I tried to draw out his trust in me.

Hesitantly he began to speak.

"I'll see what looks like shadows moving, but when I approach them, they disappear."

"You mean the shadows have a form like a person?"

"Yes."

"Has your wife seen these shadows?"

"She's never said anything about it, and I never told her about what I've been seeing. Or what I think I'm seeing."

"Being that it's a new place for you, it could be that you are just not used to the shadows that come through the windows when mixed with the lights outside," I interjected in hopes that I could give him some relief emotionally.

"Yeah, I know. That's what I kept telling myself until last week."

Instantly, fear wrapped his face like a hand slap to the jaw. He got very quiet. Whatever happened to him last week seemed to have been the last straw in living in that house.

"Go on. Tell me what happened."

"I was home alone on a Saturday. My wife took our two girls out shopping, and I was going to watch the football games that day. Around noon I went into the kitchen and got me something to eat and drink, and when I turned around to go back into the den, I saw someone standing next to the wall."

"How much detail could you make out?"

"It was an old woman. She wasn't fully formed. She didn't appear to have feet, like she was hovering above the floor. Then she started bellowing this loud scream. Her mouth was agape, and her eyes enlarged several times over what a human's should be able to do. She was hideous to look at."

"What did you do?"

"I screamed and dropped my sandwich onto the floor and ran out of the house."

He looked down at the floor as if he had just confessed the most unmanly thing he had ever done in his life.

"There's nothing to be embarrassed about. It was an honest emotion," I said.

"I still wished I had reacted a little better than that though."

He sat in the chair trying to fight back tears when he asked me, "Do you believe in haunted houses?"

"I've never encountered a home that has convinced me that it is haunted."

"I see," Mr. Gallatin whispered.

"How long did it appear to you?"

"The whole thing just took a few seconds. Five seconds at most. Then it slowly faded away."

"Did you believe it was real at the time?"

"Yes. I mean...I don't know."

A very depressed look then fell across his face before he continued.

"See, I'm getting scared that if my house isn't haunted, then I might be in the early stages of dementia."

This thought really struck at me hard, being that I have had some relatives with this terrible disease. Hallucination is one of the symptoms, but all of my relatives were up in age, this gentleman is still young.

"What makes you think that?"

"No one else is seeing it. I don't know what else it could be."

"Are you seeing these shadows or forms when you are away from the house?"

"No."

"That's a very strong indication that the short period of time that you have lived in the house, may be the main culprit here in which you have simply misinterpreted shadow play."

"I'm hoping you're right. The thought of this is really upsetting me. I don't want to go through this anymore. I just want to understand what is going on."

"We'll get to the bottom of this. Don't try and jump to any conclusions. That's very important because you might start to worry yourself so much that it will actually start to affect your health."

"Do you think...well—"

"What is it?" I asked.

"Will you investigate the house just to see if it is haunted or if I'm just, you know- like you said, just misinterpreting shadows or something like that. I know that's not really the type of work you do, but it's very important to me that I'm able to rule out any dementia."

"I can do that. It wouldn't be the first time I've visited a patient's home to help them. When would you like me to come over?"

"Maybe Friday night, I mean if that's good for you."

"I don't see any reason that it would be a problem. Of course, I'll have to ask my wife first to make sure there are no conflicts in her schedule, but I see no reason why I can't be there this Friday. Where exactly are you located in Hill Front?"

"At 328 Soldier Street, it's a three story, red brick Victorian. It has a tower on it, so I don't think you'll have any trouble finding it."

"I'm sure I won't."

"I guess I need to tell my wife why I'm asking you over," Mr. Gallatin remarked.

"That would be the best thing. While I've never met your wife, I'm sure she'll be more sympathetic than you think about what you're going through."

"I know," he said with a nod. "I guess I just wanted to figure it out on my own first."

He then stood up and we shook hands.

"I guess I'll see you Friday evening. We'll have supper for you. Do you like fried catfish?"

"That sounds outstanding."

As I prepared for my trip to Mr. Gallatin's home, I decided to make a phone call to the Lakeland County Commissioner of Revenue to verify that Mr. Gallatin does indeed live at 328 Soldier Street because I have had patients in the past (whom seemed very intelligent and in control of their actions) that did not live where they said they did.

The phone call went without a hitch, and the nice lady in the Commissioner of Revenue's office confirmed his address.

Next, I decided to call the town historian to learn the history of the house, which I believe would be very beneficial to Mr. Gallatin in that if he knew more about his home, its history, and former occupants, then it might help him feel more at ease in it.

Because I did not have permission from Mr. Gallatin to inform anyone that he was a patient of mine, I told the town historian that I was commissioned by him to write an article about the house.

However, my conversation with the local historian took a turn I wasn't expecting.

"Hello?" the voice said on the other end of the phone.

"Yes, is this Mr. Richardson?"

"Yes."

"My name is P.J. Honeywell, and I would like some information about the Victorian house at 328 Soldier Street. I've been commissioned by the owner to write an article about the house and hoped you might be able to help."

"Oh," he said, after a short pause.

His response surprised me. I couldn't help but wonder what exactly the tone meant.

"Do you know of the house?" I asked.

"Yes. It has a bit of a reputation."

"What kind of reputation?"

"Some people believe it's haunted."

This was something I wasn't prepared for, and being a man of science, I was very skeptical, even after the claims of Mr. Gallatin. Stories always get a bit out of hand over time, and I'm sure I'll be able to solve some of the ghost stories with a thorough investigation. Also, this might add to the fact that Mr. Gallatin knows of the past (in which case he wasn't completely honest with me), and it has clouded his judgment in which a strange or sudden noise or shadow takes on a more ominous presence than it would have otherwise.

"Could you give me the history of the house?" I inquired.

"Sure. It was built in the 1940s by a rich oil tycoon, but he was killed on site when the tower was being built and suddenly collapsed on him and several workers. The house was completed by his son, and he lived in it for a short time, but left it abandoned for six years. Then it was bought by a woman by the name of Gertrude Wicker, and she kept it as a girl's home until she died in the 1960s."

"What can you tell me of Ms. Wicker?"

"She was very strict with the girls, and she forbade any men on the property even the fathers of the girls. She did not like men at all."

"How did she die?"

"She jumped off the tower to her death because the home was going to be closed down for the harsh treatment of the girls."

"What sort of harsh treatment?"

"She kept the mentally ill chained up in the basement."

That statement really angered me. To take the mentally ill and completely look upon them as animals to be chained in order to control them, was the most inhumane act I had ever heard, and it took some doing on my part not to allow my anger to show. I continued on with the conversation.

"I see. After that what became of the house?"

"It changed hands many times over the years. No one would stay in it for more than six months at a time."

"You said that it was rumored to be haunted."

"Yes."

"Do you believe it is?"

"I believe I'll never live there. I'll leave it at that."

"I understand. Thank you for your help."

"You're welcome. Good luck with your article."

"Thank you."

After I hung up the phone I began to think upon a plan of action. I decided to take a video camera, a still camera (both would allow me to show how the light shines into the house, which may be causing the strange sights to Mr. Gallatin) and a tape recorder (to record observations).

I have read recently of a new theory about the possibility that mold and mildew can cause hallucinations based upon one's sensitivity to it, especially if it were near some ductwork, which would then direct its contaminants throughout the house and possibly large quantities of it. This of course is merely a theory, but I believe might have some standing.

I also cannot rule out that Mr. Gallatin simply lied to me about the old lady he saw in the kitchen. I always fall back onto my number one rule, the evidence one discovers is one's proof, not the stories of which one did not witness.

I began my trip at three p.m. The day was cool and dark clouds umbrellaed against the reaches of sky, which gave the look of a milky wash to the eyes. Rain feathered down, which brought a dreary feeling to my three-hour drive.

Night was beginning to drown the day away as I made my turn down Soldier Street. The further I went it appeared the starker the sight. Houses lit in light became fewer. A gentle rumble of thunder filled my ears and flashes of lightning backlit the trees.

Then I was there.

The house was in shadow, with the exception of a small light that pierced through a downstairs window. Two figures in silhouette stood in the window, and when my car lights shone against the glass they were gone.

I parked my car to the side of a station wagon, grabbed my bag, and walked toward the house. The side door opened, and Mr. Gallatin stood in the opening. He was smoking a cigarette which ambered bright for a faded second as seams of smoke chimneyed up in front of his face.

"Hello, Dr. Honeywell."

"Mr. Gallatin. I apologize for running late."

"No problem. Did you have any trouble finding the place?"

"I drove right to it. The only problem I had was that the weather was a little on the dreary side."

We laughed and made our way into the foyer where I was met by his two blonde, twin girls who were the figures I had seen in the window when I first drove up. They were named Jane and Jill and were as sweet as they could be. They had a small doll collection, which they showed me and brought me into telling them about my egg beater collection. Unfortunately, my enthusiasm for my hobby seemed to bore them to such long yawns that I stopped.

He introduced me to his wife, Caroline, whom was a sewing enthusiast. In fact, almost everything of cloth and fabric that was in the home she had sewn herself. I enjoyed my time with them, and they were very receptive toward me. Also, his wife made some of the best catfish and buttermilk cornbread that I have ever tasted.

After dinner I thought it best to interview the wife alone, after gaining permission from her husband, and we sat in the living room while the girls, and Mr. Gallatin washed the dishes.

"Do you know why I am here?" I asked.

"Yes, of course."

"Good. I was wondering if you have experienced anything that you couldn't fully understand?"

"In what way?"

"Shadows moving, mysterious lights, unknown sounds, anything at all."

"No. Should I?"

"Not necessarily. What about your husband? Has he acted any different lately?"

"He has been a bit despondent. Sometimes when I speak, and he doesn't know I'm around he jumps like he's scared to death. He's never done that before, but if you'll excuse me for asking, what does this have to do with termites?"

"Pardon?"

"He said you were here to investigate for termites."

"Oh. Yes, yes, I am."

I pursued my questioning no further. It was obvious Mr. Gallatin still wasn't comfortable enough to tell his family that he has asked for the help of a psychiatrist.

I tried to reassure him later that my presence shouldn't cause him any embarrassment, but for now I would play along. My duty was to understand what was causing his possible hallucinations, be it early stages of dementia or simply his misinterpretation of natural phenomena, and that I will do.

Mr. Gallatin informed me in private that his wife and daughters would spend the night with his sister which lived close by. He had told them that I might use some spray to kill the termites, and that it would be best to stay out of the home for the night.

With his wife and daughters out of the house, Mr. Gallatin and I began our investigation at seven-thirty p.m.

"What should we do first?" he asked.

"I would like for you to take me to the spot where you saw the old lady in the kitchen."

"Okay."

He then led me into the kitchen and pointed at the corner.

"She was right there. As clear to me as you are now."

I walked over to the spot and looked about. There didn't seem an explanation that could present itself to what else it could have possibly been.

"Will it be okay if I take some pictures?"

"Sure."

"Where were you standing when you saw her?"

"Right here," he said while he pointed about a foot away from the kitchen counter.

I made my way over to where he pointed and began taking pictures in the direction that he said he saw the old woman.

"This will allow me to get some sort of perspective on what you might have saw."

I snapped off a few pictures.

"Have you had any trouble with mold or mildew in the house?"

"A little here and there, not much though. Why?"

"There's a theory that sensitivity to mold and mildew might cause hallucinations."

"I've never heard of that."

"It's still a theory, but I would like to check your attic for any mold or mildew that might have been caused by a leaky roof. If it's near the ducts of the house, the pollutants could be pumped throughout the house and if you are sensitive to it, that could be causing your sightings."

"That's interesting. Well, the stairs to the attic are right this way."

As I started to follow him out of the kitchen, his phone rang. He excused himself and answered the phone in the living room. While he was away, I suddenly heard something that sounded like it had fallen upstairs in the room over the kitchen. I was startled, but the cause of the noise would consist of many possibilities and on its own, really had no effect on my investigation. However, I needed to check it out for my own curiosity.

Mr. Gallatin then came back to me.

"Mr. Honeywell, I've got to go over to my sister's house."

"Is everyone all right?"

"Oh, yeah, see they caught a mouse, and they're scared to death, so I have to go over and dispose of it. I'll only be a few minutes. They live just down the block. I'll hurry right back."

"Okay. Say, what room is upstairs here over the kitchen?"

"That's a spare bedroom. We're doing some remodeling. I'm afraid it's a bit of a mess at the moment."

"I see."

"Is something wrong?"

"I heard something fall, but being that you are remodeling, it might not be anything."

"Do you want me to stay with you until you check?

"No, that's not necessary. You go on, take your time, and I'll go on upstairs and look around."

"Okay. Do whatever you need to do."

As he left, I have to admit that the house seemed to take on a more ominous feel as I found myself alone in the house.

I made my way up the stairs, which squeaked with each stop I took, to the second floor and walked over to the bedroom that was over the kitchen, in which the door was halfway open. I opened it, felt for a light switch on the wall, and flipped it up. The bedroom looked just as he had described it.

There were wallpaper rolls and paint cans on the floor. A ladder stood near the window, the bed and dresser were placed in the center of the room to allow for easier access to the walls.

I then flipped the light off and walked back out into the hallway. I decided to make my way up to the attic.

That's when I noticed that a streetlight shone into the hallway and made some strange shadow play on the walls through the curtain fabric. This I thought might be one of the things that Mr. Gallatin is mistaking for possible ghosts.

But my satisfaction of a possible solution was immediately set back when I actually heard a voice call out, "Hello."

I stopped dead in my tracks and my heart raced at a feverish pace. My mind tried to rationalize what just happened, but I couldn't fully comprehend it.

I couldn't tell if it was a woman's voice or a child's and wondered if perhaps it actually came from outside. I walked over to the hallway window and peered outside, but the streets were empty as a light rain continued down.

I had my small tape recorder with me so I could record my thoughts (a practice I started long ago because my handwriting of notes is even difficult for me to read) in hopes that I could capture the voice again, and perhaps if I play it back repeatedly, I could figure out its origin.

"Did someone say something?" I asked.

There was no reply.

I thought that the environment was causing me to misinterpret sounds into that of a voice. It could be looked at as matrixing in which common sounds can't be identified immediately by your senses, so your brain tries to decipher the noise into something it can comprehend, thus it turns a mechanical sound into a voice.

I thought that might provide some possibility for my patient, that some of the sounds he has heard are just that.

With no more replies, I proceeded to the attic, which was on the fourth floor, but decided to leave my tape recorder running.

I got to the door of the attic and opened it. A narrow flight of stairs led upward in which a window was perched at the top. As I took the flashlight out of my jacket pocket to try and find the light switch, I heard something fall.

I looked up the staircase and saw a shadow backlit from the window, and it looked down at me.

"Who's there?" I asked.

No reply came. This silhouette of someone or something just stood there with what appeared to be something that flowed behind it like part of a garment caught in a breeze.

It took every bit of determination that I could muster to stand my ground and not give way to a flight of fright.

"What's your name?" I questioned in a confident tone, in the thought that perhaps I'm a victim of a hoax.

Then slowly the shadow began to fade away.

I leaned up against the wall and tried to gather myself. I had to be rational and realize that if my hypothesis of mold and mildew causing hallucinations or altering one's perceptions was the culprit, then I may have just experienced the same effect myself.

Upon further thought, I decided to go downstairs and retrieve my video camera and start to film the house. It would take the doubt out of my senses so that if I do see something I can play it back for better evaluation.

I got the camera, came back up to the attic, and placed it on its tripod.

"Hello?" a loud voice called out.

I jumped at the sound of the voice.

"Mr. Honeywell, are you up here?"

It was Mr. Gallatin coming back from his sister's, and I have to admit, it gave me a serious fright.

"I'm up here in the attic!" I shouted as I heard him make his way up the stairs.

I attempted to regain my composure before he arrived because I didn't want to confess my observation at the moment so that I could do a further evaluation. It is very easy to mistakenly believe you saw something which in reality you simply misinterpreted when darkness is added to the situation.

"Did you find any mold?" he asked.

"Not yet. I was just going in to look."

"What are you doing with the video camera?"

"I'm going to film anything that appears to be mold to show some people I know and ask them how to treat it. I thought it might be easier than having them have to make a trip all the way out here."

He stared at me hard for a few seconds, as if he had observed something peculiar.

"You saw her, didn't you?"

I was startled by his question.

"Saw her?"

"The woman at the window, you saw her, didn't you?"

"What makes you think that I saw someone?"

"I can tell by your face."

I didn't realize I had allowed my distress to overcome me to such a degree that he was able to pick up on it with the reflection of my flashlight beam against my face. I suppose fear isn't something you can hide, even in the dark.

"I saw something, but I'm not willing to say it was a woman."

Mr. Gallatin was clearly frightened.

"What am I going to do?" he said as he ran his right hand through his hair.

"You're not going to jump to conclusions. What I think we'll do is place the camera here and aim it up at the window. I fully believe that it's possible we are seeing something that is not a woman, but merely shadow play. I think the curtains your wife has made and the way the outside lights cast through them may actually be what you are seeing."

"I hope you're right, Dr. Honeywell."

"Let's go back downstairs and—"

"Hello?"

We both stopped any movement as the unknown voice stood our senses on edge.

"Did you hear that?" he asked.

"I did."

I listened quietly for a few seconds and then decided to try and get a reply.

"My name is Dr. Honeywell, and this is Mr. Gallatin. What's your name?" I asked.

Suddenly, we heard a quick shuffled sound on the attic floor. We both looked upward to the attic and saw something going across the floor very fast. It appeared to be a human form lying on the floor that scurried along using its fingers and toes. It would then stop and turn around and go back the other way before it seemed to actually disappear into the wall.

We were both overwhelmed with what we just saw.

"What is going on here?" Mr. Gallatin cried out.

I then proceeded up the narrow flight of stairs with my flashlight.

"Should I turn the light on?"

"Not yet," I said. "I want to see if I can figure this out first. Perhaps the outside lights are playing a trick on our eyes."

I shined my flashlight about the floor, walls, and ceiling, but saw nothing that might explain what we just witnessed. I did begin to wonder if perhaps I saw bats in flight just above the floor, but I'm sure if bats lived in the house, then I would easily have smelled the strong odor of guano.

"Go ahead and turn the light on," I ordered down to Mr. Gallatin.

He turned the attic light on and there was nothing that looked out of the ordinary. I couldn't figure out what I had just seen.

I did look along the ceiling for any signs of mold, mildew or the remnants of a leaky ceiling, but nothing showed itself.

I finally came to a rather difficult decision for me. I stopped looking for explanations of shadow play and began to do, what was for me, my very first ghost hunt.

Mr. Gallatin then insisted that we check the basement because he felt very scared down there, so I agreed to give it a look. We left the attic, but kept the camera rolling and began our way downstairs. When we got to the basement door Mr. Gallatin would go no further.

"I can't go down there."

"Why not?" I asked.

"I just can't."

"You need to tell me."

"Voices, they're all over down there. It's the worst place in the house. I'm more scared down there than I am in the attic."

"I understand."

And with that I headed down into the bowels of the house.

As I closed the door behind me, I immediately found myself on a flight of narrow stairs that headed down to a concrete floor. I directed my flashlight beam all about and saw the typical elements of a basement, webs, dirt and a musty smell. Because I was now ghost hunting, I didn't attempt to turn the light on. I assumed that I would get more evidence through the darkness.

I walked down the stairs, still a bit on edge after everything that happened in the attic, but I still had to approach this from a scientific investigation and let the events define themselves not my thoughts or feelings.

I got to the concrete floor and my light fell on a rocking chair in the center of the basement, it was rocking. It wasn't rocking a little, but at a hard pace.

A loud shriek filled my ears as if someone was in pain, it lasted for three or so seconds before it stopped.

It startled me to such a degree that I almost dropped my flashlight. My heart pounded hard in my chest as I looked all about to try and find out where this scream came from. The fear that I experienced at that moment was beyond anything I had experienced before and even after all that I had seen through the night.

As I struggled through my emotions, I felt something against my jaw line. I reached up to it and it was blood. I traced the blood trail with my index finger, and it led into my ear. Did that loud scream actually cause my ear to bleed?

The loud scream began again, but it sounded different this time. It was more muffled as if it was further away.

That's when I finally realized that it was coming from upstairs.

I hurried up the basement steps, opened the door and saw Mr. Gallatin seated on the floor with his back up against the kitchen cabinets that were beneath the sink. He was kicking his feet and trying to back up further, but the cabinets wouldn't let him. His screams were furious and constant.

I turned the kitchen light on, hurried over to where he was, and knelt down beside him.

"Calm down, Mr. Gallatin. It's going to be okay."

He grabbed my arm and held it very tight.

"You have to calm down," I told him. "Everything is going to be fine."

He tried to say something, but he just gasped for air as if he had lost his ability to speak.

"You've got to get me out of here," he finally was able to say.

"Of course."

I assisted him to his feet, and I took him outside onto the porch.

"Sit down here on the edge of the porch," I said.

"No. Get me further away from the house."

"Okay."

I have never in all my years as a psychiatrist seen someone this terrified. It was almost as if he had taken on another look, like that of a depraved man with no hope to survive into the very next moment.

I took him to my vehicle and sat him in the passenger's seat. I knelt down in front of him and tried to reassure him as tears streaked his face.

"Everything is going to be okay. You just take in long deep breaths. We're out of the house, now so try and relax."

"I can't go back in there," he struggled from his lips.

"What happened?"

"It got me."

"What got you?"

"The woman. It was an old woman. She started strangling me."

Before tonight I would have listened to such a statement with a great deal of skepticism, but now I did not. Something is in that house and I've got to try and figure out how to help Mr. Gallatin deal with it.

With such a dramatic event as my patient being attacked, I thought it best to call off any further investigation into the house. The time was two twenty-five a.m., and I went in to retrieve the camera and to make sure I had all of my belongings which I was able to do without incident.

I then took Mr. Gallatin to his sister's where he spent the night with his family.

The next morning, I began to review all of my evidence to see if I was able to back up the experiences that we both had in the house.

My tape recorder was able to pick up several voices. Those that I heard with my own ears and two of which I was not aware of when it happened.

The first voice was that of a young girl that I picked up in the attic. It said, "Don't let her see you."

The sound of the voice intrigued me greatly in that it seemed to both interact and to protect me at the same time. I wasn't sure who they meant, but then I heard the second voice which was also picked up in the attic which said, "I want you dead."

This voice was very dark and raspy. It was that of a woman, but there was no softness in it whatsoever.

After going through all the recordings, I then turned my attention to any video evidence I may have captured.

I was able to back up my experiences in the attic with the footage. The visual of some sort of creature like form that scurried along the floor, which I wasn't even aware I had filmed, was clearly visible. There was no doubt that what I saw that night was exactly what transpired. There was no shadow play or mistaken identity. They were ghosts.

I then began to review the video from where I had left it in the attic unattended. What I found disturbed me greatly.

First, I heard footsteps which began some two minutes in from when I had left the attic. Then there was a loud slam. This sound may not have been paranormal at all and could be the furnace turned on or off, so I decided that I would show it to Mr. Gallatin and see if he was familiar with the sound at all. But I am sure I never heard the sound while the investigation took place.

The next thing was the clincher that the house was not only haunted, but it was the home to something very demonic in nature.

Loud screams could be heard from what sounded like a large group of people that had gone through a great trauma. Then an evil voice cried out, "I will kill you all."

This was followed by a mist forming out of nothing and then right before my eyes I could actually see a human shape appear. It then reached behind its head as if it had reached for a hood or cape and then brought it over very quickly, squatted down and then disappeared. Then the camera turned a complete three hundred and sixty degrees, tipped over, and shut off.

I watched this over and over as I tried to rational out another explanation, but nothing would come forward other than the manifestations of ghosts.

I did more research on the house and found that the woman that ran the home for girls had attacked a man in the kitchen with a knife and injured him to such a degree that his right arm had to be surgically removed.

This made me recount the attack that Mr. Gallatin experienced in the kitchen.

With all of this now at hand, I invited Mr. Gallatin and his family to my office and showed them all that I had.

They were stunned. But what was good news for Mr. Gallatin was that he now knew that he wasn't in the early stages of dementia. However, no woman has ever witnessed or had any problems in the home. It seems that what haunts the home deems its job to protect all the women inside from the men that are in the house and doesn't care what the relationship is between the two.

After I showed them everything, we had a talk about what to do. I thought it best if they took back their home. Sit down together as a family and tell the woman that haunted the house that she is no longer wanted there or needed. Perhaps have Mrs. Gallatin confess her love to her husband and inform the spirit that she doesn't need her protection.

However, after a few days they thought it best to move out of the house and start anew in another home in another part of town. After several months there they had no more ghostly encounters and everyone was doing well.

The events of that night have stayed with me and have forced me to try and render some sort of a response. The two precious dogmas of my life are science and religion. They both guide and give me comfort in trying times, but neither gives a satisfactory answer to ghosts. Science believes you simply are no more after death. Religion teaches that you go to heaven or hell, but you do not roam around earth or a house for that matter.

So, what is happening? Is there a netherworld after death that some go to or is it a place we are all destined? Are hauntings simply evil spirits trying to convince the living that when you die you wander the earth to your own devices so there really is no need to believe in God?

Science doesn't believe in ghosts or an afterlife and look upon those that do believe in such things as simple minded people lost in their folklore. Yet, these same scientists are positive that life exists on other planets without any proof, but if I played a recording of a ghost voice or footage of a spirit, they would mock it.

Something is going on here. It should be studied by both science and religion just to try and define what it is.

I guess there is one thing about it, we will know the answer to this question of what happens to our souls as we take the final walk after life and see for ourselves. A journey, somewhat disturbingly, that we will all have to take- alone.

As for the house on Soldier Street, it's now up for sale. I heard you can get if for a very good price.

Brody stopped as his two friends just sort of nodded without saying anything.

"Well?" asked Brody, desperate for their review.

"It's not bad," said Cakes.

"A haunted house is always good for a stormy Halloween night tale," added Peter.

"I agree with that," added Kathy.

"Well, I liked it," said Brody with a hint of defense in his voice. "I don't think it was too bad considering how little time we had to write one. Though, I'm sure Mary Shelly's story will out-live mine. Now, who is going next?"

Peter looked at Cakes, and Cakes sort of decided, "I'll go. You know I almost wrote a poem for this little nightmare of ours."

"A poem?" replied Kathy. "That sounds terrible."

"But the original contest had Shelly and Byron in it. I think a poem would have fit the spirit of the competition," added Cakes.

"You know I remember a poem I wrote in college," interjected Brody. "It was called the 'Grave Robber.' Let's see if I can remember how it went…"

This was a good night
to rob a grave.
To take my place
among the mad and crazed.
So, I packed my tools,
a shovel, and a pick,
I stuffed 'em in a bag,
and a digging I went.
The nearest graveyard
was Old Soldier Field.
I went through the iron gate
to see what it would yield.
I found a grave marker,
Scotty August, it read.
Born in '33
and in '63 he was dead.
I, the intruder,
dug from dusk until two.
The digging was hard,
but I was going see it through.
I dug and dug
to where the body laid,
until I struck a wooden box
with the end of my spade.
I pried opened the top

when something caught my eye.
Scratched inside the coffin lid
were the words, "I'm alive!"
Then the body's hand grabbed my wrist
and let out a moan!
I struck him in the face,
then I was gone!
I ran through the night
screaming with fear!
Wondering in all horrors,
if the body was near!
Finding my way back home,
I curled up all afraid,
realizing in hindsight,
that there was no good night
to rob a grave.

The four friends broke out laughing.

"You might have won our little contest with that one," said Cakes.

"I agree, it wasn't bad," added Peter. "But we have a contest to conduct. So, Cakes, I believe you are up."

Cakes took stock of his story that bathed his face in the computer screen's reflected light.

"Mine is about a boy, a radio, and the end of the world."

"Night of the Sky People"

Balloons of red and blue shimmered against the breeze from the rotating fan that stood in the room. Pointy hats, chin strapped with elastic strings, centered about the kitchen counter and lay about the jutting out circle of metal chairs.

Myron swallowed his last bite of yellow cake, crowned in deep chocolate and placed the plate down on the papered table. He obsessively stared out the window as his hand swiped the corners of his mouth, and his mind drifted into promises unkept and wishes that—

"He'll be here soon. Don't worry."

"But the party's done over. Everyone's gone home."

"He called and said he would be late. Something came up at work. It couldn't be helped."

"I know."

The young boy's posture submarined into his folded arms lying beached across his chest. His mother began returning her kitchen, back to routine. A character inked plate here, a word embossed cup there, while a napkin and plastic spoon took their places inside the container of unwanted things.

A rag flashed across the table, snowing the crumbs against its fabric and depositing them into her small hand.

Myron's eyes flipped up inside a wake of sound.

"Dad's here. Look! He's got a present!"

"Calm down now."

"What is it?"

"I don't know."

"You do, too!"

"No, I don't. He wouldn't tell me."

"I hope it's a Foster 5000 Radio. Please, God, let it be a Foster 5000 Radio."

The door opened and the crash of footsteps met the father in the living room.

"Hey, there."

"Is that for me?"

"Might be for you, is the party over?"

"Yeah, it ended about half an hour ago," she said as she kissed him.

"I'm sorry about that, Tiger. Well, this is for you. I hope you like it."

"Man-o-man, this is heavy."

"Don't drop it."

Myron took it and sat down on the floor with its full weight across his lap. His hands struggled to grip the tight, glossy, wrapping paper before he was finally able to tear it loose from its hold and send rips of paper through the air like slices of madness.

"It's a Foster 5000 Radio! Look, Mom, it's a Foster 5000 Radio!"

"It sure is, isn't it?"

"Thanks, Dad!"

"You bet. You can listen to radio stations all over the world with that thing, with the short wave. It has a police scanner on it too so you can listen to what's going on with the neighbors."

"Honey—"

"Just a thought."

"It's great. Thanks, Dad."

Myron and his wish rushed to his bedroom to transition from a moment of *want*, to the forever of *have*.

"Do you need to help him set it up?"

"Oh, he knows more about it than I do. Did you know it was a Foster 5000 Radio?"

"Is it now? Hmm. I'll get your supper."

A gentle kiss and a hand that brushed slowly over the shoulder of a white shirt stirred thoughts of—

A dance of light smashed the room as Myron ran into his bedroom and cleared a table near the far wall. He opened up the box with his eyes swallowing every sight of the contents placed perfectly inside the cut-out compartments of the rigid Styrofoam.

He carefully took the radio out of its box, placed it on the table, then took out the wire antenna that was in a small plastic bag, hooked it up to the radio, and strung it along the wall using masking tape to hold it in place.

He took out the headphones, plugged them into the slot marked with an engraved headphone symbol on the side of the radio and flipped it on. He began turning the knobs and watched the bouncing red needles in front of the lighted dials, as he slowly slipped into another world.

The hours passed quickly before Myron's father walked into the bedroom and sat down on the edge of the bed. Myron pulled the headphones down, and they collared around his neck as-

"I'm listening to Chicago. Can you believe that? That's like a million miles away!"

"Or there 'bouts."

"Thanks for the radio, Dad."

"I'm glad you like it. Now, I know it's Friday night, and you don't have school tomorrow, but you need to keep it down because I have to go to work in the morning."

"Okay, Dad. I will, I promise. I'll only listen to it through the headphones. It's better that way anyhow."

His father left with a smile, and Myron continued his adventure that came from the small black box of endless sounds.

Inside the minutes that marked the passing night, Myron continued the adventure with his birthday gift and listened in on everything he could possibly ear his way into. He then switched over to 'scanner' mode and listened closely as a static of words slowly cleared with the careful tuning of a silver knob until a voice stood strong in the black speaker and-

"Unit 23 to base, over," a voice spoke.

The red needle danced as each word streamed out into the—

"Unit 23 to base, over." Again, the voice.

The small light from the radio dials reflected off Myron's face, giving a look of—

"This is officer Rogers to base. Come in, please. I'm having car trouble on the lookout pass just outside of Norton. Could you please send a wrecker? Over."

Posters of spaceships worshipped the walls. Paperback novels piled the shelves as—

"Unit 23...what's that noise?" the voice asked.

Myron sat up straight as the policeman's question made him—

"This is Unit 23, I'm hearing what sounds like military aircraft in the distance. It sounds like a fleet of fighters or something. Over."

Myron's eyes scanned the horizon, but reflected empty at the—

"I am now outside of the car and talking on my handheld. Can you hear me now? Over."

A small hand was placed on the headphones in an attempt to bring the sound closer.

"I don't know if anyone can hear me, but I'm going to keep talking anyway. The sounds of the aircraft are getting closer. I see lights shining over the mountain. Very bright lights. They look red in color. The noise is deafening. I don't know what it is." The radio sounded.

Roars of noise spanked Myron's ears to such a degree that he had to pull the headphones—

"The trees on top of the mountain are blowing wildly in all directions. I hope you can hear me over the noise! I'm beginning to hear the trees break now! It seems to be getting closer, but it is still behind the mountain! Wait a minute. I'm seeing the top of something gliding along the tree line! It's like the roof of an aircraft or something!"

Myron's eyes pulled in the night through the window, but nothing answered.

"It changed directions! It was going from left to right and now, it's going from right to...now it's going back the other way! But it won't raise above the mountain so I can get a clear view of what it is!"

Everything in the bedroom stood still in shadows.

"I'm hearing something behind me! Another aircraft of some sort! I guess it's the same kind as the one in front of me that is behind the mountain! It's getting closer! It sounds as if it is over head now, but I don't see anything!"

The boy's mind raced into the drama of the—

"My God! I see the aircraft! It looks like something from another world. I've never seen anything...it must be about five hundred yards wide by seven hundred yards long. The noise is so loud. I don't know if you can hear...it just fired a laser! I repeat, some sort of laser has been fired by the aircraft! I'm now running for cover in the woods!" The radio screeched.

Deafening engines scalded through the headset while Myron tried to listen to the—

"I'm in the woods, in a thick of pine trees. I can see the craft standing in midair. Several lights are being shone all about the ground. I don't exactly know why...is it looking for me?"

Debate raged the young boy's mind in wonder as to if what he was hearing was real.

"I don't see any traffic along the interstate which is highly unusual. The time is...my watch isn't working. I don't know if I broke it when I fell running over to the woods or if the aircraft is responsible." Panic and confusion came through the radio.

The breathless voice stumbling through Myron's ears brought his anxiety to a fevered—

"It can't be from here. It just can't. I don't know what to do."

Radio static stormed loud before clearing.

"Fire! Fire! Fire! A laser has been shot from the aircraft into the woods, and the trees are all on fire!"

Myron picked up his radio and ran to the window to look outside for any trace of—

"I'm running out of the woods! Another laser has been fired! It just missed me! They must be firing at me!"

His eyes scanned sharp across the spray of stars, but no reality matched.

"The smoke is getting in my eyes. God, it's burning."

A sharp smell entered Myron's nose as his mind began to comprehend.

"My...my side is killing me. I'm at a stream in a small valley between two slopes. I've got to get a drink of water."

Myron began to see a fog approaching above a rim of trees at—

"I'm heading up the hill now. I don't know where I'm going. I can hear the aircraft's engine. It's like it's getting further away. It must not be chasing me."

It wasn't fog. It was smoke. A dense, black smoke fostering up through the shadows.

"I'm at the top. I-I can...hardly breathe. We must be under invasion from another planet," the breathless voice spoke.

Sharps of panic rose inside Myron's mind.

"I can't believe this is happening."

Smoke enveloped the house, and Myron lowered the window as—

"I'm beginning to hear another aircraft! It's louder than the...I see 'em! I see 'em! It must be onetwothreefourfivesixseven...seven aircrafts! I repeat, seven aircrafts are flying over. I think—not *BBRRRRRRKKKKKKK ZEEEDFG* they are now flying away, due east. They are shining four lights."

Myron adjusted the knobs on his radio to drink in a clearer—

"My ears are bleeding. It must have been from the noise of the spaceships."

This isn't real. It's a radio drama of some kind. It has to be.

"I can hear my voice, so it must have not busted my eardrums."

Myron checked the setting.

"Can anybody hear me? Over."

The knob pointed at *scanner* making him believe that—

"I see something ahead. It's a dark figure on the ground. I'm lying down behind a log, looking at it."

Worlds of thought collided inside Myron's mind.

"It's not moving. I'm just not sure what it is."

Wonder argued reality's bone with—

"I'm going to take a look. I've drawn my weapon."

Danger lurked out of the radio and into the bedroom as Myron—

"It's a body. It appears to have been a man. He's burned really bad. His flesh has melted away and even his bones have started to melt. He's giving off some sort of green glow. I'm afraid to touch him. He might be contaminated. I'm going to back off."

A radio's voice formed into images that stood—

"I heard something."

Myron waited for the tension to break.

"I've got down behind a large rock. I heard a loud shriek. I have no idea what it was. It had a real high pitch. It just came out of nowhere."

No sounds came by Myron's—

"I don't hear anything now. I'm going to stand up and look around."

A boy wondered if—

"I don't see anything. I don't know what it was. I'm going to head on over here. *Ah huh ah huh ah huh*—I don't hear the—*ah huh ah huh*—the aircrafts anymore. There's complete silence."

Silence deadened the airwaves. The seconds pulsed by. No events scanned forward into his eyes or ears. Everything was still. The blackness began to—

"Explosion! Ex-losion! *Beeeeppppkrakzzzzerfffsskrrrrrrssss*—something just hit! It so-nded c-ose by. I think a dust smoke—*zkkrrk*."

Startled fears cut down Myron's brow and—

"Oh, God. That got in my...got in my lungs. I'm covered in ash or something. I can't see at all...can't hardly...breathe." The voice choked.

Myron's stare edged against the shores of the sky in an attempt to—

"I'm beginning to see now. It's not as bad as it was. I can smell something burning. I can see flames! It's off in the distance. I'd say about twenty miles away or so. It's really bright. It doesn't look like a normal fire. I can't...it's just brighter, is the only way that I can describe it. I'm going to try and walk over there to the cliff, see if I can get a better view. I have a handkerchief over my mouth right now, so if you are having trouble understanding me, that's why," the muffled voice explained.

Welts of smoke fingered about the skyline above Myron's home in stretches of—

"I'm at the cliff. I can see the fire and very dark smoke."

Chases of black plumes thickened forward toward Myron's eyes.

"There is a very terrible smell. It smells different than smoke. Something stronger. I don't know what it is. Smells like...I see a flash in the sky! It's like a comet or something. The tail is brightening out very wide! It's not that straight plume that you always see. It's wide. It just seems to be getting wider and wider. I don't—*zzkkrrbb sskkjrddd*—very bright. There's another one! It's crossing the path of the other one. It has the same...there's another one and another! I see four objects streaking across the sky."

Myron spied a flash of light, divided in three, splash the night.

"Someone is walking in the woods."

Ears strong, hard inside the radio's—

"I don't see anyone."

Silence dreads.

"I see someone. I see...wait, there's another one. They have weapons of some sort. They're wearing what looks like spacesuits. I don't know if it's us or something else. They're coming this way. God, please protect me."

Horror filled Myron's senses as he tried to—

"Mayday! Mayday! Mayday! I'm being chased through the woods by some sort of aliens! Some—*KKRRRKKZZZZ ZZZCXXXXY*—going up to the east slope just above the mountain lookout just outside of Norton, Virginia. They're on me!"

Myron flinched as gunshots filled the—

"*IIIIEEEE!*" and then silence.

Myron's eyes almost struck the window as he placed his face up against the glass and focused toward the horizon of moving trees. It looked like a storm was fully armed and charging against the spans of open sky. A shock of light in endless brightness shone through the mass of leaves and then rose upward into the swallowed sky in a funneled beam.

Myron was confused over what he was seeing, but he knew who would understand. He immediately took off to his mom and Dad's bedroom. He thundered across the room to the door when the house began to shake, as if an earthquake had hit.

He felt himself rising up into the air, banging his body against the ceiling, and being pushed from wall to wall. The windows exploded inside the house as the roaring wind blistered the air.

Myron fell hard to the floor as everything stood without sound.

He was conscious, but felt pain from the bruises all over his body. He got up slowly and walked to his bedroom door, which had been thrown from its hinges, and then he hurried to his parent's bedroom.

"Mom! Dad! What was that?" He pulled open their bedroom door and was horrified over what he saw.

His parents were elevated above the bed. Their heads propped up toward him by an unseen force, and their mouths were carved out into a ghastly, round wound.

To their right was a being.

It was tall, gangly, and with massive hands. The eyes were like that of a squid's, and its skin was olive in color.

The being was placing something into a satchel and stared dead on into Myron's eyes, which made the young boy scream in an overwhelming horror that violented out of his very being.

Myron turned to flee, but instead ran into four more beings that were walking toward him. He attempted to get away, but only found himself in the corner of the living room with no way out.

He screamed, scratched, and clawed at the walls, trying to find his way inside them to hide himself away from these monstrous sky people.

The beings were not sympathetic to his pleas. They kept walking toward him, carrying instruments of varying sharpness, and began their task in an orderly manner until the screams silenced away.

Cakes stopped in the quiet of the room and looked at his two friends, eagerly awaiting their review.

"I liked it," said Peter. "It had kind of a 'War of the Worlds' vibe to it."

"I thought it was good," said Brody.

"It was okay," said Kathy, "but I've got the winner right here."

"Do you now?" asked Brody in a fake British accent.

Kathy cleared her voice and began.

"The Room at the Top of the Stairs"

It was in the early morning twilight that Ms. Rose got up from bed to begin getting ready for her job interview. She was very nervous on how it would go, because she desperately had to have this job. Her husband recently passed away, leaving her with a great financial burden on how to make ends meet while paying off a mountain of medical costs.

For nearly forty years she had cleaned houses, and she thought she had finally put that part of her life behind her when she retired, but now it was staring her in the face all over again. With no children of her own that she could stay with, she had to come to terms with what she hated doing more than anything else in this world was now all that she had.

She found a local ad for a housekeeper on the internet, and it seemed like a good place to start. She called the gentleman who seemed very cordial and scheduled an interview with her at eight this morning.

Ms. Rose arrived at the appointed time to a farmhouse with considerable acreage. She thought it was a very pleasant house as she made her way to the front door and rang the doorbell.

The door opened and a handsome man in his early thirties greeted her with a smile.

"Ms. Rose?"

"Yes."

"Oh, do come in. You're right on time."

"I always believe in being on time," she said as she walked inside, and he closed the door behind her.

"Did you have any trouble finding the place?"

"No. You gave me very good directions."

"Good, then. Well, have a seat. I'm James Simms."

"Thank you. It's nice to finally meet you, Mr. Simms."

Ms. Rose sat in a chair as Mr. Simms sat across from her on the couch with a flight of stairs positioned behind him.

"Well, the job is fairly usual for housekeeping. I go to work at eight a.m., and that's when I would like you to be here. I get off of work at five, and it takes me about ten minutes to drive home, depending on traffic of course."

"Which day would you prefer I come each week?"

"I prefer that you come every day."

"Every day?"

"And possibly some weekends, too."

"Weekends? I usually just come once or twice a week to clean a house. Surely, you're not messy enough for me to have to come in every day," she said with a laugh.

"I'd like for you to housesit as well."

Ms. Rose thought this was odd, being that house-sitting wasn't in the internet advertisement.

"Are you planning a trip?" she asked.

"No. It's not that...house-sitting probably isn't the best term."

His eyes danced about the room as he struggled for the right words to explain his need.

"I thought this was just a housekeeping job?" Ms. Rose asked in an attempt to get to the fact of the matter.

"Oh, it is. I just need you to also make sure everything is okay with my father. He'll give you no trouble. He stays in his room at the top of the stairs and watches television all of the time. He never leaves his room."

"I'm not really qualified to give in-home care."

"Oh, no, no. You don't have to do any of that. In fact, you'll never see him. He never comes out of his room, and you are to never go in."

"Never go in? I don't understand."

"It's for the best. You don't want to go in his room. He doesn't have the best personality, if you know what I mean."

"But how can I watch him for you if I can't see him?"

"I know it sounds strange, but it would really help me out. I understand if you don't want to do it, but I just need an answer now."

"Is he sick?"

"No."

"Is he bedridden?"

"No."

"Then why do you need someone to watch out for him?"

"He fell a few weeks ago and couldn't get back up until I got home, so I thought I better try and get someone to stay with him, you know, for my own peace of mind."

"I understand that, but I'd be worried that he might become ill or something, and I'll not know what to do."

"Don't worry about that, I understand your limitations. If anything goes wrong or you just believe something might be wrong, you can call me at the office, and I'll rush right home."

"Shouldn't I call a rescue squad first?"

"No!"

Everything went silent as his hard response startled her.

"You only call me," Mr. Simms continued softer. "I'll take full responsibility. Now will you, do it?"

"I'm not sure," Rose whispered.

"What if I agree to double your pay to five hundred a week?"

"Five hundred a week?"

"And I'll only ask you to work five days a week, no weekends, if that will help you to decide to do it."

Ms. Rose thought it over in her mind, how five hundred dollars would really come in handy now, being that she had no other jobs lined up. She had to have this job, so there was really no other alternative.

"I'll do it."

"That is fantastic," Mr. Simms said with a relieved smile. "You're really helping me out here. So, can you start first thing in the morning?"

"Yes."

He reached into his jacket pocket, pulled out an envelope, and handed it to her.

"Here's the first two weeks' pay for you in advance."

"Thank you, but you don't have to—"

"Yes, I do. It's a way to show you my appreciation for you doing this for me. So, I'll see you at eight in the morning?"

"I'll be here," she said with an excited smile as she stared at the envelope of money in her hands.

The days that followed were simple for Ms. Rose. She would report every morning just before eight o'clock, and Mr. Simms would greet her, then head off to work. She would proceed to wash his breakfast dishes as well as any dishes left over from the previous evening. She would vacuum, dust, wash any clothes placed in the hamper, then when her daily tasks were done, she would sit in the living room and wait for Mr. Simms to come home.

She never ventured outside of the house for any reason because of the winter weather, nor did she ever go into his father's bedroom as Mr. Simms had requested.

As Ms. Rose worked about the house, or waited for Mr. Simms to come home, she could always hear the TV on in the father's room. There was never a time in which it was turned off. She would occasionally hear him walking around, but she never saw him, nor did she need to.

That was, until Tuesday of the following week.

It was around two o'clock when Ms. Rose sat down in the living room chair after doing all her chores for the day and slowly dozed off. Suddenly, a loud crash startled her awake. Her eyes searched around in an attempt to decipher where the noise had come from.

She then began hearing moaning coming from the father's room. She got up and walked upstairs to the bedroom door.

"Mr. Simms? Are you okay? Mr. Simms?"

But only moans answered her concerns.

She became overwhelmed with worry, and immediately pulled her cell phone from her dress pocket and called Mr. Simms' office as she paced the upstairs hallway.

"Hello, this is James Simms. I'm afraid I can't come to the phone right now, but if you leave your name and number, I'll get right back to you."

Ms. Rose's voice was in a panic as she left her message. "This is Ms. Rose. Your father sounds injured. Please come back to the house. I don't know what to do."

Suddenly, another loud crashing sound came from the bedroom. Ms. Rose hung up the phone and hurried to the door.

"Are you okay, Mr. Simms?"

She heard more moaning from inside the room. She didn't know what to do. Mr. Simms had told her to never go inside his father's room, but he sounded hurt. She had to go in, but worried that it would cost her the job and the money she so desperately needed to simply exist.

Ms. Rose debated on what to do. She kept hearing moans of pain, and felt she had no other choice. She reached for the doorknob, then turned it until the door slowly opened.

"I'm so sorry, Mr. Simms, but you didn't tell me if you were okay. I just wanted to check on you because I heard a loud noise and was afraid you had fallen. After I check on you, I'll leave straight way. I promise."

Her eyes scanned inside the darkened room where she'd seen the curtains drawn. The TV was on and inside its reflective light, she could see Mr. Simms sitting in a green cloth chair, staring at her.

She couldn't believe what she was seeing. Her eyes gorged the sight of Mr. Simms, to which she couldn't ration out what was going on, as her emotions were overwhelmed with the need to scream.

For Mr. Simms was a large frog.

He was approximately six feet tall and sat in the chair with his protruding, white, belly reflecting the soft light from the TV into her eyes. His rough, bumped skin wrapped around him in tones of grey and black, while he just stared at her with his large round eyes that sat atop his head.

Then, without warning, he shut his eyes tight, and his long, pink, tongue coated in slime shot out of his mouth until it stuck onto her face, to which she couldn't scream or breathe. She could taste his tongue tip in her mouth and became sickened immediately.

She felt herself whipped through the air toward the father's opened mouth, knocking down everything in her path as she went. Her head slammed into his upper lip, and she felt herself upside down inside his mouth, where he began swallowing her down whole.

He arched his back and bobbed his head back and forth a couple times to get her to slide down more easily. She kept kicking her legs, so he raised his front leg up to hold them down in order to protect his eyes.

Suddenly, the son ran inside the room and grabbed a hold of Ms. Rose's right foot to try and pull her out of her father's mouth.

"Let go, Dad! Don't do this!"

But her shoe came loose in his hand, and he fell backwards against the wall as he watched Ms. Rose go down his father's throat.

The son stood up, angry. He threw the shoe at his father, and it bounced off of his unflinching face onto the floor.

"I can't believe you did that!" he screamed at him. "Are you insane? I paid her in advance and now I have to run another ad! Do you know how much that costs?"

The son turned and stormed out of the room, slamming the door behind him.

The father's eyes blinked several times. His tongue wiped across his lips, and then he turned back to the television and began watching "I Love Lucy."

Kathy sat there with a big smile on her face.

"I have to admit, I wasn't expecting the ending," said Brody.

"Thank you," said a very pleased Kathy. "When I was a kid, during the summer I would sleep with the windows opened. We had a pond, and I could hear the frogs all night long. I loved that. I hadn't thought about that for a long time until this evening. I thought the story was wonderful by the way."

Peter and Cakes laughed as Peter said, "Of course, you liked it. You wrote it."

"What the writer thinks about her story matters, too," said a defensive Kathy.

"Okay, Peter," said Cakes. "It's your turn."

Peter nodded with a confident smile and said, "I'm going to take you back to a day of mad scientists and monsters."

"The Blood Letter"

Aren't we all monsters?

Mere beasts scurrying in a wrap of darkness in a desperate attempt to feed our obsessions like a demon lord?

Is what I did really so bad?

At times I believe it was necessary. At other moments, I feel decimated by my horrible actions that, in turn, isolate me inside the face of endless midnights.

I wrote this confession that lies in your hands, because I have had to come to terms with the fact that I invited the devil into my own self-inflicted gash of morality and allowed him to infect my troubled soul for an eternity.

It all seemed so rational at the time. I deemed my experiments necessary, to further the cause of all mankind, to take him to the next level of his existence. A natural step, mind you, not a step outside of his ability, but inside his basic outline.

I did not wish to find myself facing a creation that repulsed me. One that would make me lie awake at night, crying, with a pillowcase stuffed between my teeth in a vain attempt to force my tears wailing back into my soul.

My attack on all that we call being built slowly over several years. I became fascinated, even obsessed, with the idea of what would happen if you injected animal cells into a growing fetus. The reason I thought of this was to make mankind stronger and more resistant to disease, but what obsessed me more was that it might even allow us to live forever.

As our heart would slowly die out, we could have it replaced with the heart of an animal. Specific animals are bred for the very purpose of eternal life. I thought this possible, but I would have to find the right combination of animal cells, both in number and species. If every human was injected with my formula of cells, then the animal heart would not be rejected by the body, and it would be a smoother transition into our new world of endless days.

Of course, that would mean a kind of testing that I knew I could tell no one about. It would have to be done in secret and on human beings. In other words, it would need to be performed on a growing child inside the womb.

What drove me to take these black thoughts from debate and into action was the death of my soul, my precious wife Mary. The woman I loved more than anything else in this world. She was a thousand loves intertwined into one! And then one day she was gone.

Her beauty was so strong, but in her last days I held her in my arms as she coughed up blood and stared at me from behind her dark, sunken, swollen eyes. I could not stand to see her this way, so I worked endlessly at both caring for my beloved and trying to find a cure, but nothing worked. Nothing would bring her health forward from the abyss.

Then one summer night in June, she journeyed away from me and into the world that awaits us all.

I wandered the crisis point. Drifting from madness to despair and back again. There was no more hope or reason for my life. Nothing could give me purpose or standing.

But then the debate of eternal life rushed my mind. I thought of it constantly. I knew I would act upon it. Nothing could keep me from it. All I had to do was watch for my opportunity.

And come it did.

It was on the winter's midnight of January 2nd. The world had just stepped into the New Year with amplitude of hope, empowered by new resolutions and celebrations with fireworks, family, and friends gathering.

It was under this veil of happiness that I stood in my lab, determined to put my plan into motion. A plan that would eliminate the sorrow of death and allow us to stand with God as eternals!

The first thing I needed, I'm afraid to say, was a woman with child.

This was a difficult task for me to undertake because I knew what I was about to do. It was wrong, I knew it was wrong, but it had to be done in order to test my hypothesis that a new form of being could be manifested. A being that I would call the "God Man."

I walked the town at night, looking for a woman that was pregnant. I looked all about, and though I did find several, none seemed to meet my qualifications of what I would call "unwanted by society." They all seemed to be right with the world.

I had about given up (if only I had) when I saw her. She was clearly pregnant and sitting on the sidewalk obviously intoxicated. She had a front tooth missing and appeared to have no home or place, as she shouted at the people that walked by her.

I watched her for nearly half an hour when I summoned my courage and went up to her. As I approached, she looked at me and stood up.

The closer I got, the more disgusted I became. She was overweight, pock mocked, her hair was twisted and tangled, her clothes soiled and ripped. Her face was almost yellow in complexion, like a straw bottom chair. It appeared as if she had been living on the streets for some time now and didn't care about anyone or anything.

"Like what you see, sir?"

I didn't know what to say to her at first.

She stood there acting as if she was becoming bored with me.

"What's your name?" I asked, not really caring for the answer.

"Kate, and yours?"

At this point, it dawned on me that she was attempting to prostitute herself onto me. I was incensed that she would think I would want such a thing. That I would be so depraved in sexual appetite that I would settle for an ugly, pregnant woman to satisfy my cravings! But I tried to keep calm.

"Do you have a place to spend the night?"

"The night is my place."

She began laughing, people began to stare, and attention was the one thing I did not want. As I became nervous and worried, I immediately turned and hurried off.

"Where are you going? Don't you want to buy me a drink?" I could hear her yell and laugh.

I came to an alley and stood in the shadows, wondering what I was thinking? I took my handkerchief from my pocket and began to wipe the sweat from my face. Thoughts vomited my mind as to whether or not I should pursue this woman any further.

My world was in abstraction. What would people think if they knew what I was doing? How would they act toward me? Why should I care what they think? They have access to the streets as I, and they did not come down here to comfort her or lend support.

Look at how society has discarded her, ignoring her at all hours of the day and she is with a child. At least I'd be putting her and her fetus to use for science. Damn them for thinking ill of me! If they had taken care of her, she would not be here before my eyes!

The combination of the damp night's fragrance rushing through my nostrils and the urge to find my place among the greats of science began to settle my fractured nerves. The debate of right and wrong was still there, but I came to what I believed to be a rational conclusion. If it can better mankind, isn't any act reasonable?

I stared out of the alley from the dark, quiet and watched the woman walk toward me. I'm sure she didn't know that I was hiding in the shadows, because she kept stopping and asking strangers for money. No one would give her any, so she kept badmouthing them as she continued to walk toward me.

I reached into my pocket and pulled out a bottle of chloroform that I had brought with me for this very instant. My hand was shaking uncontrollably, and I spilled much of it onto the ground. She was getting closer, I fumbled with the lid, lost it in the dirt, and just out of not knowing what to do, I emptied the bottle onto the handkerchief and threw it down.

The noise of the bottle hitting the ground startled her. She looked hard into the black alley, and I knew I could wait no longer.

I lunged out of the folded shadows at her. I maneuvered behind her and quickly put the handkerchief over her face to try and sedate her. She struggled with twists, splays of convulsions, almost broke free from my grip and managed a short, half scream before I could cover her mouth again.

After a few seconds, she became lifeless. Her weight made it impossible for me to hold her up and we both collapsed onto the ground.

I held her in my arms as I sat looking into her face. The act had begun, there was no turning back now.

It took me a few minutes to catch my breath. I was exhausted from the struggle, but I was in the open, and I knew I had to get her out of the night and to the solace of my lab as soon as possible.

I stood and grabbed her by the wrists as I pulled her around the corner to the car. I found myself looking around fearing someone would see me. I was so obsessed with someone watching me that I tripped over some debris and fell into a puddle, which frustrated me with anger.

I finally made my way to the car, opened the door, and with much difficulty, pushed her into the backseat. I closed it as quietly as I could, hurried to the driver's side, and drove away.

I must confess that I had such an adrenaline rush. I had taken a woman, placed her into my car, and the power I felt was beyond anything I had ever experienced before. I was not only in control of myself, but the life of another being and I liked it.

I concentrated on the road, as I'm sure I was driving faster than usual. I just wanted to get to my lab, hide from the world, and begin my experiment. Then something fell into form ahead. I couldn't make it out at first, then it hit me. It was a sobriety checkpoint. I couldn't believe this was happening. The New Year had absolutely slipped passed me, and the possibility of coming upon a sobriety checkpoint on the outskirts of town never entered my mind once.

I didn't know what to do. Should I take off? Turn around? Should I just go forward as if nothing was wrong? What if she comes to and starts screaming?

I kept glancing in the rearview mirror at the woman, ahead at the police, and the line of cars in front of me. My heart was pounding and sweat drenched my clothes.

I determined myself to concentrate. Just relax and do what the officer says.

The wait was agonizing as each car ahead drove away, and I moved up one position. Then it was my turn to come upon the officer.

"Good evening."

"Good evening, Officer."

I handed him my driver's license. He looked it over.

"Thank you. Have a nice evening."

"Thank you," I said and drove off.

He didn't even look in the backseat. I can't believe he didn't see her lying behind me like that.

I looked at this as a sign from God, that I was supposed to conduct this experiment, for if it wasn't to be so, then He would surely have let me be found out at the sobriety check. I was sure of this.

I got her home and immediately took to removing her from my car and into my laboratory in the basement. She seemed heavier than before as I pulled her along the ground. I had to stop twice to catch my breath before pulling her along the way again. I got halfway to the door when she started to wake up.

"Where am I?" she muttered.

I said nothing and continued to drag her by her arms.

Then she got more agitated.

"What's going on?"

She began kicking and pulling to where I had to stop and sit on top of her.

"Be quiet! Do you hear me?"

I had never been this angry before. I believe it was a combination of the stress of what I was doing and the excitement of conducting my experiment, and I was not going to allow her to take that from me.

"Let me go. I'm begging you! Please!" she screamed.

I slapped her several times to get her to shut up. My violence had even shocked me, but it had to be done. I'm sure you can understand this. It was for the experiment's sake, I assure you.

I finally got her under control and pinned her arms to the ground by holding her by the wrists. I stared into her eyes as the moon flashed in and out of the clouds.

She began to cry. "What are you doing to me?"

"There is nothing to fear. You'll be okay."

"I want to go home."

"You have no home."

"Yes, I do. My husband is waiting for me."

This was something I did not expect. I figured she was all alone, but if she had a husband, then he would surely come looking for her himself, and when he cannot find her, contact the police.

I didn't know what to do. She began wiggling all about the ground trying to get loose again. She began screaming, and though I knew no one was around, I was afraid perhaps someone could be in the nearby woods, could hear her shouts and then come to investigate.

"Shut up! Do you hear me?"

"Let me go!"

She bit my arm as hard as she could, and so I hit her in the face with my fist until I had knocked her unconscious.

I was too angry to realize that I had struck a woman with child. It didn't matter. She was here for me to conduct my experiment, and her short-term horror would benefit all in a standing glory to come.

I struggled to my feet and took a deep breath. I grabbed her by the wrists and began the task of dragging her along the cold ground, until I got her into my lab and closed the door.

I turned on the lights and took her over to the gurney I had already positioned for months now, debating if I should go forward with my thoughts on this experiment. And now I would use it for the first time.

I picked her up and struggled with her weight as I placed her upon the gurney. I then strapped her down so she couldn't move.

I turned on the overhead light and just looked at her.

She was nothing to me. I didn't really even think of her as human anymore, but what she will be put through in the coming days and nights will help all of mankind.

I went to my desk and began getting out the shots that had been carefully prepared for this night. I wanted to get started right away. I had been obsessed with looking at them every night for months, making sure they would be ready just in case I went forward with the experiments.

First, I took her arm and rolled up her sleeve. I found a vein and pushed the needle in. There, I filled her with opium. This would keep her quiet, and if done often, would create an addiction, causing her to put up with anything, just to get her fix.

Then I went for the cells.

I took a knife and cut open her dress at the stomach. The signs of pregnancy were there. I was guessing perhaps five months or so.

I placed the needle into her stomach and the animal cells were injected into the fetus. She was not even bothered by it. Her mind was drifting from the opium injection, just as I had hoped.

With the first animal cell injection I settled into a routine. I would do the injections every hour, on the hour, for sixty straight days.

It only took a few days for the woman to become addicted to the opium. This simplified matters considerably. She would let me do anything to her for the feel that the drug gave her.

I gave it to her every time she asked. Sometimes, three or four times an hour. It made no matter to me. If it made her happy and kept her from thinking about what I was doing to her and what I would have to do to her in the end, then so be it.

As the sixty days progressed, the routine was becoming increasingly exhausting. I never slept. I had to tend to her addiction and the injections every hour. Then, add upon all of the sleeplessness with the fear that someone would find out what I was doing, it was enough to try the very souls of angels.

There were several times I feared I was going to be found out. I had visitors and friends come over that would surprise me. I would be so angered by them, but I had to show no temper. This was important because I didn't want to raise any questions.

As the hours washed over me, the fateful day arrived. The sixty days were up. How I kept it quiet, I do not know, but the final day came, and I was excited.

It was a trying evening for me. I was tired, but I knew this moment could change all of science. I was about to see a new being, a being that I had the forethought to create.

I had all of my instruments on a tray, I looked at her face and then at her stomach. I took the blade into my hand and began the operation.

As I cut her open, she convulsed. She was attempting to scream, but couldn't. I believe she was going into cardiac arrest. Even though she was strapped down, she was twisting so violently that it was impossible for me to continue the operation. I stood back and watched her in horror.

She finally pushed a scream out from the darkest part of her soul, like that of animal being eaten alive. It continued for several seconds and then stopped. There was no movement.

I walked over to her and looked down at her face. Her eyes stood wide open with trickles of blood soiling the crevices. She was dead, but I owed it to science to see what I had created inside of her.

I cut her open and reached down inside of her womb. I could feel flesh, but not that of a fully formed human. It was much different. It was very rough in texture and thick in folds.

I slowly pulled my hands up out of the bed of blood that leaked down onto the floor in streaming pools. My eyes gored the nightmarish monster that scorched warm in my hands, which brought shocks of emotions to my fired senses.

The body was just a massive blob of tissue, like that of a giant slug. Parts of the skin were torn away, allowing me to see reddish tissue underneath. It had no appendages, except for an unformed right hand.

It was the face that sickened me the most. The mouth of the beast was stuck on the side of its face. The gums appeared black in color with the upper gum being more prominent than the lower one. I could see what appeared to be a few teeth protruding from its wet lips. It had one developed eye, which had blood running from it, and where the other eye should have been was nothing more than layers upon layers of tissue. It had half a nose, and what little it had was lying sideways. There was a gaping hole resting in its forehead, and covering all the skin were these bumps of various sizes.

Suddenly, it began to vomit, and I immediately dropped the beast from my hand. It fell, hit the table, and bounced hard onto the floor.

What happened next horrified me to such a degree that I almost fainted from the fear.

It began crying.

I backed up against the wall of my laboratory terrified. This wasn't what I wanted to happen. I thought I could easily handle the sight of my experiment's result, but its horror has overwhelmed all of my senses. It just screamed louder and louder.

"Shut up! Shut up! Shut up!" I yelled back at it.

I crouched down onto the floor, placed my hands over my ears, and closed my eyes in a vain attempt to make everything from this night go away.

"What have I done? Dear God, what have I done?" I kept whispering to myself.

At this point, I knew what the next step was. I stood up, looked over to the corner of my laboratory, and spied my ax.

I looked at it, and with great determination, walked over and grabbed it.

I could feel the smooth sides of the wooden handle in my hands. I could hear the screams of the beast in my ears while my conscious was beating me down from all the angles of my mind.

I moved forward and headed to the other side of the table where its mother lay. I took several deep breaths. I lifted my ax into the air and moved around the table to destroy this beast, but it wasn't there.

My mind was bursting at the possibilities of where it might have gone. My eyes darted all about the room, trying to find its hiding place.

I looked under the table, and could see a slimy trail going over to the corner of the laboratory and disappearing behind a bookcase. As I raised back up, I looked into the eyes of Kate, who was staring at me as if she was cursing the very being of my soul from her never world. It upset me so much that I had to place my hand over my eyes to shield them from looking at her ghastly appearance.

I made my way around the table and was startled when the bookcase shook and jiggled about.

I walked forward with the ax in my right hand. I got to the bookcase, and with my left hand, began to pull the bookcase from the wall. As I did, I could hear the creature hissing at me.

I immediately jumped back, thinking the thing would charge at me, but everything seemed to quiet down.

I then went back, moved the bookcase out a little more, and peered behind it to see the creature lying on the floor looking up at me with a look of anger and disgust.

I moved the bookcase out just a little more, and in doing so, it snagged and fell over. Everything smashed onto the hard concrete floor as I ran away from the beast, fearing it might jump upon me.

After gathering my thoughts, I could see the creature was still in its original position. I gripped my ax as tightly as I could and walked toward it. Each step I took toward it was a challenge in courage and steadfastness. I had to fight my desire to run away screaming, because I knew this had to be done. I had to kill the creature.

I got into striking range. I lifted the ax above my head and began to swing down at the creature again and again and again with all of the force I could put behind the blows.

The creature began crying loudly as I struck at it, but I did not stop. With each blow I landed, blood and chunks of flesh sprayed all over me, the wall, and floor, to such a degree that it was difficult to actually see or stand.

I could feel the madness running through my bloodstream and brain this time. My temples throbbed and my eyes felt as if they were stretching with a tangled combination of both anger and fear. I wanted not only for this creature to die, but for this night to die with it.

Finally, I stopped swinging my ax due to utter exhaustion. I collapsed to the floor and started to cry.

"What have I done?" I said, searching for mercy, but realizing that I deserved none.

Everything was silent, except for the ticking of the clock hanging on the wall. I was covered in sweat and splattered with blood and strips of flesh. I stood up and looked over at the ghastly sight of the monster ripped up and smashed into several slices on the floor.

I turned, opened the door that led outside, and saw a bag of fertilizer against the wall. I opened it up and dumped all the fertilizer out of the sack onto the ground and brought the sack inside. I closed the door behind me, began the task of picking up the monstrosity that lay on the floor and started placing it into the sack.

I approached each piece of the organism as if I was afraid it would turn on me at any second. I reached slowly, and then snatched it from the floor and quickly put it in the sack. I was crying the whole time over all the horror. To even touch the flesh of the monster made me ill, but I had to get rid of it. I had to get it out of the lab and away from my house.

When I got all the contents into the sack, I got a rope from the drawer and tied off the top. I placed the sack in the corner of the lab and turned to look at its mother lying on the table with her belly sliced open.

I did not know what to do with her. I had to get rid of her, of course, but how?

I thought it over in my mind, but I was not rational at this time whatsoever. Please, you must understand this. I was in a state of complete madness. There is no way I would have done any of this, let alone what I was about to do, if this was not the case.

I went over to the woman and grabbed her by the arm. I pulled her down off the table and she hit with a loud thud onto the cold floor.

I was going to drag her outside, but I was so tired that I didn't have the strength. So, I thought it'd be best to divide her up into more easily manageable chunks.

I went over, got the ax again and approached the woman lying on the floor. I stood over her. She was face down, and I was very grateful that she was. There was no way I could stand to look down into her dead eyes for the fear that, somehow, she could see what I was about to do from the darkness of her soul's grave.

I took the ax and proceeded to divide her body into parts. I had no emotion while doing this. I looked at her as a problem that had to be taken care of. That's all she was to me, nothing else.

After I had finished, I stacked her remains into a pile on the floor. I then went over, got some boxes, and placed her limbs, sliced flesh, and bones inside them. The last thing I placed inside was her head. I picked it up with my eyes closed, quickly placed it into the box, closed the flaps, and taped all of them down with a roll of tape that I had on hand.

When I finished with my deed, I went upstairs to get a mop and bucket. I went into the kitchen and filled the bucket up with water. Afterwards I went back downstairs and began mopping all the blood up from the floor and walls.

Afterwards, I placed the mop into the bucket and put it in the corner. The night had fallen hours ago, and I thought this would be the best time to get rid of the creature and its mother.

I knew where I was going to take them—the cave. It was a short walk from my house and would serve as a perfect hiding place.

I headed out of the lab with the first box in my hands. I noticed a storm was approaching. The wind was blowing hard, bending the trees to their limit. I was sure this was God beginning his judgment on me.

I began my trek into the woods and up the hillside when the blinding rains came. I got halfway up, but then slipped and fell, causing her body parts to spill out onto the ground through a small opening on the underneath side which I had overlooked. I panicked.

"No, no," I cursed at myself. How could this be happening? I quickly tried to pick them up, but in the dark, I was not sure if I had gotten everything or not.

Thunder echoed through my ears as lightning pierced the blackness. The rain stung as it hit my face, but I continued up the slick face of the hill. I stopped several times to rest, but then I would head up again.

I finally arrived at the mouth of cave and collapsed in front of it.

I pushed the box into the cave as far as I could reach, repeated the event with the other two boxes that contained the sins for a thousand lifetimes, and then headed back down the hill in the killing rain.

I got back to the lab and had to get a drink of water. I was so thirsty at this moment. It hit me out of nowhere. I had become so obsessed with what I was doing, that I was pushing myself beyond the breaking point.

I quickly downed a half a jug of water that I kept in the laboratory. I then wiped my mouth and proceeded over to the sack holding the creature.

I picked it up by the end and, to my horror, the sack began twitching and twisting to such a degree that it escaped my grip.

I stood back and watched it move on the floor. I quickly went, got my ax, and hit it several times. It screamed out to almost the sound of a howl. I couldn't believe what I was hearing.

"Shut up!" I shouted and placed my hands over my ears.

Then I saw the bag begin to move across the floor. I quickly grabbed the ax and began pounding it again. This time, it stopped as blood oozed from the bag.

I looked about, got a box, placed the bag into it, and sealed the box up with tape.

I then turned and headed back to the cave.

The lightning speared the sky, and the thunder shot a loud roar through the coffin of darkness.

God was having his way with me this night. This must be how Adam felt when he ate the forbidden fruit and then had to face God with what he did.

Still, I continued up the hill and got to the cave exhausted. I placed the box inside, next to the woman, and stood back.

I gathered rocks nearby and placed them into the opening of the cave, stacking them as carefully as I could, until the opening was nearly filled. Then I took some brush, placed over it, and stood back.

When I finished, I went back to my lab and began this letter of confession for what I have done.

This is my attempt to right my wrong and hope to find mercy in the heart of God, but perhaps I am asking too much.

I will now place this letter into the cave, the very letter which you are holding in your hands at this moment.

I know that I am a truly wretched man. A man whose soul is doomed for all of eternity. I only ask that you remember me in your prayers...if they let you.

Now, I take my place inside the shadows, forever crying in the darkness, for I know that I am home.

Sincerely,

Dr. Blood

March 1971

As Peter finished, a huge explosion was heard in the distance, and all the power went out, not only in the building, but the whole neighborhood.

"Great going, Peter. Your story knocked out all the power in the world," observed Cakes with a hint of concern.

They went over to the window, and though their eyesight was limited by the dark, their senses could tell it was still snowing and it was deep. The constant sound of snow pelting the window glass and the howling wind seemed to make the night come alive like a great horror story should.

"It's never going to stop snowing," said Peter.

"What are we going to do if we can't get home tonight?" asked Brody.

Cakes smiled. "Write some more stories."

The Perfect Plan

Mark K. McClain

As daylight faded, yielding to broadening darkness, the clouds opened for a short time. The storm had rolled past. Overhead, the starless night embraced Destiny like a lover.

She was dressed in her usual gothic style, lace arm sleeves, fishnet stockings, studded choker, and knee-high boots. Naturally, like her long hair, all were black, except for the purple velvet skirt that ended just above her knees. Her full lips were covered in darkly shaded lipstick. Black circles and heavy eyeliner adorned her eyes. Her nails were raven colored.

Anticipation soared. Knowing this night had finally arrived felt like a drug rushing through her veins. Her plan seemed flawless, but only time would tell. In truth, she had only sent four invitations, each with specific instructions to keep the party and its location secret. It was meant to be a surprise of sorts. The recipients had no idea how many students would be present.

Certainly, her guests would be on time. Whenever sex, alcohol, and drugs were promised—as they were in this case—people seemed to magically appear. Tonight, would be no different. She counted on it.

The house, should one deem it as such, looked perfect. It was more of a castle than not. The enormous vertical structure had been erected during the fifteenth century, complete with rose windows, towering buttresses, and pointed arches. Each sizeable, stained-glass window was flawless, no doubt painstakingly painted by hand to reveal their multicolored glory. Not one pane was broken even after all these years.

Great gargoyles, mute in their unending observations, perched along the towering outer edges. The stony figures stared on with rigid faces. Rainwater still dripped from their open mouths.

Next were the grotesques who mocked humanity with their twisted faces. The hideously, ugly, even disgusting, distorted forms were a mystery in origin. Some bore human faces, while others were plainly animals, and yet more, a combination of the two. Their figures were strategically placed in stone corbels, keystones, and friezes. Unlike gargoyles, they were fashioned to scare and protect, at least, according to the legends.

Destiny wished to see them more clearly. The clouds, which had begun to thicken, suddenly parted as if in response from the higher powers. Pale moonlight trickled through the cloudy veil, touching upon the granite faces.

She loved them all. They were her favorite part of the old castle. If they could retell tales from the previous five hundred years, what would they say? What sort of things had they seen over the centuries, she wondered. Wars? Death? Happiness? There was no way to know.

The thick clouds reconverged to conceal the bright, first-quarter moon. Destiny moved down the graveled lane, ensuring the 'Party Inside' signs were still properly placed. From a distance, she studied the castle. It was sheer loveliness. No matter how often she came here, it looked as wonderous as the first time she laid eyes upon it.

The castle was styled after Transitoria, Nero's ancient home, aptly named the House of Passages. Destiny wished she could live within its walls. Though exploring the corridors for many months, she had yet to reach each room, walk the array of endless passages, or discover any ancient, hidden secrets, which she was certain lay within.

"You are a masterpiece," she said softly. "Workmanship like yours has long since been forgotten."

It saddened her that the old ways were dying with each passing day, replaced by people living in agitated, frenzied states, complete with modern phobias and laundry lists of mental issues. Even with belief in the ancient gods, or their evil counterparts rebounding, which encouraged her, it already had negative consequences. Just last month, her father paid for her to see a psychiatrist for having conversations with inanimate objects. Though she hated the idea of seeing a shrink, she gave in to keep family peace.

Dr. Treadmill, as Destiny named her due to her constant repetition of things the girl cared little for, said the condition was named *personification*. The affliction led to pretending inanimate objects were living things, or people. In the doctor's words, once a patient—Destiny hated being called that—applied human attributes to inanimate objects, nature, animals, or abstract concepts, they were clinically insane, or suffering from personification. In some of the worst instances, the afflicted created dramatic stories about their invented friends' social roles, emotions, and intentions.

Destiny did no such thing. She spoke to her friends, and they answered. Even from an early age she knew to keep her secret just that—secret. Otherwise, she would wind up wearing a stiff canvas jacket, being pumped full of medication, or living in a padded room. Perhaps all three. During her sessions, she had taken great care to appear anxious, yet demure, shyly seeking the help her parents longed for her to have. Yet in private, she spoke long into the night to her many acquaintances, to the voices others insisted only existed in her mind. Pure and utter gibberish, she thought. She held no intention of stopping because a doctor believed the entire scenario was a whim of fancy.

She grasped the door handle, pausing to take in a long breath, then slowly let it out. The heavy, wooden, door opened noiselessly before she crossed the threshold and closed herself inside. She looked about. Truly magnificent, she thought again. Running her fingers over the walls and railings, she made her way to the second floor to wait.

Some twenty minutes passed before two cars rumbled down the long driveway to park in the uppermost portion of the gravel-laden cul-de-sac. Destiny's back straightened as she looked on from high above, while the participants eased from their cars in fine fashion to amble toward the door.

"Looks like we're the first ones here," said Tim, the average-looking, stocky football player. He brushed hair from his eyes with an imperial sweep of his hand, as if preparing to pose for a magazine cover. But the trait he was most known for was being a cruel bully. Thanks to a combination of status and size, no one stood up to him. His twisted, sociopathic behavior had gone unchecked for years.

Conversely, Chad liked finer things, and with absurdly wealthy parents, they were easy to obtain. He drove expensive cars, wore fine clothes, and spent money at every conceivable opportunity. Though he treated women like matches—using them once before discarding them forever—he was a smooth talker and could connive his way into a girl's pants with little effort, especially if they knew he was rich, which covered nearly every female in town. Bedding women was a game to him. And if that game went awry, as it sometimes did, his parents would ensure any pending trouble vanished, usually by placing wads of cash into the right hands.

"Why are we standing around? I'm freezing," complained Hailey. She was a perfect match for Chad's affluent personality—an offensive snob who envisioned herself far above others. In reality, she was a classless, gold digger, who everyone knew would sleep with anyone who could support her fake, rich lifestyle. It was perfectly clear why she paired herself with Chad.

Jessica, though she preferred Jess, was a small, redheaded, thief and another user of men when it suited her needs, which was daily. Her methods differed little from Hailey, except that she rarely slept with her targeted victims. She merely created close relationships by quickly confessing her feelings of love, then after a short time would purloin anything of value before disappearing from her victim's lives entirely. To date, she has never worked a day in her life. Her belongings were either gifted, or came from ill-begotten gains.

Destiny sucked in a breath as Samantha—Sammy to her friends—exited Chad's car. Dressed casually in her favorite boots, blue blouse, and slim-fit jeans, the girl was the most attractive among them and a truly sweet person. She was not supposed to be here. Undoubtedly, the others were not her kind. The only reason Sammy would be invited was because they owed her. She actively helped them pass classes, doing work for five students, counting herself.

Without her, the imbeciles would be heading home to their parents as disgraced failures. They needed her. But this night, like any other with them, she seemed invisible. The four friends had already begun strolling up to the house by the time she closed the car door.

Groaning at the unexpected dilemma, while hoping her guests had not disclosed the party to others, Destiny wavered for a moment. Then she rose from her seat on the stairs. She could still go on with her plan. Sammy's presence was of little consequence. She would simply be dealt with when the time was right.

Destiny moved to the stout, wooden, railing overlooking the first floor. When observed from above, the beautiful archaic tiles caught her breath as she stared at their magnificence. The pattern, undetectable while standing upon its surface, was far more intricate and lovely from a raised vantage point. Then, the floor became not just one of colored wonder, but formed the face of a large raven surrounded by strange writings and unknown symbols. Appreciation for the ancient craftsmanship made her shiver with happiness, combined with the knowledge of what would soon take place.

The five students entered, crossing the threshold to a world they had never imagined. They closed the door and gawked at the sight.

Chad whistled a shrill sound. "Dig this old place! I could easily live here. It suits my style. Why haven't I been here before?"

"Because you're too busy shopping, or screwing, to do anything else," snipped Jess.

Chad scowled at her. "At least I can afford to buy my own stuff and don't need to steal it."

Jess flushed red and displayed her middle finger. "Asshole."

"Oh, for shit's sake! Knock it off," said Tim, guiding Jess away. "You sound like a couple of five-year-old children."

"Time has come," Destiny whispered, still unnoticed as she caressed the railing with her fingertips.

In that moment, sounds unlike any heard by the friends, filled the room. Akin to grating stone, or heavy objects being moved over granite with great effort, the hall vibrated.

"What's that noise?" grumbled Tim, puffing his chest out as if preparing for an attack.

"It's just this old house," said Chad. "Relax, dude. Do you need someone to hold your hand?" He reached out only to have his mocking effort slapped away.

"Don't be rude to my man," snapped Hailey to the football star. "He'll kick your ass if you disrespect him again." She took Chad's arm and snuggled against it. "Won't you, baby?"

Chad blushed and swallowed hard. "No need for any of that shit. We're here to have fun and get stoned. Let's find this party."

Tim snorted, then chuckled at the pair. "See, you can have common sense when you need it. Good choice."

The noises, forgotten in a moment of happy thought, returned, permeating the walls like a disease testing entrance to a new host. Scraping and clawing sounds rebounded within the chambered room from all directions, even above. The companions' eyes went toward the ceiling only to land on Destiny standing patiently at the top of the stairs.

"What is *she* doing here," asked Jess, pointing as she met her antagonist's dark eyes.

Destiny curtsied, then nodded slowly. "I am at your service. Unfortunately for you, I am tonight's party host."

"What's your game, freak. You shouldn't be here. This party is for normal people," said Tim, wagging a stiff finger her direction before checking over his shoulder, ensuring the others laughed. He enjoyed being the center of attention. "I'm going to teach you a lesson and..."

Pounding on the large front doors halted his words.

Jess sprang to Tim's side. Her eyes wide with fear. "What is that? Make it stop. It's freaking me out." Her gaze went to Destiny, and again, she pointed an accusing finger. "This is your doing, bitch."

Destiny laughed. "For once in your miserable existence, you've stated the truth. Oh, another surprise is that you are absolutely right." She descended a few steps, focusing on Jess. "Do you remember stealing my brand-new laptop from my workstation? Or maybe you have forgotten how you swiped all my money from my gym locker while I showered. My friend saw you."

Jess scoffed. "Liar! No one saw me take..." Her words faltered and she blushed, knowing she had been caught. She hung her head, remaining behind Tim as if he was a shield protecting her from her own deceits.

"Shut up, you moron. You're making things worse," said Hailey to the redhead.

Jess's face flushed. She stepped forward with a hand raised, only to flinch away as the pounding, much louder now, returned with force. Chad stepped in between the girls and Tim faced them, closing out their huddled circle. Sammy stood alone and forgotten, cowering in the shadows behind a large pillar.

"I'm leaving. This is complete bullshit," declared Chad in a shaken voice. He faced Destiny. "You're nobody and can't keep us here. Screw you." He balled up his fist and thrust it upward.

"I wouldn't open that door if you were planning to live more than a few seconds, rapist," she replied. Her last word hung in the air with a viscous feeling.

A soft gasp escaped from Sammy, as she slipped farther into the darkened corner.

The room fell into eerie silence.

Hailey backed away from the group, arms wrapped around herself. A look of confusion and disbelief registered on her face. "What is she talking about?"

Chad's expression morphed into one of forced innocence. His voice raised an octave. "I...I...don't know. She's crazy. Everyone knows it." He pushed his chin her direction. "Look at her! She's a nut job. Not to mention a certified devil lover."

"Surely you remember the night you caught me coming home late from the library," Destiny said, descending a bit farther. Her tone was soft and even. "That poor little thing between your legs must have been lonely. Maybe it got tired of seeing your hand so often. Your mistake was being stupid enough to wear your prized necklace. You know, the one your folks gave you. The one I tore from your neck as you raped me. I still have it." She patted her pocket. "By the way, I hope the wounds I gave you never heal." Her fingers curled into a claw-shape as they gently raked across her throat.

Hailey's terrified eyes darted toward Chad's neck. The scars were plain to see. "You told me you did that wrestling with Tim. You said it was an accident."

Tim scoffed. "Leave me out of it."

"Shut up, both of you," snapped Chad.

"What do you want?" Jess shouted toward the staircase.

More pounding and scratching battered the air. A howl escaped. The friends stared at each other, caught in an impasse.

Destiny resumed her slow descent. "And you, sweet little Hailey, thank you so much for posting those naked, photoshopped, pics of me. They really got everyone talking." She frowned for the first time. "Too bad you're too stupid to know about IP addresses. Did you think I couldn't find out who put that fake garbage online?"

Hailey's face drained of color. "It...it was a joke." She laughed lightly, sounding wholly unsure of herself. "I didn't mean..."

"And muscle man, Tim," Destiny interrupted while halting on a particularly creaky step. "You laid hands on my best friend. You must've felt pretty tough slapping a girl around until she needed a hospital. Very bad form, dipshit." Her eyes narrowed. "I will be sure you die most painfully."

"Wha...wha...what is she talking about?" stammered Jess. She gritted her teeth and spun. "I've had enough!" she hollered, meeting Destiny's stare. "Let us go or else."

"Or else what?" the Goth girl asked with a steady calm. "It is now time to introduce you to my friends and lay down the rules. They are simple, really—even for all of you. If you survive their wrath until dawn, you will be free to go about your miserable lives with my blessings."

"What friends? Your stupid Goth friends? I'll kick *all* their asses," proclaimed Tim, pounding a fist into his other palm. "What are they going to do, sissy slap me to death." He laughed again. The others did not.

Destiny ignored him.

"And if we're caught? Then what?" asked Hailey, her eyes darting over the room with a frightened stare. "What will they do?"

"Let's just say all your past transgressions will be absolved." Destiny smiled again. "By the way, if my words are too large for you, I can give you a minute to look them up on your phones." She laughed. "Oh, wait, there's no cell service here."

In unison, as if the concept was foreign, or totally forgotten, all four freed their phones to stare at the screens. Hailey raised hers high, then moved round the room to no avail. Chad's composure slipped with every second no bars appeared. Disappointment, mixed with hints of anger and desperation, edged onto their faces.

"That's it! I'm going to break your neck, you filthy..." Tim charged the steps.

Destiny clapped her hands to gain his attention, as he rocketed closer. "I want you to meet one of my imaginary friends. That is what my family calls them—imaginary." Another wicked grin graced her face. "Oh, Vuzarin, could you lend a hand, please," she asked sweetly.

The stone gargoyle stepped into the light to spread his great wings for an instant. Shrieks of fear rose from below. Again, the others trembled. Tim, looking far less brave, quickly retreated to rejoin them.

"What the hell is that!" cried Chad with raised shoulders, as his hands were held tightly to his chest in dread.

"It's a guy in a suit. Nothing like that exists. So fake!" said Hailey, waving a dismissive hand as she rolled her eyes.

"I...I...I'm not so sure," stuttered Jess.

"It seems the proverbial cat is out of the bag." Destiny turned to Sammy. "You have no part in this. I suggest you find cover and stay there."

As quickly as her legs would carry her, Sammy scurried into deep shadows down a long hall. The girl needed no prompting to save herself. Destiny watched her flee in the direction of the east wing, marking it in her mind.

Hailey and Chad attempted to follow, but a low, growl from Vuzarin froze them. Clawed feet advanced before Destiny lay a hand on the gargoyle's massive shoulder.

"This wonderful being, along with some of *his* friends, will hunt you until dawn. Once the sun rises above the horizon, you will be free to go. Providing you survive, of course." Another malicious smile. "May your deaths be as excruciatingly painful as what you have put me through this year." She swept a hand before her. "I suggest running instead of wasting time with your pointless words or screaming."

The quaking human prey, hurriedly understanding their dilemma, fled from sight, scattering into darkened hallways.

Taking Vuzarin's grey face in her hands, Destiny lowered her voice. "Tell the others the girl in the blue blouse must remain unharmed. I will hunt her myself."

With a graveled voice, Vuzarin spoke. "As you wish, Mistress. The sentence of death has been uttered and so shall it be bestowed upon those who have done you harm." With a quick movement, the gargoyle bound over the railing, spread his wings once more, then glided to the main floor to land with another shaking thud. Throwing his horned head back, Vuzarin let loose a call that resounded through the castle's innards.

Doors and windows flung wide as both gargoyle and grotesque alike arrived in answer. Vuzarin issued orders in a tongue even Destiny did not comprehend, though she recognized the meaning clearly enough. The die had been cast in favor of death and destruction.

Chad ran as panic narrowed his vision. Hailey kept pace beside him. Doors and hallways flew past as they sprinted the passageway. He dared a quick glance over his shoulder only to see Vuzarin bearing down on them. In that moment, an unfamiliar sensation gripped his soul—terror unlike any he dreamed possible. Not the sort of edge-of-your-seat hysteria one gets from a book or movie. Rather, one that scrambled his thoughts, sped his heart to the point of bursting, and in its full appreciation of his predicament, made him lightheaded, nearing the point of fainting. Yet, he ran on while gripping Hailey's hand.

These things are toying with us, he thought. His inclination was perfectly correct. It was a cat and mouse game of sorts, with no clear means of escape. Only barred windows and locked doors greeted them.

With every new glimpse of their hunter, who steadily drew closer, Hailey urged them into dimly shaded corners to hide behind flowing drapes or bulky furniture. Skidding round a corner to temporarily lose sight of their pursuer, the duo ducked behind a long, high-backed sofa to wait. But Chad could not remain still for long.

Though Vuzarin slowed, another pursuer—a grotesque with a large club in his sizeable, gnarled hand—lumbered into view, to join in the chase. The pair, completely unnerved by the commotion around them, bolted again.

Chad ignored Hailey's frantic protests as he hurtled forward without logic, or a solid plan in mind. His hand shook loose, and Hailey fell behind. He slid to a stop, this time behind a massive pillar. His breath was ragged. Hailey arrived seconds later, clutching her side.

Suddenly, sounds drew their attention upward. Several grotesques clung to the large wooden ceiling beams as they shadowed the fleeing humans from above. Gargoyles waited patiently, mockingly, at each end of the hall. Vuzarin approached. This pursuit had reached a pinnacle.

"I have a plan," Chad announced with confidence. He took her sweaty palm in his. "Do you trust me?"

Hailey contemplated that for a short moment. "Y...y...yes," she stammered, unconvincingly. "I trust you."

"Then come on," he answered, tugging her hand as he dashed forward once more.

Hailey resisted, trying to break his grip, but it was too tight. "You're running toward them, you idiot," she cried.

Chad's heartbeat rang in his ears, drowning out Hailey's screams and objections as he forced her along. At the end of the hall stood Vuzarin, eyes gleaming.

Forty feet separated prey and predator. Thirty. Twenty. Ten. At last, Chad stopped, jerking Hailey to a halt. Before she could speak, he took her face in his hands and kissed her warmly.

"I'm sorry. But I'm way more important than you," he said, shoving her into the gargoyle's waiting arms.

Hailey's scream never came, nor did Chad witness the unseemly sight. In that moment, as she was torn to pieces, he sprinted past. Blood splattered the walls, floor, and portions of the ceiling.

Chad's feet slapped the stone floor as he raced toward the front doors to grasp the large iron handles and pull for all his worth. They moved nary an inch. Again and again, he tried, but to no avail. The heavy entries were solid and impenetrable. Hope drained away as the crunching sound of stone on stone reached his ears. Vuzarin had returned.

Chad fought back tears of helplessness. He was going to be a victim, like an animal caught in a python's crushing grip—holding, tightening, squeezing, until all signs of his life were extinguished. The floor vibrated beneath him as he turned, backing sideways into a marbled corner as the gargoyle slowly advanced. Too petrified to make a sound, his eyes widened as the living stone creature swiped a long, clawed limb outward. Chad's partially crushed head rolled across the floor with a revolting slapping sound, coming to rest in a corner.

Jess discovered a seldom used hallway. She crept its length as silently as her stylish boots would allow. Cringing after each footfall, she slunk forward. She tested every door, but each one rejected her, forcing her deeper into despair as choices slimmed. Even if she could cry for help, none would come.

Soon, to her surprise, with the twist of a large brass doorknob, the last door opened to the outside world. The scent of fresh rain filled her nostrils as she rushed to the cars, ecstatic. No one would hear her footfalls now.

With one hand on the car door, she rounded to flip a middle finger toward the castle. "Take that, you stupid bitch! Who's trapped now!" Another obscene gesture. "I'm telling everyone what you've done. You'll be in prison forever, you psycho!"

Jess flung the door open and slid into the seat to search for the keys, only to be disappointed. They were gone. She tried the other car, as well, but met the same results. She cursed. With a quick hop, she was on her feet, running toward the road. Within fifty yards, a slow dawning came to her frantic mind. Something was following. *Should I look back*, she wondered.

Using all her willpower, she pressed forward, her thick legs striding with speed one would not expect from an unathletic person. But building fear evidenced itself in the form of a tremendous motivator.

Just then, a grotesque bolted from the woods to tangle itself in the girl's legs, biting at her ankles. Jess screamed and tripped, her face crushing hard against the graveled driveway. Her broken nose erupted with crimson spray. Small rocks cut and tore at her flesh. With a grunt, and as tears blurred her vision, she spit blood from her mouth. Two teeth followed, as she spit again.

Her hands clawed the gravel, one knee propping underneath as she struggled to a half-seated position. She looked up.

A shriek tore from her throat as the man-troll, Cractow, closed down on her. More followed. Her pleas and screams were cut short as the creatures swarmed, their hard, stony fists falling in repeated frenzy, reducing her body to a pile of bloody clothing and a crimson stain on the drive. Even her bones were flattened to tiny fragments after the thrashing.

Cractow snatched up the stained clothing and lumbered toward the castle.

Destiny bound down the stairs and moved toward the great wooden doors of the east wing. Horrific shouts and shrieks rose from behind, filling the hall with a pleasing sound—revenge. Her plan was working perfectly.

Wild yelps drew nearer as the sound of running met her ears. Destiny whirled to see Tim following in a rattled state. He was disheveled, sweaty, and looked quite insane.

Another gargoyle, Vabex, was close behind. Destiny swore she could see a smile on the stone face, the creature was enjoying her game. She could have easily finished it—quick flaps of her wings would have brought her within reach of Tim—yet she chased him farther on.

Tim dashed in Destiny's direction. Ten feet away, he dropped to his knees.

"Please," he begged, his hands clasped in the Christian prayer position, "I'll do anything you say. Just don't let that thing kill me." He glanced over his shoulder as Vabex suddenly towered over him. Bending forward, the creature's face came within inches of his head. Her breath stirred his mused hair. Tim soiled himself as tears rolled down his cheeks.

Destiny raised a hand. Vabex straightened and paused, stone eyes fixed on her victim, as the girl considered what should be done. There was no question he should die, but how?

Extending her hands wide, the goth girl brought them together with speed to clap once. Tim, thinking he had been granted reprieve, sprang to his feet in joy. But he was unaware the gargoyle had parroted the girl's actions, spreading her clawed limbs before snapping them shut.

The young man's head exploded like a balloon pierced by a sharp needle. His body fell with a thud as blood spilled from the headless corpse.

Vabex displayed a thin smile. "He was the last. It is done."

Destiny stepped forward to hug her friend. "Thank you," she whispered. "I must find Sammy now." Rounding back toward the wing, the girl ran on, calling her friend's name as she went. "Sammy, you are safe. You have my word. Come out. It's over."

Terrible disappointment welled in her stomach, thinking Sammy had escaped somehow. What would this mean for her? They had been friends for a long time, but Destiny could not ignore the burning desire to keep her friend Sammy closer anymore. Though, if the girl told of this evening's events, things could turn out poorly.

Ready to concede defeat and return to the main hall, Destiny halted when a voice came from a shadowed corner to her left.

"I...I...I don't want to die," stammered Sammy.

Destiny ran to her. "Why are you here? You do not belong with these fools."

She opened both arms to embrace her. Sammy flinched, then slowly stepped forward to bury her face in Destiny's shoulder, arms wrapping around her waist. Her eyes went to the headless body. She shuddered, then stepped back. "I know. I just wanted to fit in somewhere and thought maybe they would like me better if I hung out with them."

Destiny kissed her cheek tenderly. "You do belong somewhere." She pointed at the floor beside her. "Right here. I've waited for you to realize how much I want to be with you. I should have told you long ago. I'm sorry you had to find out this way."

Sammy kissed Destiny's lips. "It was my fault, too. I feel the same, but didn't know how to tell you. I'm ready now." She squeezed Destiny's hand after another lingering look at the corpse. "I'm so glad he's gone." Her face soured. "I never knew he did that to you. I'm so sorry."

Destiny scowled. "He got what he deserved. No more forcing himself on women or grabbing them from the shadows." She jerked her chin toward the headless body. "It all worked out in the end."

Moments passed before the pair entered the main hall. The creatures awaited their arrival.

Vuzarin tossed two objects onto the floor. They rolled like misshapen dice, until coming to rest at the girls' feet. One was Hailey's head, her mouth still agape in an unfinished scream. Both eyes were wide open, staring upward. Tim's cranium lay next to it, tipped oddly since a good piece of the skull was absent. Nonetheless, there it was.

Cractow dropped the pile of blood-soaked clothing next to the heads. "This is the one who tried to escape. We caught her and pounded her like the flesh-thing she was."

"Your wishes have been fulfilled, Mistress," announced Traxium, with a bow.

Destiny returned the gesture, then hugged each in turn, with Vuzarin last.

"Splendid work, my loyal, remarkable friends. I ask for no more than your continued alliances. You will remain in my life until I no longer draw breath." She glanced to a window. The sky was paling again. "Please return to your perches with my thanks. We shall be together soon, for I will not allow you to sit idly as time passes around you."

After bowing in unison, the creatures flung wide the doors to hurry away into the grey morning. The sound of grating stone returned as the shapes settled onto their resting spots.

"The campus will be a much better place now," said Sammy as they descended the front steps and started down the drive. "And it sure takes a load off of my schedule."

Destiny laughed. "Perfect. Now maybe you can spend more time with me."

Sammy leaned into her. "Great minds must think alike." She stopped in her tracks as if struck by a discovered error. "What about their cars?"

Destiny puffed air through her pursed lips. "It's the weekend. No one will even know they're missing until Monday at the earliest. We'll return tomorrow." She pointed to the statues. "Our friends can help us get rid of any evidence."

They kissed again. Hand in hand they walked away. Their eyes went to the gargoyles and grotesques. The girls smiled and waved, then headed for Destiny's car, hidden in the rear alcove. She parked there knowing it would come in handy. It was all part of her plan. The perfect plan.

Remember You Must Die

Mike Sherer

Baozhai parked her car before the most magnificent doors she had ever seen. She carried the case containing her art supplies up to the porch for a closer look. It was a dark night, with heavy rolling clouds blocking any celestial light. The pair of flickering torches on either side of the entrance did not provide much illumination. Yet the writhing shadows that seemed to dance across the metal drew her eyes like a magnet. The entryway was a replica of Rodin's 'Gates of Hell'. In 1880, the artist had received a commission for a set of portals for a new Museum of Decorative Arts in Paris. It was to be a bas-relief representing Dante's 'The Divine Comedy'. She had seen the bronze cast of this at the entrance to the Rodin Museum in Philadelphia.

These doors seemed just as amazing. Depicted upon their entirety were one hundred and eighty naked human forms, wriggling in anguish and unfulfilled desire as they futilely attempted to free themselves from a swirling morass. Being a student of art history, Baozhai recognized many of the agonized characters from 'The Devine Comedy' posturing upon this torturous surface. The Three Shades stood above the doors pointing down to the suffering below. Directly under them sat Rodin's 'The Thinker' pondering the misery at his feet. There was Count Ugolino and his sons, who endured starvation locked up in a tower until the boys died, at which time Ugolino ate their flesh. The tragic lovers, Paolo and Francesca, were depicted. Even Rodin himself, at the bottom, amid the most frenzied contortions of suffering ever portrayed.

Baozhai was so intent upon her inspection of the doors that she jumped back at their opening. Before her stood a towering skeleton. The foul bones were draped with rotted flesh. A black spider of considerable heft emerged from an eye socket. Her right hand covered her nose and mouth as the stench threatened to deprive her of consciousness. She nearly shrieked when it stretched out its bony right hand toward her. It grasped her case instead, which she released without protest. It carried the case back into the house, leaving the doors open.

Baozhai recovered her nerve enough to lean inside the doorway and peer about. The skeleton had disappeared into the gloom of the cavernous interior, lit by only a few scant candles. *What had she gotten herself into? The thing had seized all her creative tools. She couldn't abandon them.*

She stepped across the threshold. "Hello?"

"Greetings, Miss Chao."

The weak, raspy voice echoed from the grand staircase sweeping in a great arc down from the second floor. A candle flickered weakly as it descended, floating unaided through the air.

Baozhai was rooted to the cracked tiles just inside the door. It was as if she had lost control of her body. She was only able to move a hand up to one of the open doors to steady herself. Until she realized it was resting upon a perverted tangle of twisting naked forms attempting to snake their way up out of the abyss. It was almost like they had taken hold of her hand and were trying to pull her down into the Pit with them. She jerked back, which sent her stumbling inside.

Regaining her balance, she glanced fearfully up. The candle had reached the bottom step. At this distance, the outline of the body holding it could be discerned in the murk. As it continued toward her, she could make out an extremely old man clad in a shabby suit of approximately the same age as its wearer. She steeled herself to confront who she assumed to be her employer. "What was that? At the door?"

The pale centenarian lowered the candle as he shuffled up to her. "My butler, Lars."

"Your butler? It looked like a skeleton."

"A good costume, eh? Not one you'd find at Spirit of Halloween."

"What did he do with my supplies?"

"Took them into the room where you'll be working." The old man extended a gnarled bony hand.

Drawing a deep breath, she took it. The twisted loose flesh was cool, dry, papery.

Yet the grip was firm. He escorted her through the shadows. "We've gone to great pains to set the mood."

Baozhai jerked to a halt, emitting a squeal. She swiped at the spider web she had been led into.

The old man responded with a cackle that sounded like a death rattle. "Perhaps we have gone too far. Lars!"

A chandelier as grand as the one in the Paris Opera put to such deadly use by Erik blazed on to light up the entire room. As Baozhai's pupils adjusted, she could see most of the furnishings were covered in once-white sheets. The few tables and chairs left uncovered were draped in cobwebs and coated in dust and grime. One grand Victorian chair was ruined with splotches of mold. She began to cough.

"Allergic to mold?" Mister Pestis swiped a finger across the seat and held it up to her face for inspection. The tip was discolored with grey and green. "It's not real. Pastel chalk." He swiped the side of his face with the same hand, leaving a dark streak across his convoluted ashen skin. "This, I am afraid, is not a product of Lars's craft. I am as old as I appear to be."

He led her into a small reading room, where her easel and canvas were set up. The case containing her painting supplies had been set on a table next to the easel. "Will this do, Miss Chao?"

The cozy room was well-lit, which wasn't necessarily a good thing. She saw a human skull, topped with a lit candle dripping red wax down across the pale bare bone. Also, a dark oil painting, a still life, hanging on the wall. But what seized her attention and held it in a vise, was the cadaver in the corner.

"Ahh, I see you have found my prize possession." He walked over to it. Even though he had released her hand by this point, she was irresistibly drawn to the body in his wake. Lying face-up upon a cement slab was a stone rendering of a badly decomposed corpse. Most of its rib cage, pelvic structure, and sharp bones of its legs and arms, protruded through thin rotten skin. Squirming upon it and wriggling up out of it were numerous recreations of fat well-fed worms. "'L'homme aux moulons'. In English, 'Man Eaten By Worms'. A sixteenth century cadaver monument." Mister Pestis ran light fingers across it. "A reproduction, of course. The original is in Boussu, Belgium."

Baozhai retreated.

Relishing her reaction, he croaked on. "You might wonder why I delight in such a morbid artistic creation. Momento mori. Remember you must die. A cadaver monument like this is a stark reminder of what awaits us all. In the hurly burly of life, it is easy to forget our ultimate fate. At my age, though, I've come to dwell upon the topic. Today that is considered an unhealthy practice, but the stoics, and many others throughout the centuries, thought it normal, in fact imperative, that we contemplate our demise."

Baozhai found a less disturbing subject to focus her attention upon. The still-life on the wall depicted an assortment of odd items haphazardly arranged upon a table, such as world globes, books, assorted manuscripts, musical instruments, a watch, and other small trinkets and baubles.

Mister Pestis joined her before it. "'Vanitas Still Life, 1662', by Edwaert Collier. It depicts real-world luxuries of 17th century European elites. This painting is meant to remind us how devoid of value what we strive to accumulate all our lives really is." He turned from assessing the painting to assess her. "What shabby shit to place such importance upon."

Baozhai retreated to her blank canvas. "We should get started." She was surprised to find a tray with a decanter of wine and two glasses sitting on the table next to the skull and candle. It hadn't been there before. She gazed about. They were alone.

"Lars can be disquietingly quiet." The old man creaked over to the tray and poured a glass.

"I can't drink. I have to keep a clear head."

He poured the second glass despite her protestations. "Sometimes a cloudy head can produce better results. Like Samuel Coleridge, or Phillip K…"

"…Not while I'm painting," was her adamant reply.

The old man left a filled glass on the tray and carried the other with him to the daybed. He sat, leaned back, and stretched out his legs.

As she studied his pose, she noticed a dark stain on the back. *It could be wine. Although it would have taken quite a quantity to make a stain that big.*

"Shall we begin, Miss Chao?"

When Baozhai stepped back from the canvas, she was surprised the room was brightly lit from the just-risen sun coming through a low window. Not only were both wine glasses empty, but also the decanter. *Had she drunk wine last night after all?* It wasn't until she set her brush down that she felt her right hand cramping. She clasped both hands and flexed them backwards to stretch out her overtaxed fingers while evaluating the painting. The old man on the canvas didn't appear much different than the cadaver monument behind him. She saw she had painted an indistinct form mirrored in the dark, uncurtained window.

"I see you painted Lars looking in on us last night."

Startled, she jerked around to find Mister Pestis at her side.

"He seemed concerned we were working too hard."

"I must have fallen asleep on my feet. I've never done that before." She stumbled across the room.

Proving surprisingly quick and nimble, Mister Pestis caught her by the arm to steady her. He guided her to the daybed he had posed on and settled her safely onto it.

Baozhai squinted at the dazzling dawn light flooding the room. "What happened last night?"

"You painted a masterpiece."

She stared at the completed canvas. There was no denying it was finished, and that Mister Pestis was pleased with it. "I worked through the night?"

"You were in a creative zone. I didn't want to disturb that." He motioned to a tray with a coffee service, fruit, rolls and Danish that had been brought in. "Would you like some breakfast?"

Baozhai looked around. The tray with the empty wine glasses and decanter was absent. Apparently, Lars had once again entered and left unnoticed. He was elusive for such a big man. "No." She dug knuckles deep into her eyes. She couldn't seem to come to her senses. As her blurry vision cleared, she saw that in the bright light of the low sun blazing through the window, the articles that had so disturbed her in the nighttime looked innocuous in daylight. The candle on the skull had melted down to a nub, the dried wax that had run down over the skull giving it a comical appearance. The still-life on the wall seemed dull and pedestrian. Even the cadaver monument seemed nothing more than a Halloween display.

"You are welcome to stay here, Miss Chao. If you are too weary to drive home. There are many unused bedrooms."

"No, thank you." She stood and began gathering up her supplies. "I need to go home."

"Won't you have some coffee? I fear for you driving in such an exhausted state. The lane through the woods is narrow and twisting. It can be treacherous at the best of times."

"Thank you." She doubled her efforts to pack away her things. "I can manage."

He sighed. "If you must." He led her out of the room. The hall she had walked through upon arriving the night before did not appear ominous any longer, merely untidy. "The fee we agreed upon has been deposited into your Pay Pal account." He chuckled. "Despite appearances, we do live in the twenty-first century here. Lars is capable of conducting online transactions."

As if summoned, Lars appeared. He had shed the skeleton costume and was dressed in normal casual clothes, yet he still appeared to be of formidable height. She hadn't imagined that. He opened the front door for her.

Baozhai looked over the doors. The many horrid images were gone. Nothing but ordinary wood panels. "What happened to your doors?"

Mister Pestis joined her at the entryway to see what she was referring to. "What about them?"

"They were different last night. Covered in horrible figures. A recreation of 'The Gates of Hell'."

The old man looked from both doors, to Lars, to Baozhai. "I appreciate Rodin's masterpiece, but these doors are only doors. They've been here for as long as I've owned the house."

Baozhai turned her attention to the pair of torches that had been lit. In the bright morning, she could see they were not actual torches, merely electric lights designed to resemble open flames.

Baozhai hurried on out to her car. Tossing her case and collapsed easel into the back, she lunged in behind the wheel. The young woman couldn't get out of there fast enough. She looked back to the house. The doors were shut, the old man and his servant had gone back inside. The large disintegrating two-story manse appeared much less sinister in the daytime. It was merely a run-down collapsing hovel. She started her car and drove away. Digging out her phone, she checked her bank account. The payment they had agreed upon had been deposited.

Rounding a bend, the huge low early morning sun shone through the bare branches to dazzle her. In this blinding light, she saw a tortured figure like those in the doors last night, reaching out for her from the trunk of a tree on the side of the gravel drive. She screamed as both ghastly arms smashed through the windshield to embrace her. The last thing she remembered was the ghostly form pulling her to its bosom.

She kicked at whatever had trapped her legs. She twisted all about as she tried to free her arms.

"Miss Chao."

She calmed a bit at the familiar voice of Mister Pestis. Calm enough for her to realize her legs were tangled up in a sheet. She focused on Lars looming over her. He was holding her down by the arms. "Let me go!"

"You will hurt yourself."

She looked to see the old man seated beside her.

"Settle down. Lars will release you as soon as you are calm."

With an effort, Baozhai calmed and looked herself over. A wadded sheet lay discarded at her side. She was in just her underwear. Accusing eyes shot from Lars to Mister Pestis. "Why did you take my clothes off?"

The old man nodded at Lars, and he released her.

She snatched the sheet back over her.

Mister Pestis helped her tug it into place. "There was a lot of blood. We had to see how badly you were injured."

Only at that point did Baozhai register the pain. "What happened?"

"You wrecked."

She closed her eyes to remember. Driving down the lane. Checking her bank account on her phone. The sudden sharp bend. The blinding sun in her eyes. The monster in the tree reaching for her.

"You ran off the road and hit a tree. You must have been driving too fast. You tore out of here when you left. I warned you that lane was treacherous, and you seemed to be half-asleep. You shouldn't have been driving."

Baozhai touched the bandage on her head. She lifted the sheet to find a heavy bandage on her left side, and a smaller one on her right thigh. "Did you call nine-one-one?"

"No. I did not know what kind of medical insurance you have. An unnecessary trip to the emergency room..."

"Unnecessary?"

"...can be quite expensive," the old man doggedly continued. "Lars is a qualified EMP. He has taken good care of me through several harrowing episodes. He assessed your condition was not life-threatening."

"Where are my clothes?"

"We threw them away." Seeing the fury mount on her face, the old man hurried on. "They were bloody rags." Seeing the fury wasn't abating, he continued. "There are plenty of clothes here for you to wear."

Baozhai took a deep calming breath. "How bad is my car?"

"Pretty bad. You were going too fast. If you'd had your seat belt on and hadn't been texting..."

"I wasn't texting." Seeing the doubt on the old man's face, she qualified. "I was checking my bank account. I wasn't texting." She paused a moment. "How did you know what I was doing?"

Mister Pestis smiled. "As I said before, we do live in the twenty-first century here. There are security cameras in the trees along the lane. So we can keep track of who comes and goes. Would you like to see?"

Taking her silence as assent, he motioned to Lars. He turned on a screen. A black and white video began playing. From above, Baozhai's car could be seen approaching a sharp curve. The footage was paused, the frozen image zoomed in on. Baozhai, without seatbelt, was looking down at the phone in her hands as she drove. "Whatever you were doing with your phone, you shouldn't have been doing it while driving." The video zoomed back out and resumed. Her car ran off the lane and crashed into a tree. Without any ghostly arms reaching out of a tree trunk for her. The video was paused once again.

"Where is my phone?"

"Somewhere in the woods, I presume. We couldn't find it. It must have been thrown from the car."

"Find me something to put on and I'll leave."

"You really shouldn't, Miss Chao."

"The hell with you." She threw the sheet aside. "I'll go home like this." She started to sit up, grimaced, then collapsed back down.

"You are in no condition to walk, let alone drive." Mister Pestis drew the sheet back over her. "Here's what I propose. Stay here until you are recovered enough. While you're here we'll get your car repaired."

Baozhai glared up at him. "Why would you do that? You are not responsible for what happened. You urged me not to drive, I didn't have my seat belt on, and I was fooling with my phone when I wrecked."

"But I feel responsible." He smiled in a way meant to reassure, but it failed miserably. "Now let me finish my proposal. While you are healing I would like you to do some more paintings for me. I am impressed with your skill. The one you did last night is very good. I want more like it. I will pay you for each the same sum as we agreed upon for the first one and cover the repairs of your car as a bonus."

She considered the offer. Briefly. "I need to see a doctor."

"Lars examined you. He is not a doctor, but as I said he is a qualified EMP. Despite the pain, your injuries aren't life-threatening. I searched your wallet for personal information in case we needed to take you to the emergency room. I didn't find a medical card. Do you even have medical insurance?" Interpreting her silence as a no, he continued. "Going to the emergency room would cost you a lot of money. As would the increase in your premium if the auto insurance company became aware you wrecked while texting."

"Is that blackmail?"

"Of course, not. The security video will be written over, like always. I'm merely trying to make clear to you why we took the actions we did. It was for your benefit."

Baozhai released a long exasperated breath out between tight-pressed lips. "What have you got for me to wear?"

Baozhai sat wrapped up in the sheet, in a chair, in another dusty, dank room. Lars stood unobtrusively behind her. In front of her stood Mister Pestis before the open doors of a large ornate antique wardrobe filled with evening gowns. "I apologize for the selection. You will not find any modern clothes here. No women have lived here for decades."

"I don't care. Anything that will cover me."

He pulled out a floor-length evening dress in a protective plastic bag. "This one is enchanting, and it is clean. All of these clothes have been well taken care of."

Baozhai shrugged.

He spread it out on the bed. "This will be your room. It is on the first floor so you won't have to deal with steps. Is it acceptable?"

"Is there a lock on the door?"

"Yes."

"Which you most likely have a key to?"

"There is a deadbolt you can turn that doesn't have a key."

Baozhai looked all around. The bedroom was spacious. Nearly all the furnishings were covered with sheets. The heavy carpet was surprisingly clean. The wallpaper, although of ancient design - *Victorian, Edwardian, Neolithic?* - appeared intact. A large brilliant dust-free electric chandelier hung from the pristine ceiling. "In a house like this there is probably a secret passage."

Mister Pestis smiled as if she were joking. He motioned to the bed. "Lars has changed the linen. It is very comfortable." He walked to the door. "Rest. After dinner tonight, if you are up to it, we can begin on the next painting."

That night, Baozhai was escorted by Lars down a well-lit hall. She was wearing the selected evening gown, a black 1930s style elegant mermaid sleeveless dress. The material clung to her upper body and hips like a second skin, flowing loosely down her legs to the floor. Other than that, it was not revealing at all. The front covered her to the neck, while the back was open only mid-way down. Lars walked at her side dressed in an old-fashioned suit with his arm offered for support. Baozhai leaned on it as she shuffled slowly at his side.

Reaching the end of the hall, Lars opened the double doors. Before her was a brightly lit ballroom filled with people all attired as she and Lars were in formal gowns and evening suits of vintage styles. Although the people embraced one another, none of them danced. A small orchestra was at the front of the room.

Mister Pestis emerged from amid the crowd of immobile dancers. He, like Lars, was dressed in ancient formal wear. "You look wonderful, Miss Chao." He stopped before her. "Are you feeling up to this?"

"I'm not up to dancing."

"No, no, this is only to stage the background for your painting tonight. No one here is actually dancing."

Upon closer inspection, she saw all the attendees were well-dressed manikins topped with skulls, with bony hands extending from the sleeves on the men and bony arms from the sleeveless gowns on the women. Each wore a mask, some small and covering only the eye sockets, others large and ornate of fantastical designs covering the entire death's head.

"Do you know the tune?"

Baozhai attempted to focus on the music. "It's familiar."

"'Danse Macabre', by Saint-Saens." He took her arm from Lars and led her into the ballroom. They threaded their way through the well-dressed skeletons posed to dance. "Your easel is set up in front, but I want you to see this first." He led her to a drawing in stark, black, pencil hanging on the wall. " 'The Dance of Death (1493)', by Michael Wolgemut." On the canvas five dead bodies cavorted. Two were skeletons with a few wisps of hair still attached to their bare skullcaps. An upright half-rotted body clad in shreds of cloth, with its intestines trailing out and a full head of long hair, twirled one of the two dancing skeletons by its bony fingers. A fully-clothed body with only its fleshless skull uncovered played an instrument providing the music the others were dancing to. A fifth body was on the ground emerging from underneath a death shroud, with worms falling off its badly-decomposed form.

"The Danse Macabre consists of the dead summoning representatives from all walks of life to dance along to the grave. This was typically a pope, or emperor, or king, dancing with commoners, such as a child or a laborer. It was produced as memento mori, to remind people of the fragility of their lives and how vain are the glories of their brief time on earth. It was enacted at court masques. Like this." He swept his arm wide, indicating the entire ballroom. "The Danse Macabre may have been the origin of dressing up in costumes for Halloween. The practice began during the Black Plague. The cultural impact of mass outbreaks of the disease were not fleeting. The effects endured long past the initial outbreak in its deep etching upon culture and society. Think how the effects of Covid still influences life today."

Mister Pestis led Baozhai to her easel. "The deathly horrors of the 14th century such as recurring famines, the Hundred Years' War, and most of all the Black Death, were culturally assimilated throughout Europe. The omnipresent possibility of sudden and painful death evoked a hysterical desire for amusement while still possible."

Something brushed Baozhai's shoulder as she passed between dancers. Out of the corner of her eye she caught a couple spinning about, but when she focused on them, they were motionless. Yet there was a mocking leer on their bony visages as they both stared directly at her.

Mister Pestis eased Baozhai down into a chair before a blank canvas. "I don't expect you to stand while you work, and if you get too tired to continue, we can finish this another night."

"I feel okay. I slept all day, and the Tylenol you gave me helped."

He smiled. "Tylenol. Yes."

She saw her pencils, brushes, and oils had been set up on a table next to her easel.

Mister Pestis struck his pose by embracing a lone skeletal form clad in a luxurious ballroom gown.

"No mask for you?" Baozhai asked as she prepared her palette.

"No. I am not hiding from death, as the masked participants were at a Danse Macabre." He pulled his partner closer. "I am embracing death."

Baozhai went to work painting the ballroom scene, with Mister Pestis and his partner in the foreground. Throughout the long night, the music continued. As the orchestra obviously wasn't performing, she assumed she was hearing recorded music. Mister Pestis kept her informed of what was being played—Bach's 'Toccata & Fugue' on organ, Gounod's 'Funeral March of a Marionette', Mussorgsky's 'Night on Bald Mountain', Chopin's 'Funeral March', Schubert's 'Death of a Maiden', Berlioz's 'March to the Scaffold,' and 'Dream of a Witches' Sabbath', both from Symphonie Fantastique, Grieg's 'In the Hall of the Mountain King', List's 'Mephisto Waltz', and Dukas' 'The Sorcerer's Apprentice'.

Upon regaining her senses, Baozhai saw morning light streaming in through the tall windows. She looked to the canvas. The painting appeared completed. She looked around in a daze. Mister Pestis whirled up to her, still dancing with his inanimate partner. He bent around the canvas to see. "Incredible. It looks like they are really dancing."

"There are techniques to convey movement."

His partner brushed her bare shoulder with its bony fingers.

Startled, and still only half-conscious, she jerked away from the couple. Into Lars' arms. She looked up to see him looming above her.

"Lars has been watching over you all night. In case this endeavor became too much for you."

Baozhai smiled her appreciation up at the towering stoic form as she righted herself. She looked back to the half-alive couple. "*You* must be exhausted."

"Just the opposite." He spun away with his partner, whose feet actually seemed to move on their own. "Seeing how fantastically exquisite your painting is, I am invigorated anew." The two bodies twirled around the other stationary couples. As they came around one couple, Baozhai could see his partners' rectal grin had widened.

That evening Baozhai rose from her bed feeling refreshed. She found herself clad in an opaque white cotton sleep dress with lace trim that reached to mid-calf, very comfortable and conservative. A different evening gown was laid out for her. *So the old man was now selecting her clothes for her.* She walked over to pull back the curtain and look outside. The sun was setting. She had once again slept the day away. She saw also laid out for her were several more Tylenols. *They must be maximum-strength. She felt fine.*

Baozhai limped over to a free-standing mirror to inspect the bandage on her head. It was smaller. *Lars had changed it? She didn't remember him doing that.* She probed it with a light touch. *Not too much pain.* She pressed on the other bandages. *They felt smaller, also. Lars had changed them, too?* She pulled off the nightdress and stood naked before the mirror. *He* had *changed them. Lars must have removed her clothes to do that.* Surprisingly, she didn't feel violated. *He was a doctor. Or at least an EMP. She had been examined by male doctors before. He must have put the nightdress on her after treating her injuries and then tucked her in bed, since she didn't remember doing any of that.* She moved about, testing her mobility. *Still a bit of a limp, but better.*

This was actually working out for her. She was healing. Earning more money from her artwork than ever before. And the paintings! She had never painted so well. Or so fast. Last night was all a blur. She closed her eyes to remember. *The eerie music, Mister Pestis dancing around with his skeleton partner, all the other dancers waltzing throughout the night. She knew that hadn't really happened. She had envisioned it, so she could impart their movements in oil on the canvas. It had been a long magical night, which she had masterfully captured. She must have been exhausted from the sustained intense effort, and had fallen into such a deep sleep at the end of it that she couldn't remember Lars changing her bandages and tucking her into bed.*

In the following days, Baozhai fell into a comfortable routine. The pain grew to be negligible and she soon regained full mobility. She continued to sleep the days away and remain active throughout the night, as that was the routine of the household. She painted all night long, retaining scant memory of her brush-strokes, but the paintings continued to be vivid and fascinating, if horrific. Each evening after a hearty meal cooked by Lars, as the sun set, Boazhai faced a new blank canvas. All of her art supplies were replenished during the day while she slept. Lars was proving to be a man of many talents.

One evening Lars led Baozhai outside into the woods on the property. He illuminated the narrow twisting path they followed with a lantern held high. As on every night, she was wearing what had been laid out for her. This night it was a black, form-fitting evening dress, low-cut in front, and so low in back that folds lay bunched loosely upon the top of her hips, while the skirt, which reached mid-calf, was slit all the way up one leg. She was walking better than before, with only one hand in her companion's hand. "My injuries seem to be healing nicely. Thank you for taking care of them."

Lars nodded.

"I hope it's not discomfiting you."

Lars shook his head.

"You don't talk much, do you?"

Lars shook his head.

"Where are you taking me?"

"To your next tableaux."

Emerging out from under the tangle of twisted arthritic tree limbs, they stepped into a small clearing, brightly-lit by a blazing full super moon in a starry night sky. Lars doused the lantern. A ring of mushrooms sparkled in the spectral light. She stepped up to the edge of the small meadow where a canvas was set up on an easel beside a folding table upon which her pencils, brushes and paints were arrayed.

A faint light shined within the fungus circle. It seemed to come from two sources. One was fairy lanterns, plants standing three feet high with clusters of a half-dozen or so long lantern-shaped blooms glowing orange beneath green leaves. The other source were actual lanterns, fashioned of twisted vines containing a softly glowing orb within each. Music floated out from the trees surrounding the meadow. "What is that?" Baozhai asked Lars.

"The scherzo from Mendelssohn's 'A Midsummer Night's Dream'."

Across the meadow, a troupe of small faeries danced out of the trees across the open meadow into the ring of mushrooms. Their hazy appearance made Baozhai assume they were a projection of some sort, perhaps a hologram. She began sketching the magical scene.

Before she got far, the music changed. It grew slower, darker, more somber, with a pipe organ the dominant instrument. She glanced questioningly at Lars.

"Mendelssohn again. 'The Wedding March'."

"Doesn't sound like any wedding I've been to."

"This is a dark epic version of it."

The faeries flickered away. In their place a solemn procession of thirteen nude women of all ages, from teen to tottering, made its way into the faerie ring. The coven was followed by a goat-like incarnation of Mister Pestis. With horns and a tail, the winged hairy demonic figure followed the beauties into the meadow on cloven hooves. Appearing more spry than she had ever seen him, the old man danced with one after another of the witches.

"Walpurgis Night," Lars provided without being asked. "A spring celebration."

Mister Pestis seemed tireless. He danced through the night as Baozhai labored to catch the Witches Sabbath in oil.

In the deepest darkest hour of the night, a transformation took place. Mister Pestis jettisoned his devilish accouterments. The horns came off, the tail discarded, the hooves kicked from his feet, nearly all of the hair shed. With only a pelt remaining about his loins, he stretched out on the ground in the middle of the faerie ring. The thirteen witches danced around him.

When a distant bell peeled, they fell upon him with tooth and nail. The old man shrieked as blood and torn flesh flew through the air. The screams subsided to moans, then to silence. The thirteen women lifted his limp lifeless body from the ground and carried it out of the mushroom circle, out of the meadow, and into the trees.

Baozhai looked back in concern. "Is he okay?"

"Yes." Lars stood immediately behind her. "Finish. Before you lose the night."

She went back to work.

Baozhai was putting the finishing strokes on the canvas just as the sky brightened in the east.

"Yes, that's it."

Baozhai spun around to find Mister Pestis standing behind her. He was fully dressed, and appeared unharmed and unwearied.

"Another nightmarish masterpiece."

"Are you okay? I saw you get ripped to shreds."

"A good performance."

"You mean that wasn't real?"

"The faeries weren't. The witches were." He turned toward the meadow. "Come out and take a bow."

The thirteen women, fully clothed and free of gore, filed into the ring of mushrooms to do as bidden. They then dispersed into the trees and out of sight.

On another night Baozhai, wearing a full-length black dress open in back from her ankles to the top of her thighs, and with a scooped bodice so low it hardly concealed anything, was led by Lars into a small chapel deep in the sprawling house. Mister Pestis, in only a torn and filthy loin cloth, was chained face-up upon a blood-stained altar. Towering above the altar was an inverted cross. Gathered around were cloaked hooded figures. Next to the altar stood a manikin designed with Baozhai's face and dimensions. This likeness of Baozhai was clad in narrow straps of black leather, concealing little of her form. On her face was a malicious grin. She held a wicked dagger high in the air, poised to plunge down into the old man's chest. He smiled up in anticipation, eager to receive the blade into his heart.

Baozhai looked back at Lars. "You reproduced my body well. You've been assessing more than just my injuries whenever you treated them." Merely a statement of fact. She did not seem upset with the notion. She picked up a sketching pencil and went to work.

On another night, Lars and Baozhai, clad in a flimsy white shift with a plunging neckline and a skirt that just covered her hips, descended into the basement. They came to a dark dank cell. Mister Pestis, clad in shredded rags, was chained to the stone wall. His flesh was scored with whip marks, cuts, bruises, burns. Nearly all his hair had been yanked out or burned from his body. All ten broken, bloody, nail-less fingers had been bent into improbable positions, while half his toes were missing.

Sconces flickered on either side of him, producing dense oily smoke. Filling the cell were the well-used instruments of his torture, all caked in blood. An array of blades. A hand axe. A pruning shear. A brazier with several metal tongs whose tips glowed red hot. An assortment of whips hung on the wall. An elaborate rack. An open iron maiden with its many spikes dripping blood. In the midst of all this was a towering manikin of a bare-chested man with a black executioner's hood completely concealing his face.

"The torturer looks like you."

Lars shrugged.

Baozhai began sketching out the scene. "Good job with the make-up. Those scars look real. Did you do them?"

"Yes. All of them. The ones that are cosmetic and the ones that aren't." When her mouth gaped open, he continued. "Mister Pestis strives for realism."

On another night, Baozhai stood before the full-length mirror in her bedroom with a red whalebone corset, trimmed in black hanging loose on her, and matching red panties. She held the front of the stiff garment in place while Lars laced up the back. "Deep breath."

"It's already deep," she gasped.

He pulled harder.

"My God," she squeaked. "How did women wear these?"

"They suffered for their beauty." Lars inexorably drew the corset together in back as he worked his way up the many laces. "Don't waste your breath talking."

At last, he knotted the topmost laces. "Let me see."

Baozhai turned. Her stomach had disappeared, and her nearly-bare breasts were forced up to jut out horizontally.

"I've been very compliant with your wardrobe choices…" She ran out of breath before she could complete her complaint.

"Not my choices."

"I feel like I'm going to pass out."

"Many women did."

"What's next? Me painting while naked?" She looked over her shoulder to assess the reflection of her back side. "Why does Mister Pestis want me dressing like this."

"It inspires him. He is not ignoring you all the long night while you work at your canvas. He enjoys your beauty." He extended his arm.

She took it. "Be ready to catch me if my knees buckle."

Lars led her outside. It was a dark, starless night. A brisk, warm wind buffeted the heavy clouds about. A flash of lightning in the distance. He led her into the trees and down a path illuminated by candles. After a short trek, the trees began to thin. They came upon a cast-iron fence. Peering between the tilted rusting staves, she saw it enclosed a small graveyard. The tombstones looked ancient, much of the inscriptions worn off. Coming to a gate, they entered.

A huge pit gaped open before them. Supported by Lars, she leaned over to peer in. It was piled full of naked bodies in various stages of rot. White powder, most likely lime, had been shoveled over them. Huge mice crawled about feasting. At the top of the heap lay Mister Pestis. He was as naked as the rest, only not yet decomposing. He smiled up at her in all his wrinkled hairless glory. "I hope you are not offended."

"Not at all. I've worked with nude models before." She studied the scene. "Are those rats real?"

"Yes, they are."

"Won't they bite you?"

"Not me. I've doused myself with a rat repellant."

"I hope those aren't real corpses you've dug up from somewhere."

"I assure you they are not. Merely manikins. With meat tucked away amid them, to keep the rats interested." He peered out of the ground in another direction. "We'd best get started. A storm is brewing."

Baozhai stepped up to her easel positioned at the edge of the pit. Only then did she notice the figure posed on the far side. A manikin covered to his feet with a heavy dark cloak and wearing a plague mask. It concealed the entire face, with two open holes spanned by glass for the eyes, while below them was a half-foot long nose hooked like a beak.

"I've seen that mask in paintings," Baozhai said.

Mister Pestis called up from the pit. "Medico della peste. Plague doctors wore them to treat victims of the Black Death. The beak identified him as a doctor while preventing him from coming into contact with the sickness. It was filled with a perfume to help him endure the stench of the putrid bodies he attended to."

She surveyed the gruesome scene. "This is the most horrendous pose yet."

"I have faith you will capture it. Pit graves like these were common throughout Europe during the Plague years. People died in such numbers, and there were so few healthy people to dig graves, that burials became haphazard and unceremonious. The bodies had to be put in the ground as quickly as possible in a futile attempt to limit the contagion. Mozart's burial in the final scene of that excellent movie 'Amadeus' was a good depiction."

Somber music began playing. Baozhai looked to see Lars had turned on a boombox. A slow mournful tune, accompanied by a plaintive Latin chorus.

"Mozart's 'Requiem Mass in D Minor'. One of the most anguished tunes ever composed. Listen to those strings. Don't they sound desolate? And the power of that chorus singing in Latin. I can't decide if I want this played at my funeral, or Beethoven's 'Mass in C'."

Baozhai went to work. "Isn't that what this is? A rehearsal for your funeral?"

"No. Mozart was buried in a pauper's grave. My corpse will fair better."

The storm threatened throughout the long night, yet dawn came without it breaking on them. As always, Baozhai could recall little of the night. In the early dawn light, she saw she had completed another masterpiece. She could practically see the fattened rats scurry across the canvas, could practically smell the stench that would have arisen from real bodies. Could they have been real? She wasn't about to descend into that ghastly open grave to see for herself.

Mister Pestis scrambled up out of the ground. Lars draped a sheet about him as he inspected the completed horror. "Wonderful, Miss Chao."

She noticed blood soaking into the sheet. "Were you bitten?"

He pulled the sheet open to inspect the various bites oozing blood. "The repellant wasn't very effective."

Baozhai was surprised upon awakening the following evening to find Mister Pestis seated at the side of her bed. This was a variation of the pattern they had established. "Why aren't you preparing for our night's painting?"

"There isn't to be one. We are finished."

Baozhai propped the pillows up behind her so she could lean back onto the headboard.

"You have produced six incredible depictions of my death. Six exquisite corpses, masterfully detailed. A powerful gallery of heroic endings for me to contemplate. I am quite pleased."

She produced an honest smile. "I'm happy to hear that."

"Lars is preparing a final feast for us. Dress and pack, then come down to dinner."

"Any particular outfit?"

"No. You have been very obliging to an old man's whims. Tonight, it is your choice."

Later, Baozhai entered the dining room in the first dress that had been chosen for her, the one she had worn on the night she painted the Danse Macabre. She saw all six of her paintings were on display around the table. She made a circuit of the room examining each. "Do you have a favorite?"

"No, they are all masterful." Mister Pestis, already seated at the table, said. "Do you?"

She lingered before the last painting she had done. "Yes. This."

"Does that mean you like seeing me naked? Or that you enjoy seeing my corpse nibbled on by rats?"

"Neither. It's because I was oxygen-deprived that evening. I think my condition imparted a hallucinogenic effect to the painting. Made it more fantastical than the others." She turned to smile at him. "I didn't know if I could finish it before passing out."

"Lars was watching over you, like always. He would have caught you. He wouldn't have let you fall into the pit on top of me and the rats and all the dead rotting bodies."

Her smile faded. "Those were manikins? Right?"

"Manikins. Of course."

Lars arrived with the first course. Baozhai sat next to Mister Pestis, and the final supper began.

Later that night, Mister Pestis led Baozhai out the front. She noted the doors appeared as they had that first night she had arrived. "The Gates of Hell are back."

He rapped one door with his knuckles. "Two molded metal panels that can be easily mounted and removed."

"Are you setting the mood again?"

"One last time. For your departure." He led her out onto the porch. Her repaired car was parked in the driveway. Lars was loading her belongings into the trunk.

Baozhai broke into her brightest face yet. "It looks brand new."

"I don't know about that, but it looks better than before you wrecked it."

She walked up to take a closer look. "I seem to have acquired more than I arrived with."

The old man followed her. "Lars packed up all the outfits you wore for our sessions. Souvenirs of our time together."

She laughed. "Thank you, but I am never putting that corset back on."

"You never know."

She opened the driver door. "It doesn't squeak." She swung it back and forth. "It used to squeak." She spied her phone on the dash. "You found it!"

"It was in the trees near where you wrecked. It must have been flung out of the car in the crash."

She snatched it up and turned it on.

"You must promise not to text while you are driving."

"I promise. At least until I get off your property."

"While it's on, check your bank account. You have been paid what we agreed upon."

"I trust you." She set the phone back down. "Besides, I know where you live."

"Yes, you do. I hope you'll come back and visit us sometime."

She smiled pleasantly, and noncommittally. "Thank you for everything." She pulled up the long skirt to expose the inside of the top of one thigh. "Hardly a scar." She released the bunched-up skirt and touched her side. "Anywhere."

"Lars took good care of you."

She turned to the big man, who had been standing silently beside the car, and hugged him. "Thank you, Lars." She turned to hug Mister Pestis. Without another word, she climbed in her car and drove away.

Lars stepped up alongside Mister Pestis to watch her go. "How long does she have?"

"It's hard to say. The Chinese have developed a high resistance to infection. So many of the world's deadliest pandemics originated in China. Covid 19 that killed over three million, the Flu Pandemic of 1968 that killed one million, the Asian Flu of 1956 that killed two million, the Flu Pandemic of 1889 that killed one million, the Plague of Justinian of 541 that killed twenty-five million. And, of course, the deadliest of them all. The Black Death, that killed two-hundred million. On top of that, several more of the worst that are thought to have originated in India could easily have come from across their common border with China."

Baozhai's taillights receded down the twisty lane.

"She made it past the site of her wreck," Lars noted.

"Yes," Mister Pestis chuckled. "No special effects tonight. No arms reaching out of a tree to grab her." He looked up to Lars. "Your technological skills are impressive."

"As will be your death."

"Yes. I wonder who will pass first? Me or Miss Chao?"

"Yours will be the celebrated death."

"With retainer sacrifices. Like in ancient Egypt. When a Pharaoh died, servants, court officials, wives and concubines were sacrificed at his funeral. In the time of ancient Ur mass human sacrifices were offered at the death of a king."

"Yours will be grander than any of them."

"That is because Yersinia Pestis thrives yet today. There are outbreaks of Plague around the world. The Black Death has not been eradicated, it is merely in hiding, biding its time. Especially within the bodies of the Chinese. Which was why I chose one to be my artist." It was the old man's turn to smile. "While you were treating her injuries, she never knew you were giving her additional doses of the bacteria she already harbored." His smile turned even more malicious. "Or that you inflicted the wounds she believed came from the wreck. Her actual injuries weren't that bad. You were careful not to damage her permanently, yet enough to prevent her from leaving."

"We had to keep her alive to die another day."

"To instigate the human sacrifices to honor my passing. My retainer sacrifices."

By this time the taillights had disappeared.

"Miss Chao has carried death out into the world." He turned to go back into the old house.

Lars followed him inside. "Your death will be honored like the Egyptian Pharaohs and Mesopotamian kings of old. With mass carnage."

The Gates of Hell closed on the pair.

Penance

Natasha Grodzinski

Then the Lord God said, "It is not good that man should be alone."
— Genesis 2:18

I think my favorite thing about this time are the bars.

I adore these dark, secret, places with music so loud you feel its beat at the base of your skull, flashing neon lights, and poorly lit bathrooms. Their chaos makes me feel giddy.

And there are boys. So many boys inside every single bar, all of them just waiting for their cue, a lingering glance, an accidental brush at their arm, a perfectly timed ass drop followed by a coquettish *ohmigosh did I do that?* over the shoulder.

I've learned that's all it takes before they swarm. Boys with their pink mouths open, their bodies sweating just enough, and looking so fucking sweet to touch that I can feel myself drooling.

Yes, the bars are my favorite thing.

But iced coffee is a close second. I really like iced coffee.

Depending on the circumstances, it can be unpleasant to be yanked out of the aether by the whims of humans. Almost as unpleasant as it is to be catapulted back by the anger of celestial beings, after they condemn you to demon-hood for all eternity.

Here's how it happened.

I woke up face-down on a wooden floor, already coughing from the amount of dust saturating my throat and nose. I pressed my hands onto the floor and pushed up, at once aware of three things.

I was naked.

I was starving.

I was in the center of a shitty pentagram that looked like it was drawn with chalk, in a candlelit room, each one emitting a different artificial, cloying scent.

It was humiliating. I used to be worshiped, feared, revered, but now, apparently, the world is a place where I can be summoned by any idiot with a laptop. The sight of my summoner before me didn't inspire any more confidence. Tall and thin with a patchy beard. Jean shorts and a flannel button-down open over a t-shirt with another bearded guy's face on it.

Long gone were the days of being called to the woods for orgies, of human sacrifices amidst choirs of Gregorian chanting. Tragic.

"Oh, my God," the idiot said. Which, really, was the dumbest thing he could have said.

He unzipped his shorts, and at first, I couldn't tell if he was going to piss himself or come in his pants, but the burning sensation of a smudged Unholy Union sigil kissing at my heels told me it would be the latter. My gaze skirted over the other sigils, but I didn't see my name, only the symbol for a common demon. A *common demon*. Brutal. As though I didn't even exist anymore. As though I was just another limb of the dark mass.

I squinted at him. "You meant to summon a succubus, yeah?"

He didn't speak but bobbed his head up and down so fast it looked painful.

"You wanted to get laid? Hand not doing enough for you?"

Bobbing again. "I'm involuntarily celibate, so I—"

"I'm gonna stop you right there," I said, holding up a flat hand. I almost felt sorry for him, for how much he fucked up without even realizing, how unfortunate it was that he had been craving any old succubus and was given me. How could I explain it? "You don't happen to know anything about praying mantises, do you?"

He stopped, his shorts and underwear pulled down to his ankles.

"Uh," he said.

I rode him on the floor, right in the middle of the sub-par pentagram. The sex wasn't good—it took too long to get him hard and too little before he came—but it was still sex. And I was hungry, so hungry that as soon as my orgasm hit, I grabbed his head between my hands and snapped it off his neck. I tossed the head aside and started in on the exposed muscle and bone with my tongue already out, moving from neck down to trapezes down to deltoids. Once I started eating, I was in a frenzy, barely letting myself swallow before I was chewing my next mouthful. I picked up one of his arms and tore the triceps away with my teeth. Everything became soaked with blood. I couldn't get a good grip on him anymore, hands slipping, my knees skidding across the slick linoleum floor, but still, I didn't stop.

He tasted *good*. Good in a way I hadn't experienced in ages. He tasted lick-your-fingertips *may I have seconds pretty please* good, but it was also more than that. I felt him on my body's tongue, down the throat, in the pit of the stomach—but I also felt him in my body's veins, its brain, its heart.

It tasted like rage and barbecue sauce. Like ill-intent and self-righteousness, the molten sweetness of sickening thoughts and profound shame.

I wiped at my mouth, smearing blood and saliva down my chin. I licked the length of my palm, continuing all the way down to my elbow, groaning at that taste.

I wanted more.

It wasn't until I stood up on shaking legs, until I stepped over the edge of the summoning circle, hissing at its scorching touch, that I saw it.

A silver ring with a broad skull, teetering precariously on the edge of a coffee table. There was a hum emanating from the ring, something that rattled my head until I picked it up, turning it over in my blood-soaked fingers.

One touch, and I could feel the tug of it, beneath my corporeal form to my very essence, to the smoke and sin of me.

The idiot bound me to it. The same idiot in pieces at my feet.

I'm thinking of it as an opportunity, not a crisis.

I'm here, and bound to an object with no living owner. It's been a while since I've been able to go hunting properly, and on such rich grounds. I might as well make the most of it.

But I can tell I'm being watched—whenever I'm blinded by a bright patch of sunlight or feel the faint touch of a warm breeze carrying whispers of hymns. They're keeping an eye on me. Angels.

I can tell they're whispering to the Big Man, probably letting him know He *could* pull me right out of this world if He only *wanted* to. A little binding magic is *nothing* to Him.

He hasn't done anything yet, though. I like to think He might feel bad for what He did to me and is letting me have some fun, letting me off the leash for a while. Maybe one of them, the Big Man or Daddy Dearest Satan, sent me themselves for some kind of reckoning, but that's depressingly unlikely. They've become too alike, the pair of them. They like to sit back and watch shit unfold.

Even if they did want me here, I'm not doing it for them. I do it because I'm hungry. I violently crave that same taste my summoner had, that smoky-sweet lushness, and I find it in them—those who believe themselves to be predators. It's a delightful game to turn them into prey. This, more than sex, more than the muscles and skin on their bones, is what fills me. When I kill them, I do it for myself. I do it for the self I was before this curse and the self I am after it, the being that was born for pleasure and reborn for death, and now is a servant to both.

I've been watching humans long enough to know they are creatures of habit. It shouldn't surprise me that this is something else they've held onto. Sex as power. Sex as violence. Violence as sex. Violence as power. I don't appreciate its consistency, but I like the sweet little space it leaves for me to slither into. Being able to instill fear in the hearts of men is the closest I've ever felt to being a god.

Right now, I'm watching from the dance floor as a guy comes up behind a girl at the edge of the bar. I recognize him, a slippery motherfucker I tried to catch last week when I saw him try to force a drunk girl into a cab. The girl's friends made a scene, and in the chaos, he managed to get away.

And look at how he's just fallen into my lap, carelessly approaching someone else right in front of me, his smile bright and broad, his hair slicked back off his forehead. He looks mature, expensive, in a silky black shirt and fitted trousers, but I see the reality of him stripped bare of his layers as clear as night.

I've known hundreds of men like this. They're the same in every century, only their hair and their methods change.

He bumps into the girl, causing her phone to fall to the floor. She crouches to get it, and I see him drop something in her drink before stooping down, putting on a big, apologetic show and I can't fucking *believe* how bold he is, how uncaring of being seen or caught.

"Sorry, baby," I say to the boy who's had his hands on my hips and his breath on my neck for the last three songs. "Gotta run."

One. I launch myself between them so quickly I don't even let the girl see him, taking care to brush right up against the guy's denim-encased semi.

Two. I snatch the girl's drink off the bar and down it in one gulp. The cocktail is overwhelmingly sweet, and while the remains of the dissolving drug feel like sand on my tongue, I know they'd be undetectable to a human.

Three. The girl stands back up, and I can see her trying to figure out what's happening through her drunken confusion.

Four. I pull the guy away from the bar by his arm.

"Hi, handsome," I say, at the same time the girl notices her empty glass and yells *What the fuck!* over the pounding music. Good. I prefer her to think she had a shitty encounter with a rude girl rather than a close call with a nightmare.

I take him to the dance floor first, ignoring the pathetic, pouting look my last dance partner sends my way as I latch myself onto another body.

It works like this. Sometimes I go weeks without eating properly, sometimes only a day, and it all depends on what I catch out here, in this grotesque nighttime world. It's easy to find men, yeah, but not always easy to find *these* men. They don't like to be hunted, and they definitely don't like to be found.

He, him, my midnight snack, is currently grinding against my backside, grunting into my ear. *You're a little crazy, huh? You're such a little slut, aren't you?* He probably thinks he sounds seductive, cool, but it comes across as forced. Like he's playing a role.

I make a show of laughing. I turn my head to whisper into his ear, "You have no idea."

I can play a character, too. I swivel my hips back into his crotch, and he groans, grips me tightly at my sides. I rest my head on his shoulder, playing up my panting into his ear. I tell him *I'm horny, I'm so horny I think I'll explode* and I'm not even completely lying when I say that. My hunger is a sharp pain in my gut, and the close proximity to a warm, moving body makes my eyes roll back into my head, saliva pooling in my open mouth.

I tell him I want us to find somewhere private, and I don't need to wait for his response before I leave. I know he's following me, away from the thumping music, past the bar, the impatient line for the bathroom, and the leering bouncers at the entrance into the thin, cold air.

I take him to my summoner's apartment—something I've turned into a base on the mortal plane. It looks the exact same as it did they day I arrived, but it doesn't matter to my guest, who can't separate his mouth from my neck for more than a few seconds. He's so focused on getting his dick out that he doesn't even notice the pile of dried bones in a corner of the living room.

I let him bend me over the edge of the sofa. I say *you're such a slut, aren't you?* and I eat him alive before he can even finish.

I change out of my tight dress, high heels, temporary face, and frown at the corner of bones, which is beginning to grow alarmingly tall.

I really need to do something about that.

"I don't want to know," Maggie the Necromancer says as she lets me in the back door of her shop. The heavy wooden door slams shut behind us. I grunt as I haul the garbage bag full of bones into her office. There's a tear in it, and I can see the edge of a femur starting to slip out. "I really don't want to know. Did anyone see you? How can anyone not see you. You're hauling around a *plastic bag* full of body parts."

I stop just inside the door to Maggie's office, which also acts as a kitchen, spell room, and morgue, and drop the bag. The bones rattle together like toys. "You never want to know," I say, annoyed.

I like Maggie, I do, but her constant attempts at convincing herself she sits on a higher moral ground than me are exhausting. Sure, I'm cursed to hunger for the flesh of men, but Maggie takes their bones from me to do Satan knows what.

"And you're being dramatic. No one ever sees me."

I'm wearing my usual face, the one that I prefer to have on during the day, something close to what I was before. It's nondescript for a human. Average enough that no one looks at me twice. Humans are obsessed with uniqueness, as if they weren't all created from the same exact crap. When I make myself a face that's beautiful, or ridiculous, or both, the type of face I create when I go hunting, that's when humans notice me.

Maggie motions at the crumpling black mass on the floor. "At least, like... push it towards the freezer."

I oblige. Because I like Maggie. We're business partners. She was the first decent witch I could find in this town after days of following around teenage girls who meet behind train cars to read spells off their phones.

"The last one was a bastard," I tell Maggie while she begins sorting through the bag. It doesn't feel like something I want to say, only something I should say. "They all are."

Maggie doesn't respond, but I can guess what she would ask.

So, you think you get to decide whether they deserve to die?

And I know what I would ask in return.

Why do all humans think death is something that has to be earned?

It takes a few months, but she does start asking questions eventually.

"I thought your kind didn't eat people." She says with such practiced nonchalance that I know it's something she's been thinking about for a while.

I shrug. I'm leaning against a shelf in her store and drinking an iced coffee with enough sugar in it to make my teeth ache. There are no customers browsing, but there never are. The only people I've ever seen enter her shop come in with their hands held tightly to their chests, their eyes nervous. They approach Maggie's counter with shaky steps, and say something like:

I... um... I've heard that you, you... have ways of, well. I-I heard from someone, and I swear I don't even believe in this kind of thing, but...

And Maggie asks, with as much tact as a plastic knife, "Who died?"

She's very pointedly not looking at me now, her eyes are fixed on the appointment book open on her desk. She's wearing a long dress patterned in fat sunflowers. Her right hand is nervously tapping a pen on the page. It betrays her. She's frightened of me.

I've been wondering whether Maggie knows who I am. She's not an idiot, and she is a performer of Dark Magic. The closest we've come to talking about it was the first day I walked into her shop, looked her in the eye and asked whether or not she was interested in receiving a large donation of human bones.

I see no point in lying, so I say, "They don't. But I do."

I keep drinking my coffee, leaning against the shelf, watching sunlight dance on the floor, wondering if Angels are listening in right now.

I know it must all be connecting inside Maggie's little mortal brain, maybe confirming something she already knew, maybe telling her something she didn't want to know.

"What did you do?"

I frown. I don't like that. Why do humans always assume I did something? It's always my fault, isn't it? I had to do something really *really* bad to become this, didn't I? Why else would anyone be cursed to become a demon who can only survive by getting fucked and eating human flesh? It's such a typically human question.

I cross over to her desk and plant my hands flat on the top. Slowly, I lean into her space. She's staring at a point over my shoulder, but I wait her out with a closed, flat smile until she finally meets my eyes.

"All I did," I say cheerily, "was get pulled from the dirt to marry a man who never learned how to give a woman an orgasm."

Maggie visibly gulps. She whispers, "Lilith."

My smile widens. *Yes. I still exist.*

Another night.

I'm leaning against a streetlight outside of a bar, finishing off a frankly disgusting beer, and waiting for the guy I'm following to finally stop smoking and go inside. It's been too long since I last ate and I'm getting impatient.

I'm building a fantasy in my mind of this next meal, turning myself on from the very thought of it, when suddenly I'm interrupted by a man walking by, who stops, looks me over, and asks, "How much?"

I smile slightly. "Not for sale, man. And I'm sure you wouldn't want to buy it anyway."

The man scoffs, as though he's heard that kind of response before, as though he's fed up with continuously being fooled by women standing alone in public. "Maybe you shouldn't be dressed like a slut, then."

I think a line like that is supposed to make me feel bad or make me want to go home and change into a turtleneck and never venture outside again. Firstly, latex is comfortable, fuck off. Secondly, even if I was working this corner, that doesn't mean he can speak to me however he likes. Thirdly, what he could never understand is that I have an entire existence consisting of answering to the names men have given me.

Woman. Wife. Slut. Demon. All true at one time or another, and all wrong. Too simplistic in their generalizations.

My guy finally goes inside the bar. I toss my can aside and follow him, already dying for a taste, but I wait a little bit longer, until he's ordered another drink and is standing at the edge of the room, scouring the crowd for something tempting.

I slide up next to him. I press myself against his side. *Hello.*

He grins down at me, wrapping an arm around my waist.

Got you.

Honor Among Thieves

Pamela Kenney

If you stuck a gun to my head, I'd have to say I wasn't too surprised when Hank shot me.

I was mad as hell.

But not really surprised.

After all, I could see it from Hank's point of view. The rest of us *did* leave him behind at the scene of a bank robbery.

It wasn't anything we planned. It wasn't as if the four of us schemed to throw Hank to the wolves.

It was just that we found ourselves in the getaway car with no sign of Hank anywhere. The sirens were getting closer, and he was nowhere to be seen.

I can't remember who said, "Where the hell is he?"

But I do remember Vinny behind the wheel, saying, "He's been caught."

I like to think I raised a protest when Vinny slammed his foot down on the gas, but really, I was just so relieved to get out of there. The sirens were closing in so fast I thought for sure we'd only make it as far as the corner.

I do remember turning around in my seat as we peeled out of there and seeing Hank emerge from the brick building. The look on his face when he realized we were leaving him behind. So much pain, anguish, and fury.

The same fury I was seeing on Hank's face right now, in the back alley where he'd cornered me, after a chase through the streets of our old neighborhood.

"Hank," I gasped, trying to catch my breath, holding up an index finger to indicate there was more I wanted to tell him as soon as I could talk again.

But Hank just said, "I don't give a damn what you have to say."

Then he shot me.

I stared down at the hole in my gut. It seemed so weird to see all that blood spurting out. It looked like a gag someone would pull on Halloween. I was shocked I was still standing upright.

Hank must have been surprised, too, because he advanced a few steps towards me. I staggered back to keep away from him.

That's when I realized there were now two versions of me.

One of me was still standing, sporting a new hole in my gut, but not feeling any pain at all, while the other one was lying in a heap on the ground, staring into space, not breathing.

No, I thought. *That can't be right. That would mean I was...dead.*

How could I be dead? When I was alive not two seconds ago.

There must be some mistake.

That's when Hank savagely kicked me in the face.

And I didn't feel a thing.

By that point, I'd retreated to a dark corner next to a dumpster and I could see Hank stomping away at the body, but it seemed as if it was happening to someone else. As if I was watching a movie about my life and the person playing me *was* me.

Hank took one last savage kick then turned and ran off down the alleyway.

I tiptoed out of my hiding place. Maybe if I lay down on top of myself, I could fix the whole "being dead" problem. But as I got closer, I could see I was in really bad shape. Even if I could figure out how to come back to life, I knew it would be a very painful existence, what little of it there was. Hank had done quite a number on me.

The bastard.

There was no way I was having an open casket. It would be way too upsetting. For my girl. My ma. The guys from the neighborhood.

Holy shit, I thought, standing bolt upright. The guys from the neighborhood. Exactly the guys that Hank was gunning for. *Shit.* I had to warn them.

It might be hard to believe, but I left without a second glance back at myself. It's funny how your body becomes just one more piece of clutter you leave behind when you move on. Like the two hundred pound armoire that's been in the family for generations. It just becomes more stuff you're sick of moving around.

I took off running.

When I got to Vinny's place, the front door was hanging by one hinge and the living room was a mess. Vinny was standing in the middle of the chaos with a confused look on his face and a gaping wound in his chest, pointing down at the second version of himself crumpled at his feet.

I could understand his confusion, but there wasn't any time to talk it over. We had to act.

"Vinny," I said.

He tore his eyes away to look in my direction.

"We have to warn the guys. You go to Phil's place. I'll go to Stan's."

"But I don't understand," Vinny said, his eyes returning to the floor.

Which was when it appeared.

It looked like a man in all respects, except for the horns. And the glowing red eyes. And the evil smile on its face. It appeared in a puff of smoke right behind Vinny and latched on to his arm.

"Time to go, Vinny," it said.

"What?" my friend asked, cringing away from the pain caused by its talons digging into his flesh.

"He doesn't get it, does he?" it said, talking directly to me.

I felt terror grip my throat as I tried to shrink myself into a vanishingly small dot. Terrified that it could see me. That it knew of my existence.

"But then again, I always knew Vinny wasn't the brightest light on the tree," it said. "You wouldn't believe what he sold his soul for. Pathetic really."

Just then, Vinny started to cry. The tears of a terrified soul in utter agony. One who was all alone, completely friendless.

"C'mon, let's go," it said with disgust, unmoved by tears from yet another human. "I haven't got all day."

Then they were gone in a puff of smoke.

My dry heaves continued for quite a while after that, so it took some time before I made it to Stan's place. I held out little hope for what I would find there, so I was immensely relieved to discover Stan alive and kicking.

"Stan, you gotta get out of here," I said, forgetting for a minute.

Of course, Stan continued about his day, walking right through me as I tried to block his path. It was then I felt a tingling sensation in my spine that could only be caused by someone staring at you intently, unrelentingly. I whirled around quickly, eyes bulging, searching to see if it had followed me, but only Stan and I stood in his living room. Well, the two of us and his cat.

A fat, gold tabby sat on the back of the couch, prime real estate for watching the bird feeder, full of birds, out in the front yard. Only he wasn't watching the birds, he was staring directly at me. I took three paces to the right. His eyes followed me.

"Can you see me?" I asked.

"Meow," he said, stating the obvious, with a patented feline shrug.

I ran over to the cat.

"You gotta do something," I said.

The cat swivelled his head to look back out the window.

"C'mon, you little fucker," I said, poking at him with my index finger.

At first, he tried to ignore me, but I could tell I was getting under his skin. His tail started twitching like crazy. Soon enough, he was standing up and arching his back.

"What's the matter, kitty witty?" Stan asked.

Kitty witty, I thought, looking to see if I was in the right apartment. But no, it really was my old friend Stan, showing a whole new side to his personality.

"Do you need to go to the vet?" Stan asked with concern, trying to pet his cat.

"Yes! Take him to the vet. He really needs to go to the vet. Right now," I yelled.

The tabby hissed at me and tried to strike with his claws.

"Okay, that's it. Outside with you," Stan said, snapping his fingers and clapping his hands in order to herd the cat toward the door.

When he opened it, I heard Hank say, "Hello, Stan."

Stan wasn't able to slam the door shut before Hank got his foot in to block it.

I turned my back on the scene and headed for Phil's house. There was nothing else I could do for Stan.

Soon enough, I was at Phil's, where thankfully he was at home. And still alive.

Before long, I was wearing myself out, flapping my arms and shouting, trying to get his attention. I tried moving stuff around with no luck. I tried stomping on the floorboards. Even the curtains wouldn't rustle, as hard as I tried to move them.

So, when the front doorbell rang, I hung my head with defeat.

"Don't do it, Phil," I said wearily, sinking down onto the sofa.

He put his eye to the spy glass and I cringed to think I was about to see my friend lose his head.

Instead, he pulled back and quickly opened the door, saying, "Jane."

I stood up and stared at my girlfriend, her face red from crying.

"Jane, what's wrong?"

"What happened, Phil? What did you guys do?"

"What do you mean?" he asked, backing away, but unable to hide the guilt on his face.

Jane burst into tears.

Phil walked to the other side of the room to get the box of tissues and tried to compose himself.

I ran over to Jane.

The only girl I'd ever loved. I wrapped my arms around her. I could feel her warmth, but was certain she couldn't tell I was there.

"You want coffee? Tea?" Phil asked from the kitchen, keeping his distance.

Jane silently shook her head, tears flowing down her cheeks.

Some hair came loose from behind her ear and fell in front of her face, something that happened a million times a day. Without a second thought, I reached out to tuck it back, just as Jane did the same.

It was in that moment I felt her hand and it seemed as if she felt mine, too. She held her breath, her eyes looking up into mine.

I trailed my finger along her cheek, and her eyes closed as if she could feel my touch. My heart leapt in my chest. Could it be true? Her eyes opened, locking on mine.

"I love you," I said.

A tear escaped as she nodded briefly, a wrinkle creasing her brow at the thought that maybe she was losing her mind. Hearing voices, isn't that the first sign?

In the next moment, she was startled out of her reverie by a pounding at the front door.

"No! Jane, run!" I screamed, trying to grab her shoulders, but the connection was lost. She only moved a little farther into the living room, rubbing her arms as if she were cold.

Phil came out of the kitchen and was halfway to the door when it was kicked in, the sound of splintering wood making them both jump with alarm. Jane screamed at the sight of Hank coming into the apartment with a gun.

"Run, Jane!" I screamed at the top of my lungs, but she couldn't hear me.

That's when I saw it again. A cloud of smoke, and suddenly, it appeared. Leaning against the wall, its arms crossed, staring at me with one eyebrow raised. Not saying a word. Just staring at me with a knowing expression on its face, a sardonic smile playing about its lips.

Behind me, I heard Phil shriek as the gun went off. To my left, Jane stood, staring in horror, shaking with fear, unable to move. I heard Phil's body slam back against the kitchen cabinets before sliding down to the floor. Then Hank saying, "What are you doing here, Jane?"

Jane numbly shook her head, tears streaming down her face, unable to say a word.

"I'm sorry, Jane, but I can't have any witnesses," Hank said, advancing toward her.

I turned to look at it.

"Yes," I said.

"Good," it replied.

I heard the gun go off again, only this time, it was Jane who was screaming as we watched in slow motion, the bullet heading directly towards her. But somehow in mid-flight, the trajectory of the bullet changed, and instead of hitting Jane, it lodged into the wall beside her.

The next gunshot I heard was Phil pulling out his own weapon, and with his last ounce of strength, shooting Hank.

Jane and I both drew in long, shuddering breaths and locked eyes. It was over.

I felt its presence behind me moments before its talons started digging into my arms.

Jane was crying and shaking her head.

"No!" she screamed.

The cloud of black smoke engulfed us, and we were gone, moving through a dark, bewildering landscape, its talons digging deeper and deeper into my flesh.

"At least you had a good reason," it said begrudgingly with just the slightest touch of admiration. "You wouldn't believe what some people sell their souls for."

But I wasn't listening to anything it said. All I could hear was Jane yelling at the top of her lungs, "I love you!"

I closed my eyes, savoring those three little words, knowing they were enough to sustain me for an eternity.

Those three words were having the completely opposite effect on it, however. Howling in agony, it released me, then clamped its hands over its ears as if daggers were piercing its eardrums. I guess I shouldn't have been surprised. It probably never heard those words in its line of work.

But the instant it released my arms, I started to float away towards the heavens, accelerating faster and faster the further I got. I looked back, and all I could see was the fury written all over its face when it realized I was leaving it behind.

The Big League

RIK HOSKIN

"Cancer's popular this year."

"Cancer's always popular," Paul groused. "I hate it."

Mina couldn't hide the expression of surprise on her youthful face. "Why do you say that?" she asked.

Paul shook his head. "They've been riding high for so long, they think the world revolves around them."

The pair were standing in the grand lobby of the conference center, along with two dozen other corporate representatives, waiting for the conference to start. Sunlight streamed through the wall of windows that ran two stories tall all the way along one side. A handful of conference attendees could be seen out there, enjoying a chat and a last cigarette in the warm sunshine.

"Everyone loves cancer," Mina said. "You can't hate success."

Paul gave her a withering look. Fresh out of university, this was Mina's first conference and, to his eyes, she looked like a teenager dressed up for the prom, a child trying to pass for an adult.

"Let me tell you something," he said in a hushed voice. "When my great-great-great grandfather started this company, he got infant mortality way up there, so people took notice. Thanks to him, the population was constantly being culled from the very moment people were born. It was simple and efficient. Cancer's messy. It tracks people down, insinuating itself, and then it works at them, taking little chunks, needling them until they succumb to it. Who wants that?"

"Everybody's got to die of something," Mina said. "That's why we're here, isn't it?"

"And that's the other thing," Paul said. "Cancer's too diversified now. It's taken over multiple markets. Lung cancer, pancreatic cancer, skin, tits, ass. There's nowhere they've not gotten their claws in."

"It's called product recognition, darling," a familiar voice said from behind Paul, and he blushed, realizing he'd been overheard.

He turned to see Bella, head of brand management at Cancer Inc., standing five feet behind him, silver-blonde hair cut to perfectly frame her face. Her hair might be a little more silver this year, but that face never seemed to age. She wore a power suit in brilliant red. Paul wanted to say it made her look like a clown or a kid's entertainer, but it didn't. She carried it off with style, and she knew it. She always smelled good, too. He hated that.

"Cancer," Bella said, spreading her hands over her head as if unfurling a banner, "nine-point-five million people a year can't be wrong. And that's just the deaths."

"Well, we prefer to specialize," Paul mumbled. "There's more dignity in that, I find."

Bella scoffed. "Didn't your father expand into cot death?"

"That was my grandfather," Paul corrected.

"And where is that today? Cot death?"

"It's still happening," Paul said defensively. "We do all right."

Bella took in Mina when she spoke. "Trust me, brand recognition is the future. Look at Heston."

Mina raised her eyebrows querulously. "Who's Heston?"

"Corona virus," Paul said glumly.

Bella elaborated. "His company developed it, but they had a rebrand post-launch. Covid, they called it. It was set to be a world beater, and then they go and rebrand. Madness."

"You never know what your marketing department will come up with," Paul admitted. "It's fraught with potholes."

"Not for us," Bella told him, patting his arm just below the shoulder. "Have you seen G.R.? Someone told me he was here already."

Paul inwardly winced at the way she called their paymaster "G.R." Why did she do that?

"He's meant to be here in—" he checked his watch "—ten minutes. Maybe he arrived early."

"Maybe," Bella agreed. "I'll catch you in the bar later?"

"Yes, I'm sure," Paul agreed. How he loathed the woman.

Mina watched Bella walk away. "She seems friendly," she said.

"Don't be fooled. She's a snake," Paul said.

They waited in silence for a half minute or so, Paul feeling unsure what to say to the younger woman, she awaiting his lead in any conversation. In the end, the seething rage he felt at Bella's barbs ebbed, and he smiled tightly once more as he saw another familiar face making his way in through the crowd of up-and-comers and old hands. It was Heston Porter, wearing a suit that looked like he'd slept in it, an expression of consternation on his lined face.

"Heston, how are you?" Paul asked, striding to intercept the man.

"Dying on my feet," Heston admitted. "I just got an impromptu going-over by our illustrious leader."

"We have a meeting with him at three," Paul said. "How is he?"

"He's not happy," Heston said. "I tried to tell him the Covid mess wasn't my fault. Blasted idiots in PR told me to rename it. I should've known it was too late in the product cycle for that. Idiots."

"They all are," Paul agreed.

Mina smiled. "I liked the name Corona."

"So did I," Heston said. "I wanted Krona originally, you know? But they changed that, said Corona rolled off the tongue easier. And then they went and changed it, anyway. Idiots."

"Why Krona?" Mina asked.

"My late grandmother was Swedish," Heston said, warming to his subject. "It's the currency over there."

"A disease named for a currency," Paul mused. "Funny, that."

"You said 'late'," Mina said. "What did she die of, your grandmother?"

"Not cancer," Paul interjected hopefully.

"No, she was hit by a tram," Heston stated.

"Road death," Mina said. "Retro."

"It's a diminishing field," Paul observed. "Through the 1960s and 70s and into the 80s, road casualties were a booming market. But, what with safety features and better roads, it's become low yield."

"It never made much impact on the overall stats," Heston said. "People pinned their hopes on it for a while, but it proved to be a blind alley. You're young. You'll find trends come and go in this business."

"Not cancer," Paul groused bitterly.

Heston laughed. "You and Bella still at each other's throats then?" He addressed Mina before Paul could answer. "They went to the same university. U-Mass, wasn't it?"

"Yes," Paul said.

"They're contemporaries, you see," Heston went on. "Little bit of competition keeps you on your toes, right?"

Paul didn't answer. He just smiled.

As Heston walked away, chuckling to himself with more of a spring in his step, Mina asked about Bella. "Were you and the cancer woman in the same classes? Wait! Did you date? Is that why you're so funny with her?"

"We didn't date," Paul said. "I graduated a year before her."

"Oh," Mina said, realizing what that meant. Bella was younger and more successful than Paul. "It doesn't matter, it's all cyclic. Cancer won't be around forever."

"What about you?" Paul asked. "Which university did you attend?"

"Columbia," Mina said. "I majored in Creative Writing. It seems so different when you come out into the real world."

"It does," Paul agreed. He was still seething about Bella and Cancer Incorporated. He just wanted this conference to be over.

The lecture hall was huge with stepped seating that angled down towards the stage where slides would be projected on a big screen. Though it seated over a hundred, the hall was less than a third full. Paul and Mina sat two rows back from the front, but no one took up a position in front of them.

The man that they had come to see arrived from a set of doors to the left of the stage, striding in silent tread like a wraith. He looked like you'd imagine—a black hood over his head, skeletal face beneath with two bottomless pits for eyes. But he wore a suit these days instead of robes, black to match his hood, and he no longer carried his scythe around with him.

The Grim Reaper began by introducing himself to everyone, even though he recognized most of the people here.

"The rising population continues to present a problem," the Reaper outlined as images of crowds flashed up on screen behind him. "Consider: in 1803, the world's population topped one billion for the first time. That's barely two hundred years ago. It took until 1928 before it had doubled to two billion, but by 1987, it was at five billion. Today, we have a population on this planet of seven-point-seven billion human beings. This level of growth is impossible to sustain, and yet what are we doing about it?"

Behind him, a selection of graphs showed the rapid increase in the population, and a projection for where the line would be in thirty years. It looked bad.

"Now, we've had successes, and I know that all of you are tackling the problem. I was just speaking with Heston Porter less than an hour ago about the limited success of his Corona/Covid initiative. We need to be more imaginative, people, be bolder, take risks. The human population won't cull itself. We need to bring it down to a level that's sustainable."

The Grim Reaper held his fist to his chest, and Paul noticed for the first time that he wore a discreet pin there in the shape of a scythe. *Old habits.*

"You are my most trusted allies. I know you can make this happen."

The audience applauded, and then the Grim Reaper opened the floor to questions, fielding queries about the possibility of another global war, of a new disease, and even of outside intervention. One woman across the aisle from Paul and Mina proposed instilling a kind of madness into wild animals and making them turn on humans, but while the Grim Reaper admired the style, he dismissed it as too slow and too random.

"Random deaths are good," he reminded the audience. "The more random they are, the harder they are to prevent. But it needs to be large scale. Drastic times call for drastic solutions."

Paul smiled when he heard this. He'd show the Grim Reaper a drastic solution. Oh, yes. Then Bella could take her cancer brand recognition and shove it.

After the lecture, Paul and Mina were among the many corporate representatives invited for a one-on-one session with the Reaper. These sessions offered a rare chance to present prospective ideas that were already in the development stage directly to the Reaper of souls himself. They were the third group in, and they had watched each of the first two enter excitedly, only to exit a short period later looking deflated and demoralized. The Grim Reaper could be cutting if he didn't warm to an idea.

"Baby Mortality Industrial," the Reaper's assistant called, a tall and painfully thin woman who reminded Paul of a praying mantis.

Paul shot Mina a tight smile. "This is it," he whispered.

"Good luck," Mina replied.

They walked into the Grim Reaper's temporary office, a room he had taken over simply for the duration of the conference. *This is where Heston received his going over*, Paul realized. Next week, it would be in-use as someone else's meeting room for an opticians' conference or chemical engineers or comic book fans. But when the Reaper was in a room, it took on an atmosphere that Paul had come to associate with him—the feeling of cold in the air, like morning frost on winter stone. When Paul breathed out, he saw his breath in a white cloud.

The Grim Reaper sat at the far end of the conference table, his hood down to expose his fleshless skull. It was unsettling the way he presented as just a skeleton with those bottomless pits for eyes that seemed to look right through you. He grit his teeth in an approximation of a smile as he saw Paul and Mina approach.

"Paul," he said cheerfully. "It's been far too long. And who is this?"

"This is Mina, she joined my organization just before Christmas," Paul said.

Mina dipped her head in greeting, and offered a shy, "Hello."

"What happened to Robert?" the Reaper asked.

"Robert retired for health reasons," Paul said. "Cancer."

"I'm sorry to hear that," the Reaper said. "Well, let's get started. Do you have something new for me? A new baby death idea, perhaps?"

"No, infant mortality's passed its peak. I accept that. We've been exploring some new possibilities outside of that field," Paul explained. He drew out a presentation book and passed it across the desk. The Grim Reaper plucked it up with a skeletal hand.

"Tell me," the Reaper said, flicking through the booklet.

"We're considering doing something viral," Paul said. "Big reach, big rewards."

The Reaper looked up from the booklet. "It's been tried. Recent endeavors like SARS, MERS, Covid. They all burn out. Ebola's the same. Influenza is hanging in there, but it's statistically less and less significant."

"Ah, but this is a new virus," Paul said. He could feel he was losing his patron's interest. "Let me explain. This one affects the brain with a very rapid take up that debilitates almost immediately."

"Go on."

"We already had the basic components. It's actually an adaptation of my great-grandfather's old designs," Paul went on, feeling he was on firmer ground now. "But we needed to update it, modernize the whole thing, and Mina here came up with a failsafe delivery system."

The Grim Reaper smiled at Mina. "Ah. New blood, new ideas. What's this delivery system?"

"It manifests through the written word," Mina explained, picking up where Paul had left off. "A hidden cue taps the amygdala section of the brain, inducing disorientation that rapidly takes hold, resulting in confusion, loss of appetite, the urge to self-harm, and, ultimately, death."

The Grim Reaper laced his skeletal fingers together and leaned forward, his attention rapt. "I see. And how does it transfer? How does it manifest?"

Mina drew a deep breath. "The virus can be delivered via any written word. So, a book, a newspaper, even onscreen. Its symptoms exhibit initially as the words no longer making sense to the reader."

"Not phasing lense?"

"Tes coltival frenton."

Depth grimmed. "O'mendia!"

Tourist Trap

TERRY CAMPBELL

Trevor Brayson could see his own reflection in the Arizona State Trooper's sunglasses, and he hoped he didn't look as scared and nervous to the lawman as Trevor looked to himself. *Oh shit,* he thought. *Mirrored sunglasses. Every* cop in *every* TV show or movie he'd ever seen wearing mirrored sunglasses was a corrupt, mean, and murderous asshole. Always. You could take that to the bank. He wasn't sure what unnerved him more, the evil sunglasses, or the fact that Trooper Cadaverosa—boldly emblazoned on his nametag—was sucking on a chicken leg bone like it was a cherry popsicle. *We are so fucked.* The air inside the Tesla felt like it had suddenly risen twenty degrees. He could feel sweat beads forming on his forehead, sensed the tiny salty rivulets creeping toward his eyes. In the passenger seat beside him, Trish sat motionless, stuck to the crinkling vinyl seat.

The trooper leaned his head closer to the window. Trevor's frightened eyes grew larger in the reflection. Could he actually see his own sweat in the cop's glasses? The imposing figure studied them for a moment, then his hand moved up to the sunglasses, and the trooper whipped them off his face.

Trevor wished he had left them on.

The trooper's eyes were black. Like a shark's eyes. No hint of white. Black and round and ready to strike.

Then, Trooper Cadaverosa did something totally unexpected.

He smiled.

"You folks headed to Tombstone?" he asked.

"Uh..." Trevor stammered, glancing at Trish. "Yeah, yes. Tombstone."

"For the day," Trish added.

"Well, I'm sorry to put a damper on your day, but I'm going to have to write you a citation for speeding." Every third or fourth word out of his mouth was accentuated by a series of slurping, sucking sounds.

The trooper's eyes were blue now. Had that been a trick of the light? Deep shadows from his hat?

"Yes, sir. I understand."

The officer handed Trevor's license and insurance papers back to him. He then presented the traffic ledger for Trevor to sign. "You know, Tombstone has gotten pretty touristy. It's not like it used to be."

"Oh, yeah? Well, neither one of us has ever been, so we thought we'd check it out."

"You folks ever heard of Vulture's Craw? Heck of a lot closer."

Trevor grinned and looked at Trish, then back to the trooper.

"Vulture's...Craw?"

"Sure, it's an old mining town, just like Tombstone and Bisbee. A lot older, though. And, like I said, a lot closer. And not nearly as...touristy."

"I've never heard of it," Trish said.

Trevor shot her a look.

"No, not surprising. It's a little off the beaten path. In the shadow of the Dragoon Mountains that way." He motioned back over his shoulder. "I have some friends who run a couple of the businesses there in town. Their motto is "Once you go to Vulture's Craw, you'll never go anywhere else."

There was an uncomfortable silence for a moment.

Trevor slowly handed the signed citation back to the officer. He took the ticket and folded it, then stopped. "Tell you what," he began. "You folks follow me to Vulture's Craw, spend the day—and your money—there, and I'll tear up this ticket."

"Really?" Trevor asked. He was seeing dollar signs behind his eyes. That ticket would cost him at least three-hundred bucks, he was sure of it. Trish mouthed the words "Vulture's Craw" as a question.

"On my word," the trooper said, placing his hand over his heart.

"Show me the way," Trevor said.

"We go back the way we came about a mile, and we'll veer off to the east. Just follow me."

Trevor watched the trooper walk back to his patrol vehicle and slide into the seat. He continued to watch as he killed the lights and made a U-turn on the desolate desert highway. When the police car had headed back up the road, Trevor pulled the Tesla around and followed behind.

He could feel Trish's eyes burning into him. He knew that sensation all too well.

"Why the hell did you agree to that?" she asked.

He knew that was coming. Trevor shrugged. "Got me out of a speeding ticket."

"Really? That was your deciding factor? We've been planning this Tombstone trip for months. We've always wanted to see Tombstone."

"But what if this is like he says, an old mining town. Less crowded than Tombstone?"

"Less touristy?" Trish said, sarcastically. "Asshole."

Trevor dismissed her remark and took note that Trooper Cadaverosa was exiting onto a reddish, sandy road. The clouds of the dust kicked up by the officer's tires made it difficult to follow the patrol car, but Trevor managed to steer the course.

He noticed that Trish was on her phone. He glanced over, attempting to catch a glimpse of the screen.

"Trevor, there is no 'Vulture's Craw' on the map," she said. "Google search, either. Are you sure about this?"

"Maybe you don't have any data way out here. It's gotta be out here. Why would he tell us about it?"

"I don't know," Trish said. "All I know is, there is no mention of the town on the internet. Nothing on any map. You can't even see any buildings out this way on Google Earth. Nothing but mountains and desert. It's like it doesn't exist."

Trevor thought about it for a moment. "Well, he did say not many people knew about it."

Trish gave him that exasperated look, and he knew better than to push it.

"How far did he say it was?"

"He didn't," Trevor answered. "He just said it was a lot closer—"

"Than Tombstone. Right. I was really looking forward to Big Nose Kate's Saloon."

"I'm sure they'll be an even cooler saloon here," Trevor said, hoping to lighten her spirit.

"Yeah, Buzzard's Blood."

Trevor focused on the road and attempted to peer through the dust cloud, looking for any signs of the trooper's taillights. The dust had seemingly gotten thicker in just the past few seconds. In fact, the entire sky had suddenly darkened around them, as if a total eclipse had just swallowed southern Arizona. Trevor grabbed a tissue and wiped at the interior of the windshield, but it didn't help.

"Trevor! Look out!"

Trevor hit the brakes just as he noticed the trooper's brake lights directly in front of him. He could tell by the swirling, colored reflections on the opaque clouds that the car's emergency lights had been activated.

"Jesus!" Trevor mumbled, slamming the Tesla into park.

"What the hell?" Trish said, trying to peer through the dust.

Slowly, the dust began to settle. The lights from the patrol car began to grow brighter, and soft shapes formed in the distance.

And then, as if the dust cloud had never been, the town of Vulture's Craw loomed ahead like a literal oasis in the desert.

Weathered-board buildings lined either side of a reddish, dirt road, several two-story, but mostly single, disappearing eventually into a vanishing point. A few of the exteriors were painted in bright, southwest colors. There was another street in the center of the town, forming a cross for the layout of the town. Trevor squinted into the bright sunlight. In the center of the four-way intersection was an odd construction of thick round timbers that seem to have been cut from fallen trees, jutting up into the air with similar sections branching in all directions and random angles. It reminded Trevor of perches in a bird cage, which caused him to think of Tombstone. A tinge of regret crept into his brain, but nevertheless, he pulled the Tesla over and stepped out. Trish followed, using her hand to shield her eyes and peering down the street. He knew she was already checking out the shops.

"Well, folks, here we are," Trooper Cadaverosa said, approaching them. "Downtown Historic Vulture's Craw."

"Wow," Trevor said. "I was beginning to think you were leading us on a goose chase."

The trooper chuckled. "She springs out of nowhere, don't she?"

Trish happened to glance down at the rear bumper of the patrol car. A bumper sticker from a saloon called 'The Empty Gullet' in Vulture's Craw, Arizona proclaimed, 'Save a Tree. Eat a Critter.'

"Really?" she said, disgusted.

"Ma'am?" the lawman asked before realizing what she meant. "Oh, great place. I recommend it. I know the owners. They're good people."

"Well, I'm vegan," Trish said, jutting out her hip with attitude.

The officer seemed a bit taken aback. "Well, I'm sure they have some lettuce or something like that."

Trevor suppressed a laugh. Trish was already pissed enough.

"Well, you folks enjoy your day. I have to get back out to the highway," Trooper Cadaverosa said. "And remember, once you visit Vulture's Craw, you'll never go anywhere else." He tipped his hat to them, still gnawing on the chicken bone and slid back into his car.

Trevor watched him drive away and turned back toward Trish. He could feel her eyes stabbing into him.

"Two hours," he said. "Two hours and if you don't like it, we'll head to Tombstone. There'll still be plenty of time to hit the saloons."

"And the shops?" she grinned, standing on her toes and shifting.
"And the shops."
"Okay, then. Let's check out Vulture's Craw."

It turns out Trish loved the shops. By the time they decided to head down to the Empty Gullet Restaurant and Saloon for a bite to eat and a few adult beverages, she had walked out of the boutiques with three bracelets, a pair of earrings, a candle and a copper and turquoise colored trucker's cap. Three and a half hours had passed.

Trevor was surprised at how crowded the town was. Cars lined the dirt streets. Quite a few people flitted from shop to shop, ducking in and out of the handful of saloons that lined either side of the street. Trevor had struck up conversations with several groups of people, and the general consensus among them all was that none of them had ever heard of Vulture's Craw before that day. None had seen it online or found it on Google Maps. Most of them had heard of the town while stopping for gas along the desert highway, or somewhere in towns passed along the way. Even a few, like Trevor and Trish, had been told of the town's location by a member of law enforcement.

"Oh, my gosh," Trish suddenly squealed.

Trevor was pulled from his thoughts as Trish trotted along ahead of him. Outside a Native American jewelry store was a young man and woman pushing an extra wide baby stroller that transported a set of triplet girls dressed in matching pink outfits.

"They are so adorable. Trevor, come and look at these precious babies."

The parents beamed proudly, as Trish pinched chubby cheeks and blew kisses. Trevor, not really one to codger over babies, agreed that they were cute and peered down the boardwalk to see how close they were to the saloon. Right now, a mug of ice-cold draft beer seemed much more dote-worthy.

"Can I take a selfie with them?" Trish asked.

The parents told her of course she could. You could tell they were the type who craved the attention a cute set of triplets always provided.

As Trevor waited for Trish to get her fill of the preciousness, he noticed a man in full gunfighter regalia standing against one of the support columns. The man tipped his hat to Trevor. Trevor returned the gesture with an obligatory head nod and walked over to the man.

"Where you folks from?" the slinger asked.

Ten to one that was the first question he would ask, Trevor thought. "Glendale."

"Come to see Tombstone, did you?"

Trevor grinned. "Actually, yes. But a state trooper informed us of your lovely little town."

"You'll like the shows here a lot better," the man said.

"Oh, was there a famous gunfight that took place on the streets of Vulture's Craw?"

"Not a gun show. A tribute rodeo. It's a little demonstration we put on commemorating the great winged creatures that chased the Apache out of the Dragoon Mountains and allowed our ancestors to settle this town."

"Winged creatures?"

"Oh, don't worry. They're long gone these days. But their lore lives on forever in Vulture's Craw."

"Oh," Trever said. "Okay, cool."

The man pointed back to the buildings as if to indicate an area beyond them. "The arena is on the back side of town. In the shadow of the mountains. Rodeo starts at sundown."

"Oh, well I don't know if we'll be here that late," Trevor said. "But if we are, we'll definitely check it out."

Trevor started to turn back toward Trish to pry her in the direction of sustenance when the strange contraption in the center of the intersection caught his attention again. "Say," he said, spinning back to the gunman, "what is that thing?"

"That?" the man said, pointing to the wooden structure. "That's for them."

Trish walked up behind him. The family of five were rolling back up the wooden walkway. Trevor turned and followed the man's finger.

He hadn't noticed them before.

Scores of vultures were perched along the tops of the buildings all up and down the town's main drag. They sat in silence, some preening their feathers, some picking at their talons, some just staring into space at something only vultures can see.

"Trevor?" Trish asked, taking his arm.

Trevor's gaze followed the line of buildings all the way to the end. All along the stretch, the birds sat motionless. Once in a while, the ruffle of wings could be heard when another joined the group.

"What are they doing?" Trevor finally asked.

"They're gathering," the gunfighter said. "It's almost feeding time."

"Feeding...feeding time?"

"Sure, three o'clock, every afternoon."

"You feed the vultures?" Trish asked. "But why?"

"Well, they're a very important part of the ecosystem around these parts. They take care of the roadkill, die-offs in the desert, and the rodent population. We celebrate their existence every afternoon with a ritualistic feeding. Usually around three o'clock. It's tradition, and one of our biggest draws."

"Usually?" Trevor asked.

"Yeah, well," he said, then paused. The cowboy stepped out of the shadow of the storefronts and peered along the rows of buildings as if looking for something. "Oh, there he is."

Trevor and Trish joined the man to either side and squinted into the sun. "That one. See the red growth hanging over his beak? He's the one all the others answer to. They won't move until he does."

As if on cue, the bird in question spread its great black wings and lifted into the air. They watched it soar in the sky for a moment, circling the wooden structure, then drop down from the air currents and light on the topmost beam.

Suddenly, a loud electronic squeal pierced the quiet air. Trevor turned in time to see one of the shop's proprietors step onto the sandy soil with a megaphone in his grip. "Caw! Caw! Caw!"

Trevor laughed aloud. "What the hell?"

"He's signaling for the carrion," the gunslinger answered.

"The carrion?" What kind of hokey tourist bullshit had they stumbled onto?

They were aware that all the buildings up and down the drag were being vacated. Store workers and customers alike spilled out onto the streets of Vulture's Craw.

That's when Trevor and Trish were hit with the foulest stench imaginable. Suddenly, an ATV pulling a trailer zipped by them, headed toward the wooden structure. Piled inside the trailer were numerous decaying and overly ripe animal corpses. The vehicle pulled up beside the giant feeding perch, where the men jumped out and began staging the putrefying remains in various areas of the crossbeams. When finished, they piled back into the vehicle and headed back toward the direction from which they had come.

One by one, the perched vultures took flight and began soaring over the city's street. Their numbers were so numerous that their shadows darkened the road. Circling high above the carrion, the birds watched and waited. When the red-crested vulture dropped down to one of the dead animals, the others began to swoop in.

The sounds of all the feathers and wings flapping were loud in the open air. The birds squawked and bustled for position, blood and grue splattered through the air as talons and beaks tore into moldering flesh.

Trish leaned against Trevor and whispered, "You made me miss the *OK* Corral shootout for this? Oh, you are gonna pay."

Trevor grinned. "Fair enough."

"Quick," she said. "Feed me before my appetite is completely destroyed."

He took her hand and led her back toward the Empty Gullet.

Their dinner was magnificent. The drinks took any edge off that the feeding of the vultures might have instilled in them. They both felt completely relaxed and at peace. Trevor stood near the front door and peered out into the streets of Vulture's Craw, waiting for Trish to come out of the bathroom. The shadows outside were getting longer. Looking back into the bar area, something was bothering him, but in his calm state, it seemed insignificant and trivial.

Just then, Trevor detected movement out of the corner of his eye. He turned and looked up, mesmerized. A lone vulture was gliding down the street, a mere few feet off the dirt surface. No flapping of the wings, no other movement. It was almost animatronic. Trevor watched as the scavenger reached the cross intersection, tilted its wings ever so slightly, and coasted to the left down the side street. Its wings never moved, as if it had found its own private wind tunnel. Trevor was still watching the empty street corner when Trish came bouncing out the saloon doors.

They stepped out of the Empty Gullet and headed back toward the Tesla.

"That was the best daiquiri I've ever had," Trish said. "So good."

"Well, I only had beer, but I can say it might've been the coldest beer I've ever had."

Trish laughed and took his hand. The happy couple strolled along the boardwalk. The day had turned out all right, but that vulture-robot was eating at him.

Then something dawned on Trevor. "Hey," he said, stopping and turning in a circle. "Where are all the people?"

Trish looked around and shrugged. "It is after five," she said. "You know, just about everything in Tombstone closes at five. Probably no different here."

"Yeah, but all the cars are still here."

Up and down both sides of the street, the same number of cars remained where they were when Trevor and Trish had first arrived with the trooper. Then Trevor recalled the thought he'd had back at the restaurant waiting for Trish, which had made him so uneasy. The restaurant had suddenly emptied out. Only the employees had remained. All the customers were gone.

"I don't know what to tell you," Trish said, poking him in the ribs. She took a few steps farther and suddenly stopped. "Trevor."

He looked down at her. He was about to make some comment when he noticed her eyes. They were wide and staring.

He looked away and followed her gaze.

The baby stroller that had carried the cute triplets stood blazing in the late afternoon Arizona sun. It was empty.

Both Trevor and Trish looked around. No one was in the streets.

"Where are the parents?" Trevor asked.

"Where are the babies?" Trish answered.

They were both aware of the oppressive silence.

"Where is anyone?"

Not even the townspeople were about. Trevor turned, raced back up to the Empty Gullet, and pulled on the door handle. Locked. A *Shut* sign hung in the window.

He started to walk back to Trish when he heard a loud clanging sound in the near distance, and then remembered what the cowboy had told him before the ritualistic feeding of the buzzards had commenced.

He sighed in deep relief.

"The rodeo," he said, laughing at himself.

"What?"

"That's where everyone is," he said. "When you were cooing over those stupid babies, a guy was telling me about this festival they have at the rodeo. They reenact some ceremony celebrating these winged creatures that chased the Indians away."

"Sounds stupid," Trish said.

"Well, evidently, it's the thing to do. What do you say? Let's go check it out. Then we'll leave. I promise."

Trish rolled her eyes and took her man's hand, and the couple strolled in the direction the gunslinger had pointed at earlier. They could hear the bustle and chatter of the crowd and the beat of music, and as they neared the rodeo, the voices became clearer.

"Well, glad you could make it," a voice called out.

It was the same gunslinger Trevor had spoken with earlier. "Well, after that wonderful feeding frenzy earlier, we couldn't wait to see what the grand finale might be."

The cowboy grinned. Trevor could see bits of food trapped in his bushy moustache. "You won't be disappointed. You folks head on in. Got a spot for you down in front."

Trevor and Trish exchanged amused glances. Trevor just shrugged and led his girlfriend into the arena.

The bleachers were filled to capacity. Trevor recognized some of the faces from town, workers and fellow tourists alike. Vendors were navigating the narrow steps slinging cold beer. Down on the sandy arena floor, several rodeo clowns were busy warming up the crowd. Another sort of strange wooden contraption was sequestered in the center of the floor. A large metal ball completed the ensemble. Trevor felt an odd chill scurry up his spine. *Now what are they feeding?*

Another dressed up performer directed them to two open spots near the front railing, positioned in front of the peculiar display. They took their seats and shifted to get comfortable. In the distance, beyond the small arena, the sun was setting over the Dragoon Mountains. It was a spectacular sight, and Trevor was glad they had decided to skip out on Tombstone. He would have to thank Trooper Cadaverosa if they ever crossed paths again.

At that moment, the clowns scurried away, and a tall man dressed in black trousers and duster with a striped black and white shirt and matching black satin puff tie strode leisurely up to the center display, stepping up onto a wooden platform. He held a microphone in his hand.

"Denizens of Vulture's Craw," he said, his magnified voice booming throughout the small structure. "The hour of the Thunderbird draws near."

Thunderbird, Trevor thought. Winged creatures.

"For the visitors of our fair town unfamiliar with our history, Vulture's Craw owes our very existence to the Thunderbird. Long ago in antiquity, it was the Thunderbirds, an ancient race of winged and feathered creatures, that drove the Apache from this land and allowed our ancestors to settle here.

"However, this was not without a cost. The Thunderbird demanded sacrifice. With this sacrifice, our ancestors were allowed to stay, spread roots, and settle in this area. This tradition has continued to this present day. Once a year, on the eve of the summer solstice, a sacrifice is offered."

The crowd erupted in cheers. Trevor and Trish looked around. It was evident not everyone was cheering. The people they had met in town, the ones in the shops, lunching at the Empty Gullet, the ones who had driven all the vehicles still parked in town, gazed around with uneasy looks on their faces.

At that point, a large gate opened behind the MC, and two gunslingers stepped forth with a young man. The man was slumped over. His clothes were disheveled, and his face appeared beaten and bruised. Trish recognized him as the father of the triplets.

"Trevor?" she said, apprehensively.

Trevor tapped her shoulder. "I think it's just part of the show, hon."

"But he's bleeding, Trevor. I can see it from here. This is not part of some lame show."

The men led the father up the platform and stretched him across the metallic ball. Nervous and frightened murmurs arose from the town visitors. Anticipation swelled within the townspeople.

"As the sun sinks behind the Dragoon Mountains, the Thunderbird will rise, and it will feast."

The tall man then produced a long stiletto from a leather scabbard tied to his waist. He held the knife up in triumph, and half the crowd erupted in cheers, the other half in screams, as the blade was drawn across the restrained man's abdomen. The last of the orange fiery ball slipped behind a distant craggy peak. Terrible shrieks filled the air, and a sprawling shadow swept over the rodeo arena.

The creature that landed on a wooden support was nothing short of an abomination. It was vaguely humanoid, with sinewy spindly legs ending in taloned feet, and wiry arms with long fingers, tipped with sharp claws. Its overall color was a sickly pale-orange/flesh color, and the great wings that sprouted from its back were both leathery with tracings of blood vessels dissecting through them like a long-forgotten roadmap and great course feathers sprouting along the edges. Its head, much like a vulture's, but with a long knobby protrusion formed at the rear of the skull, seemed overly large for the body. The creature flapped its enormous wings twice and dropped down onto the victim, its great beak tearing into and eviscerating the man.

Suddenly, the thumping of many wings sounded overhead, and the sky grew dark with dozens of like creatures swooping in to join the feast.

This was no tourist show.

Finally snapping from his trance, Trevor grabbed Trish and pulled her upward. All around, the tourists were attempting to flee but were restrained by the citizens of Vulture's Craw.

"Where do you think you're going so soon?"

It was the gunslinger.

His eyes were huge and round, with giant black pupils.

It was then that the sky went completely black.

"Trevor!" Trish shouted.

"I've got you!" he answered back. "Let's get out of here!"

Trevor fumbled for his cell phone to give them some light for escape, but failed to hold it in his jittery fingers, and it dropped to the floor. Arms and legs flailed all about. In total darkness, it was useless attempting to locate it. He stood back straight and realized he had lost Trish's hand.

"Trish!" he called into the blackness.

He heard her answer from somewhere close, but it might as well have been a mile away. He tried to move toward her, straining his ears to hear Trish over all the noise. Suddenly, he became aware of another sound piercing the night, above all the screams and shouts.

It was the shrieks and calls of birds.

The arena was suddenly bathed in an eruption of bright light as the arena lights kicked on. Taking advantage of the sudden gift of sight, Trevor wheeled about looking for Trish.

When his eyes completely adjusted to the light, Trevor felt a warm gush as his bladder let go.

All of the townsfolk in the stands had transformed into smaller, slightly more humanoid versions of the winged creatures that had descended upon the triplets' father. The arena had turned into a bloodbath.

Trevor watched in horror as the tourists were ripped to pieces by sharp beaks and deadly talons. Some were lifted into the air and carried away.

Trevor tried to call out once more for Trish, but his voice was cut short when he felt scaly avian toes wrap around his throat. He was lifted into the air, and he twisted and conformed his body in order to look down upon the chaotic scene below.

He didn't know how long he'd been out. Trevor stirred in the complete darkness. His hand immediately went to his throat. It felt wet and sticky, and he had no idea how severe the damage might be. He whispered for Trish, but there was no response. He could sense movement around him. He heard scraping noises, and some sort of strange mewling sounds, like kittens or newborn animals.

Oh fuck, he thought.

Slowly, he began crawling toward the sounds. He bumped into a rock, and his hands felt along the rough, rocky flooring. He didn't know why, but he felt as if he were inside the mountains, deep within a cave system in the Dragoons.

Where the Thunderbird lived.

The air was cool, damp, and musty smelling. Trevor slid himself forward. It made sense to him to keep low. He didn't know what kind of eyesight these things had, but the less of him they could see the better.

He realized that his surroundings were gradually becoming more visible. He could see light flickering on the cavern walls. Trevor pulled up against a large rock and peeked over the top.

It was a breeding chamber.

Large eggs lay scattered throughout the massive area, resting atop piles of discarded clothing and foam stuffing. There must have been hundreds of eggs, if not thousands. That pitiful mewling found his ears again, and Trevor directed his attention beyond the nests.

He had never seen a more horrendous sight.

The hatchlings were pink and bruised looking. They looked like deformed human babies with beaks for mouths and stubby growths sprouting from their backs. They rolled, kicked, and made those horrible sounds. When one of the adult creatures approached, they began moving and hopping frantically.

Feeding time, Trevor surmised.

The giant bird-creature hacked and gagged while its head spasmed back and forth repeatedly. The terrible pink things jumped and flapped their appendages. The great beast threw its head back and coughed, then its head jerked forward, and it regurgitated the contents of its gullet at the hatchling's feet.

Trevor did the same with the Gullet-Buster Double Cheeseburger he had slaughtered at the Empty Gullet hours earlier.

Before the deformed beings could pounce on the vomitus, Trevor saw the tiny bones, tufts of blonde hair, and the scraps of pink cloth.

"Trevor!" He heard a fierce whisper call out. It was Trish.

He turned away from the grisly scene and grabbed her. She pulled him away and directed him to his feet. "Come on," she said. "I saw a shaft of light back here in the cavern wall. I think it's a way out."

Before they could get there, they were spotted by a couple of the Vulture's Craw denizens turned monsters. Trevor and Trish dashed forward, him following her blindly to wherever she was leading him. Trevor could see the light just before Trish dove into the hole. He was right behind her. He felt a talon grab at his ankle as he slithered down the shaft.

They managed to crawl forward a few feet when gravity took over and they felt themselves sliding. Bones and blood vessels were bruised and banged as they bounced down the rocky slide for what seemed an eternity. When they finally crashed to a halt, Trevor looked up and could see the moon.

"Hurry, we don't know how long it will take them to come after us!"

Trevor and Trish scurried up the rocks and found themselves at the foot of the mountains. Ahead of them was open desert, lit adequately by the full moon. Ahead in the distance was some form of artificial light. They could only assume it was the city lights of Vulture's Craw.

They ran like they had never run before and found themselves on the outskirts of town. It was difficult to gain their bearings, but Trevor felt they were headed toward where they had left the Tesla parked.

They raced past a line of parked cars when Trish suddenly stopped. She still had her phone, so she used its flashlight and trained it on the bumper of the closest car.

Save a Tree. Eat a Critter.

Trish held the light toward the top of the car, and the illumination glinted off the top of the red and blue lights.

The exhausted and broken couple started to pick up the pace once again when a sudden gust of wind blew in circles around them, kicking up a billowing cloud of dust. The sounds of enormous wings flapping in the night sky above them blended with the desert wind.

There was a rattling of earth, as the Thunderbird landed behind them. Frozen in their steps, Trevor and Trish turned to face the ancient unholy creature.

"Remember the town'ssssss motto," the humanoid vulture creature hissed, a bloodied and mangled human femur protruding from the corner of its mouth. Hot saliva dripped from the curved beak between the sucking and slurping on the bone. *"Once you visssssit Vulture'ssssss Craw, you'll never go anywhere elsssssssse......."*

The Pyro

TRACY FALENWOLFE

George Rockaway opened one eye and viewed the smoldering pit of ash in his backyard. Untended, the inferno he'd built had died during the night, but not before consuming three felled oaks from his property, several pieces of discarded furniture, and his old computer, which hissed, stank, and probably poisoned the air a little as it melted. How else were you supposed to get rid of the thing and be guaranteed the memory was really wiped and the information on it not sold to the highest bidder, or used in some other plot against you?

George righted himself on the stone bench where he'd slept, banished from the house and the bed he shared with his wife. His head throbbed. His mouth felt like it was stuffed with ash, and he was chilled. Cold to the bone, which was no wonder, given the heavy frost adorning the lawn and shrubs in between the fire pit and house.

He considered the A-frame chalet he'd built from the ground up, debating the pros and cons of going inside to take a leak, but decided he was still too mad at Debbie to go up there and act like nothing had happened, because something had, he just couldn't remember what.

He watched a few stale, frozen breaths curl around his head, then grabbed the rake from the shed and staggered back to the pit. The ashes near the middle still glowed an orangey-red and could have lit the rake handle like a giant cigar, if he'd have held it there long enough. The power of last night's fire had been almighty. It had destroyed, sucking everything that had gotten close inside itself like a vortex. It had been the biggest and best bonfire any of his people had ever seen. A real show.

Something shiny caught his eye as he smoothed the ashes out to cool. He propped his rake against the bench and stooped to pluck a gold ring, still warm to the touch, out of the vestiges of the fire. His heart stopped.

Frantic, he dropped to his knees. He sifted through the warm ash, combing through the silt with his hands, searching for something he knew was there but couldn't quite put his finger on. Until he did.

He held it up like a macabre trophy. A human tooth. A molar, or a wisdom tooth, maybe. And then he found three shards of bone and laid them all out on the stone bench next to the ring.

Twenty-four hours earlier, the sun shone as George maneuvered a little skidsteer around the bonfire site he'd carved out on his property. It wouldn't be his first fire, but this one was important, so he wanted to enlarge the area. Size mattered, no matter what people said.

He ringed the fire pit with boulders, which would serve as a break to keep the fire in, as well as an obstacle to keep drunken assholes out. When he finished with the boulders, he arranged stone benches around the pit in tiers, like his own private amphitheater. Then he sat on one of the benches and took out his pocketknife. Earlier, he'd cut branches off a scraggly oak and stood the pieces that were at least a yard long and about the same diameter as his thumb, in a metal bucket next to the pit. He whittled one end of each branch into a sharp point. When he was done, he had a bucket full of spears, lethal enough to harpoon a rabbit. But it wasn't that kind of party. His guests would get a kick out of threading uncooked hot dogs onto the sticks and roasting them over the fire.

Satisfied with his preparations, George drove the skidsteer back up to the garage and hosed it off. Then he parked it in between his mini excavator and his plow. He stood back and admired the lineup in the structure he'd built special, to house his personal equipment. It reminded him of the Tonka trucks he played with as a boy.

"How's it going?" George's wife, Debbie, walked toward him. She wore a white apron at her trim waist and smelled like a combination of apple pie and homemade chicken soup. At five-foot, ten, she was two inches taller than he was, but she made him feel like a giant.

"Goin' good," he said, trying to hide how lucky he felt every time he looked at her.

Debbie wore tight skinny jeans today, which were much sexier than the scrubs she wore to work. He would have loved her to wear one of those old-fashioned, white, nurses' uniforms on occasion, but those weren't a thing anymore.

Today, a thin t-shirt stretched across her chest calling attention to her breasts. The ends of her long dark hair landed just about there and made it impossible to look away. "You want some lunch?" she asked.

"Don't have time."

Debbie came closer. "Nervous?"

The breeze picked up and ruffled the dried cornstalks tied to the porch.

"No." George had nothing to be nervous about. He'd taken steps to ensure he'd get what he wanted, otherwise, he wouldn't have planned the party for tonight. He wrapped one arm around Debbie's waist and pulled her close for a kiss. Then, he brushed her hair away from her face so it would rain down her back, not her front. "You're gonna change before they get here, right?"

She squinted at him in answer, and then got serious. "If you do get this contract, are you going to have to bring Eddie back into the business?"

George let his arm drop to his side. His brother, Eddie, had bowed out of Rockaway Excavating shortly after they'd inherited it. "Why would I?"

Debbie looked at the garage. "I was wondering if that's why you invited him tonight. It's such a big job. Between the ordering and the billing—"

George snorted. "Cathy'll just have to get the lead out of her ass and move a little faster. I don't need Eddie for that."

Debbie didn't reply.

"Eddie's invited tonight because he's my brother. He wants to be here to celebrate with us, but he doesn't want back in. He doesn't want anything that came from our father."

A crow cawed overhead, punctuating Debbie's silence.

"Don't worry." George kissed her again. "We'll be okay without him."

She rubbed her hands up and down her arms, where goose bumps had erupted.

George frowned at her. "Go inside and get a better shirt on. It's going to get cold tonight."

She turned around and flitted off, while George grabbed a can of lighter fluid and headed back toward the pit. He watched Debbie out of the corner of his eye, and when she went inside, detoured to his pickup truck and grabbed a little box out of the glove compartment.

George worked all day and had just changed his own shirt when Frank Piscaletti arrived. It was dusk, and the fire was roaring. Frank was a tall, gangly, man with hair like yellow straw on the right side of his head, and something like peach fuzz on the left. His half a head of hair—and his half a brain—were the result of an accident he had on the job eleven months ago. Frank had dug up a gas line with a backhoe and was trapped inside the cab while it burned. George could have put him out to pasture then, but instead he gave Frank an office job. Now the guy had a purpose, which George figured was better than lying on the couch obsessing over being a freak, but he also played an important role in the shop. Frank Piscaletti was a walking, bumbling, reminder to his people to be careful, and that was important since another reportable accident would put Rockaway Excavating out of business.

"Frank." George snapped his fingers to get the guy's attention. "It's okay."

The breeze had become a steady wind out of the west, and Frank had volunteered to move the western facing row of benches back a few feet, but he was mesmerized by the fire. "It's hot," he said to George.

"I know, buddy." George clapped Frank on the back. "Watch this." George drained the beer he'd grabbed after he'd finished building the fire and leaned across the boulders with it.

"Be careful." Frank whimpered like a frightened eight-year-old girl.

"It's all right." George positioned the bottle in the center of the fire. "Watch that for a while. When it gets hot enough it's going to start melting."

Frank's good eye darted back and forth, while the glass on the side of his face that was scarred and puckered just reflected the flames. "How hot is hot enough?"

"Fourteen hundred degrees."

Frank shook his head back and forth. "Too hot, too hot."

"It's okay, buddy. Just stay on this side of the boulders, okay?"

Frank was still shaking his head.

"Come on with me." George led Frank around the pit to the other side of the fire where the wind was at their backs. He dug a beer out of the cooler and handed it to Frank. "Here."

Frank took the beer.

"Go on, drink it," George said.

Frank took a sip.

"You'll be all right."

Frank nodded. "You're the boss."

"That's right," George said.

Frank took a longer pull of the beer this time. "A legend in your own mind."

George opened another beer for himself. "Who told you that?"

"JD."

When George didn't respond, Frank hurried to explain. "That's Cathy's husband. You know, Cathy from work. She's married to JD."

"I know," George said.

Something in the fire popped and Frank stumbled backwards. He was all arms and legs and reminded George of the scarecrow from the *Wizard of Oz,* though he wasn't sure if it was because of the way he shied away from the flames, or because he needed a brain.

George clapped him on the back and went to the other side of the fire to finish moving the benches, quietly enjoying the smell of wood smoke, which he personally found more appealing than any perfume or cologne Debbie could have worn.

"That's a big-ass fire, Rockaway." JD Daniels picked up one end of the bench George was about to move. JD looked like a jarhead who juiced, and then bought his shirts two sizes too small, so you would notice his biceps. He kept his hair cut to regs, as if he might be called back to active duty at any time and had to be ready. Or maybe it was just so people wouldn't notice he was going gray.

"Hey, Sparky," George goaded. Electricians hated that nickname as much as his people hated being called lever pullers. "Beer's over there." George motioned with his chin.

JD didn't take the hint. He folded his arms across his chest after he'd set down the bench and pointed his own chin toward the fire. "You've got a lot to celebrate."

"Yup."

"The Spectrum job is massive."

"Yup."

"Cathy says you're not planning to subcontract."

"Nope."

"How are you going to pull it off without hiring a second crew? Or a third, even."

"I'll get it done."

JD smiled but squeezed the back of his own neck.

George knew he was like sand in the guy's shorts, but he didn't care. This was George's house, George's party, and George's victory. If JD didn't like it, he should have stayed home.

JD shrugged. "If you went union, you wouldn't have to worry about it. You could call the hall and get as many skilled people as you need for as long as you need them."

"My people are skilled."

JD made a show of looking across the fire at Frank, who was staring at the flames, trembling. "Uh-huh."

George was about to tell JD where to stick it, when his fat-assed wife, Cathy, and their two fat-assed kids appeared behind him. George just smiled then, figuring it was no wonder JD was so irritable—the guy's wife bore a striking resemblance to a hippo. There was so much lard in her rear end that George worried it would ignite if she waggled it too close to the fire.

There was one plus to having such a woman for an office manager, she kept that behind in her chair and got the job done. She didn't get up a whole lot, didn't go out for smoke-breaks, wasn't one of those people who went out for a walk on her lunch. The only thing hindering her job performance was her mouth—it ran constantly.

"Hey kids." George stooped in front of Cathy and JD's boys and held out a fist for a knuckle bump. "Hot dogs are over there in the cooler. Go on, get a couple, and you can cook them over the fire."

Their eyes lit up and they ran off.

George liked the kids. They couldn't help who their parents were. He'd let them fill up on hot dogs and soda and at the end of the night, he'd give them each one of the jack o' lanterns lining the path from the house down to the fire.

"So." Cathy smiled and looked back and forth between George and JD. She worked so hard to make sure George and JD liked each other, which only seemed to magnify the fact that they didn't. She held out her fingers. "I've got everything crossed. I don't think I'll sleep tonight."

George shook his head. "Ye of little faith."

JD snickered.

"It's not that I don't think we'll get it." Cathy worked to get her foot out of her mouth. "I just want it to be official before I believe it, you know?"

No, he didn't. True, Spectrum Development wasn't announcing the winner of the contract until tomorrow morning, but did she really think he would throw this huge rally if he didn't have the inside track?

"Spectrum has used Whitehead for so many years, I find it odd they'd cut him out of this one to go with you," JD said, draping his arm across Cathy's shoulders.

George just shrugged. "I guess they have their reasons. I heard that Luke Pearson likes to think outside the box."

The rug rats came back waving hot dogs in the air. George grabbed two sticks out of the bucket and gave one to each boy. They immediately aimed them at one another and began jousting. "Holy moly," Cathy cried. "Those are sharp. Dylan, Dougie, stop it!" She took the sticks from the boys and pushed the hot dogs over the points, then gave them back. "Hold them over the fire. And be careful."

George stooped in between the kids. "Pull it back a little." He helped little Dougie pull his wiener out of the flames and to the edge of the fire. "You'll cremate it if you put it in too far."

JD took over helping his kids and George stepped back. "Have fun," he said and smiled to himself as he went to get more fuel for the fire.

The bottle he'd thrown on the fire earlier slumped now, but George wasn't satisfied. A couple of his foremen were here now, and some of the crew started showing up. He wanted the fire to be a spectacle. An event. This gathering was a celebration, a show of Rockaway Excavating's strength and power, and George wanted the bonfire to reflect that. He threw three chunks of a huge old oak on the fire, breaking a sweat in the process. Oak burned hot. It would put on a good show for his guys.

He was admiring his work when Vanessa Martino, a young grunt on Larry Lutz's crew, caught his eye. Vanessa wasn't married, or gay, and wasn't hard to look at either, which meant she got the hormones on the jobsite raging. She could hold her own with the guys, but as far as he knew, she hadn't been involved with any of them so far.

Her lips hinted at a smile as she tipped her beer toward George. Frank Piscaletti sat behind her, talking, and she nodded occasionally, pacifying him. Vanessa wasn't a bitch, but she wasn't that nice, either. Sitting with Frank Piscaletti kept the rest of the crew at a distance. Some of the guys looked at Frank and figured how it could have been them in that backhoe. And no one wanted to see themselves as a deformed half-wit.

George smiled back at Vanessa and caught himself thinking that with her dark hair and eyes, she was a younger, hotter, version of Debbie. It was pitch black outside now, and orange flames licked the empty space between them. George wondered about the token female on his crew. Maybe power was what turned her on. Maybe she wasn't interested in any of his crew because she wanted the top dog. Which would be him. He thought of the box he had in his pocket and wondered if she would be impressed by its contents.

Debbie must have had some kind of spousal radar, because she appeared at his side just as George was thinking some thoughts that could have gotten him in trouble. "Look who's here," she said, and stepped aside.

"Benny!" George bobbed and weaved, and threw a punch that he pulled before it landed square on Benny's jaw. "I didn't think you were coming."

Benjamin Rockaway was George's son from his first marriage. At least that's what his ex told him. George had dark hair and a compact build, while Benny was tall, blond, and lanky, but George loved the kid either way. Benny shrugged. "I ended up getting a ride."

"Well, we're glad you made it." George took Benny by the arm and led him toward the fire. "So how you been, man?" He turned back to Debbie before Benny had a chance to answer. "Did you see Eddie yet?"

"He's on his way."

George stopped walking and patted his pocket for his phone.

"You left it in kitchen," Debbie said. "He couldn't get a hold of you, so he called the house."

George turned back to Benny and led him to the cooler. "You want a beer?"

Benny sighed, just like his mother.

"What? You're not driving." Not since he'd gotten that DUI last month.

"Mom'll be pissed."

"Mom's not here."

"She's picking me up later."

"So, what's the problem?"

He shrugged again. "She said if she catches me drinking again before I'm twenty-one she won't pay for my insurance anymore. And if I have to pay for my insurance I can't pay for school."

George slapped a beer into Benny's hand. "If you're old enough to enlist and fight for your country, you can have a damn beer. You're at my house and you're not driving anywhere. If your mother has a problem with that, she can deal with me."

Benny looked at the bottle in his hand. "I gotta ask you something."

"Yeah, anything. You know that. Whatever you need, you just ask." George glanced over to where Vanessa had been sitting and saw that she was gone. Larry Lutz had taken her place and was quizzing Frank Piscaletti about something.

George clapped Benny on the back. "I'll be right back, and then we'll talk. Meantime, have a beer. Have a hot dog. Debbie made soup and a couple of pies. Anything you want, you help yourself. You're the heir to the throne, man. You're royalty around here."

George left Benny by the beer and made a beeline for Larry Lutz.

Larry had been on the job for forty years. The greasy weasel had been one of George and Eddie's father's employees, and he was a pain in the ass. He was never without the cigar stub clamped between his teeth. He didn't smoke it, just chewed on it for something to do.

Once, Eddie had asked him when he planned to retire, and the guy went off about age discrimination and all that crap. Shortly after, one of the jobs had an OSHA visit. George had had prior notice thankfully, since whoever called them had wanted to remain anonymous, but he always thought it was Larry who'd brought the hammer down.

Larry had been talking to Frank a lot since his accident, and George wanted to know why, since Frank had no memory of the actual event. George had spared him the details, except to tell him that on the day it happened, he'd hit the bar at lunchtime for one of the crews' fortieth birthday, which was true.

"Gentleman." George sidled up behind Larry.

Frank blinked and stopped talking.

Larry turned around.

"Glad you could make it," George said.

Larry grinned around the cigar stump. "Didn't see how I had a choice."

"I don't know who gave you that impression."

Larry ignored the comment. "I was just asking Frank here about the Spectrum Development contract."

"What about it?

"Safety classes," Frank spat out. "He wants to know about safety classes."

"Really?" George said.

Larry narrowed his eyes and clamped down on his cigar. "You get this much new work and you're going to have to hire a bunch of greenhorns. If you don't train 'em proper I don't want to work with 'em and neither do a lot of the other guys."

"Then maybe you and those other guys should work somewhere else."

Larry shook his head. "Your father would be ashamed."

"My father's dead."

"He won't be the only one dead if you cut the wrong corners."

They'd gotten loud. George realized everyone else had stopped talking and were craning their necks to try to catch a piece of the action. The only person who dared approach was JD Daniels. "Problem?"

"Maybe," George said. "But not yours."

"Mark my words," Larry went on as if JD hadn't joined the group. "You already maimed one." He jerked a thumb toward Frank. "You keep up like this and you're going to kill someone."

When George stepped closer to Larry, JD stepped in between them.

"This is none of your concern, JD." George tossed his beer bottle into the fire. It wasn't completely empty, so a few seconds after he tossed it, steam shot out of the mouth of the bottle like a rocket.

Frank Piscaletti screamed and covered his ears with his hands. He took off running just as Cathy waddled up to her husband. "What's going on?"

JD shook his head.

"Go after Frank and see if he's okay," George said to Cathy.

"She's not at work," JD huffed out.

George ignored him. "Maybe blow him for old time's sake."

Cathy's face stretched into a horrified yawn. JD was about to land one on George's face, until he got a look at his wife and realized it was true. She burst into tears. "You're a bastard, George."

Maybe. But what was she gonna do about it? And what was Larry Lutz gonna do about it? Everyone complained about something, but they all wanted something from him, too. Larry wasn't going to leave. He had four more years to beef up his pension. No other outfit would even offer him one. And as for Cathy, she needed the health benefits for her and the kids. JD was a big cheerleader for the union, but what had they done for him lately? He'd been laid off for so much of the past two years, he'd lost his benefits and had to pay for them himself now.

Cathy clawed at JD's overinflated chest. "Honey."

He shrugged her off. Now he looked like a jarhead who juiced *and* raged. "Go get the kids. I'll meet you at the truck."

"I can explain."

"Not here." JD turned and walked away.

"It was long before I met you," she called after him.

He'd stopped listening.

Larry Lutz got right up in George's face. "I'll go find the kid," he said, pushing the cigar stub to the corner of his mouth with his tongue. "Somehow you have him believing the accident was his fault, but you and I both know it wasn't like that. You didn't get those permits, and I know it."

George would have fired Larry right on the spot, but his brother Eddie appeared out of nowhere and put his mouth to George's ear. "Luke Pearson just got here."

Seeing Eddie had been giving George a start lately. He was built a little less like a fireplug than George was and had recently sprouted a skunk-like shock of white hair right around his left temple, which meant he was the spitting image of their father.

George tamped down his temper. He was in the process of taking a deep breath when Vanessa Martino caught his eye. She showed him a broad smile, and for a minute he was pissed off, but then he realized how much she was enjoying herself. How much she was enjoying watching him.

He put his hand on Eddie's shoulder. "Go find Frank, will you? Larry Lutz took off after him and I'm not sure I want the two of them talking."

"I'll take care of it," Eddie said, and walked away.

George looked around. Cathy and JD's kids were parked on a bench near the fire, while the two of them had a conversation near the tree line. Judging by the way both of their arms were flapping, it didn't look pleasant. Benny sat alone with three empty beer bottles next to him. His scowl made sure no one tried to join him. All of George's men had broken up into their respective crews and looked tentative. He could see they were debating whether to stay or go. And Frank and Larry and now Eddie were all MIA.

Debbie was headed down the hill from the house, toward the fire with Luke Pearson in tow. The candles in some of the jack o' lanterns had gutted out and now the path looked like a mouth with a couple of missing teeth. "Hey guys, do me a favor?" George said to one of his crew. He pointed to three old bureaus. "Throw those on the fire."

"Really?"

"Really," he said. "Have some fun."

By the time George met Luke Pearson and walked him down to the fire, the guys and their wives were mingling again, oohing and aahing over the flames as they threw drawers into the pit one at a time and watched them incinerate.

Luke Pearson followed George to the boulders circling the fire. He wasn't dressed for a bonfire, khakis, loafers, and a ski jacket that had Spectrum Development embroidered over the heart, he had clearly arrived on business. "This is quite a party," he said to George. There was something going on at his hairline, like he'd just gotten new plugs or something.

George ignored it. "It's a rally, more or less. My guys are excited to work for Spectrum. Tonight is an opportunity for them to kick back, eat, drink and have a little fun before we get to it."

Pearson rubbed a hand across his newly-shaven face. "You know, there were a lot of bidders on this job. And yours wasn't necessarily the lowest." He smelled like Old Spice. And bullshit.

George's gut clenched anyway.

Pearson met his eyes. "But that's not the only thing we take into consideration when awarding a contract this big."

George nodded like he knew exactly what Pearson was talking about.

"If we have a reason to believe the contractor with the best bid won't be able to finish the job, for instance, we may go with the second-best bid."

Now Pearson was talking about the bug George had put in his ear. Good.

"The problem is that we have shareholders to answer to. And they want to know what those reasons are. It's hard to tell them that I know something that I shouldn't know."

Yada, yada, yada. The way George saw it, that was on him. George had had lunch with Pearson before bidding on the contract had opened. He'd managed to mention that he'd just come from seeing his wife who was an oncology nurse at work and had also bumped into Joseph Whitehead there. Then he played it off as a slip of the tongue. Whatever Pearson took away from the conversation was his problem.

"I'm sure you made the right decision," George said.

Pearson smiled and stuffed his hands into his pockets. His mouthful of caps gleamed in the firelight.

Of course, Frank Piscaletti, Larry Lutz, and George's brother Eddie, picked that moment to emerge from the woods behind George. Pearson's smile fled and he reflexively stepped back when he caught sight of them. It was no wonder.

Frank's gruesome side was illuminated by the flames. He looked so unnatural, he might as well have been a Sasquatch stepping out from the trees.

"George. Can I talk to you?" Frank was agitated and stuttering. There were tears in his eyes. Eye. The one that was real, anyway.

George clapped him on the back. "Sure, Frank." He pointed to the cooler. "Go get yourself a beer. I'll be right over."

"But I have to talk to you now."

Eddie stepped up to the plate and introduced himself to Pearson. They shook hands. "We met on the Southside mall project, I think," Pearson said. "Both of us worked for our fathers back then if I remember correctly."

Eddie said he remembered.

"So, you and your brother here inherited the family business?"

Eddie shook his head. "I got out of the game a while back." His patch of white gleamed. It said, "I'm distinguished," or "I'm better than you," or maybe just "I'm old." Eddie turned to George. "Why don't you go take care of Frank," he said. "I'll make sure Luke here gets a beer and something to eat."

Debbie called out to George at that moment. She trudged down the hill toward the three of them. The firelight silhouetted her perfect body and made her hair glow. George felt a moment of immense pride. He wondered what Pearson's wife looked like and would have bet the entire contract that she was nothing like Debbie.

She stopped fifty feet from the fire and called out again. "George, someone's here to see you." He could see by her alarmed expression that it wasn't anybody he wanted to see. He also noticed someone following along behind her in the dark.

Apparently, so did Eddie, because he shuffled Luke Pearson over to the beer cooler just as Debbie stepped aside and Joseph Whitehead, looking hale and hearty as ever, came into focus behind her. Whitehead said something to Debbie, and then put his hand on her arm as he moved past her toward George.

George wanted to punch the guy in the face for touching Debbie. For talking to her, even, but she didn't seem to be bothered. "And Linda is here for Benny," she called.

Jesus, Joseph Whitehead *and* his ex. At least Linda had the decency to stay up at the house since she wasn't invited to the bonfire.

"Benny!"

The kid lifted his head and looked at George.

"Hey, man, your ride is here."

Benny threw the four empty beer bottles into the fire and stood.

George shook his hand and clapped him on the back. "Come back soon, okay? We'll talk then, right?"

The kid shrugged and walked away. He was just like his mother. But George had bigger problems to deal with right now. Joseph Whitehead had closed the gap from the house to the fire and stood nose to nose with him. "You have some nerve. How dare you spread lies about me."

"I did no such thing." Whatever Luke Pearson gleaned from George's comments was his own doing.

Whitehead's face went bright red, as he poked a finger into George's chest. "You're a bastard."

The fire cracked and popped next to them. "You're gonna want to take your hand off of me before I break it off," George said under his breath.

Everyone had gone quiet, but Whitehead's voice boomed. "I know what you did, Rockaway. Because one of your own people told me about it."

George's men looked at each other, but no one spoke.

"I'm not dying of cancer," Whitehead yelled. He poked George in the chest again. "And how dare you tell people I am."

Everyone at the fire was quiet. From somewhere in the distance a squeaky, whiney voice screamed, "George!"

George's ex, Linda, charged down the hill repeating his name again and again. She pointed at him as she bobbled closer in her high-heeled boots. "You let him drink? An underage kid with a DUI?"

George had provided the beer, the food, and the fire, but the last thing he was going to give his people was a show. He looked at Whitehead. "You want to talk about this like men, feel free to sit down and wait for me to come back. You want to beat your chest and make accusations, get off my property."

George started up the hill and hooked Linda's elbow, forcing her to do an about face. She started in on him again, but he wasn't in the mood. "Shut up," he spat, and hauled her back to her car. Leaves crunched under their feet.

It was cold away from the fire. Debbie stood with her arms wrapped around her middle, talking to Benny who sat inside the car. George could see Debbie's breath.

"Now." George let go of Linda's arm and she stumbled backward into her car door. "You have something to say to me, say it here. You don't come down to where I'm conducting business and try to make trouble for me."

"Me make trouble for you?" Linda dusted off her leather coat. "You're delusional. What about your son? If he gets busted for underage drinking while he's already had a DUI, he will go to jail! Don't you get that?"

"How's he gonna get busted? You're driving him home to your place where he's going to sleep for the rest of the night."

"That isn't the point!" Linda bent her head and looked inside the car at Benny. "Did you ask him about the money for school? Did you ask him for a job?"

"He already has a job," George said.

"No," Linda said. "He *had* a job. Until he got the DUI. You can't make deliveries without a driver's license."

"Mom let's just go," Benny screamed from inside the car.

"You're such a deadbeat," Linda said to George. "Can't even give your own kid a job." She spun to get into the car, and George grabbed her arm again.

"He didn't ask me for a job. He didn't ask me for anything."

"He shouldn't have to ask." Linda pulled away and shoved George. "And don't touch me or I'm calling the cops. You touch me, that's assault."

"Mom," Benny yelled again. "Just get in the car."

"You touched me back," George said. "You think it doesn't go both ways?"

"Fine. I'm still calling them." She shot a finger toward the massive fire. "You think that's legal? There are ordinances, George. You can't have a raging inferno in your back yard. But you think the rules don't apply to you. You always thought that."

Debbie stepped in between them. "George." She put her hands on his chest.

He shrugged her off, and she stumbled back.

Eddie stepped out of the darkness looking more like their father than ever. "That's enough, George." He had a hand on Debbie's elbow. It didn't bother George as much as when Whitehead had done it, but the way Debbie's body curled toward Eddie did.

Linda picked that moment to jump in the car and stomp on the gas. She flew backwards down the drive and locked up the tires as she turned the wheel and lined up with the street. Then she lurched forward and sprayed stones at the three of them left standing there.

George stared at his wife and brother, trying to comprehend why they were looking at him like he was a monster. He wanted to take out the box in his pocket and give it to Debbie right then. But he planned to do it down at the fire when everyone else was gone and it was just the two of them. It was supposed to be a gift to her. A symbol of what was to come when he scored the big Spectrum Development contract. But if he didn't get his ass back down to the fire the deal ran the risk of falling apart.

"What are you doing up here?" he asked Eddie.

"I came to warn you that I couldn't keep Whitehead and Pearson apart."

George left Eddie and Debbie in the driveway and went back down the hill. Cathy, JD, and the boys were nowhere in sight, and most of the other guys were packing up to leave. Frank Piscaletti and Larry Lutz sat with their backs to the fire on a stone bench near the beer cooler, facing Luke Pearson and Joseph Whitehead. The conversation looked intense.

Larry Lutz stood and grinned around the cigar stump in his teeth when George joined the group. He put a hand on Frank's shoulder. "Come on, Frank. Time to go."

Frank wouldn't meet George's eyes. He skittered past him and ran up the hill after Larry. Luke Pearson and Joseph Whitehead rose. Luke shook Joseph's hand and then George's. "Gentleman," he said. "I promise an announcement before nine am." He turned to George. "Thanks for having me."

George nodded.

Joseph Whitehead said nothing, but he and Pearson walked up the hill together, and neither one of them looked back.

George waited until he heard four car doors, four engines turn over, and four vehicles pull out of his drive. Then he screamed every curse word he could think of at the top of his lungs, dumped the rest of the beer out of the cooler, and threw the cooler into the fire. It turned black instantly, and then melted like ice cream. Within minutes of tossing it into the flames there was no sign of it ever existing. But George felt better for having watched it burn.

He saw movement through the flames. Someone was on the other side of the fire. He cocked his head to see who it was, since he'd thought everyone left. Vanessa Martino circled toward him. She picked a beer up off the ground. "Sounds like you need one of these." She handed a bottle to George and picked up another one for herself.

"I thought everyone was gone," George said.

She shrugged. "I thought it was just getting good." She threw the twist off top to the beer into the fire.

George did the same.

"Guess it didn't go the way you planned," she said.

George drank half his beer. "Never does."

Vanessa tapped the neck of his bottle with hers. "I hear ya."

George was leery. He'd never sat and talked to Vanessa. He'd never been this close to her, as a matter of fact, and now that he was, he saw that he'd been wrong when he'd thought she was a younger hotter version of his wife. There was no way Debbie had ever looked this good.

"What now?" she asked.

George wondered how she meant it. He was a little drunk, but not so drunk he was foolish enough to go with the first thing that crossed his mind. "I guess we'll find out tomorrow. Pearson said he'd announce who got the contract before nine."

Vanessa looked at her watch. "Guess that'll be a tough eight hours for you."

"Yeah."

"Was that your son earlier? The kid who sat alone and drank?"

"Benjamin. Yeah, why?" Before he finished asking, he realized she was young enough to be interested in his son and not him. That would blow.

"He hates you," she said.

George snorted. "He gets that from his mother."

Vanessa finished her beer and smiled to herself.

George watched. "What?"

"Nothing." She shook her head.

"Didn't look like nothing."

"Because it wasn't. But if I say what I was thinking I'm likely to end up fired."

"Not tonight." George got them each another beer. "Try me."

She twisted off her cap and threw it into the fire. "I was going to say that maybe she wouldn't hate you, if you knew how to treat a woman."

George choked on his beer.

She held up her hand. "It's nothing personal. I'm just warped like that."

George wiped his mouth with the back of his hand. "You think I don't know how to treat a woman?" He set his beer on the bench next to him and reached into his pocket. "Take a look."

He pulled out the tiny ring box he'd been carrying around all night and handed it to Vanessa. "This is for my wife. It's a thank you. For her part in getting this contract."

Vanessa took the ring out of the box and slipped it onto her finger. "And what was her part?" She held out her hand and admired the ring. Seeing it on her finger reminded him of the ring he'd bought for Linda when Benjamin was born. She still wore that ring, and George hoped Debbie wouldn't make the connection too.

Vanessa was still waiting for an answer.

"She puts up with a lot."

Vanessa met his eyes. She took off the ring and put it back in the box.

Something in the fire hissed, and then squealed like someone was slowly letting the air out of a balloon. Then it stopped. George heard crunching on the other side of the fire. He stood up. "Who's over there?"

Vanessa stood, too.

A figure moved into view. George furled his brow. "I thought you were gone."

George blinked at the tooth, the ring, and the three shards of bone he'd laid out on the bench. He watched another one of his breaths float heavenward, as he wracked his mind to fill in the blanks from last night. Someone had ended up in the fire, he was sure of it, and hangover aside, he had a real terrible feeling about who it was.

He ran up to the house. "Debbie?" He looked in every room. "Debbie, honey?" She wasn't there. She wasn't anywhere. He ran out to the garage and fell to his knees when he saw her Volvo parked there. "Debbie," he screamed. Jesus, it had been her, hadn't it? He'd pushed his wife into the fire.

He knelt there alongside the garage with his head in his hands and tried to remember. He was a lot of things, but he wasn't a murderer, and he loved his wife. Why would he do such a thing?

As he knelt there on the grass, a car pulled into the drive. Debbie got out of the passenger side. George was so relieved he couldn't speak. He followed her into the kitchen. "Debbie. Debbie, honey?"

She wouldn't look at him. He probably deserved the silent treatment after what a jerk he'd been. That was fine. She could ignore him. At least she was alive.

He begged again, but she wouldn't listen. Then George heard a noise coming from down at the fire pit. It sounded like a piece of his equipment. He looked outside and saw someone driving his mini excavator.

He ran down to the fire pit and when he saw the ring, tooth, and the shards of bone again, he remembered everything.

He thought he'd seen his father step out of the woods last night. "I thought you were gone," George said to him.

Vanessa got up to leave then. She slapped the ring box into George's hand, and he put it back in his pocket. The fire crackled and popped. "We need to talk," George's father said, but by then George realized it was Eddie standing there, and not an apparition.

"About what?" George said.

"About the business."

"What about it?"

"Wait till we're all here."

George was confused. "Who else is coming?"

Eddie looked up toward the house. Debbie was on her way down. When she joined them, Eddie told George to sit down.

He refused.

"Fine. Have it your way."

"What's this all about?" George asked.

"Debbie has concerns about the business if you get the Spectrum Development contract."

George looked back and forth between the both of them. "Why does she need you to speak for her?"

Debbie sighed. "I don't, George. I went to Eddie to ask him about some things. He agreed with me and volunteered to be here when we talked."

George didn't like the sound of that.

"I asked you if you would bring him back into the business, because I'm worried about what will happen if you don't."

"What do you think is going to happen?"

Debbie stepped closer, and George backed away. He was right up against one of the boulders. The heat of it warmed the back of his legs.

Debbie backed off. "I'm worried someone else is going to get hurt, or worse. I don't like how you cut corners. It's dangerous."

George couldn't believe what he was hearing. He turned to Eddie. The ripples of heat distorted his face so that George once again thought it might have been his father he was looking at. "You filled her head with this."

"He didn't have to, George," Debbie snapped. "I talked to Cathy after you lied to Luke Pearson about Joseph Whitehead. You used me, George. You took advantage of my job to get what you wanted."

"For us," he cried. He lunged forward to take her arm, to make her understand, and Eddie got in between them and put his hand on her elbow again.

At that moment George hated Eddie as much as he'd hated their father. Thomas Rockaway had been a beloved businessman in public, but a cruel bully at home. Neither George, Eddie, nor their mother had escaped his bruising words, or punishing fists. And now he had his hands on Debbie.

"Don't touch her." George took a swing at Eddie and lost his footing as he pivoted. He stumbled over the boulder and flew face first into the fire. He felt propelled, but he'd never know if the fire had grabbed him and pulled him in, or if he'd been pushed from behind. For a moment he felt like he was flying. He was weightless. Powerful. Omnipotent. The flames were glorious. Beautiful. They danced, sparkled, and undulated. They lapped his skin. Worshiped him.

But that was last night. Now Eddie drove George's mini excavator to the edge of the fire pit. Debbie walked up behind him. "Are you sure this is what you want?" Eddie asked.

Debbie nodded. "It's best for everyone."

George couldn't breathe anymore. Couldn't see through the violent, persistent flames consuming him.

Eddie turned the earth under and pushed the boulders, along with the ring, tooth, and the shards of bone onto a giant pile in the center of the pit. He climbed down and stood next to Debbie. "You're going to tell everyone he's in the Midwest cleaning up after the tornado?"

She swallowed. Smiled. "Anyone who asks."

"When should we tell the crew that Rockaway got the Spectrum Development contract?"

"They'll know soon enough." Debbie was still staring at the pile of boulders. "It really was his best fire, wasn't it?"

"Yes." Eddie put his arm around her. Squeezed her shoulder. "It really was."

George tried to reach out, but it was just then he felt his skin start to burn.

ABOUT THE AUTHORS

Brigid Barry

**Brigid is a lifelong resident of Maine.
A disabled Air Force veteran and blessed parent
of twins, she lives on a small hobby farm with
her favorite husband and a collection of animals.**

Chris Campeau

Chris writes dark fiction and creative nonfiction from Canada's capital. His works has appeared in 34 Orchard Magazine, The Globe and Mail, Cargo Literary, The Horror Tree, Parhelion Literary, and others. He's also the author of *The Vampire Who Had No Fangs*, a children's picture book that's not even remotely scary, and the novella *Resisters*, a wintery version of *Psycho* meets *The Fog* set in rural Ontario during the Ice Storm of 1998.
Find him at chriscampeau.com.

C.W. Stevenson

A native of San Antonio, Texas,
C. W. "Clint" Stevenson resides there with his
wife, son, and their retinue of furry companions.
In his spare time, he spends time with his family
and collects too many books.
His work can be found in Alien Dimensions,
Illustrated Worlds Magazine, and Creepy Pod.

Gayle Siebert

Gayle has been writing stories all her life.
Now retired and living on an acreage
on Vancouver island,
she devotes her time to caring for her two horses,
and has published 12 suspense/mystery novels.

Glenn Dungan

Glenn Dungan is currently based in Brooklyn, NYC.
He exists within a Venn-diagram
of urban design, sociology, and good stories.
When not obsessing about one of those three,
he can be found at a park drinking
black coffee and listening to podcasts about murder.

Jessica Clem

Jessica Clem is a writer and editor based out of Minneapolis with a love for running, horror, and any movie by Robert Eggers.
She also volunteers as a Super Advocate with the Planned Parenthood Minnesota, North Dakota, and South Dakota Action Fund.

Jonathon Palmer is an Aurealis Award-Winning
author of weird fiction.
He's got a thing for unstable astronauts in fiction,
but he thinks the real-life ones are heroes.
He lives in Western Australia where
he teaches English and tolerable Japanese.

Jonathon
Palmer

Justin Alcala

Justin Carlos Alcala (he/him) is an award-winning American novelist & short story writer. His works are most notable for their appearance in Publisher's Weekly, the SLF Foundation Awards, and the University of British Columbia project archives. Justin is a folklore fanatic, history nerd, tabletop gamer, and time traveler. Alcala's thirty plus short stories, novellas, and novels can be found in anthologies, magazines, journals, podcasts, and commercial publications. He currently resides with his dark queen, Mallory, their fey daughter, Lily, changeling son, Ronan, goblin-baby, Asher, and hounds of Ragnarök, Fenrir and Hilda in Bigfoot's domain. Where his mind might be is anyone's guess.

Kaye George

Kaye George has had a prolific career spanning many years in the mystery genre, and also writes under the name Janet Cantrell.
She's accrued four Agatha Award nominations, won a Silver Falchion, a Derringer short story nomination, as well as achieving national bestseller status. She's also a violinist, arranger, and composer. She is a member of Sisters in Crime, the online Guppies chapter (where she was president), as well as the Smoking Guns Knoxville Chapter, which she helped organize.
www.kayegeorge.com

Ken Foxe

Ken Foxe is a writer and transparency activist in Ireland. He's the author of two non-fiction books based on his journalism and is a member of the Horror Writers Association.
www.kenfoxe.com/short-stories

Ken Teutsch is a writer, filmmaker,
and humorist living in North Arkansas.

Ken
Teutsch

Kent Priore

Kent Priore writes dark literature where romanticism
meets modern psychology for a macabre
but hopeful depiction of inner struggle,
and the human ability to endure.
He is a fierce advocate for mental health awareness
and for greater acceptance of neurodivergence.
For this reason, themes of mental health
are pronounced and ever present in his work,
both the devastating and the hopeful aspects of it.
He graduated with honors from Bard College with a
BA in the Written Arts, and is a proud
marginalized voice in the neurodivergent community.
www.kentpriore.com

Mister Bad

Kyle Owens has books published by Books to Go Now,
Clash, and Next Chapter Publishing, as well
as appearing in several short story anthologies.

Mark K. McClain

As a teenager, Mark wrote stories for pleasure,
influenced by authors such as J.R.R. Tolkien,
David Eddings, Isaac Asimov, Agatha Christie,
Stephen King, and others. As a former newspaper
columnist, Mark has penned more than forty
outdoor-related articles. He has also published
several magazine pieces. He now writes
both Fantasy and Horror. Currently, he
resides on an island near northwest Washington
where he operates Next Journey Books,
his thriving editing business.
Mark is a retired U.S.A.F. veteran.

Mike Sherer

Mike lives in West Chester in the Greater Cincinnati area of southwest Ohio. His screenplay "Hamal_18" was produced in Los Angeles and released direct to DVD, and is now available for free viewing on Tubi. He has published more than twelve novels and novellas, and 35 short stories.

Natasha Grodzinski

Natasha Grodzinski is a writer based in
Toronto, Canada. Her work has been
previously published in Three Drops from a
Cauldron, From Arthur's Seat, Luna Station
Quarterly, and Dream Glow Magazine.
She never outgrew making up stories on her
long walks in the woods,
and it's led her all the way here.

Pamela Kenney

Pamela Kenney writes many things from short stories
to novels to plays, but no matter what she writes,
the end result always has a touch of humor.
She is thrilled to be included in this collection
of horror stories, which will add to her growing
list of anthologies. Her cozy mystery series
(of which there are many) can be found on Kobo.

Rik Hoskin is a multi-award winning writer of novels,
graphic novels, video games, and animation.
He's written comics for Star Wars, Doctor Who,
and various other properties, and won the
Dragon Award for Best Graphic Novel 2018
for White Sand (with Brandon Sanderson),
which also made the New York Times Bestseller list.
He writes SF and horror novels and short stories
under his own name and as "James Axler". He
also writes video games, where he has served
as head writer, and has written animation
for BBC television in the UK.

Rik Hoskin

Terry Campbell

When he's not writing, Terry Campbell enjoys e-bike riding, exploring small towns, abandoned places, haunted buildings, and antique wandering. He was a finalist in the inaugural Longhorn Prize from Saddlebag Dispatches Magazine. He resides in Texas.

Tracy Falenwolfe

Tracy Falenwolfe writes mystery, horror, suspense, and whatever strikes her fancy. She is the winner of the 2014 Bethlehem Writers Roundtable Short Story Award.

CHECK OUT THESE OTHER GREAT READS FROM ROWAN PROSE!